P9-EMG-801

RANDOM
HOUSE
LARGE
PRINT

Ghosted

Ghosted

A NOVEL

Rosie Walsh

RANDOM HOUSE
LARGE PRINT

Copyright © 2018 by Rosie Walsh Ltd.

Published in the United States of America by Random House Large Print in association with Viking, an imprint of Penguin Random House LLC, New York.

Cover design: Jaya Miceli
Art direction: Roseanne Serra
Cover art: shuoshu / Getty Images

The Library of Congress has established a Cataloging-in-Publication record for this title.

ISBN: 978-0-5256-3191-0

www.penguinrandomhouse.com/large-print-format-books

FIRST LARGE PRINT EDITION

Printed in the United States of America

10 9 8 7 6 5 4 3 2 1

This Large Print edition published in accord with the standards of the N.A.V.H.

ACKNOWLEDGMENTS

Thanks first and foremost to George Pagliero and Emma Stonex, for that strange hot day when we all agreed that I was to write this book without further delay. For the tremendous support and enthusiasm that followed.

Warmest thanks to Pam Dorman, my editor, for brilliant editorial wisdom and such strong vision for, and deep understanding of, the book. To Brian Tart, Kate Stark, Lindsay Prevette, Kate Griggs, Roseanne Serra, Jeramie Orton, and the rest of the team at Pamela Dorman Books / Viking. It really is an honor to be a part of such an exceptional list.

Endless gratitude to Allison Hunter, my tireless U.S. agent, who nearly killed me in an exercise class but then turned it around and secured me the book deal of dreams. To my UK agent, Lizzy Kremer, who masterminded everything so superbly, and without whom I would be quite lost. Thanks also to Harriet Moore and Olivia Barber.

Thank you to Sam Humphreys of Mantle, UK, for loving this story from the get-go, and for the incisive and thoughtful editing that made it so much better than it could have been. Thanks also to the other editors around the world who acquired it, too. I still can't believe it! My gratitude to Alice Howe of David Higham Associates, and her mighty translation rights department: Emma Jamison, Emily Randle, Camilla Dubini, and Margaux Vialleron.

Sincere thanks to Old Robsonians, a real football team of whom I am inordinately fond. They donated a very generous sum of money to the children's charity CLIC Sargent for a mention in this book.

To Gemma Kicks and the wonderful charity Hearts & Minds, for their generous help when I was researching Clowndoctor charities. I was amazed and inspired by the real difference their Clowndoctors make to children's lives, each and every day. Thanks also to Lynne Barlow of Bristol Children's hospital.

Thank you to Emma Williams, community psychiatric nurse; James Gallagher, cabinet maker; and Victoria Bodey, parent of young boys. Thanks to the many friends who answered a neverending stream of (often very personal) questions on Facebook.

To Emma Stonex, Sue Mongredien, Katy Regan, Kirsty Greenwood, and Emma Holland for valuable feedback on the manuscript in its various stages. And most of all to my dear writing partner, Deborah O'Donoghue, without whom I'm not sure I could have written this book. So many great ideas in this book came from you, Deb—thank you. I can't wait to see your own novel on the shelves.

Thank you to my SWANS—South West Authors and Novelists—for support, great lunches, and laughter. To the ladies of CAN for the same. Thank you to Lindsey Kelk for my LA research trip and mostly very un-writerly discussions. Thank you to Rosie Mason and family for the many memorable days playing in that beautiful valley, and Ellie Tinto, for keeping the spirit of Margery Kempe alive and very impious.

Thank you to Lyn, Brian, and Caroline Walsh, who have always encouraged me in everything I do, and who've been so proud of me as I've forged ahead as a writer under my own name. And thank you, above all, to my darling George and our tiny, funny, perfect little man, who has changed forever my understanding of love.

We can perhaps only ever fall in love without knowing quite who we have fallen in love with.

Alain de Botton
Essays in Love

Part I

CHAPTER ONE

Dear You,

It's exactly nineteen years since that luminous morning when we smiled and said good-bye. That we would see each other again was never in doubt, was it? It was a question of when, not if. In fact, it wasn't even a question. The future might have seemed as insubstantial as the curled edge of a dream, but it unequivocally contained us both. Together.

And yet it didn't. Even after all these years I find myself stunned by that.

Nineteen years since that day. Nineteen whole years! And I'm still looking for you. I will never stop looking for you.

Often you appear when I expect it least. Earlier today I was trapped in some pointless dark thought or other, my body clenched like a metal fist. Then suddenly you were there: a bright autumn leaf cartwheeling over a dull pewter lawn. I uncurled and smelled life, felt dew on my feet, saw shades of green. I tried to grab hold of you, that vivid leaf, cavorting and wriggling and giggling. I tried to take your hand, look straight at you, but like an optical black spot you slid silently sideways, just out of reach.

I will never stop looking for you.

CHAPTER TWO

Day Seven: When We Both Knew

The grass had become damp. Damp and dark and full of industry. Stretching away toward the blackened ridge of the woods, it quivered with battalions of ants and ponderous snails and tiny, gossamer-spinning spiders. Underneath us, the earth drew to itself a last residue of warmth.

Eddie, lying next to me, was humming the **Star Wars** theme tune. His thumb stroked mine. Slowly, gently, like the clouds moving across the fine clip of moon above us. "Let's search for aliens," he'd said earlier, as the violet sky had thickened to purple. We were still there.

I heard the distant sigh of the last train disappearing into the tunnel farther up the hill and I smiled, remembering when Hannah and I used to camp out here as children. In a small field in this same small valley, hidden from what still felt like a small world.

At the first sign of summer Hannah would beg our parents to put up the tent.

Sure, they said. As long as you camp in the garden.

The garden was flat. It was at the front of our house, overlooked by almost every window. But it was never enough for Hannah, whose spirit of adventure—even though she was five years my junior—had always exceeded mine. She wanted the field. The field straggled up the steep hill behind our house, flattening just enough at the top to fit a tent. It was overlooked by nothing other than the sky. It was speckled with hard Frisbees of cowpat and was so high up you could almost look down our chimney.

Our parents were not so keen on the field.

"But I'll be perfectly safe," Hannah would insist, in that bossy little voice. (How I missed that voice.)

"I'll have Alex with me." Hannah's best friend spent most of her time at our house. "**And** Sarah. She can protect us if any murderers come."

As if I were a well-built man with a reliable right hook.

"And you won't have to make our dinner if we go camping. **Or** our breakfast . . ."

Hannah was like a tiny bulldozer—she never ran out of counterarguments—and our parents inevitably gave in. At first they camped in the field with us, but eventually, as I fought on through the knotted jungle of adolescence, they allowed Hannah and Alex to sleep up there alone, with me as bodyguard.

We would lie in Dad's old festival tent—a lumbering thing made of orange canvas, like a small bungalow—and listen to the symphony of sounds in the grass outside. Often, I'd stay awake long after my little sister and her friend had slackened into sleep, wondering what kind of protection I'd actually be able to offer were someone to burst in. The necessity of protecting Hannah—not just as she slept in this tent, but always—felt like molten rock in my stomach, a volcano barely contained. And yet what would I actually do? Karate chop them with my teenage wrist? Stab them with a marshmallow-toasting stick?

Often hesitant, not entirely certain of herself, was how my form tutor had described me on a report.

"Well, that's really bloody useful," Mum had said, in the voice she normally reserved for telling off our father. "Ignore her, Sarah. Be as uncertain as you like! That's what your teenage years are for!"

Exhausted, eventually, by the competing forces of protectiveness and powerlessness, I'd fall asleep, waking early to assemble whatever disgusting combination of things Hannah and Alex had packed for their infamous "breakfast sandwich."

I laid a hand on my chest; dimmed the lights on the memory. It wasn't an evening for sadness; it was an evening for now. For Eddie and me, and the great, still-growing thing between us.

I concentrated on the sounds of a woodland clearing at night. Invertebrate rustle, mammalian shuffle. The green whisper of moving leaves, the untroubled rise and fall of Eddie's breath. I listened to his heart, beating evenly through his jumper, and marveled at his steadiness. "More will be revealed," my father always liked to say about people. "You have to watch and wait, Sarah." But I'd been watching this man for a week, and I hadn't sensed any disquiet. In many ways he reminded me of the me I'd trained myself to be at work: solid, rational, untroubled by the shifting tides of the nonprofit sector—but I was someone who'd spent years practicing, whereas Eddie seemed, simply, to be that way.

I wondered if he could hear the excitement careening around in my chest. A matter of days ago I'd been separated, approaching divorce, approaching forty. Then this. Him.

"Oh! A badger!" I said, as a low shape shuffled across the darkened edge of my vision. "I wonder if it's Cedric."

"Cedric?"

"Yes. Although I suppose it probably isn't him. How long do badgers live?"

"I think about ten years." Eddie was smiling: I could hear it.

"Well, then it's definitely not Cedric. But it could be his son. Or maybe grandson." I paused. "We loved Cedric."

A vibration of laughter traced through his body, into mine. "Who's we?"

"Me and my little sister. We used to camp quite near here."

He rolled over onto his side, his face close to mine, and I could see it in his eyes.

"Cedric the badger. I . . . you," he said quietly. He traced a finger along my hairline. "I like you. I like you and me. In fact, I like you and me very much."

I smiled. Right into those kind, sincere eyes. At those laughter lines, at the heavy angle of his chin. I took his hand and kissed his fingertips, rough and mottled with splinters after two decades of woodworking. Already it felt like I'd known him for years. For a lifetime. It felt like someone had matched us, maybe at birth, and nudged and aligned and planned and schemed until we finally met, six days ago.

"I just had some very mushy thoughts," I said, after a long pause.

"Me too." He sighed. "It feels like the last week's been set to a score of sweeping violins."

I laughed, and he kissed my nose, and I wondered how it was that you could spend weeks, months—**years**, even—just chugging on, nothing really changing, and then, in the space of a few hours, the script of your life could be completely rewritten. Had I gone out later that day I would have got straight on the bus and never met him, and this new feeling of certainty would be no more than an unheard whisper of missed opportunities and bad timing.

"Tell me even more about you," he said. "I still don't know enough. I want to know everything. The complete and unabridged life story of Sarah Evelyn Mackey, including the bad bits."

I held my breath.

It wasn't that I hadn't known this would happen at some stage, more that I still hadn't decided what I'd do when it did. **The complete and unabridged life story of Sarah Evelyn Mackey, including the bad bits.** He could take it, probably. There was an armor on this man, a quiet strength that made me think of an old seawall, an oak tree, maybe.

He was running a hand along the curve between my hip and rib cage. "I love this curve," he said.

A man so comfortable in his own skin you could probably sink any secret, any truth into him, and he'd be able to hold it without sustaining structural damage.

Of course I could tell him.

"I have an idea," I said. "Let's camp out here tonight. Pretend we're still young. We can make a fire, cook sausages, tell stories. Assuming you have a tent, that is? You seem like a man who'd have a tent."

"I am a man who has a tent," he confirmed.

"Good! Well then, let's do it, and I'll tell you everything. I . . ." I rolled over, looking out into the night. The last fat candles of blossom glowed dully on the horse chestnut at the edge of the woods. A buttercup swayed in the darkness near our faces. For reasons she'd never deigned to share, Hannah had always hated buttercups.

I felt something rise in my chest. "It's just so lovely, being out here. Brings back so many memories."

"Okay," Eddie smiled. "We'll camp. But first, come here, please."

He kissed me on the mouth and for a while the rest of the world was muted, as if someone had simply pressed a button or turned a dial.

"I don't want tomorrow to be our last day," he said, when the kissing came to an end. He bandaged his arms more tightly around me and I felt the cheerful warmth of his chest and belly, the soft tickle of his cropped hair under my hands.

Closeness like this had become a distant memory, I thought, inhaling the clean, sandy smell of his skin. By the time Reuben and I had called it a day, we were sleeping like bookends on either side of our bed, the stretch of untouched sheets between us an homage to our failure.

"Till mattress us do part," I'd said, one night, but Reuben hadn't laughed.

Eddie pulled away so I could see his face. "I did . . . Look, I did wonder if we should cancel our respective plans. My holiday and your London trip. So we can roll around in the fields for another week."

I propped myself up on an elbow. **I want that more than you will ever know,** I thought. **I was married for seventeen years and in all that time I never felt the way I do with you.**

"Another week of this would be perfect," I told him. "But you mustn't cancel your holiday. I'll still be here when you get back."

"But you won't be here. You'll be in London."

"Are you sulking?"

"Yes." He kissed my collarbone.

"Well, stop it. I'll be back down here in Gloucestershire soon after you get back."

He seemed unappeased.

"If you stop sulking, I might even come and meet you at the airport," I added. "I could be one of those people with a name on a board and a car in the Short Stay."

He seemed to consider this for a moment. "That would be very nice," he said. "Very nice indeed."

"Done."

"And"—he paused, looked suddenly uncertain— "and I know it's maybe a bit soon, but after you've told me your life story and I've cooked sausages that may or may not be edible, I want us to have a serious conversation about the fact that you live in California and I live in England. This visit of yours is too short."

"I know."

He tugged at the dark grass. "When I get back from holiday, we'll have—what, a week together? Before you have to go back to the States?"

I nodded. The only dark cloud over our week together had been this, the inevitability of parting.

"Well then, I think we have to . . . I don't know. Do something. Decide something. I can't just let this go. I can't know you're somewhere in the world and not be with you. I think we should try to make this work."

"Yes," I said quietly. "Yes, me too." I slid a hand inside his sleeve. "I've been thinking the same, but I lost my nerve every time I tried to bring it up."

"Really?" Laughter and relief spilled into his voice, and I realized it must have taken some courage for him to start the conversation. "Sarah, you're one of the most confident women I've ever met."

"Mmmm."

"You are. It's one of the things I like about you. One of the many things I like very much about you."

It had been a great many years since I'd had to start nailing confidence to myself like a sign on a shop. But even though it came naturally now—even though I spoke at medical conferences around the world, gave interviews to news crews, managed a team—I felt unsettled when people remarked on it. Unsettled or perhaps exposed, like a person on a hill in a thunderstorm.

Then Eddie kissed me again and I felt it all dissolve. The sadness of the past, the uncertainty of the future. This was what was meant to happen next. **This.**

CHAPTER THREE

Fifteen Days Later

Something terrible has happened to him."

"Like what?"

"Like death. Maybe not death. Although, why not? My grandmother dropped dead at the age of forty-four."

Jo turned round from the passenger seat. "Sarah."

I didn't meet her eye.

She looked instead at Tommy, who was driving us west along the M4. "Did you hear that?" she asked.

He didn't respond. His jaw was clenched shut, the pale skin by his temple pulsing as if someone were in there, trying to break out.

Jo and I shouldn't have come, I thought again. We'd been convinced Tommy would want the support of his two oldest friends—after all, it wasn't often that you had to stand shoulder to shoulder with your school bully while the press took photos—but as each dreary, rain-spattered mile passed, it had become evident that we were doing little more than increasing his anxiety.

What he needed today was the freedom to peddle synthetic confidence without being watched by those who knew him best. To pretend it was all water under the bridge. **Look how I became a successful sports consultant, delivering a program to my old school! Look how happy I am to be working alongside the head of PE—the very man who punched me in the stomach and laughed when I turned my face into the grass and cried!**

To make matters worse, Jo's seven-year-old, Rudi, was next to me on the backseat. His father had been offered a job interview and Jo hadn't had time to find childcare. He had been listening with great interest to our conversation about Eddie's disappearance.

"So, Sarah thinks her boyfriend's dead and Mum's getting cross," Rudi surmised. He was going through a phase of distilling awkward adult conversations into neat one-liners, and he was very good at it.

"He's not her boyfriend," Jo said. "They spent seven days together."

The car fell silent again. "Sarah. Think seven-day boyfriend dead," Rudi said, in his Russian voice. Rudi had a new friend at school, Aleksandr, who had recently come to London from somewhere near the Ukrainian border. "Killed by secret service. Mum disagree. Mum cross with Sarah."

"I'm not cross," Jo said crossly. "I'm just worried."

Rudi considered this, and then said, "I think you tell lie."

Jo couldn't deny it, so remained silent. I didn't

wish to antagonize Jo, so I remained silent as well. And Tommy hadn't said anything for two hours, so he remained silent, too. Rudi lost interest and returned to his iPad game. Adults were rife with baffling and pointless problems.

I watched Rudi obliterate what looked like a cabbage and was blasted suddenly by a great longing: for his innocence, his seven-year-old's worldview. I imagined Rudi Land, in which mobile phones were gaming stations rather than instruments of psychological torture, and the certainty of his mother's love was as solid as a heartbeat.

If there was any point to becoming an adult, it eluded me today. Who wouldn't prefer to be killing cabbages and talking in a Russian accent? Who wouldn't prefer to have had their breakfast made and their outfit chosen, when the alternative was malignant despair over a man who'd felt like everything and somehow become nothing? And not the man I'd been married to seventeen years; a man I'd known precisely seven days. No wonder everyone in this car thought I was mad.

"Look, I know it sounds like a teenage saga," I said eventually. "And I don't doubt that you're pissed off with me. But something has happened to him, I'm certain of it."

Jo opened Tommy's glove compartment to extract a large bar of chocolate, from which she snapped off a chunk with some force.

"Mum?" Rudi said. "What's that?"

He knew perfectly well what it was. Jo handed her son a square without saying anything. Rudi smiled at her, his biggest, toothiest smile, and—in spite of her growing impatience—Jo smiled back. "Don't ask for more," she warned. "You'll only end up being sick."

Rudi said nothing, confident she'd give in.

Jo turned back to me. "Look, Sarah. I don't want to be cruel, but I think you need to accept that Eddie is not dead. Nor is he injured, or suffering a broken phone, or battling a life-threatening illness."

"Really? You've called the hospitals to check? Had a chat with the local coroner?"

"Oh, God," she said, staring at me. "Tell me you haven't done any of those things, Sarah! Jesus Christ!"

"Jesus Christ," Rudi whispered.

"Stop that," Jo told him.

"You started it."

Jo gave Rudi more chocolate and he went back to his iPad. It had been my present to him from America, and he told me earlier on that he loved it more than anything else in the world. Which had made me laugh and then, to Rudi's bafflement, cry a little, because I knew he'd have learned that phrase from Jo. She had turned out to be a remarkable mother, Joanna Monk, in spite of her own upbringing.

"Well?"

"Of course I haven't been calling hospitals," I sighed. "Come on, Jo." I watched a row of crows scattering from a telephone wire.

"Are you sure?"

"Of course I'm sure. My point was just that you don't know any more than I do what's happened to Eddie."

"But men do this all the time!" she exploded. "You know they do!"

"I don't know anything about dating. I've been married the last seventeen years."

"Well, you can take it from me: nothing's changed," Jo said bitterly. "They still don't call."

She turned to Tommy but found him unresponsive. Any residual confidence he'd feigned about today's big launch had evaporated like the morning mist and he'd barely said a word since we'd set off. There had been a brief display of bravado at Chieveley Services when he'd had a message telling him that three local newspapers had confirmed attendance, but a few minutes later he'd called me "Sarah" in the queue at WHSmith, and Tommy only called me Sarah when he was extremely anxious. (I had been "Harrington" since we turned thirteen and he'd started doing push-ups and wearing aftershave.)

The silence thickened, and I lost the battle I'd been fighting since we left London.

I'm on my way back to Gloucestershire, I texted Eddie, quick as a wink. **Supporting my friend Tommy; he's launching a big sports project at our old school. If you wanted to meet up, I could stay at my parents'. Would be good to talk. Sarah x**

No pride, no shame. I'd somehow moved beyond

that. I tapped the screen of my phone every few seconds, waiting for a delivery report.

Delivered, it announced perkily.

I watched the screen, checking for a text bubble. A text bubble would mean he was writing back.

No text bubble.

I looked again. No text bubble.

I looked again. Still no text bubble. I slid my phone into my handbag, out of sight. This was what girls did when they were still in the tender agonies of adolescence, I thought. Girls, still learning to love themselves, waiting in mild hysteria to hear from a boy they'd kissed in a sweaty corner last Friday. This was not the behavior of a woman of thirty-seven. A woman who'd traveled the world, survived tragedy, run a charity.

The rain was clearing. Through the crack of open window I could smell the tang of wet tarmac and damp, smoky earth. **I am in agony.** I stared vacantly at a field of round hay bales, squeezed tightly into shining black plastic like pudgy legs into tights. I would tip over the edge soon. I would tip over the edge and go into free fall if I didn't find out what had happened.

I checked my phone. It had been twenty-four hours since I'd taken out my SIM card and rebooted. Time to try again.

Half an hour later we were on the dual carriageway coming into Cirencester and Rudi was asking his mother why the clouds were all moving in different directions.

We were a matter of mere miles from where I'd met him. I closed my eyes, trying to remember my walk that hot morning. Those uncomplicated few hours Before Eddie. The sour-milk sweetness of elderflower blossom. Yes, and scorched grass. The drift of butterflies, stunned by the heat. There had been a barley field, a feathered, husk-green carpet panting and bulging with hot air. The occasional explosion of a startled rabbit. And the strange sense of expectation that had hovered over the village that day, the boiling stillness, the littered secrets.

Unbidden, my memory fast-forwarded a few more minutes to the moment I actually met Eddie—a straightforward, friendly man with warm eyes and an open face, holding court with an escaped sheep— and misery and confusion tangled like weeds over everything else.

"You can tell me I'm in denial," I said to the silent car. "But it wasn't a fling. It was . . . it was everything. We both knew. That's why I'm sure something's happened to him."

The idea made my breath stick to the inside of my throat.

"Say something," Jo said to Tommy. "Say something to her."

"I work in sports consultancy," he muttered. Embarrassment bloomed on his neck. "I do bodies, not heads."

"Who does heads?" Rudi asked. He was still keeping close tabs on our conversation.

"Therapists do heads," Jo said wearily. "Therapists and me."

Ferapists. She pronounced it **ferapists**. Jo was born and bred in Bow, was a proper, salt-of-the-earth Cockney. And I loved her; I loved her bluntness and mercurial temper, I loved her fearlessness (lack of boundaries, others might say), and most of all I loved the tremendous fury with which she adored her son. I loved everything about Jo, but I would still have preferred not to be in a car with her today.

Rudi asked me if we were nearly there yet. I told him yes. "Is that your school?" he asked, pointing at an industrial estate.

"No, although there are some architectural similarities."

"Is **that** your school?"

"No. That's Waitrose."

"How long till we get there?"

"Not long."

"How many minutes?"

"About twenty?"

Rudi slumped back into his seat in self-conscious despair. "That's **ages**," he muttered. "Mum, I need some new games. Can I have some new games?"

Jo said he could not, and Rudi set about buying some anyway. I watched in awe as he matter-of-factly typed in Jo's Apple ID and password.

"Er, excuse me," I whispered. He looked up at me,

his little blond Afro an unlikely halo, his almond-shaped eyes cartwheeling with mischief. He mimed a zip being shut across his mouth and then pointed a warning finger at me. And because I loved this child far more than I wanted to, I did what I was told.

His mother turned her attention to the other child on the backseat. "Now look," she said, putting a plump hand on my leg. Her nails had been painted in a color called Rubble for today. "I think you have to face facts. You met a bloke, you spent a week with him, then he went on holiday and never called you again."

The facts were too painful at the moment; I preferred theories.

"Fifteen days he's had to get in touch, Sarah. You've been sending him messages, calling him, all sorts of other things that quite frankly I'd never expect of someone like you . . . and yet—no response. I've been there, love, and it hurts. But it doesn't stop hurting until you accept the truth and move on."

"I'd move on if I actually knew that he simply wasn't interested. But I don't."

Jo sighed. "Tommy. Please help me out here."

There was a long pause. Was there any humiliation greater than this? I wondered. A conversation like this, at the age of nearly bloody **forty**? This time three weeks ago I'd been a functional adult. I'd chaired a board meeting. I'd written a report for a children's hospital with which my charity was soon to start working. I'd fed and groomed myself that day, made jokes, fielded calls, responded to e-mails. And now here I was with less command of my emotions than the seven-year-old sitting next to me.

I checked Tommy's eyebrows in the rearview mirror to see if he was likely to throw anything in. His eyebrows, which had taken on a life of their own when he'd lost his hair in his early twenties, were nowadays more reliable barometers of his thoughts than his mouth.

They were creased together. "The thing is," he said. He paused again, and I sensed the effort it was taking to extract himself from his own problems. "The thing is, Jo, you've assumed I agree with you about Sarah. But I'm not sure I do." His voice was soft and careful, like a cat skirting danger.

"What?"

"I predict a riot," Rudi whispered.

Tommy's eyebrows worked up his next sentence. "I'm sure the reason most men don't call is that they're just not interested, but it sounds to me like there might be more to this. I mean, they ended up spending a week together. All that time, can you imagine? If Eddie was just after you-know-what, he'd have disappeared after one night."

Jo snorted. "Why leave after one night if you can pack in seven days' you-know-what?"

"Jo, come on! That's what twenty-year-old boys do, not men of nearly forty!"

"Are you talking about sex?" Rudi asked.

"Er, no?" Jo was thrown. "What do you know about sex?"

Rudi, terrified, returned to his fraudulent iPad activity.

Jo watched him for a while, but he was bent studiously over the screen, muttering in his Russian voice.

I took a long breath. "The one thing I keep thinking about is that he offered to cancel his holiday. Why would he—"

"I need to wee," Rudi announced suddenly. "I think I've got less than a minute," he added, before Jo had time to ask.

We pulled up outside the agricultural college, right across the road from the comprehensive Eddie had gone to. A gray mist of pain hovered as I stared at its sign, trying to imagine a twelve-year-old Eddie bouncing through the gates. A round little face; the smile that would crease his skin into laughter lines as the years passed.

Just passing your school, I texted him, before I had time to stop myself. **I wish I knew what happened to you.**

Jo was suspiciously upbeat when she and Rudi got back in the car. She said it was turning into a lovely day and that she was very happy to be out in the countryside with us all.

"I told her she was being mean to you," Rudi whispered to me. "Do you want a piece of cheese?" He patted a Tupperware of rejected cheese slices from the sandwiches Jo had given him earlier.

I ruffled his hair. "No," I whispered back. "But I love you. Thank you."

Jo pretended not to have heard the exchange. "You were saying that Eddie offered to cancel his holiday," she said brightly.

And I felt the fissures of my heart open wider, because, of course, I knew why she was finding it so hard to be patient. I knew that of the many men to whom Jo had given her heart and soul (and, often, her body) in the years before Rudi, almost none had called her. And the ones who had called always turned out to have a collection of other women on the go. And each and every time she had let them string her along, because she could never quite give up the hope of being loved. Then Shawn O'Keefe had arrived on the scene, and Jo had got pregnant, and Shawn had moved in, knowing Jo would feed and house him. He hadn't had one single job in all that time. He'd disappear for whole nights without telling her where he was. His "job interview" today was pure fiction.

But Jo had been allowing this for seven years, because she somehow convinced herself that love would blossom if she and Shawn worked just a little harder, if she waited just a little longer for him to grow up. She'd convinced herself they could become the family she'd never had.

Yes, Jo knew all about denial.

But my own situation seemed to be too much for her. She'd tried to humor me since Eddie had disappeared off the face of the earth, forced herself to listen to my theories, told me he might just call tomorrow. But she hadn't believed a word of it, and now she'd cracked. **Don't allow yourself to be used the way I have**, she was saying. **Walk away now, Sarah, while you still can.**

The problem was, I couldn't.

I had tried out the idea of Eddie simply not being interested. Each and every one of the fifteen days my phone had remained silent. I'd combed through every glowing, lambent moment of my time with him, searching for cracks, tiny warning signs that he might not have been as certain as I was, and I'd found nothing.

I barely used Facebook these days, but suddenly I was on it, all of the time, scouring his profile for signs of life. Or, worse—someone else.

Nothing.

I phoned and messaged him; I even sent him a pathetic little tweet. I downloaded Facebook Messenger and WhatsApp and checked throughout the day to see if he'd surfaced. But they told me the same thing every time: Eddie David had last been seen online just over two weeks ago, the day I left his house so he could pack for Spain.

Flattened by both shame and desperation, I'd even downloaded a bunch of dating apps to find out if he was registered.

He wasn't.

I craved control over this uncontrollable situation.

I couldn't sleep; the thought of food made my insides convulse. I couldn't concentrate on anything and I jumped on my phone with the frenzy of a starving animal when it buzzed. Exhaustion pressed at me throughout the day—great fibrous wads of it; a suffocation, at times—and yet I spent most of the night wide awake, staring into the pitchy darkness of Tommy's spare room in west London.

The strange thing was, I **knew** this wasn't me. I knew it wasn't sane behavior, and I knew it was getting worse, not better, but I had neither the will nor the energy to stage an intervention on myself.

Why didn't he call? I typed into Google one day. The response was like an online hurricane. For the sake of any remaining sanity, I had shut down the page.

Instead, I'd Googled Eddie, again, had gone through his carpentry website, looking for . . . By that point I didn't even know what I was looking for. And of course I hadn't found a thing.

"Do you think he told you everything about himself?" Tommy asked. "Are you certain he isn't with another woman, for example?"

The road dipped down into a little bowl of parkland, in which stately oaks had gathered like gentlemen in a smoking lounge.

"He's not with another woman," I said.

"How do you know?"

"I know because . . . I know. He was single; he was available. Not just literally, emotionally."

The flash of a deer vanishing into a beech wood.

"Okay. But what about all the other warning signs?" Tommy persisted. "Were there any inconsistencies? Did you sense he was holding anything back?"

"No." I paused. "Although, I suppose . . ."

Jo turned round. "What?"

I sighed. "The day we met, he canceled a few incoming calls. But that was the only time it happened," I added quickly. "From then on he answered every time his phone rang. And he didn't have anyone strange calling him, either; it was all friends, his mum, business queries . . ." **And Derek**, I thought suddenly. I had never quite got to the bottom of who Derek was.

Tommy's eyebrows were engaged in some complicated triangulation.

"What?" I asked him. "What are you thinking? It was just the first day, Tommy. After that he picked up when anyone rang."

"I believe you. It's more that . . ." He trailed off.

Jo was noisily silent, but I ignored her.

"It's more that I've just always thought Internet dating to be risky," Tommy said eventually. "I know you didn't meet him online, but it's a similar situation—you have no friends in common and no shared history. He could have recast himself as almost anyone."

I frowned. "But he made friends with me on Facebook. Why would he do that if he had anything to hide? He's on Twitter and Instagram for his work, and he's got a business website. Which includes a photo of him. And I stayed at his house for a week, remember? His post was addressed to Eddie David. If he wasn't Eddie David, cabinet-maker, I'd know."

We were now deep in the old woods that spread across Cirencester Park. Pennies of light flashed across Jo's bare thighs as she gazed out of the window, apparently at a loss. Before long we'd emerge from the woods, and soon after that we'd reach the bend in the road where the accident had happened.

At that thought, I felt my breathing change, as if someone had thinned out the car's oxygen.

A few minutes later we emerged into the postrain brightness of country fields. I closed my eyes, still unable, after all these years, to look at the grass verge where they said the ambulance crew had laid her out, tried to stop the inevitable.

Jo's hand found its way to my knee.

"Why are you doing that?" Rudi's antenna was up. "Mum? Why is your hand on Sarah's leg? Why are there flowers tied to that tree? Why is everyone being—"

"Rudi," Jo said. "Rudi, what about I spy? I spy with my little eye something beginning with 'W'!"

There was a pause. "I'm too old for that," Rudi said humpily. He didn't like being kept out.

My eyes were still pressed shut, even though I knew we'd passed the spot.

"A whale," Rudi began reluctantly. "A watering can. A wobile phone."

"Okay, Harrington?" Tommy asked, after a respectful pause.

"Yes." I opened my eyes. Wheat fields, tottering drystone walls, footpaths like lightning forks across horse-cropped grass. "Fine."

It never got any easier. Nineteen years had sanded down its edges, planed over the worst of the knots, but it was still there.

"How's about we discuss Eddie some more?" Jo suggested. I tried to say yes, but my voice trailed off. "In your own time," she said, patting my leg.

"Well, I do keep wondering if he's had an accident," I said, when speech felt possible. "He was off to southern Spain to windsurf."

Tommy's eyebrows considered this. "I suppose that's a reasonable theory."

Jo pointed out that I was friends with Eddie on Facebook. "She'd have seen something on his page if he'd got hurt."

"We shouldn't underestimate his phone having died, though," I said. My voice wilted as each avenue of hope shut down. "It was a mess, he—"

"Babe," Jo cut in gently. "Babe, his phone isn't dead. It **rings** when you call him."

I nodded miserably.

Rudi, eating crisps, kicked the back of Jo's seat. "Borrrrrrrred."

"Stop it," she said. "And remember what we agreed about speaking with your mouth full."

Rudi, unseen to Jo, turned toward me and offered me a view of his half-masticated crisps. Unfortunately, and for reasons unclear, he had decided that this was an in-joke between us.

I slid my hand into the side pocket of my bag, closing my fingers around the last piece of hope I had. "But Mouse," I said pathetically. Tears were hot and close. "He gave me Mouse."

I cupped her in the palm of my hand; smooth, worn, smaller than a walnut. Eddie had carved her from a piece of wood when he was just nine years old. **She's been with me through a lot**, he'd said. **She's my taliswoman.**

She reminded me of the brass penguin Dad had given me as a desk mate during my GCSE exams. It was a stern-looking thing that had scowled ferociously at me from the moment I'd opened each paper. Even now, I loved that penguin. I couldn't imagine trusting anyone with it.

Mouse meant the same to Eddie; I knew it—and yet he had given her to me. **Keep her safe until I get back**, he'd said. **She means a lot to me.**

Jo glanced back and sighed. She already knew about Mouse. "People change their minds," she said quietly. "It might just have been easier for him to lose the key ring than to get in touch."

"She's not just a key ring. She . . ." I gave up.

When Jo resumed, her voice was gentler. "Look, Sarah. If you're certain something bad has happened to him, how's about you scrap all these private communications and write something on his Facebook wall? Where everyone can see it? Say that you're worried. Ask if anyone's heard from him."

I swallowed. "What do you mean?"

"I mean exactly what I just said. Appeal to his friends for information. What's stopping you?"

I turned to look out of the window, unable to reply.

Jo pressed on. "I think the only thing that **would** stop you is shame. And if you really, truly, honestly believed something terrible had happened to him, you wouldn't give a rat's about shame."

We were passing the old MOD airfield. A faded orange wind sock frilled over the empty runway and I suddenly remembered Hannah's great hoots of laughter when Dad once observed that it was like a big orange willy. "Willy sock!" she'd yelled, and Mum had been torn between helpless laughter and reproach.

Rudi opened Jo's music library on the iPad and selected a playlist called "East Coast rap."

If I was as worried as I said, why **hadn't** I written something on Eddie's wall? Was Jo actually right?

The Cotswold stone cottages of Chalford were sliding into view, clinging determinedly to their hillside as if awaiting rescue. Chalford would give way to

Brimscombe, which would turn into Thrupp and then Stroud. And in Stroud a large committee of teachers, pupils, and press were waiting for Tommy at our old school. I had to pull myself together.

"Hang on," Tommy said suddenly. He turned down Rudi's rap and looked at me in the rearview mirror. "Harrington, did you tell Eddie you were married?"

"No."

His eyebrows had become quite wild. "I thought you said you told him everything!"

"I did! But we didn't go through our roster of exes. That would have been . . . well, tacky. I mean, we're both nearly forty . . ." I trailed off. Should we have done? "We were meant to tell each other our life stories, but we never got round to it. Although we did establish that we were both single."

Tommy was watching me through the rearview mirror. "But have you and Reuben updated your website?"

I frowned, wondering what he could be getting at. Then: "Oh, **no,**" I whispered. Freezing fingers brushed my abdomen.

"What?" Rudi shouted. "What are you talking about?"

"Sarah's charity's website," Jo told him. "There's a whole page about Sarah and Reuben, about how they started the Clowndoctor charity in the nineties when they got married. And how they still run it together today."

"Oh!" said Rudi. He put the iPad down, delighted at last to have been able to solve the mystery. "Sarah's boyfriend read it and his heart got broken! That's why he's dead, because you can't be alive if your heart doesn't work."

But: "I'm sorry—I don't buy it," Jo said quietly. "If he spent a week with you, Sarah, if he was as serious about you as you are about him, that wouldn't be enough to put him off. He'd confront you. He wouldn't just slink off like a dying cat."

But I was already on that confounded Messenger app, writing to him.

CHAPTER FOUR

Day One: The Day We Met

It was furnace-hot the day I met Eddie David. The countryside had begun to melt and pool into itself; birds holed up in stock-still trees and bees drunk on soaring Fahrenheit. It didn't feel like the sort of afternoon for falling in love with a complete stranger. It felt exactly like every other June 2 on which I'd made this walk. Quiet, sorrowful, loaded. Familiar.

I heard Eddie before I saw him. I was standing at the bus stop, trying to remember what day of the week it was—Thursday, I decided, which meant I had nearly an hour to wait. Here in the livid heat of the day, for a bus in which I would certainly fry. I started to wander down the lane toward the village, looking for shade. On a boiling current I heard the sound of children in the primary school.

They were interrupted by the blast of a sheep from somewhere up ahead. **BAAA**, it shouted. **BAAA!**

The sheep was answered by a great gale of male laughter, which barreled off into the compressed heat like a jet of cool air. I started to smile, before

I'd even seen the man. His laughter summed up everything that I felt about sheep, with their silly faces and daft side-eyes.

They were a little way away, on the village green. A man sitting with his back to me, a sheep a few feet away. Staring at the man through those side-eyes. It tried another baa and the man said something I couldn't hear.

By the time I'd reached the green, they were deep in conversation.

I stood on the edge of the scorched grass, watching them, and felt an old slide of recognition. I didn't know this man, but he was a charming replica of so many of the boys with whom I'd been to school: a big, pleasant loaf of a thing; cropped hair and biscuity-brown skin; the West Country uniform of cargo shorts and faded T-shirt. He would be capable of putting up shelves, would doubtless know how to surf, and would quite probably drive a clapped-out Golf donated by his pleasant but batty mother.

The sort of boy whom, I'd stated in my teenage diaries, I would one day marry. (The "one day" referred to an unspecified time in the future when, like a butterfly from a scrubby chrysalis, I would resign my post as average-looking, socially unsuccessful sidekick to Mandy and Claire, and would emerge a bold and beautiful woman with the power to attract any man she had time to notice.) The husband would come from this village—Sapperton, or one of the others nearby—and he would definitely drive a Golf. (The Golf was quite a thing, for some reason. In the fantasy, we drove it down to Cornwall for our honeymoon, where I amazed him by charging fearlessly into the sea with a surfboard under my arm.)

Instead I'd married an effete American clown. An actual clown, with boxes of red noses and ukuleles and silly hats. In a couple of hours he'd be stirring, as the bright Californian sunshine began to bleach the walls of our apartment. Maybe he'd yawn, roll over, and nuzzle at his new girlfriend before padding off to ramp up the air-conditioning and make her some gruesome green juice.

"Hello," I said.

"Oh, hello," the man said, glancing round. **Oh, hello.** As if he'd known me for years. "Found myself a sheep."

The sheep let off another foghorn baa, never turning from the man's face. "It's only been a few minutes," the man told me, "but we're both very serious about each other."

"I see." I smiled. "Is that legal?"

"You can't legislate love," he replied cheerfully.

An unexpected thought came to me: **I miss England.**

"How did you two meet?" I asked, stepping onto the green.

He smiled at the sheep. "Well, I was sitting here, feeling a bit sorry for myself, when this young lady appeared as if from nowhere. We started talking.

And before I knew it, we were discussing moving in together."

"This young **man**," I said. "I don't know anything about sheep, but even I can tell you he's not a lady."

After a moment the man leaned backward and checked the sheep's undercarriage.

"Oh."

The sheep stared at him. "Is your name not Lucy?" he asked. The sheep remained silent. "He told me his name was Lucy."

"His name is not Lucy," I confirmed.

The sheep **baa**ed again and the man laughed. A delirious jackdaw flapped out of a tree on the lane behind us.

Somehow I was standing right by them. The man, the sheep, and me all together on the bleached village green. The man was looking up at me. He had eyes the color of foreign oceans, I thought, full of warmth and good intentions.

He was rather lovely.

It will be many months before you can expect to develop authentic feelings toward another man, I'd been told this morning. The advice had come courtesy of a preposterous app called the BreakUp Coach, which my closest friend in LA, Jenni Carmichael, had downloaded (without permission) to my phone, the day after Reuben and I had announced our separation. Every morning it sent me dire push notifications about the state of emotional trauma I was in right now, and how that was totally okay.

Only I wasn't in any sort of emotional trauma. Even when Reuben told me he was sorry but he felt we should divorce, I'd had to force myself to cry so as not to hurt his feelings. When the app told me about my shattered heart and my broken spirit, I felt as if I were the recipient of someone else's mail.

But it made Jenni happy when she saw me reading the messages, so I kept the app. Jenni's emotional well-being—increasingly delicate, as her thirties came to a close, taking with them her hopes of reproduction—was heavily dependent on her ability to look after the needy.

The man turned back to the sheep. "Well, it's a shame. I thought we had a future, Lucy and I." His phone started to ring.

"Do you think you'll be okay?"

He pulled his phone a little way out of his pocket and canceled the call. "Oh, I expect so. At least, I hope so."

I busied myself scanning around for another sheep, a farmer, a helpful sheepdog. "I feel like we should do something about him, don't you?"

"Probably." The man pulled himself up to standing. "I'll call Frank. He owns most of the sheep around here." He dialed a number on his phone and I swallowed, suddenly uncertain. Once the sheep had been dealt with, we would have to stop joking and conduct an actual conversation.

I stood on the green and waited. The sheep was picking unenthusiastically at the coarse spokes of grass around him, keeping tabs on us. He'd been shorn recently, but even his cropped coat looked suffocating.

I wondered why I was here. I wondered why the man had been feeling sorry for himself earlier. I wondered why I was raking a hand through my hair. He was talking to Frank on the phone now, chuckling easily. "Okay, mate. I'll do my best. Right," he said, looking at me. He really did have lovely eyes.

(Stop it!)

"Frankie's not going to get here for a good hour. He says Lucy's broken out of a field down by the pub." He turned to the sheep. "You came a long way. I'm impressed."

The sheep carried on eating, so he looked at me instead. "I'm going to try and get him back down the lane. Fancy helping me?"

"Sure. I was heading down there for lunch anyway."

I hadn't been heading down there for lunch. I'd actually been waiting for the 54 to Cirencester, because there were people in Cirencester and there was no one at my parents' house. Last night an emergency room nurse from the Royal Infirmary in Leicester had called to say my grandfather had been admitted with a hip fracture. Granddad was ninety-three. He was also infamously offensive, but had nobody other than Mum and her sister, Lesley, who at the moment was in the Maldives with her third husband.

"Go," I'd told Mum when she wavered. Mum

didn't like letting me down. Every June she would put on a towering production for my visit: seamless logistics, a house full of flowers, exquisite food. Anything to persuade me that life in England was far better than anything California could offer.

"But . . ." I watched her sag. "But you'll be on your own."

"I'll be fine," I said. "Besides, Granddad will be thrown out of hospital if he doesn't have you there to apologize for him."

Last time my grandfather had been admitted to hospital, he'd had an unfortunate showdown with a consultant to whom Granddad kept referring as an "imbecilic medical student."

There was a pause as Mum struggled with her filial and parental responsibilities.

"Let me get the next couple of days out of the way," I'd said, "and then I'll come up to Leicester."

She looked at Dad, neither of them able to choose. And I thought, **When did you two become so indecisive?** They looked older this time, smaller. Especially Mum. As if she didn't quite fit her body anymore. (Was this my fault? Had I shrunk her, somehow, with my insistence on living abroad?)

"But you don't like being in our house," Dad said, unable to find a better way of putting it. And his inability to find something funny to say—for once—made the space in my throat swell until it felt like nothing could get past.

"Of course I do! What nonsense!"

"And we can't leave you our car. How will you get anywhere?"

"There's the bus."

"The bus stop's miles away."

"I like walking. Seriously, please go. I'll relax, like you're always telling me to. Read books. Eat my way through this mountain of food you've brought in."

And so this morning I'd waved them off down the track and found myself alone suddenly, in—yes—a house I didn't like being in. Especially on my own.

Which meant I had not been heading to the Daneway for a solo pub lunch. The fact of the matter was that I was trying to coerce this complete stranger into having a drink with me, in spite of this morning's app notification that flirtation with other men would only end in tears. **Try to remember, you're stratospherically vulnerable right now**, it had said, with an accompanying soft-focus picture of a girl crying into a mountain of comfy pillows.

The man's phone rang again. This time he let it ring out.

"Right, let's be having you," he said. He moved toward Lucy, who glared at him before turning and running. "You go over there," the man called at me. "Then we can funnel him into the lane. Ow! Shit!" He hopped awkwardly over the grass and then ran back for his flip-flops.

I swung round to the left, as fast as I could in the syrupy heat. Lucy swerved off to the right, where the man was waiting, laughing. Accepting he was trapped, Lucy grumbled off toward the little lane that led down to the pub, offering the odd baa of protest as he went.

Thank you, God, or the universe, or fate, I thought. For this sheep, this man, this English hedgerow.

What a relief to talk to someone who knew nothing of the sadness I was meant to be suffering. Who didn't put his head sympathetically to one side when he talked to me. Who simply made me laugh.

Lucy made several breaks for freedom on the road down to the pub, but with some strong teamwork we managed to return him to his field. The man snapped off a branch from a tree and braced it across the gap in the fence through which the sheep had escaped, then turned to me and smiled. "Done."

"Indeed," I said. We were standing right next to the pub. "You owe me a pint."

He laughed and said that seemed reasonable.

And so that was that.

CHAPTER FIVE

Seven days later Eddie and I had said good-bye. But it was a French good-bye: an **au revoir**. An **until the next time!** It was not a farewell. It was not even remotely a farewell. When did "farewell" involve the words "I think I've fallen in love with you"?

I had followed the river Frome home to my parents' house, happy and humming. The water was brilliantly clear that day, brindled with green, mossy cushions and clean gravel riffles, watched over by spiked clusters of cattails. I passed the spot where Hannah had once fallen in trying to pick crowfoot flowers and surprised myself by laughing out loud. My heart was full, singing with memories of the last week: late-night conversations, cheese sandwiches, belly laughs, bath towels drying on a rail. The broad mass of Eddie's body, the wind sifting gently through the trees outside his barn like fine trails of flour and, over and over again, the words he had said when I'd left.

I'd arrived that evening in Leicester. In the taxi to the hospital, a rainstorm had broken; the town turned dark and the red lights of A&E had slid down the windscreen like soup. I'd found my grandfather up in a hot ward, surly but shaken, and my parents exhausted.

There had been no call from Eddie that night. No message detailing his return flight. Briefly, as I put my pajamas on, I'd wondered why. **He was probably in a hurry,** I told myself. **He was with his friend.** And: **He loves me.** He'd call!

But Eddie David hadn't called. And he hadn't called, and he hadn't called.

For a couple of days I'd convinced myself it was fine. It would be absurd—deranged, even—to doubt what had happened between us. But as the days bled painfully into a week, I found it harder to hold at bay the rising ocean of panic.

"He's having a great time in Spain," I lied, when I arrived in London for my planned stay with Tommy.

A few days later, over lunch with Jo, I'd cracked. "He hasn't called," I admitted. Tears of panic and humiliation fattened in my eyes. "Something must have happened to him. It wasn't just a fling, Jo; it changed everything."

Tommy and Jo were kind to me; they listened, told me I was "doing really well," but I sensed they were shocked by the disintegration of the Sarah they knew. Was I not the woman who'd turned her life around after running off to LA in a black cloud of tragedy? The woman who'd started a brilliant children's charity, married an all-American man; the woman who now flew round the world making keynote speeches?

That same woman spent two weeks skulking around Tommy's flat, reduced to stalking a man with whom she'd spent seven days.

In that time Britain had nearly exploded in the pressure cooker of the EU referendum, my grandfather had undergone two surgeries, and my parents had become virtual prisoners in his house. My charity had won a substantial grant, and Jenni was well into the last cycle of IVF for which her insurers would pay. I was in a landscape of very real human highs and lows, yet I'd struggled to register any of it.

I had seen friends do this. I'd watched in amazement as they claimed that his phone was broken; his leg was broken; **he** was broken, wasting unseen in a ditch. They insisted that some careless comment they'd made must have "scared him off," hence the need to "clear up any misunderstandings." I had watched them shred their pride, break their heart, lose their mind, all over a man who would never call. Worse, a man they barely knew.

And here I was. Sitting in Tommy's car, my pride shredded, my heart broken, my mind lost. Composing a desperate message saying that I really wasn't married anymore. That it had been a **very amicable breakup**.

Tommy pulled up near the gates of our old school just as rain began to print gentle patterns on the windscreen. He parked uncharacteristically badly, one wheel on the curb, but—even more uncharacteristically—made no attempt to straighten out. I took in the fat beech hedge, the yellow zigzags on the road, the sign up by the gates, and an old bass line of unease strummed in my pelvis. I put my phone in my handbag. Texting Eddie would have to wait.

"So, here we are!" The weight of unfelt enthusiasm made Tommy's voice sag in the middle like an overburdened washing line. "We should get going. I'm due to speak in five minutes!"

He didn't get going, so neither did we. Rudi stared at us. "Why aren't you getting out of the car?" he asked, incredulous. Nobody answered. After a few seconds he exploded from the backseat, running at speed toward the school gates. We watched in silence as he slowed to a hands-in-pockets saunter, stopping casually at the entrance to assess the possibility of fun on the school field. After squinting for a while, he turned back to the car. He wasn't pleased.

Poor Rudi. I didn't know how Jo had sold today to him, but I doubted she'd told the whole truth. A sports program launch at a secondary school might have held some appeal if he'd been in with a chance of wearing one of the fitness watches or heart-rate vests that were part of the project, or even if there had been children his age to play with. But the tech toys that formed the centerpiece of Tommy's program were to be showcased by a tribe of "promising athletes" selected by the head of physical education, and the youngest participant was fourteen.

Rudi stood near the car looking grumpy. Jo got out to talk to him, and Tommy, suddenly wordless, leaned over to check his reflection in the rearview mirror. **He's terrified**, I thought, with a swell of sympathy.

The boys at our mixed grammar had not been kind to little Thomas Stenham. One of them, Matthew Martyn, had accused Tommy of being gay when he had turned twelve and his flashy mother installed a fashion hairstyle on his head. Tommy had cried, and so, of course, it had stuck. Matthew and company had sprayed Tommy's seat with a "de-gaying" formula every day; they stuck pictures of naked men to the inside of his desk lid. He had started going out with Carla Franklin at age fourteen; they had called her a beard. Tommy had taken to spending hours in his mother's home gym, but his new muscles made things a good deal worse: they took to casually punching him on the school field. By the time his family emigrated to the States in 1995, he had had an exercise disorder, a mild stammer, and no male friends.

Years later—long after he'd returned to England—a wealthy tech lawyer named Zoe Markham had hired Tommy to be her personal trainer. He'd had a large number of successful London women on his books at the time, many of whom flirted quite openly with him. "I think it's a sort of fantasy," he'd told me. He was caught somewhere between flattery and disgust. "I'm like a sexy handyman with a tool belt. Blue collar with muscles."

Zoe Markham, apparently, was different. They got on "fantastically well" and had a "genuine connection," and, crucially, she saw him as a "whole person," not just an employee who had the power to make her look slim and beautiful. (She was already both.)

After a few months of casual flirting she had offered him a leg up into sports consultancy via an old friend. Tommy had taken her to dinner to thank her. She had taken him home and removed her clothes. "I think it's time for a real one-on-one, don't you?" she'd said.

She was his first girlfriend of any real significance; certainly the first he believed to be entirely out of his league. To him, she was a goddess, a marvel—the liniment for each and every one of his old wounds. "I wish I could tell those bastards at school," he'd told me, the day she invited him to move into her Holland Park flat. "I wish I could show them I'm capable of attracting a girl like Zoe." And I'd said, "Yes, wouldn't that be brilliant?" because I never imagined it could happen. That sort of thing never did.

Except, in Tommy's case, it did.

About a year ago he'd sent a brochure for his secondary sports program to every head teacher in the

UK. The program included a donation of wearable sports technology—heart-rate vests, fitness watches, that sort of thing—from one of Zoe's biggest clients, a tech multinational, and was Tommy's pride and joy. When he received a call from the head of our old school, he was touchingly delighted. "She wants me come and meet her head of PE!" he told me during one of our Skypes. "Isn't that **brilliant**?" He had found the situation to be marginally less brilliant when he discovered that the head of PE was his teenage bully, Matthew Martyn.

But it had been a good chat, Tommy assured me. A bit awkward, at first, but Matthew had said something about how they'd all been dickheads when they were teenagers, and punched Tommy on the arm and called him "mate." Later, like two old friends, they had compared notes: Matthew showed Tommy a photo of his family, and Tommy—unable to believe his luck—showed Matthew a picture of his beautiful, smartly liveried, fiercely toned girlfriend in her splendid London kitchen.

By the time I arrived at Tommy and Zoe's London flat earlier in June, already distraught about Eddie, Tommy had delivered the program. He told me his old ghosts had been laid to rest; that he was "over" what had happened to him at school; that he was actually looking forward to seeing Matthew Martyn again at the program launch. Then: "Zoe's coming," he added, as if it were a mere afterthought. "It'll be great to introduce her to Matt."

I had wanted to hug him then. To tell him that he was fine, just as he was. That he didn't need Zoe on his arm to increase his stock. But I went along with it, of course, because he needed me to.

Zoe had pulled out four days before the launch. "I have to go to Hong Kong for one of my clients," she'd said. "It's really important. Sorry, Tommy."

Not sorry enough, I thought. She knew what this meant. Tommy's face was the color of recycled paper.

"But . . . but the school's expecting you!"

She frowned. "I'm sure they'll survive. They're showing off to the rural press, not to me."

"Can you not fly a day later?" he pleaded. I could hardly bear to watch.

"No," she said levelly. "I can't. But you'll thank me for going on this trip. There's going to be a delegation from the Department for Culture, Media and Sport. I still think I've got a good chance of getting you onto one of their advisory committees."

Tommy had shaken his head. "But I told you. I'm not interested."

"And **I** told **you**, Tommy, that you are."

Jo and I had stepped in to replace her.

Did I want to return to my old school? Of course not. I'd hoped never to see the place again. But Tommy, I thought, needed me, and helping someone in need was just about the only decent distraction I knew. Besides, what did I have to fear? Mandy and Claire had left that school in the nineties. Neither they nor any of the people I'd fled would be there today.

"**Harrington.**" Tommy had twisted round to look at me. "Are you there?"

"Sorry. Yes."

"Look, there's something I need to tell you."

I watched him. Tommy's eyebrows were not carrying glad tidings.

"When I got that message about the local press earlier, Matthew told me something else. He—" Tommy broke off, and I knew then that it was bad.

"Matthew married Claire Peddler. I didn't mention it before because I didn't think you'd want to hear her name. But when he texted to say that the local press were coming, he also said that . . ."

No.

". . . that Claire had decided to come, too. And she's . . ."

Bringing Mandy.

". . . bringing a little group of friends from our year. Including Mandy Lee."

I sank forward and rested my head against the back of his seat.

CHAPTER SIX

Day One: The Drink That Lasted Twelve Hours

Sarah Mackey," I said. "M-A-C-K-E-Y."

The landlord handed me a pint of cider.

The man from the village green just laughed. "As it happens, I know how to spell Mackey. But thank you. My name's Eddie David."

"Sorry." I smiled. "I live in America. It's a more American surname, I think: when I'm over here, I often have to spell it. Plus I'm fond of clarity."

"So I see," Eddie said. He was leaning sideways on the bar, watching me. Tenner folded between large brown fingers. I liked the scale of this man. That he was so much taller, so much broader, so much stronger than me. Reuben and I had been the same height.

We sat in the pub garden, an oasis of flowers and picnic tables in the little valley below Sapperton village. The thin ribbon of the river Frome spooled unseen around the meadow fringing the pub's car park; briar roses toppled from a tree. A couple of walkers were slumped over half-pints, a panting cocker spaniel staring at me from under their legs. As soon as I sat down under a large umbrella, the dog came and sat by my feet, settling itself with a great huff of self-pity.

Eddie laughed.

Somewhere along the valley, the abrasive cracking of a chain saw started and stopped. A few stunned birds called dazedly from the woods above us. I sipped the cold cider and groaned. "Yes," I said.

"Yes," Eddie agreed. We clinked glasses and I felt an uncurling of pleasure. Being alone in my parents' empty house this morning had been more upsetting than I was willing to admit, and the walk along Broad Ride had done nothing to improve my mood. But here, taking the rough edge off it all, was cold cider and a very agreeable man. Maybe it could be a good day.

"I love this pub," I said. "We used to come here when I was a kid. My little sister and I would roam feral and poke around in the stream while my parents and their friends got a little too jolly."

Eddie took a good draft from his pint. "I grew up in Cirencester. Bit trickier to roam feral in the middle of a town. But we did come here once or twice."

"Oh, really? When would that have been? How old are you?"

"Twenty-one," Eddie said comfortably. "Although people say I look younger."

He didn't mind when I laughed. "Thirty-nine," he said eventually. "I remember running around this garden when I was about—what, ten? Then my mum moved here in the late nineties, so I started coming here quite a lot. How old are you? Maybe you and I were feral together."

A small fleck of suggestion. My app must be going mad.

"Oh, probably not. I moved to Los Angeles when I was still a teenager."

"Really? That's quite a move."

I nodded.

"Did one of your parents take a job out there?"

"Something like that."

"And are they still out there?"

"No. They live near here. Over toward Stroud."

I angled my face away, as if that excused me skirting the edge of a lie. "So. Eddie. Tell me what you were doing on Sapperton Green on a weekday afternoon."

He leaned down to stroke the walkers' dog. "Visiting my mum. She lives up near the school." A tiny hairline fracture passed through his voice. "What were you doing?" he asked.

"I walked from Frampton Mansell." I nodded in the direction of my parents' village.

He frowned. "But you didn't come along the valley—you came from up the hill."

"Well . . . I wanted to get some proper exercise, so I hiked up the hill and walked along the top. Along Broad Ride, in fact—it's changed a lot," I added quickly. **This is becoming a minefield.** "So overgrown! It used to be so wide and stately; people would bring their horses from all over for a gallop. Now it's little more than a pathway."

He nodded. "They do still gallop up and down it, even though it's been banned. One of them came very close to mowing me down earlier."

I smiled at the thought of anyone being able to mow down this big mass of man, horse or otherwise. It pleased me that he, too, liked to walk along that secret green corridor.

"I was like Moses of Sapperton," he said. "Parting a Red Sea of cow parsley."

We both sipped our drinks.

"So do you live round here?"

"Yeah," Eddie said, "although I get a lot of commissions from London, so I'm there a fair bit." He slapped me suddenly on the calf.

"Horsefly," he said softly, flicking the dead insect off his palm. "Eating your leg. Sorry."

I took a long draw on the cider and felt the heady, sensual purr of alcohol and mild shock. "They're bastards here in June," he said. "They're bastards all year, but especially in June."

He showed me two angry bumps on his forearm. "One of them got me this morning."

"I hope you bit it back."

Eddie smiled. "I didn't. They spend quite a lot of time sitting on horses' private parts."

"Of course. Yes."

Before I'd asked permission of myself, I touched

the bites on his skin. "Poor arm," I said, although in a very matter-of-fact tone, because I was already embarrassed.

Eddie stopped laughing and turned to look at me. He met my gaze, a question in his eyes.

It was me who looked away first.

Sometime later I was comfortably drunk. Eddie was inside getting our third, or maybe fourth pint. I heard the beep-beep of the till as the landlord rang up his order, the crackle of something I hoped might be crisps, and the lazy whine of a plane dragging across the sky.

The lichened surface of our old picnic table had begun to feel like sandpaper on the soft backs of my thighs. I looked around for another, less abrasive table, but found none, so I flopped down in the grass like the ramblers' dog from earlier on. I smiled, happy and intoxicated. Grass tickled my ear. I wanted never to leave. I wanted simply to be here; no phone, no responsibilities. Just Eddie David and I.

As I gazed up at the sky, the earth warm underneath me, I caught an old ripple of memory. **This**, I thought lazily. The smell of warm grass, the soft patter and rustle of it, layered with buzzing insects and snatches of hummed songs. This had been me once. Before Tommy had moved to America and adolescence had exploded under my feet like a landmine, **this had been enough**.

"Man down," Eddie said, coming down the steps with a beer, a cider and—worshipful praises!—crisps! "You claimed to be a hard drinker."

"I forgot about cider," I admitted. "But it should be noted that I haven't passed out. I just got fed up with that prickly bench." I hauled myself up on my elbows. "Anyway, you must open those crisps straightaway."

Eddie sat on the grass next to me, removing from his pocket what looked like an uncomfortable bunch of keys. They were held together by a little wooden key ring in the shape of a mouse.

"Who's that guy?" I asked, as Eddie handed me a pint. "I like him."

Eddie turned to look at the key ring. After a little pause he smiled. "She's called Mouse. I made her when I was nine."

"You made her? Out of wood?"

"I did."

"Oh! Gosh, how lovely."

Eddie ran a finger along Mouse. "She's been with me through a lot," he smiled. "She's my taliswoman. Anyway. Cheers." He leaned back on his elbows, turning his face to the sun.

"So we're just drinking in the middle of the day," I surmised happily. "While everyone else is working. We're just sitting here, drinking."

"I'd say so."

"We're drinking in the middle of the day and now

we are quite drunk. And we are having a nice time, I think."

"Will we resume conversation, or are you going to spend the afternoon making statements?"

I laughed. "As I said earlier, Eddie: clarity. It keeps me on the straight and narrow."

"Okay. Well, I'm going to just eat some crisps and drink my beer. Let me know when you're done."

He opened the crisps and passed them over.

I like him, I thought.

Since arriving in this secret garden, Eddie and I had sifted through our childhood memories and discovered hundreds of historical intersections. We'd walked the same hills, been to the same sweaty nightclubs; we'd sat on the same towpath at sunset and counted dragonflies dancing above the reed beds in the old Stroudwater canal.

All of this had been separated by only a couple of years. I imagined sixteen-year-old me meeting eighteen-year-old Eddie, and wondered if he would have liked me then. I wondered if he liked me now.

Earlier on I had told him about my nonprofit organization and he'd been delighted, had asked me endless questions. He understood straightaway the difference between our Clowndoctors and the regular entertainers who'd visit a children's hospital. And he understood that I did it because I couldn't not, no matter how many funding cuts we suffered, no matter how frequently our guys were treated as mere party clowns. "Wow," he'd said, after I'd shown him a clip of two of our Clowndoctors working with a child who'd been too afraid to go into surgery. He looked actually quite emotional. "That's incredible. I . . . Good for you, Sarah."

He had shown me pictures of the furniture and cabinetry that he made in a workshop on the edge of Siccaridge Wood. That was his job—people commissioned him to make beautiful things out of wood for their homes: kitchens, cabinets, tables, chairs. He loved wood. He loved furniture. He loved the smell of timber wax and the crack of a biscuit joint tightening in a clamp, he told me; had given up trying to force himself to do something more profitable.

He showed me a picture of an old barn: small, stone, with a gently pitched roof, sitting in the sort of forest clearing that'd be right at home in a Hans Christian Andersen tale.

"That's my workshop. It's also my home. I'm a real-life hermit; I live in a barn in a wood."

"Oh, good! I've **always** wanted to meet a hermit! Am I the first human you've talked to in weeks?"

"Yes!" Then: "No," he added quickly. In his eyes I caught the edge of something I couldn't grasp. "I'm not actually a hermit. I have friends and family and a busy life."

After a pause he smiled. "I didn't need to say that, did I?"

"Probably not."

He cleared the picture of the barn from his phone,

just as it started ringing. This time, he switched it off, although without any visible irritation. "Well, that's my job, anyway. I love it. Although there have been years when I've earned almost nothing. They've been less fun." A tiny spider crawled up one of his arms and he watched it, pushing it gently away when it tried to enter the sleeve of his T-shirt. "A few years back I even thought about getting a proper job, something with a guaranteed pay packet. But I can't do a nine-to-five. I'd . . . Well, I suspect I'd struggle. Maybe die. Something bad would happen; I wouldn't survive it."

I considered this.

"I find it rather annoying when people say things like that," I said eventually. "I think only a tiny handful of people would actually choose to be in an office nine to five. But you have to remember, most people don't have a choice. You're quite privileged, being able to do something like cabinetry out of a workshop in the Cotswolds."

"True," Eddie said. "And of course I know what you mean, but I'm still not sure I agree. It's my contention that everyone has a choice, in everything. On some level."

I watched him.

"What they do, how they feel, what they say. It's just somehow become the received wisdom that we don't have a choice. About anything. Jobs, relationships, happiness. All beyond our control." He shooed the tiny spider back into the grass. "It can be frustrating, watching everyone complaining about their problems, never wanting to discuss solutions. Believing they're a victim of other people, of themselves, of the world." That tiny hairline fracture had returned to his voice.

After a beat he turned to me, smiling. "I sound like an arsehole."

"A bit."

"I didn't mean to sound unsympathetic. I just meant . . ."

"It's okay. I know what you meant. And it's an interesting point."

"Maybe. But expressed very poorly. I'm sorry. I've just . . ." He paused. "I've been quite worn down by my mother recently. I love her, of course, but I sometimes wonder if she even **wants** to be happy. And then I feel awful because I know that it's pure brain chemistry, and of course she wants to be happy."

He scratched his shins. "You're just the first person I've talked to in the last few days who hasn't been feeling sorry for themselves. I got carried away. Sorry. Thank you. The end."

I laughed, and he leaned back, letting one of his knees fall sideways so it landed on my leg. "I'm having an even better time than I would have done with Lucy the sheep. Thank you, Sarah Mackey. Thank you for giving up your Thursday afternoon to drink pints with me."

My chest filled with thick spirals of pleasure. And I let it, because it felt good to be happy.

Eddie went to the loo soon after and I deleted Jenni's app from my phone. Rebound or not, I hadn't felt this happy in a man's company—in anyone's company, really—in a very long time.

"There's something in this valley, isn't there?" Eddie said later. Even he wasn't sounding sober anymore. The landlord had locked up for the afternoon and told us we were welcome to stay in the garden as long as we wanted.

"The devil's furnace?" I suggested, fanning my face. "For someone who lives in southern California, I'm unconscionably hot. Where's the Pacific when you need it? Or a pool. An air conditioner at very least."

Eddie laughed, angling his head toward me. "Do you have a pool?"

"Of course not! I run a nonprofit!"

"I'm sure some charity executives pay themselves enough to have a pool."

"Well, not this one. I don't even own an apartment."

He looked back up at the hot bar of sky. "Yes, the devil's furnace is here," he said thoughtfully. "But there's something else, don't you think? Something old, or secretive. It's always felt to me like a back pocket, this little valley. Somewhere where all sorts of stories and memories are shoved. Like old ticket stubs."

I couldn't agree more, I thought. I had more ticket stubs shoved down the back of this valley than

I cared to think about. And it didn't matter how many years I had spent living away from the place: they were still here, every time I returned. Echoes of my sister at every turn of the tiny river Frome; snatches of song in the old beech trees; the feel of her hand in mine. The mirror-stillness of the lake, just like the day we drove back from the hospital. It was all still here. Just out of sight, but never out of mind.

We lay there talking for hours, a part of him always touching a part of me. My heart expanding and contracting like hot metal.

Something was going to happen. Something had already happened. We both knew.

At some point Frank the farmer arrived to check his sheep and repair his fence, and gave us some cola and a packet of Cheddar from his shopping. "I owe you," he'd said, and then winked at Eddie as if I couldn't see him.

We drank the entire bottle of Coke and ate almost all the cheese. I wondered if Reuben's new girlfriend—who had apparently taken him on a date to a juice bar—had ever drunk several pints of cider, passed out in a pub garden with a stranger, and then snacked on Coke and Cheddar. I found that I couldn't have cared less.

I felt like I was at home. Not just with Eddie, but here, in this valley, where I'd grown up. For the first time since I was young, I felt like I was somewhere I belonged.

Our secret valley finally cooled as the broiling sun dropped off the side of the world. A twilight fox skeetered across the car park. Small groups of people came and went, the quiet clink of glasses and cutlery muffled by the sluggish rustle of trees. Bright stars stapled an inky sky.

Eddie was holding my hand. We were back at our table. We'd eaten something—lasagna? I barely remember. He was telling me about his mother, and how her depression was beginning to spiral downward again. He was going on holiday in a week with a friend, windsurfing in Spain, and was worried about leaving her, even though she'd told him she would be fine.

"Sounds like you're very good to her," I said. He hadn't replied, but he'd lifted our locked hands up and just kissed one of my knuckles.

And now the pub was closing, for a second time, and even though we hadn't discussed it, even though I was still technically married, and meant to be suffering deep emotional trauma, even though I had never gone home with a stranger before—especially to a barn in quite literally the middle of nowhere—it was as clear as the cloudless night that I was going home with him.

Using the light of my phone, because his was so

cracked the torch no longer functioned, we walked hand in hand along the tangled, silent towpath, past forgotten lock workings and glassy black pools of water.

He let me into his hermit's barn—which really was in a woodland clearing, flanked by beautiful old horse chestnuts and dimly glowing cow parsley—but there were no elves or satyrs or silken-haired faeries here, just an old army Land Rover and a small patch of darkened lawn, at which Eddie stared suspiciously while he got out his keys. "Steve?" I thought I heard him whisper. I didn't question him.

He opened the door. "Come in," he said, and neither of us could quite look at each other, because it was happening, now, and we both knew already that it was bigger than the next few hours.

As we walked through the stilled machines in his workshop, I breathed in the pungent scent of cut wood and imagined Eddie in here: planing, hammering, gluing, sawing. Making beautiful things out of beautiful materials with those large brown hands. I thought of those hands on my skin and felt quite foggy.

We passed through two heavy doors—essential, he told me, for sawdust control—and finally up a flight of stairs to a big, open-plan space, full of old lamps and shadowy beams and gentle creaks. Outside, the trees moved slowly, black against black, and a fine twist of cloud wandered across the headlamp moon.

I got a glass of water in his kitchen and heard him behind me. I stood there for a while, eyes closed as I felt his breath on my bare shoulder. Then I turned round and leaned against the sink as he kissed me.

CHAPTER SEVEN

Dear You,

Look, I'm married. And I've a horrible feeling you already know.

I wasn't lying when I told you I was single. And I definitely wasn't lying about how you made me feel.

Reuben and I separated about three months ago. The thing that finished us off was that I couldn't give him a baby, but I think we'd both known for a very long time that we'd come to the end of the road. It's a long story— probably beyond the scope of Facebook Messenger—but it was very hard for him.

I was so horribly relieved when he sat me down; I knew what he was going to say. I only wished I'd had the courage to say it myself, years earlier. I sat there opposite

him with a phone charger in my hand,
weaving the cable round and round my
fingers until he took it, and then I cried,
because I knew he needed me to.

Is that it, Eddie? Is my marriage why
you didn't call me? If it is, please try to
remember how it felt when we were
together. I meant it all. Every kiss, every
word, every everything.

I read the message three times and then deleted
the whole thing.

Dear Eddie, I wrote instead.

I suspect you've found that I am married.
I would dearly love the opportunity to
explain the whole thing to you, face-to-
face—although I want you to know right
now that I am not married any longer: the
website is out of date. I was—and still
am—single. And I want to see you, and
apologize, and explain.

Sarah

Tommy, Jo, and Rudi were long gone. I had been
crouching in the back of Tommy's car for nearly half
an hour.

I was going to have to get out.

CHAPTER EIGHT

Tommy was standing on a sad little platform in the middle of our old school field, talking into a PA system. He was pretending to find it funny that the equipment was punctuating his speech with burping noises.

I scanned the assembled crowd. Why were Mandy and Claire here today? Did they not have better things to do? Did they not have **jobs**? My lungs felt like they'd been bundled into a tiny chamber behind my nose. I couldn't stand the prospect of seeing them. Not now. Not in this state.

"Hey." Jo appeared from nowhere. "How are you doing?"

"Great."

"It'll be fine," she said quietly. "Even if Tommy feels he has to hang around, we'll be done within the hour. And I'll keep an eye on you."

We watched in silence as Tommy talked about Matthew Martyn. A real inspiration to his pupils . . . Has worked tirelessly on this program . . . Makes all the difference to work with people like Matt . . .

"Look, I . . . um, are they here?"

Jo slid her hand into the crook of my elbow. "I don't know, Sarah," she said. "I don't know what they look like."

I nodded, trying to breathe deeply.

"What have you been up to, anyway?" she asked. "Hiding on the car floor?"

"Mostly. I messaged Eddie. About being married. Then I put on too much makeup. And now I'm here."

There was a short gust of applause, and we turned to watch as Tommy handed the microphone over to Matthew Martyn. Matthew was one of those men who'd spent so much time working out that he had to carry his enormous arms at an angle, like a penguin. He and Tommy slapped each other on the back as they swapped places.

"Right," Jo said. "I think I'd better go and wait for him. After Matthew's speech it's mingling time." I watched helplessly as she walked away.

After a few minutes Rudi sauntered up, holding a glass of champagne. "This is **so** boring, Sarah," he said.

"I know."

"And Tommy's being weird."

"It's because he's nervous," I told him, removing the champagne from his hand. "Do you ever behave?"

"No." Rudi smiled, then pointed at an all-weather

running track that hadn't existed in my time. Hurdles were arranged across the lanes closest to us. "Can I go and jump over those things?"

"If you promise you'll stick to the lower ones."

"Epic!" He ran off.

Wretched memories oozed from my skin like sweat as I scanned around me again. I **hated** this place. And no matter how juvenile it was, I hated Matthew Martyn. I didn't care that he'd been a teenager: he'd made another boy cry, again and again and again, and he'd derived pleasure from it. He was talking now as if he'd designed the bloody program, not Tommy.

I was halfway down Rudi's champagne when I saw Mandy and Claire at the back of the crowd. Ten yards away, maybe less. I darted my gaze away before I was seen, taking with me a few fragmented details: a blue-and-yellow dress, a fringe, back fat straining over a bra strap. I lowered the glass, my arms moving like those of a robot in a crude animation. My face flared red.

Then: "Sarah Harrington?" a voice whispered near my left shoulder. "Is that you?"

I turned to find myself face-to-face with my English teacher, Mrs. Rushby. Her hair was a little gray now, but still scrolled into that elegant twist that we'd all tried to copy at some point during our school years.

"Oh, hello!" I whispered. My voice was laced with hysteria.

Mrs. Rushby, without warning, gave me a tight hug. "I wanted to do that years ago," she said, "but you'd gone off to America. How are you doing, Sarah? How have you been?"

"Great!" I lied. "And you?"

"Very good, thank you." Then: "I am so pleased to hear you're well. I really hoped it would work out for you in California."

I was touched. Not just that she'd hoped for better times for me, but that she had remembered me at all. Then again, I thought, I hadn't been a very ordinary pupil by the time I'd left.

For a short while, protected from the crowd by Mrs. Rushby, I started to feel a faint whisper of confidence. I made a couple of jokes and felt pathetically happy when she laughed. Did anyone ever lose the desire to impress their favorite teacher? I wondered. More than nineteen years had passed since I'd been in her A-level English class, and yet here I was, trying to make clever gags about revenge tragedies.

Mrs. Rushby, thankfully, changed the subject when she realized I couldn't remember John Webster's name. She told me she'd seen a news piece about my charity when she'd taken her family on holiday to California. "Something to do with entertaining hospitalized children, isn't it? Clowns?"

I relaxed as I slipped into even safer territory: work. Clowndoctors, I explained, as I had done a thousand times before. Not clowns. Trained to support the kids, normalize their medical experience, make the hospital environment feel less intimidating.

As I spoke I glanced over at Mandy and Claire, still there at the back of the crowd. The blue-and-yellow dress and the fringe had belonged to Claire; the back fat to Mandy. Her once-spiky little frame had expanded by at least five stone since school, something I'd probably have prayed for back then. Now I felt nothing. She looked over at me, then quickly away.

Mrs. Rushby excused herself to hand something to another teacher and I downed the rest of Rudi's champagne, just as the railway level-crossing alarm—a sound I hadn't heard in years—started up in the distance. And for a second I was back in the midnineties again, a teenager wading through uncertainty and emotional hubris, exhausted by the effort of just living. A ladder in her tights, a thin attempt at a knowing smile smeared across her face. Trying so hard to get it right with Mandy Lee and Claire Peddler.

Mrs. Rushby was still busy and I was now exposed, so I checked my Facebook messages. I made myself look tense and focused, as if I were responding to a critical work e-mail.

Still nothing from Eddie.

I put my phone away and watched Rudi, who was sizing up a far too big hurdle. "Rudi," I called. "No." I mimed slashing my throat.

"I can do it," he shouted at me.

"No, you can't," I called back.

"Yes, I can!"

"If you move one more inch toward that hurdle, Rudi O'Keefe, I'll tell your mum you've been using her password."

He stared at me in disbelief. Aunty Sarah would never be so mean!

I stood my ground. Aunty Sarah would absolutely be so mean.

He returned angrily to the smaller hurdles and I noticed someone watching him from the grassy island in the middle of the track. Someone slim, boyish, wearing shapeless jeans and a khaki-colored mac. The hood was pulled up, even though the rain had cleared. A sixth-former? Photographer? After a few seconds I realized his gaze was directed not toward Rudi but toward my part of the field. In fact—I turned round, but the only people nearby were Mrs. Rushby and the other teacher—it seemed oddly as if he were looking at **me**.

I squinted. Male? Female? I couldn't tell. For a second I even wondered if it was Eddie, but he was broader than this person. Much taller.

I turned round again, to make certain there was nobody else he could be watching. There was not. Abruptly, the figure started walking away, toward a new entrance gate onto the main road.

"Sorry, Sarah." Mrs. Rushby returned. "So, tell me, how's your husband? I remember him from the television piece. He seemed like a very talented man."

I checked over my shoulder one last time, just as the person in the khaki mac did the same. It was me he was looking at. It was **definitely** me. But after a split second he turned back and walked off the school grounds.

An electric bus whined past on the main road. Slender planks of sun splintered out from between clouds, and something moved uneasily in my abdomen. Who was that?

I watched Mrs. Rushby's face drop as I told her Reuben and I had recently separated. This, I thought, would take some getting used to. "We're still running the company together, though. It's all very amicable and grown-up!"

"I'm sorry." She frowned, folding her arms self-consciously. "I shouldn't have asked."

"Not at all." I wished I could explain to her how easy it was—how embarrassingly easy—for me to talk about Reuben. **Why had a person in a hood been watching me?** That's what I wanted to know.

"Well, Sarah, I'm quite sure you'll find happiness with someone else."

"I hope so!" I said. And then, to my horror: "Actually, there is a someone else, but . . . It's difficult."

Mrs. Rushby was clearly taken aback. "Right," she said, after a pause. "Oh, dear."

What was **wrong** with me? This had been my first shot at a normal conversation in two weeks! "I'm sorry," I sighed. "I sound like one of your GCSE students."

She smiled. "One is never too old to yearn," she said kindly. "I can't remember who said that, but I endorse it wholeheartedly."

I couldn't think of a single thing to say, so I apologized again.

"Sarah, if we didn't have thousands of years' writings on the pain of love—not to mention the questioning of faith, the loss of self it precipitates—I'd be out of a job."

Yes, I thought miserably. That was it. The loss of self. How could I ever admit that I preferred the idea of Eddie being dead than I did that he'd simply changed his mind? I was a monster.

I missed Sarah Mackey. She'd been so **regular**. She'd—

"ARGHHHH!"

I whipped round. Rudi must have tackled the too-high hurdle. He was curled on the ground, clutching his leg.

"Oh, fuck," Jo hissed, right into the silence that followed. She ran over to him, and all the parents and the teachers and the local journalists, all of Matthew Martyn's junior sports troupe—not to mention Matthew himself—turned as one, sending javelins of disapproval across the field. **Who was this woman who'd turned up with Tommy? Why wasn't her child in school? And why was she using the F-word?**

"Charming," I heard a woman say. It was Mandy Lee. I'd know that voice anywhere.

I hurried over to the screaming heap of Rudi and helped Jo inspect his leg. "Mummy," he wailed, a word I hadn't heard him use in years. Jo caved herself around him, kissing him, telling him he was safe. A tall man with a pointed face marched up to Jo and announced that he was the designated first aider.

"Let me take a look at him, please," he said, and Rudi's wails increased to siren pitch. He never did accidents by halves.

After Jo had taken Rudi off in a taxi to the minor injuries unit at Stroud Hospital, I slunk off to the toilet with the vague notion of collecting myself.

I ran my hand over the brick cubicle wall, knowing that, under layers of paint, my name was scratched alongside Mandy's and Claire's and some fierce words about how nobody would ever come between us. Ironic, really, given that a few days after we had committed our indestructibility to the toilet wall, they had decided to eject me from their block of desks for the day and I'd ended up having to eat my lunch in the very same cubicle. It had been raining outside; I'd had nowhere else to go. I recalled the burst of misery as my crisp packet had rustled and someone—some girl who'd never identified herself—had peered under the door to see what I was up to.

I flushed the loo, thinking about the unidentifiable person watching me from under the hood of his coat earlier. Who even knew I was in Stroud today, beyond Eddie? Could he—or she—really have been looking at me? And if so, why?

I checked Messenger before leaving the cubicle, but there was nothing from Eddie. He still hadn't been online since the day we met. Maybe Jo was right, I thought. Maybe I should write a public post on his wall. The only thing stopping me, after all, would be fear of what people might think. What Eddie might think. And if I was as certain as I said I was that something bad had happened, that should be the least of my worries.

The idea pitched around me like a bird trapped in a room.

But then: No! came the answer. It's not as simple as that. The reason I haven't written on his page is that . . .

Is that **what**?

I was going to have to write something. If Eddie really had been wasting away in a ditch, if he really had drowned in the Strait of Gibraltar, I was being pretty damned casual.

I opened up his Facebook page, took a long breath, and typed.

Has anyone seen Eddie recently? Have been trying to get in touch with him. A bit worried. Let me know if you've heard from him. Ta. And before I had a chance to stop myself, I pressed "Post."

Suddenly the loo was filled with sounds I remembered. High-pitched chatter, makeup bags being unzipped, mascara wands being pumped. Several women talking through curved mouths as they smeared on lipstick. They shrieked with laughter about how they were still doing their makeup in the toilet mirrors after all these years, and I smiled despite myself.

Then: "Have you seen Sarah Harrington?" someone asked. "That was a surprise."

And then Mandy's voice: "I know! Pretty brave to just turn up like that."

Murmurs of agreement. "Can I borrow your mascara? Mine's gone clumpy." Taps being turned on and off; the useless sigh of the hand dryer that had never worked.

"If I'm honest, I was a bit disappointed to see her," Claire said. The other women went silent. "I just wanted to have a nice afternoon, support Matt—know what I mean?"

Know what I mean? I'd said it for a while, to fit in.

"Yes," Mandy said. "And of course she's got as much right to be here as anyone else, but it's . . . well, difficult. For us, at least."

Claire agreed that it was.

"She pretended not to have seen me earlier," Mandy said. "So I'm afraid I did the same. And so should you, Claire, if it's going to stress you out." This was the kind of leadership that had made her popular at school. **Let's ignore Claire tomorrow.**

Let's make some fake IDs. Although not for you, Sarah—you don't look old enough. "I've got too much on my plate at the moment—I haven't the mental space for Sarah Harrington."

Further murmurs of agreement.

Then: "Tommy Stenham's looking well," Claire said lightly. "Don't you think?"

Oh, she'd been deadly at that! Drop some poor person into the conversation—tone innocuous, intentions murderous—and wait, quivering, for Mandy to take the lead.

"Looking very well indeed," Mandy agreed, "although I was a little confused by his girlfriend." Her voice just skirted laughter.

I tried to breathe quietly.

"Oh, that's not his girlfriend," Claire said. "His girlfriend's a lawyer. Matt's seen a photo of her. Apparently she's much better looking than the woman with the kid."

Mandy said, "I suppose the real surprise is that he has a girlfriend at all."

Witchy cackling. More taps. More towels. And then they started recounting, voices thick with guilty pleasure, all the things the boys used to say about Tommy. Through gales of laughter they agreed it had been **very cruel**. On a roll, now, they moved on to the length and appropriateness of Jo's dress, the generous proportions of her body, the embarrassing spectacle Rudi had made, and I began to boil. Hearing them talk about me had been bad enough, but it was nothing I hadn't spent years imagining them saying. Tommy, though? Jo? No.

So I wrenched open my cubicle door and I faced them: this row of thirty-seven-year-old women, with their carefully done hair and their perfume and their outfits that they wouldn't admit to having bought especially for the occasion. They all turned round, mascaras in hand, lip gloss sparkling sickly. They all stared at me, and I stared at them.

And I said nothing. Sarah Mackey, keynote speaker, lobbyist, campaigner. She stood there in silence in front of her old friends, and then she fled.

CHAPTER NINE

Day Eight: The Day I Left

This has been the best week of my life," Eddie said, the day I left his house.

I loved this about him. He seemed always to say what he was thinking; nothing was edited. Which was a novel experience for me, because everyone edited everything when I came back to England.

Smiling, he placed two big hands round the sides of my face and kissed me again. My heart was wide open and my life was starting over. I had never been more certain of anything.

"I do want to meet your parents," he said, "because they sound very nice, and because they made you. But I'm quite glad they had to go away."

"I agree." I traced a finger along his forearm.

"It feels like the most extraordinary act of providence—there I was, sitting on the village green, talking to a sheep—and you just marched into my life, as if you'd been waiting in the wings for a cue. And then you came to the pub, and you . . . liked me." He smiled. "Or at least you seemed to."

"Very much." I reached round and slid my hand into his shorts pocket. "Very much indeed."

Outside, the song of a blackbird fluted down from a branch. We both turned to listen.

"Final time," he said. He handed me a flower of hawthorn blossom from the pot on his windowsill. Spring had been slow, and the flowers were still blanketed across the trees like whipped cream. "Final time. Should I cancel my holiday?"

"You should not," I made myself say. I twirled the tiny stem between my fingers. "Go and have a wonderful time. Forward me your flight details and I'll be at Gatwick a week today."

"You're right." He sighed. "I must go on this holiday, and I must actually enjoy it. Normally I'd be over the moon at the thought of a week in Tarifa. But I can call you, can't I? From Spain? I don't care about the cost. Let me take your mobile number, and numbers for everyone you're likely to be near until I can see you again. We can FaceTime. Or Skype. And talk."

I laughed, squinting through cracks to put my number in his mangled old phone. "It looks like you've driven over this on a tractor," I said, putting the little sprig of blossom on the windowsill.

"Put in the landline at your parents' house," he said. "And the landline where you're staying in London. What's your friend's name? Tommy? Put his address in, too, so I can send you a postcard.

Although you're going up to Leicester to see your granddad first, aren't you?"

I nodded.

"Well, give me his number and address, too."

I laughed. "Trust me, you don't want to end up on the phone to Granddad."

I handed back his phone.

"Let's make friends on Facebook, too." He opened his Facebook and typed in my name. "Is this you? Standing on a beach?"

"That's me."

"Very Californian." He looked at me and my stomach pitched. "Oh, Sarah Mackey, you're lovely."

He bent down and kissed my shoulder. He kissed the crook of my elbow. The pulse at the bottom of my neck. He pulled my hair up and kissed my spine as it dropped into my vest.

"I'm crazy about you," he said.

I closed my eyes and smelled him. His skin, his clothes, the soap we'd used in the shower. I couldn't imagine surviving without this for seven days. And as much as I'd loved Reuben, I had never seen separation from him as a matter of survival.

"I feel the same." I held him tightly. "But I think you know that. I'll miss you. A lot."

"And I'll miss you." He kissed me again, pushing my hair back off my face. "Look, when I get back, I want to introduce you to my friends and my mother."

"Great."

"And I want to meet your parents, and your British friends, and your terrifying granddad, if he ends up coming to stay."

"Of course."

"And we'll work out what to do from there, but it'll involve us being together somehow, somewhere."

"Yes. You, me, and Mouse." I slid my hand back into his pocket, felt the little wooden key ring.

He paused. Then: "Take her," he said. He pulled out his keys. "Keep her safe until I get back. I'm always scared of losing her on the beach. She means a lot to me."

"No! I can't take your lovely Mouse. Don't be mad . . ."

"Take her," he insisted. "Then we know we'll see each other again."

He placed Mouse in my palm. I looked at her jetty eyes, then at Eddie's.

"Okay." I closed my fingers around her. "If you're sure?"

"I'm very sure."

"I'll take good care of her."

We kissed for a long time, him leaning against the newel post at the top of the stairs. me pressed tight into his chest, Mouse in my hand. We'd agreed that he wouldn't see me off at the front door. It seemed too final, too much like a proper separation.

"I'll call you later today," he said. "I'm not sure what time, but I'll call. I promise."

I smiled. It was sweet of him to acknowledge that: the old, crabby fear of not being called. But I knew he would. I knew he'd do everything he said he'd do.

"Bye," he said, kissing me one last time. I took the blossom stem and walked down the stairs, turning at the bottom. "Don't watch me go," I said. "Make it feel like I've just popped out for some milk or something."

He smiled. "Okay. Good-bye, Sarah Mackey. See you in a few minutes, with some milk or something."

We both paused, watching each other. I laughed, for no reason other than sheer happiness. Then: **Say it**, I thought. **Say it, even though it's crazy, even though we've only known each other a week. Say it!**

And he did. He leaned against the newel post, crossed his arms and said, "Sarah, I think I might have fallen in love with you. Is that too much?"

I breathed out. "No. It's perfect."

We both smiled. A point of no return had been crossed.

After what felt like a long, long time, I blew him a kiss and drifted off into the bright morning.

CHAPTER TEN

Dear You,

I've been missing you so much today, little sister.

I miss your naughty laugh and those milky sweets you always used to buy with your pocket money. I miss that keyboard you had when you were little, the one that played that infuriating tune when you pressed the yellow button. You'd pretend you were playing it yourself and you'd laugh yourself silly, thinking you'd fooled me.

I miss finding evidence of you having had a root around my bedroom when I wasn't there. I miss the way you used to splodge jam right over the edge of the bread crust so you wouldn't have any jamless mouthfuls.

I miss the sound of you sleeping. Sometimes I'd pause from my busy schedule of teenage angst and just listen at your door. Soft breaths. Stars on the ceiling. The rustle of your spaceship duvet, which you insisted on, even though the man in the department store said it was for boys.

Oh, my Hedgehog. How I miss you.

Things aren't all that good for me at the moment. I don't know what to do with myself—I feel like I'm losing my mind.

Let's hope not, eh?

Anyway, I love you. Always. Sorry I couldn't find anything more jolly to say.

Me xxx

CHAPTER ELEVEN

If you can't reach me on my mobile, I may well be in my Gloucestershire workshop, it said on Eddie's "Contact Me" page.

I keep things pretty simple down there: there's a wood-burning stove, a temperamental kettle, and a desk, and that's it, as far as luxuries go. But I do have a phone, in case I'm attacked by bears or bandits. Try me on 01285 . . .

I highlighted the number. "Call?" my phone asked.

"Sarah?" It was Jo, calling from the kitchen. "Can you check this soup?"

"Coming!" I pressed "Call."

The phone started ringing and adrenaline mushroomed, pressing out at my skin like gas in an over-filled balloon. I leaned against the wall, hoping he wouldn't answer, hoping he would. Wondering what I would say if we spoke, wondering what I'd do if we didn't.

"Hello, this is Eddie David, cabinetmaker. Sorry I'm not here to take your call. Leave a message and I'll get back to you soonest, or try my mobile. Bye!"

I hung up. Flushed the toilet. I wondered if it would ever stop.

I had been spending the month of June in England for nineteen years. Normally, I stayed three weeks in Gloucestershire, with my parents, and one in London, with Tommy. London was close enough to Gloucestershire for this to work well. This trip, however, had turned out to be quite different. Granddad's sudden and total immobilization had prevented Mum and Dad from coming back. Trapped three hours away in Leicester, they divided their time between caring for him, trying not to kill him, and searching for a carer who would also try not to kill him. Any spare moments were spent on the phone to me. "We feel so awful that you're there and we're here," Mum had said miserably. "Is there **any** way you could stay a bit longer?"

I had agreed to stay an extra two weeks and moved my return flight to July 12. I'd promised Reuben I'd start working remotely as soon as my holiday finished, and to prove it, had accepted an invitation to speak at a palliative care conference organized by our one and only British trustee.

Until I resumed work, however, I was staying here in London. The prospect of my parents' empty house—with Eddie's place a mere mile away—was too appalling to consider. Zoe had been away most of this time, so it was just me and Tommy: exactly what I'd needed.

But the lady of the house was back now, just in from an EU roundtable on tech law; tired yet immaculate as she stood by the stove in a sleeveless silk blouse, stirring the ramen I'd made to welcome her home.

I hovered embarrassedly in the doorway, watching her. She was one of those people who had no need for an apron, even when wearing silk. A woman of precision and economy, Zoe Markham, not just of speech but of body. She took up only a slim column of space and seldom saw fit to enlarge it with gesticulation or noise. In fact, had it not been for her behavior around Tommy during the first year of their relationship, I wouldn't even have been able to swear that we were of the same species. She'd been reassuringly human back then; hadn't been able to take her hands off him, was always forcing him into sentimental selfies, and even hired a pro photographer to take pictures of them training together.

"Ah, Sarah," she said, looking up. "I rescued dinner." She gave me a smile that made me think of cold cream.

You never knew what anyone did behind locked doors, I thought, but the idea of Zoe hiding in a toilet, calling some man's workshop at 8 P.M.—in spite of him having cold-shouldered her for three weeks—made me suddenly laugh.

Tommy, who had no idea what I was laughing at, but who was nervy as a cat this evening, joined in.

Zoe sat still as marble as I served, watching me through gray eyes. It was one of the things about her that unsettled me most. The lack of speech, the incessant bloody **watching**. (Tommy once said it was this quality that made her such a successful lawyer. "She misses nothing," he'd told me, as if this were a trait to be celebrated in the real world.)

"I hear you're pining for a man," she said.

"I don't think **pining**'s the right word," Jo said quickly. "She's more . . . confused."

Zoe's eyes swiveled over Jo, but she said nothing.

I'd been surprised to see Jo tonight. She didn't like Zoe and it never seemed to have occurred to her to pretend otherwise. (I didn't love Zoe either, but I'd agreed with myself that I'd keep on trying. Zoe had lost both of her parents in the King's Cross fire of 1987, and you had to forgive people with an excuse like that.)

Zoe tucked a wedge of ice-blond hair behind an ear. "So what's going on?"

"The story's just as Tommy probably reported," I said. "We had a week together. It was . . . well, special. He went on holiday, said he'd call me before his plane took off, but he didn't, and I haven't heard from him since. I think something has happened to him."

A tiny frown crossed her face. "Such as what?"

I smiled weakly. "I've driven Tommy and Jo quite mad with my theories. There's probably no point going over them again."

"Not at all," Tommy said. "We're as baffled as you are, Harrington."

And Jo, who was not as baffled at all, but who couldn't bring herself to stand shoulder to shoulder with Zoe, agreed.

"It's quite a mystery," she said. "Sarah's put a note on his Facebook page asking if anyone's heard from him, yet nobody's replied. He hasn't been on WhatsApp or Messenger for weeks and all of his social medias are quiet."

"Media," Zoe smiled. "'Media' is the plural." With a small, skillful movement of her wrist, she lifted a perfect coil of noodle from her broth. She ate for a moment, looking thoughtful. Then: "Let him go," she said, decisively. "He sounds weak to me. You deserve better than a weak man, Sarah."

The conversation turned to the bombings in Turkey, but I realized that I'd drifted back to Eddie after a few minutes. **What is wrong with me?** I wondered desperately. **Who have I become?** No matter what I did, no matter how serious the events around me, I seemed able to focus on only one thing.

I might have to let go of him, was the thought that kept circulating. **I might have to accept that he simply changed his mind.** The idea left me immobilized, torpid with disbelief. And yet three weeks had passed since we'd said good-bye, and in that time I'd heard nothing from him. And nobody had replied to—nobody had even **acknowledged**—my appeal for information on his Facebook wall.

"We've lost her again," Zoe said.

I blushed. "No, no, I was just thinking about Turkey."

"We've all loved and lost," Zoe said briskly. "And at least your BMI is down."

"Oh." I was thrown. "Is it?"

It was not impossible. My appetite was terrible, and I'd been out running every day, solely because it gave me a different type of chest pain to deal with.

"I could look at any woman on earth and tell you her BMI." Zoe smiled.

I didn't dare look at Jo, but I was pretty certain that "I could look at any woman on earth and tell you her BMI" would make an appearance in conversations to come.

"One of the key benefits of a broken heart," Zoe went on. "Slimming down, toning up. You look fantastic!" She crossed her perfectly slim, perfectly toned legs and fished a prawn out of her bowl.

I was exhausted by the time I cleared the table. Too exhausted to unwrap the artisan chocolates I'd bought with the intention of pretending I'd made them myself. Too exhausted, even, to care about openly checking Eddie's Facebook wall while I made coffee.

So I ended up staring emptily at his profile for a good while before I realized that someone had finally replied to my appeal for information. Two people, in fact. I read their posts once, twice, three times, then moved across the kitchen and slid my phone into Tommy's vision.

Tommy read the posts a few times before handing my phone to Zoe, who read them once, said nothing, and handed the phone to Jo.

Thoughts spiraled like a tornado.

"Well," Tommy said, "I think we might owe you an apology, Harrington." He glanced at Zoe, who had probably never apologized to anyone.

Hot. I was too hot. I took off my cardigan and it fell to the floor. My head thrummed as I bent down to pick it up. **I was too bloody hot.**

"Blimey," Jo said, looking up from the phone. "Maybe you were right."

"Oh, come **on**!" Zoe laughed. "This post doesn't mean anything!"

But for the first time in as long as I could remember, Tommy took her on. "I don't agree," he said. "I think this changes everything."

This afternoon someone whose name I didn't know, an Alan somebody, had replied to my post:

I just looked up his profile for the same reason and saw your post, **Sarah**. He went AWOL after canceling our holiday the other week. Has anyone messaged you about this? Let me know if you hear anything.

Then someone else, a Martin someone, had written:

Was wondering the same. He hasn't
turned up at football for a few weeks.
Admittedly, he is not known for his
reliability, but this is beyond the pale.
I'm sorry to say that tonight we were
thrashed 8–1. A shameful episode in our
long and magnificent history. We need
him back.

A few seconds later the same guy, Martin, had
posted a photo of Eddie and had written:

Find this man. **#WheresWally**

And, finally:

It doesn't sit well with me that you can't
punctuate hashtags.

I stared at the photo of Eddie, holding a pint.
"Where are you?" I whispered, horrified. "What's
happened?"
Into the ensuing silence, my phone rang.
Everyone watched me.
I picked it up. It was a withheld number. "Hello?"
There was a silence—a human silence—and then
the line went dead.
"They hung up," I told the room.
"I think you were right," said Jo, after a long pause.
"Something very odd is going on here."

CHAPTER TWELVE

Day Two: The Morning After

I should have been jet-lagged. Deeply exhausted and probably hungover; certainly uninterested in waking before midday. Instead, I woke at seven o'clock feeling like I could take on the world.

He was there. Asleep next to me: Eddie David. A hand snaked out in my direction, resting on the soft shelf of my stomach. He was dreaming. The hand on my navel twitched occasionally, like a leaf in a halfhearted wind.

His curtains frilled at the bottom as the morning moved silently through the open window. I drew in a great lungful of air, drawn straight from the valley like water from a spring, and looked around the room. Mouse was sitting with Eddie's keys on an old wooden campaign chest.

I hardly knew this man, of course. I'd met him less than twenty-four hours ago. I didn't know how he liked his eggs, what he sang in the shower, whether he could play guitar or speak Italian or draw cartoons. I didn't know what bands he'd loved as a teenager or how he was likely to vote in the referendum.

I hardly knew Eddie David, yet I felt like I'd known him for years. Felt like he'd been there too when I'd been running around the fields with Tommy and Hannah and her friend Alex, building dens and dreams. Exploring his body last night had been like returning to the valley here; everything familiar and right and exactly as I'd left it last time.

My first time with Reuben had been confused, brief, and hopeful; the bonding of two lost little souls in someone's spare room with the thunder of an air conditioner and a carefully planned sound track on the CD player. And it had meant everything to us at the time, but in the years that followed we'd smiled ruefully at how bad it had been. There had been no such awkwardness last night. No misplaced fumblings or self-conscious questions. I bit my lip, smiling shyly at Eddie's sleeping face.

He made a snuffling sound, stretched out, and rolled in closer toward me. He didn't wake up. Just reached out an arm and hooked it round me. I closed my eyes, committing to memory the feeling of his skin on mine, the gentle weight of his hand.

The world and its unsolvable problems seemed a very long way away.

I went back to sleep.

When I woke up again, it was gone midday and the air smelled richly of baking bread.

I put on a sweatshirt of Eddie's and crept out of his bedroom into the big space he lived in. Light streamed in through skylights and dusty windows, spliced and jigged by a network of old beams, full of rivets and pits and rusty hooks.

Eddie was moving around the kitchen at the other side of the room, talking to someone on the phone. Fine particles of flour lifted off the work surface he was wiping down with his spare hand, shifting in a sunny cloud under the roof lights.

"Okay," he said. "Okay, Derek, thank you. Yeah, you too. Speak soon, okay? Bye."

After a brief moment of stillness he turned on a radio hiding behind glass bottles on a windowsill. Dusty Springfield was coming to the end of "Son of a Preacher Man."

His phone rang again.

"Hi, Mum." He rinsed a cloth and ran it over the surface. "Oh, she's there already? Brilliant. Good. Yes, I . . ." He paused, leaning against the worktop. "That sounds nice. Well, have a great time, okay? I'll pop over on my way to the airport if I don't hear from you before then." A pause. "Of course, Mum. Okay. Bye."

He put the phone down and wandered over to the oven to peer through the window.

"Hello," I said eventually.

"Oh! Hello!" He spun round. "I'm making bread!" He beamed at me and I wondered if this was all just some sort of psychedelic dream, a desperate escape from the quotidian trudge of divorce papers and accommodation searches. This ebullient, handsome man, sweeping into a part of the world I'd come to dread and painting everything in bright colors.

But it wasn't a dream; it couldn't be, because the commotion in my chest was too great. Somehow, it was real. (Would we kiss on the mouth? Would we hug, as if we'd known each other for years?)

There was a breakfast bar separating the kitchen from the rest of the room, a wide, polished plank of something beautiful. I took a seat at it and Eddie smiled, throwing his tea towel over his shoulder and walking toward me. He leaned across the bar and answered my question by kissing me decisively on the mouth. "I like you in my sweatshirt," he said.

I looked down at it. It was gray, worn ragged at the wrists. It smelled of him.

Dusty Springfield gave way to Roy Orbison.

"I'm very impressed that you made bread," I said. "It smells incredible." Then I frowned. "Oh, hang on a minute. Are you one of those terrifying people with hundreds of skills?"

"I'm a person who can do a lot of things badly but with great enthusiasm," he said. "You can call that skilled, if you like. My friends have other names." He pulled up a stool on the other side and sat opposite me, pushing some orange juice in my direction.

I felt his knees press against mine. "Tell me some of your nonskills," I said.

He laughed. "Um . . . I play the banjo? And the

ukulele. I'm teaching myself the mandolin, which is trickier than I thought. Oh, and I learned to throw an ax recently. That was brilliant." He mimed it, making a thwacking noise.

I grinned.

"And . . . well, sometimes I challenge myself to try to make things out of bits of limestone I find in the woods, only I'm especially bad at that. And I bake bread quite often, although again without any great skill."

I started to laugh. "Anything else?"

He ran a finger round one of my knuckles. "Don't invent some fiction in your head about me being a high achiever, Sarah, because I'm really not."

An alarm went off and he got up to check the bread. Eddie's sense of place was so strong, I thought, imagining him combing the local woods for things to carve. It was almost as if he were a part of this valley, like an oak. Pieces of him would be flung into the wider world during season change or wild weather, but his core stayed in the earth. This earth, in this valley.

The thought came to me suddenly that I didn't feel like that about LA. I loved it: it was my home. I loved the heat, the scale, the ambition, the sense of anonymity it gave me. But I wasn't the dust of its deserts or the waves of its ocean.

"Bread needs a little more time," Eddie said, sitting back down. "What are you thinking about?"

"I was thinking about you as a tree and me as a desert."

He smiled. "That doesn't make us very compatible."

"It wasn't like that. It was . . . Oh, ignore me. I was being weird."

"What sort of tree was I?" he asked.

"I went for an oak. An old one."

"Can't go wrong with oak. And I'm forty in September, so old's reasonable."

"And I was just thinking how rooted you seem to be. Even though you say you still work in London quite often, it's like . . . I don't know. Like you're a part of the landscape."

Eddie looked out of the window. Below us, clumped lavender leaned on the breeze.

"I hadn't thought about it like that," he said. "But you're right. No matter how many times I go up to London to fit a kitchen, play football, see friends—and find myself thinking, **I love this city**—I come back to this valley. I can't not. Do you get that same wrench when you leave LA?"

"Well, no. Not entirely. But it's where I've chosen to be."

"Right." There was a slight pinch of disappointment in his voice.

"But it's funny," I went on. "Listening to you talking about all these things you do, these hobbies you have, I realized how much I miss all of that. You can get anything and everything in LA, at any time of night, have it delivered, downloaded . . . I mean, they're talking about deliveries by **drone** at the moment. There're no limits to what's possible. But for all that, I can't remember the last time I made anything, other than my bed. I rarely exercise, I don't play an instrument, I don't go to evening classes."

How flat I sound. How two-dimensional.

Eddie just looked thoughtful.

"But who cares about hobbies, if you're spending all your time doing a job you love?" He twirled a strand of my hair into his fingers.

"Mmmm," I said. "I do love it, but it's . . . challenging. Nonstop. Even when I come back to the UK for my holiday, I work."

Eddie smiled.

"Choice," I said, eventually. "You're going to remind me I have a choice."

He shrugged. "Look, not many people set up a children's charity from scratch. But everyone needs downtime. Nonthinking time. It keeps us human."

He was right, of course. I seldom delegated. I held my work close, cloaked myself in it: I always had; it was the only approach I knew. But for all that activity, all that industry, was I **there**? Was I really there, in my life, the way Eddie seemed to be in his?

This is not the conversation to be having with a man you've barely known twenty-four hours, I told myself, but I seemed unable to stop. I'd never had this conversation with anyone, including myself. It was like I'd turned on a tap and the bloody thing had come off in my hands.

"Maybe it's not a city-living thing, or even a job thing," I said. "Maybe it's just me. I do sometimes look at other people and wonder why I can't find time to do all the things they seem to do outside of work." I poked at a cuticle. "Whereas you . . . Oh, ignore me. I'm rambling. It's just that it all feels very natural, being here . . . Which is confusing, because normally when I come home, I can't wait to leave."

"Why?"

"Oh, I'll tell you another time."

"Sure. And I'll teach you the banjo. I'm terrible, so you'll be in great company." He turned over his hand and put mine in it. "I don't care what hobbies you do. I don't care how hard you work. I could talk to you all day. That's all I know."

I stared at him with wonder.

"You're great," I said quietly. "Just so you know."

We looked straight at each other, and Eddie leaned over again and kissed me. Long, slow, warm, like a memory brought back by music.

"Do you want to hang around for a while?" he asked, afterward. "If you don't have anything to do, that is? I'll show you my workshop downstairs and you can make a mouse of your own. Or we can sit around kissing. Or maybe we can take potshots at Steve, a little bastard of a squirrel who lives on my lawn." He rested his hands on my legs. "I just . . . Sod it. I just don't want you to go."

"Okay," I said slowly. I smiled. "That sounds lovely. But your mother . . . ? I thought you were worried about her?"

"I am," he said. "But she—well, she doesn't have explosive breakdowns, more just gradual declines. My aunt's come to stay because I'm off on holiday on Thursday. She'll be keeping a close eye on her."

"You're sure?" I asked. "I don't mind if you need to go and see her."

"Quite sure. She called earlier, said they're off to the garden center. She sounded well." Then: "Trust me," he added, when I looked doubtful. "If things were even approaching serious, I'd be there. I know what to look for."

I imagined Eddie watching his mother, week in, week out, like a fisherman watching the sky.

"Okay," I said. "Well then, I think you should start by telling me about Steve."

He chuckled, flicked a crumb, or maybe an insect, out of my hair. "Steve terrorizes me and just about every species of wildlife that tries to live here. I don't know what's wrong with him; he seems to spend almost all of his time in the grass, spying on me, rather than up a tree where he belongs. The only time he gets off his backside is when I buy a bird feeder. No matter where I hang the bloody things, he manages to bust in and eat everything."

I started laughing. "He sounds great."

"He is. I love him, but I also dislike him very intensely. I have a machine-gun-grade water pistol—we can have a go at him later if you like."

I smiled. A whole day with this man and his squirrel, in this hidden corner of the Cotswolds that reminded me of all the best parts—and none of the worst—of my childhood. It was a treat.

I looked around me at the vestments of this man's life. Books, maps, handmade stools. A glass bowl full of coins and keys, an old Rolleiflex camera. At the top of a bookshelf, a collection of garish football trophies.

I wandered over toward them. **The Elms, Battersea Monday**, said the closest one. **Old Robsonians— Champions, Division 1.** "Are these yours?"

Eddie came over. "They are." He picked up the recent one; ran a brown finger along the top. A little ruler of dust slid off the edge. "I play for a team in London. Which might sound a bit odd, given that I live here, but I'm up there quite a lot doing kitchens and . . . well, they've proved very difficult to leave."

"Why?"

"I joined years ago. When I thought I was going to give London a proper go. They're . . ." He chuckled. "They're just a very funny group. When I moved back to Gloucestershire, I couldn't quite bring myself to retire. Nobody can. We all love it too much."

I smiled, looking again at the jumble of trophies.

One went back more than twenty years. I liked that he'd held friendships so long.

Then: "No!" I breathed. I plucked out a book from farther down his shelves: the Collins Gem **Birds,** the exact same edition that I'd had as a child. I'd spent hours poring over this little tome. Sitting in the fork of the pear tree in our garden, hoping that if I stayed there long enough, the birds would come and roost with me.

"I had this, too!" I told Eddie. "I knew every single bird off by heart!"

"Really?" He came over. "I loved this book." He turned to a page near the middle and covered the name of the bird with his hand. "What's this?"

The bird had a golden chest and a burglar's mask across his eyes. "Oh, God . . . No, hang on. Nuthatch! Eurasian nuthatch!"

He showed me another.

"Stonechat!"

"Oh, my God," Eddie said. "You are my perfect woman."

"I had the wildflowers one, too. And the butterflies and moths. I was a precocious little naturalist."

He put the book to one side. "Can I ask you something, Sarah?"

"Of course." I loved hearing him say my name.

"Why do you live in a city? If you feel like this about nature?"

I paused. "I just can't live in the country," I said eventually. Something about my face must have told him not to pry further, because, after watching me for a few seconds, he ambled off to get out the bread.

"I had the trees book." He looked around for an oven glove, settling eventually for the tea towel on his shoulder. "Dad got it for me. It was he who got me into woodwork, in fact, although he certainly never imagined I'd make a career of it. He used to take me to help him collect firewood from the log man in autumn. He let me smash up some of the logs to make kindling."

He paused, smiling. "It was the smell. I fell in love with the smell at first, but I was fascinated by how quickly you could turn a tough-looking log into something completely different. One winter I started pinching bits of the kindling to make stick men. Then there came the toilet-roll holder, and the worst mallet in history."

He chuckled. "And then there was Mouse." He opened the oven; pulled out the baking tray. "My pride and joy. Dad wasn't particularly impressed, but Mum said it was the most perfect little mouse she'd ever seen."

He put a round, fragrant loaf onto a wire rack and closed the oven.

"He left when I was nine. Dad. He has a family on the Scottish border, somewhere north of Carlisle."

"Oh." I sat back down. "That must have been rough."

He shrugged. "It was a long time ago."

An easy silence fell while he retrieved butter,

honey, a jar of what looked like homemade marmalade from the fridge. He passed me a plate with a deep crack running through it ("Sorry!") and a knife.

"Does your mum know I'm here?" I asked, as he started slicing the bread.

"Ow!" He wrenched his hand away from the loaf. "Why am I so greedy? It's far too hot to eat."

I laughed. If he hadn't gone straight in, I would have.

"No," he said, protecting his hand this time with the tea towel. "Mum doesn't know you're here. I can't have her think her only child is a dirty old mating goat."

"I suppose not."

"Maybe if I'm really good, we can do some more mating," he said, throwing a red-hot slice of bread in the direction of my plate.

"Certainly," I said, sticking my knife into the butter. It was full of crumbs. Reuben, who liked to serve butter hipster style, smeared onto a piece of slate or some ridiculous rock or other, would have hated it.

"You're great at mating," I added, and I didn't blush.

Eddie did. "Really?"

And, because I didn't seem to have any choice in the matter, I got up, marched round the planky island thing and closed my arms around him, kissing him hard on the mouth. "Yes," I said. "This bread is too hot even for me. Let's go back to bed."

CHAPTER THIRTEEN

Dear Alan,

Please forgive this message from out of the blue.

You replied to my post on Eddie David's Facebook wall earlier today. I'm a bit worried, and wanted to share what limited information I have.

Prior to your holiday with Eddie, I spent a week with him in Sapperton. I left on Thursday, June 9, so that he could pack, and he said he'd call me from the airport.

I never heard from him again. After trying several times to contact him, I gave up, assuming that he had changed his mind. I never fully believed it, however, and when I saw your reply to my post I knew I hadn't been deceiving myself. Below is my phone number. I would really

appreciate you sharing any thoughts
or info that you might have. I am not a
stalker! I just want to know he's okay.

Best wishes,
Sarah Mackey

Eleven P.M. leached silently into midnight. My
phone buzzed and I hurled myself at it, but it
was just Jo saying she'd got home safely. No
reply from Alan. I lay back in bed and felt my heart
straining in my chest. It hurt. It **actually hurt**. Why
did nobody tell you that a broken heart wasn't just
a metaphor?

Midnight turned into one, then two, then three.
I imagined Tommy and Zoe in their giant bed
along the hallway, and wondered if they held each
other while they slept. I remembered Eddie's body,
wrapped around mine, and felt a longing so fierce
it seemed to bore through my skin. Then I spent a
while intensely disliking myself, because in Istanbul
there were bodies in bags, whereas Eddie was—quite
probably—a man who simply hadn't called.

At four, having caught myself in the act of searching online for death notices in Eddie's area, I let myself quietly out of Tommy's flat. Dawn was pressing
gray smudges into the sky, and a lone street sweeper
was already at work, shuffling slowly past Zoe's
smart Georgian terrace. It would be another couple

of hours until the city reached full throttle, but I couldn't take another moment of the suffocating silence and the buzz of dark theories, each more terrible than the last.

At Holland Park Avenue, I started running. For a short while I sailed effortlessly past bus stops sheltering tired-looking migrants on their way to work, cafés with grilles still down, an inebriated man stumbling back from Notting Hill. I tuned out the whine of night buses and taxis, allowing only the slap of my trainers and the warble of the dawn chorus.

My effortless sailing didn't last long. As the road began to climb toward Notting Hill, my lungs started to burst, as they always did, and my legs gave up. I walked up to the Portobello turnoff.

There's nothing crazy about what I'm doing, I thought, when I could force myself to run again. **London is awake already.** A workers' café was packed out with tradesmen in hi-vis vests; a man was opening a coffee cart on Westbourne Grove. London was on the move. Why shouldn't I be? This was **fine**.

Only, of course, it was not, because my body felt tired and miserable, and I was the only runner I saw for the duration. And because it was still only 4:45 A.M. by the time I got back to Tommy's.

I showered and slid into bed. I tried for five minutes not to check my phone.

One missed call, the screen advised, when I gave in. I sat up. It was a withheld number, at 4:19 A.M. A message had been left.

The message comprised two seconds of silence, followed by the sound of a human pressing the wrong button. After a brief scrabble, the caller managed successfully to hang up.

Briefly, I wondered if it was Eddie's friend Alan, but according to Facebook he had not yet read my message.

Then who?

Eddie?

No! Eddie's not that person! He's a talker! Not some shady crackpot who calls at 4 A.M.!

By the time I woke at lunchtime, Alan had read my message. He had not replied.

I stared at my phone dementedly, refreshing it again and again. He couldn't just ignore it. Nobody would do that!

But he had read it, and he had ignored it. The day passed; I heard nothing. And I felt frightened. Less, as each day passed, for Eddie, and more, as each day passed, for myself.

CHAPTER FOURTEEN

Rudi was absolutely still.

He stood and stared at the two meerkats closest to the fence, and they stood and stared at him, paws resting casually on their soft bellies. Rudi, without realizing what he was doing, had straightened up and had rested his own little paws on his own little belly.

"Hello," he whispered reverently. "Hello, meerikats."

"Meerkats," I corrected.

"Sarah, be **quiet**! You might frighten them!"

Tommy alerted Rudi to the arrival of another meerkat and Rudi whipped round, forgetting in an instant that I existed. "Hello, meerikat three," he whispered. "Meerikats, hello! Are you a family? Or just best friends?"

Two of the meerkats started burrowing in the sand. The third shuffled over his sandy hill to give what looked like a hug to another member of the tribe. Rudi almost trembled with wonder.

Jo took a photo of her son. Five minutes ago she'd been telling Rudi off about something; now she smiled at him with a love that had no edges. And watching her, trying to imagine that sort of towering, immeasurable devotion, I felt it again. An acute poke from the lumpy cluster of feelings I kept in a remote corner. It was right that I wasn't going to be a mother, of course, but the pain of lost possibility sometimes left me breathless.

I extracted my sunglasses from my bag.

My parents had found a carer for Granddad and would be back in Gloucestershire tomorrow. Rudi wanted a farewell tea at Battersea Park Children's Zoo before I left to go and see them, although this, I suspected, had more to do with a recent television program he'd watched about meerkats than it did saying good-bye to Aunty Sarah.

I checked my phone, a reflex as common now as breathing. After the dropped phone call I'd had in the middle of the night last week there'd been another one, a few days ago, and it had lasted a full fifteen seconds. "I'll call the police," I'd said, when whoever it was refused to say anything. The caller had hung up immediately and there hadn't been anything since, but I was certain it had something to do with Eddie's disappearance.

I wasn't sleeping very much at all now.

Tommy unpacked the little tea he'd made and Rudi came running over to eat, recounting a poorly remembered joke about eggy sandwiches and eggy farts. Jo told him off for talking with his mouth full.

A child nearby was whining about missing out on feeding the coati. And I sat in the middle of them all, unable to eat my sandwiches, a miserable churning in my stomach.

Not long before leaving the sixth form, I'd studied **Mrs. Dalloway** for my English A level. We'd taken turns narrating the book, exploring Woolf's "unique narrative technique," as Mrs. Rushby called it.

"The world has raised its whip," I read aloud when my turn came; "where will it descend?"

I had paused, surprised, and then read the sentence again. And even though my classmates were watching me, even though Mrs. Rushby was watching me, I had underlined the sentence three times before moving on, because those words had described so perfectly how I felt, most of the time, that I marveled that anyone other than me could have written them.

The world has raised its whip; where will it descend?

That was it! seventeen-year-old me had thought. That perpetual alertness! Watching the skies, sniffing the air, bracing for calamity. **That's me**. And yet here I was now, nineteen years on, feeling exactly the same. Had anything actually changed? Had my comfortable life in California been mere fantasy?

I had another look at my egg sandwich but it made me heave.

"Oi," Jo said, in my direction. "What's going on?"

"Nothing. I'm just enjoying my tea."

"Interesting," said Jo, "given that you're not actually eating it."

After a pause I apologized. Told them I knew I must seem insane. Told them I was trying so very, very hard to pull myself together, but that I wasn't having much luck.

"Did he break your heart?" Rudi asked. "The man?"

Everyone stopped talking. Neither Jo nor Tommy could look at me. But Rudi did, Rudi with his little almond eyes and his perfect child's understanding of the world.

"Did he break your heart, Sarah?"

"I . . . Well, yes," I said, when I found my voice. "Yes, I'm afraid he did."

Rudi wheeled from side to side on his heels, watching me. "He's a villain," he said, after careful consideration. "And a fart."

"He is," I agreed.

Rudi gave me a hug, which brought me to the very edge of tears.

Tommy was holding my phone, staring thoughtfully at Eddie's Facebook page. "I do wonder about this man," he said, after a long silence.

"You and me both, Tommy."

"The WheresWally hashtag, for starters," Tommy said. "Isn't that a bit odd? His name's Eddie."

Jo opened a packet of dried fruit and nuts for Rudi. "Eat them slow," she told him, before turning to Tommy. "**Where's Wally?** is a series of books, you plonker," she said. "Don't you remember? All them pictures of crowds with Wally hidden in them?"

Rudi began picking out raisins and discarding the nuts.

"I know what **Where's Wally?** is," Tommy said. "I just think it's a strange thing to say about someone whose name is meant to be Eddie."

I shook my head. "That's just what you say when you're looking for someone. Scouring crowds. Needle-in-haystack job."

Tommy shrugged. "Maybe. Or maybe not. Maybe he's someone else entirely."

Rudi perked up. "Do you think Eddie is a murderer?" he asked.

"No," Tommy said.

"A vampire?"

"No."

"A gas man?" Jo had recently explained Stranger Danger.

Tommy stared thoughtfully at my phone. "Oh, I don't know," he said. "But there's something fishy about this man." Then suddenly he sat up straight. "Sarah!" he whispered. "**Look!**"

I took the phone from him and found he'd opened up my Messenger. Then everything surged forward and into free fall, like water from a weir. **Eddie was online.** He had read my messages. Both of them. He was online now.

He was not dead. He was somewhere. "What were you doing in my messages?" I hissed.

"I was being nosy," Tommy said. "I wanted to see what you'd been saying to him, but **who cares**? He's read your messages! He's online!"

"What did he say?" Rudi was trying to grab the phone. "What did he say to you, Sarah?"

Jo confiscated the phone and took a good long look.

"I hate to tell you this," she said, "but he read your messages three hours ago."

"Why hasn't he written back?" Rudi asked.

It was a good question.

"I'm getting tired of your boyfriend, Sarah," Rudi said. "I think he's a really horrible person."

There was a long silence.

"Let's go down the meerkat tunnel," Jo said.

Rudi looked at me, and then at his precious meerkats, ten yards away—ten yards too far.

"Go," I told him. "Go and be with your people. I'm fine."

"Just walk away, Sarah," Jo repeated, as her son scampered off. She sounded exhausted suddenly. "Life is too short to run around after someone who makes you miserable."

She went to join Rudi. Tommy and I stared at the screen. Impulsively, I typed, **Hello?**

Seconds later, Eddie's picture dropped down next to the message. "That means he's read it," Tommy said.

I won't bite, I wrote.

Eddie read the message. And then—just like that—he went offline.

I stood up. I had to see him. Talk to him. I had to **do something**. "Help," I said. "What do I do, Tommy? What do I do?"

After a beat, Tommy stood up and put his arm around my shoulders. If I closed my eyes, we could be back in 1997 at LAX, me crumpled against him in the arrivals hall, him carrying the keys for a huge, air-conditioned car, telling me everything would be okay.

"Maybe his mum got really bad with her depression," I said desperately. "He told me she was on a downward spiral when I met him. Maybe it got really scary."

"Maybe," Tommy said quietly. "But, Harrington, if he was serious about you two, he'd still have sent a message. Explained. Asked you to give him a few weeks."

I didn't argue, because I couldn't.

"See if he replies," Tommy said, squeezing my shoulder. "But unless he does soon, and unless something really quite extraordinary has happened to him, I think you should consider very seriously whether or not you want to see him again. It's not kind to have put you through this."

Awkwardly, but with much tenderness, he kissed the side of my head. "Maybe Jo's right," he said. "Maybe you do need to let go."

My oldest friend had his arm around my shoulder. The man who'd helped me glue myself back together, all those years ago, who'd watched me lose everything and somehow rebuild my life. And now we were only a few short years from forty, and it was happening again.

"She **is** right," I said dully. "You both are. I have to let go."

And I meant it. The only problem was, I didn't know how.

CHAPTER FIFTEEN

This is not just a broken heart, I thought, later that night. I was standing in Tommy and Zoe's kitchen in my pajamas, eating crisps. **It's more than that.**

But what?

The accident? **Is it something to do with the accident?**

There were so many blanks in my memory of that awful day. Distance, or trauma, or perhaps the vast difference between my English and American lives had helped me block out a lot of what happened. And yet the feelings I was having now, I knew them. They were like bad old friends.

At 1:30 A.M. I decided to use this surfeit of energy to attempt some work. My colleagues had been too polite to say anything, but I knew I'd have someone on the phone if I didn't process the backlog soon.

I got back into bed and opened my e-mails. And my brain—finally—ignited. I made big decisions; I made small decisions. I authorized spends and sent a report to our trustees. I checked our Web mail folder, because nobody ever remembered to check it, and found an e-mail from a little girl asking if some of our clowns could visit her twin sister, who was very sick in a hospital in San Diego. **Of course! I wrote, forwarding the e-mail to Reuben and Kate, my deputy. Send in the clowns! It's a hospital we know! Let's have our guys in there by Friday, please, team!**

By three in the morning I realized that my brain was running at a speed I didn't like.

By four I felt quite mad.

At a quarter past four I decided to call Jenni. Jenni Carmichael would know what to do.

"Sarah Mackey!" she said. I could hear the soaring violins of an old romantic film in the background. "What the hell are you doing awake at this time of night?"

Thank you, I thought, closing my eyes. **Thank you, God, for my dear Jenni Carmichael.**

My wedding to Reuben had been something of an embarrassment. His side of the congregation was full, whereas mine contained only Mum, Dad, Tommy, Jo, and a couple of waitresses from the café on Fountain where Reuben and I had held our first charity meetings. No Hannah. Just a silent space on the bench next to Mum. And no friends either, because nobody in England knew what to say to me anymore, let alone wanted to fly across the world for the pleasure of still not knowing what to say.

I'd told Reuben's family that "none of my English

friends could make it" and shame had sloshed all over me like beer from an overfull glass.

Reuben and I had a beautiful honeymoon in Yosemite. Hidden away in a bell jar of love, we were happy. But when toward the end of the trip we found ourselves in San Francisco, surrounded by laughing groups of young people, my friendlessness had taunted me again.

Then Jenni had arrived in my life, as if shipped in by courier. Jenni was from South Carolina. She had no interest in the film industry, unlike most out-of-towners: she just "wanted to try something new." While Reuben and I were wandering around northern California as newlyweds, Jenni was being installed as the manager of the office building where Reuben and I rented a desk, a gray concrete block crouching in the shadow of the Hollywood Freeway.

Upon our return, she had come to ask me if we were planning to pay our overdue desk rental anytime soon. I handed over cash and apologies the very same day, hovering guiltily beside her as she counted the dollar bills. On her desk I noted half a cake wrapped in cling film and a small CD player on which she was playing what sounded like a "Greatest Love Songs" compilation. She glanced up at me and smiled as she thumbed through the money with a rubber thimble. "I suck at numbers," she said. "I'm counting the bills to look efficient." She went back to the beginning of the pile twice before giving up.

"I'll trust you," she said, putting the money in a cash box. "You look honest. Would you like some cake? I baked it last night. I'm scared I'm going to eat the whole damned thing."

The cake was outstanding, and, as I ate it by her desk, Jenni recounted her interview with the very strange man who owned the building. She did a near-perfect impression of him. **I want her to be my friend,** I thought, as she skipped a modern power ballad in favor of Barbra Streisand. She was nothing like me, or anyone I'd ever known, and I liked her all the more for it.

I'd have got there. I'd have found friends eventually. I still carried the scars of my past but was emerging already as Sarah Mackey, charity executive: pleasant, ultrareliable, sometimes witty. But Jenni Carmichael was the conduit; through her I began to meet people, to believe that I could belong here in this city I so needed to call home.

Three years later Jenni had become not only a firm friend but a valuable asset to our charity. When Reuben and I signed a long lease on a building on Vermont, just two blocks down from the Children's Hospital, she quit her job and came with us. Our new HQ wasn't much to look at, surrounded by dicey-looking medical clinics, coin laundries, and takeaways, but the rent was low, and it had a big, open ground floor that would become Reuben's training academy for new Clowndoctors. She came first as our office manager, then as "someone who helped with grants," until eventually, after several years, we made her our VP of fund-raising.

A year or so after we met, she had forged her own perfect love story and now lived happily on the edge of Westlake and Historic Filipinotown with a man called Javier, who fixed wealthy folks' SUVs and bought her flowers every week. She lived for their romantic getaways and talked about Javier as if he were God Himself.

They had been trying for a baby for eleven years. She refused to complain, because complaining was not something she had much time for, but it was killing her. Slowly, and from the inside, it was destroying my friend. For her I had even prayed to a god I'd never believed in. **Please give her a baby. It's all she wants.**

If this final round of IVF didn't work out, I had no idea what she'd do. Neither she nor Javier had the money to fund treatment once her insurers had stopped paying out. "Last-chance saloon!" she'd said stoutly, when we hugged good-bye at LAX.

Jenni had been shocked by my break with Reuben. I think it shattered her assumptions about love: sure, people divorced all the time, but not those in her immediate life. She got around it by taking on the role of rescuer, for which she'd been designed. She downloaded apps to my phone, moved me into her spare room, and made a vast number of cakes.

"So!" she said now. "Eddie reached out to you, right? Everything's back on track?"

"Actually, no," I said. "It's the opposite. He's back in the world—assuming he went anywhere in the first place—but he's not replied to any of my messages. He's cut me dead."

"Hang on, honey." I heard the music stop. "Just pausing my movie. Javier, I'm just gonna take this call out on the deck." I heard the screen door snap shut behind her. "Sorry, Sarah, could you repeat all of that?"

I repeated all of that. Jenni perhaps needed a moment to take on board that my second shot at a love story had gone up in flames.

"Oh, shit." Jenni never swore. "**Really**?"

"Really. I'm a bit of a mess. As you can probably tell, it being gone four in the morning over here."

"Oh, shit," she said again, and I laughed bleakly. "Tell me everything that's happened since we last messaged. And step away from that computer, too. You've sent some crazy messages in the last few hours."

I told her everything that had happened.

"So that's it," I said, when I got to the end. "I think I'm probably going to have to let him go."

"No," she said, a little too sharply. Jenni didn't like seeing anyone turn their back on love. "Don't you dare give up. Look, Sarah, I know most folks'll be telling you to leave that man well alone, but . . . I can't give up on him yet. I'm as certain as you are that there's an explanation."

I smiled briefly. "Such as?"

"I don't know," she said slowly. "But I'm determined to get to the bottom of it."

"So was I."

She laughed. "We'll figure it out. For now, hang on in there, okay? Which reminds me—how're you feeling about tomorrow?"

"Tomorrow?"

"Your meeting with Reuben and Kaia. At some film place by the river Thames, right?"

"Reuben's in London? **With his new girlfriend?**"

"Uh . . . yes? He said he'd e-mailed to set up coffee tomorrow. Introduce you to Kaia, so you don't meet for the first time back home in Cali."

"But why is she in London? Why are either of them in London? I'm meant to be going to back Gloucestershire tomorrow! I—**What?**"

"Kaia wanted to come," Jenni said helplessly. "She hasn't been to London in years. And Reuben already had a flight to London for your vacation together . . ."

I sank back in bed. Of course. Reuben and I had booked tickets to the UK back in January, when we were still playing that lonely game of husband and wife. I came home every year for the anniversary of the accident, and he had often come with me— although it had been a few years since he'd made it. "This year, I will," he'd promised. "I know how much you miss your sister. I'll be there for you this year, Sarah." And so the tickets had been booked.

Then, later, he had asked me for a divorce. "I've

changed my London flight to a different date," he'd said, a few days later. He was watching me, face smudged with guilt and sadness. "I didn't think you'd want me to come with you."

And I'd said, "Sure, that's a good idea; thanks for thinking of it." I didn't really consider when he might have decided to go instead. In all honesty, I had thought about very little around that time; I had mostly been stretching cautious limbs, flexing tiny new muscles. Experimenting curiously at Life Without Reuben. The ease, the fluidity, the sense of future and space in this brave new world had felt oddly shameful. Where was the mourning?

"He booked a ticket for Kaia," Jenni said. She wasn't enjoying this exchange. "I'm sorry. He said he'd e-mailed you."

"He probably did. I just haven't got to it yet." I closed my eyes. "Well, that'll be cozy. Me, Reuben, Reuben's new girlfriend."

Jenni laughed bleakly.

"Sorry," I said, after a pause. "I wasn't snapping at you; I'm just shocked. And it's my own fault anyway. I should have stayed on top of my e-mails."

I heard her smile. Little offended Jenni. "You're doing great, honey. Apart from the being up in the middle of the night thing. That could do with some work."

I closed my eyes. "Oh, God, and I haven't even asked you how the IVF cycle's going. Where are you at? How long until they harvest your eggs?"

Jenni paused. "Oh, they did that. I went in last week and they harvested the hell out of me. I sent you a message? On WhatsApp? They implanted three embryos, because it's my last chance. I'll find out next week."

She took a breath as if to say something else, but then stopped. In the silence swung a thousand-ton weight of desperation.

"Jenni," I said softly. "I'm so sorry. I thought you were still on the ovary stimulation bit. I . . . God, I'm sorry. It excuses nothing, but I am not myself at the moment."

"I know," she said brightly. "Don't feel bad. You've been there for me, every cycle. You're allowed to make one mistake!"

But her voice was too cheerful, and I knew I'd let her down. In the sooty darkness of Zoe's spare room, I felt my face flush livid with self-loathing.

Jenni replied to something Javier shouted, then said she would have to go soon. "Listen, Sarah, here's my suggestion," she said. "I think you should start over with Eddie. Like you've just met. Why don't you send him a letter? Tell him all about yourself, as if you were on a first date? All the things you never had a chance to tell him. Like . . . does he know about the accident? Your sister?"

"Jenni—let's talk about you. There's been far too much chat about me and my pathetic life."

"Oh, honey! I'm taking good care of myself. I'm visualizing and chanting and doing fertility dances and eating all sorts of gross, healthy stuff. That's all I can do. But there's plenty you can do." She paused. "Sarah, I will never forget the day you told me about the accident. It was the most awful thing I ever heard, and it made me love you, Sarah. Really, really love you. I think you should tell Eddie."

"I can't send him a sob story to make him change his mind!"

"That's not what I'm saying. I just think . . ." She sighed. "I just think you should let him get to know you **properly**. All the parts of you, even the ones you don't like people seeing. Let him know what an extraordinary woman you are."

I paused, the phone hot against my cheek. "But, Jenni, I was lucky you reacted the way you did. Not everyone would."

"I don't agree."

I pulled myself up on my pillows. "So . . . He cuts me out for nearly a month and suddenly I start writing to him about my childhood? He'd think I was crazy! Certifiable!"

Jenni chuckled. "He would not. Like I said, he'd fall in love with you. Just like I did."

I slumped back down again. "Oh, Jenni, who are we trying to kid? I have **got** to let go of him."

She burst out laughing.

"Why are you laughing?"

"Because you have no intention of letting go of him!"

"I do!"

"You do not!" She laughed again. "If you wanted to let go of Eddie, if you **really** wanted to let go, Sarah Mackey, the last person on earth you would have called for advice would have been me."

CHAPTER SIXTEEN

Day Five: A Beech Tree, a Wellington Boot

Eddie was on the phone to Derek again. I didn't yet know who Derek was, but I imagined he had something to do with Eddie's work: Eddie sounded more formal talking to him than he had when a friend called yesterday. Their conversation this afternoon was brief, mostly Eddie saying, "Right," or "Okay," or "Sounds like a good idea." After a few minutes he was done. He went inside to replace the phone.

I was sitting on the bench outside his barn, reading an old copy of **Our Man in Havana** from his shelf. It turned out that I still loved reading. I loved that a novelist on the payroll of MI6 had dreamed up a hapless vacuum-cleaner salesman, drafted into the Secret Intelligence Service so that he might better fund the extravagant lifestyle of his beautiful daughter. I loved that I could read about this man for hours and never once pause to overthink my own life. I loved that, with a book in my hand and no urgent need to be anywhere, or to be doing anything, I felt like a Sarah I'd entirely forgotten.

The hot weather had not yet broken, but it would soon—the air was still and curdled, hovering like a bird of prey before attack. My clothes hung motionless on the washing line above a thick cluster of rosebay willowherb, which didn't move an inch. I yawned, wondered if I should go and check everything was okay at Mum and Dad's.

I knew I wouldn't. The second night Eddie and I had gone to bed together, it had become quite clear that we would stay here, in this suspended world, until either my parents came back from Leicester or Eddie went on holiday. I didn't want to be apart from him even for the hour it would take to walk home and back. The universe I knew had stopped, for now, and I had no desire to bring it back.

From the edge of Eddie's lawn, the squirrel, Steve, was watching me. "Hi, you criminal," Eddie said as he came back out. He looked at the squirrel, mimed shooting a gun. Steve didn't move a muscle.

Eddie sat next to me. "I like you in my clothes," he smiled, pinging the elastic of his boxer shorts against my side. I was wearing them with a T-shirt of his, worn thin at the shoulders. It smelled of him. I yawned again and reached over to ping his own boxer shorts. I had stubbly legs. Nothing mattered. I was stupid with happiness.

"Shall we go for a walk?" he asked.

"Why not?"

We stayed on the bench for a while, kissing, pinging elastic, laughing about nothing.

It was a little after two by the time we set off. I was back in my own clothes, which smelled of Eddie's washing powder and sunshine.

After a few yards following the river, Eddie left the path and started striding up the hill, into the heart of the wood. Our feet sank deep in the untouched mush of the forest floor. "There's a thing I wanted to show you up here," Eddie said. "A bit of a silly thing, but I like to come and check it's still there from time to time."

I smiled. "It can be our noteworthy activity for the day."

We hadn't completed many noteworthy activities since this affair had begun. We had slept a lot, made love a lot, eaten a lot, talked for hours. Not talked for hours. Read books, spotted birds, made up an extended narrative about a dog who'd nosed around Eddie's clearing while we'd eaten Spanish tortilla on the bench one day.

In short, even though everything was happening, nothing was happening.

I squeezed his hand as we climbed up through the woods, struck again by the dazzling simplicity of everything. There was birdsong, there was the sound of our breath, and there was the sensation of sinking into the mulch. And, beyond a deep feeling of contentment, there was nothing else. No grief, no guilt, no questions.

We'd walked nearly to the top of the hill when Eddie stopped. "There," he said, pointing up at a beech tree. "A mystery Wellington."

It took me a while to see it, but when eventually I did, I laughed. "How did you do that?"

"I didn't," he said. "I just spotted it once. I have no idea how it got up there, or who was responsible. In all the years I've lived here, I've never seen anyone in this part of the woods."

A very long way up—probably more than sixty feet—a branch, once heading skyward, had been snapped off. A black Wellington boot had been placed over the remaining stump. Since then, a few younger limbs of pale green had grown below, but the trunk was otherwise smooth: impossible to climb.

I stared up at the welly, puzzled by its existence, delighted that Eddie thought it was something he should take me to see. I slid an arm around his middle and smiled. I could feel his breath, his heart, his T-shirt just on the brink of damp after a hot uphill climb. "A proper mystery," I said. "I like it."

Eddie mimed throwing a welly a few times but then gave up. It was inconceivable. "I have no idea how they managed it," he said. "But I love that they did."

Then he stepped round and kissed me. "Such a silly thing," he said. "But I knew you'd like it." His arms wrapped tight around me.

I kissed him back, harder. All I wanted to do was kiss him.

I wondered how I could possibly go back to LA when happiness of this sort was right here. Here, in the place I'd once called home.

Eventually we found ourselves in the leaves without any clothes on.

I had mulch in my hair, probably insects. But I felt only joy. Deep, radial branches of joy.

CHAPTER SEVENTEEN

Dear Eddie,

I've thought long and hard about writing this letter. How can I possibly reach out—yet again—now you've made such a conspicuous show of being alive but unwilling to communicate? How can I be so desperate, so unwilling to heed your silence?

But last night I found myself thinking about the day we walked up to see that welly. What a silly, lovely thing it was to do; how we stared up at it and laughed. And I thought, **I'm not ready to give up on him. On us. Not quite yet.**

So this is it: my last-ditch attempt to find out what happened. To work out how I could have got it so wrong.

Do you remember our last night together, Eddie? Outside in the grass, before we hauled your enormous tent outside and then spent the next few hours trying to put it up? Do you remember that, before we both collapsed with exhaustion in the damned thing, I was meant to tell you my life story?

I'm going to start it now, from the beginning. Or at least the edited highlights. I figured that maybe it would remind you why you liked me. Because whatever else you might have managed to hide from me, the liking-me bit wasn't made up. Of that much I'm certain.

So. I am Sarah Evelyn Harrington. Born Gloucester Royal at 4:13 p.m. on February 18, 1980. Mum taught maths at a grammar in Cheltenham, and Dad was a sound engineer. He did a lot of touring with bands, until he started to miss us too much. After that he did all sorts of soundy things locally. He still does. Can't stop himself.

They bought a wreck of a cottage in the valley below Frampton Mansell, about a year before I was born, and they've lived there ever since. It's about fifteen minutes' walk along the footpath from your barn. You probably know it. Dad and his friend reopened that old path the summer he and Mum moved in. Two men, two chain saws, several beers.

Being in that valley with you made the place feel very different. Reminded me of a Me I'd forgotten. And as I said to you on our first morning, there is a good reason for that.

Tommy, my best friend, was born a couple of months after me to the "slightly fraught"

(Dad's words) couple in the house at the end of our track. He and I became best friends and we played every day until that strange, sad moment in adolescence where playing just isn't the thing anymore. But until then, we forded streams, stuffed ourselves on blackberries, and made tunnels through blankets of cow parsley.

When I was five, Mum had another baby—Hannah—and after a few years Hannah joined in our adventures. She was utterly fearless, my sister—far braver than Tommy and I, in spite of being several years our junior. Her best friend, a little girl called Alex, was quite literally in awe of her.

It's only now, as an adult, that I realize quite how much I loved my sister. How I was in awe of her, too.

Tommy spent a lot of time at our house because his mum was—as he put it—"crazy." I'm not sure, in hindsight, that was fair, although she was certainly preoccupied on a very deep level with very surface things. She moved their family to LA when I was fifteen and I was heartbroken. Without Tommy I had no idea who I was anymore. Who were my friends? What group did I belong to? I knew only that I had to latch on to someone fast, before I wheeled off the school social scene and became a confirmed loner.

So I latched on to two girls, Mandy and

Claire, with whom I'd always been friendly—if not exactly friends—only now it was more intense. Intense and exposing. Girls can be so cruel when they're young.

Two years later I was on the phone to Tommy at five in the morning, begging him to let me come and stay. But I'll get to that later.

I'm going to leave it there. I don't want to just vomit my entire life story all over you, because you may not want to hear it. And even if you do, I don't want it to sound like I think I'm the only person on earth with a past.

I miss you, Eddie. I didn't think it was possible to miss someone you'd known for only seven days, but I do. So much I can't seem to think straight anymore.

Sarah

CHAPTER EIGHTEEN

There he was: Reuben. Right there at a table in the BFI café, talking to his new girlfriend, whose face was just out of sight. The brown-husked remains of a coffee next to his hand, all about him the simmer of self-possession and new masculinity.

I remembered the shy, skinny boy I'd found quaking outside a Mexican restaurant all those years ago, his hair gelled and his neck sheathed in cheap aftershave. The crushed and trembling quality of his voice when he'd asked me out a few hours later. Now look at him! Broader, stronger, quite the Californian hero with his tapered fashion shorts, his sunglasses, his deliberately careless hair. I couldn't help but smile.

"Hello," I said, arriving at their table.

"Oh!" Reuben said, and for a second I saw the young man I married. The man I thought I'd be with forever, because a permanent life with him in that sunny, cheerful city was all I thought I'd ever need.

"Hey! You must be Sarah." Kaia stood up.

"Hello," I said, and held out my hand. "It's very

nice to meet you." Kaia was slim and clear-eyed. The soft imprint of old acne scarring on her jawline faded into smooth cheeks; dark hair trailed smoothly down her back.

She ignored my extended hand and kissed me on the cheek, clasping my shoulders and smiling warmly, and I knew in that moment that she would hold the balance of power today. She was complete, this woman, and I was not. "It's great we made this meeting work," she said. "I've been looking forward to putting a face to your name for a long time now."

Kaia was quite some woman if she hadn't put a face to my name through Google Images. I was not quite some woman, and had googled her as soon as I knew her surname, but Kaia, of course, had no online footprint. Too bloody pure.

She sat down, smiling as I found a space for my bag under the table and took off the cardigan that was forcing out beads of sweat across my forehead. She was the sort of woman I'd sometimes see meditating on the beach at sunset, I thought, as I freed my arms. Good and grounded, with salt on her skin and wind blowing through her hair.

"So . . . ," Reuben said, sitting down too. "So here we are, hey?" He took a breath, then closed his mouth, realizing he didn't know what to say.

Kaia glanced at him and her face softened. That's my look, I thought childishly. I'd look at him just like that when he lost his way, and he'd feel okay.

"I've heard so much about you, Sarah," she said,

turning back to me. She was wearing a long dress with a bold ikat pattern and an assortment of silver bracelets, and she was somehow more elegant than anyone else here. "And I know there's a lot more to you than your outfit"—was she reading my mind?—"but I have to say that's a beautiful skirt you're wearing."

I smoothed it down. It was one of my nicer ones, actually, but I felt rather self-conscious in it today. Like it was a casual Friday and I'd tried too hard.

"Thank you," I said. I tried and failed to think of something to say that proved there was more to me than that.

Kaia got out her wallet. "I'm going to go get us some drinks. What would you like?"

"Oh, that's kind." I checked my watch and was disappointed to see that it wasn't yet midday. Reluctantly, I ordered a lime and soda.

She slid out of her seat and Reuben got up too. "I'll help!"

"I've got this," Kaia said. "You two go ahead and catch up."

But Reuben insisted and I found myself alone at the table.

This is it, I thought, wiping my forehead with a napkin. **This is my future. Running a business with my ex-husband who's now dating a yogi. One of the really nice ones.** I watched them walk to the bar. Reuben slipped an arm around her waist and then turned guiltily to check I hadn't seen.

This is my future.

He had come into the office six weeks after we split up, ostensibly on the verge of an anxiety attack. "You okay?" I'd asked him, watching over my computer as he crashed around in one of the props cupboards.

He spun round, eyes wild. "I've met someone," he blurted, cowering in the doorway of the cupboard.

A large bag of red noses fell off the shelf behind him and he picked it up, hugging it to his chest. "I'm so sorry," he whispered. "I did not plan this."

He came toward me like a bomb-disposal technician approaching a device, his face frantically searching mine. A little trail of noses was falling on the floor alongside him, but he didn't notice.

"I feel so bad to be telling you this so soon after our breakup," he'd said. "Do you need to sit down?"

I pointed out that I already was.

It had stunned me how little I'd felt. It was odd, certainly, but I found myself more curious than jealous. Reuben was dating! My Roo! "Are you sure you want to know?" he kept asking.

I'd managed only to ascertain that Kaia worked part time in a juice bar in Glendale, that she was a yoga teacher and trainee naturopath, and that Reuben was totally gone.

I watched her order drinks. She wasn't beautiful, in an obvious, western sense, which in a way made it worse. She just glowed, in a slow-cooked, wholesome way. And she was good, I sensed. Kind and Good, in sharp contrast to my Manic and Dark. Reuben pressed down the tip of her nose and laughed. He used to do that with me.

This would have been much easier, I thought churlishly, **if Eddie and I had worked out.** Even if Reuben got down on one knee and proposed to Kaia, right here in the bar, I'd have cheered and clapped and probably offered to organize their bloody wedding.

If Eddie had called.

My stomach pitted miserably and I checked my phone, as if that would help anything.

Then I froze.

Was that . . . Was it . . . ?

A speech bubble. A little gray speech bubble, which meant Eddie—real, living, breathing Eddie, somewhere in the world—was typing a reply to my messages. I sat perfectly still, watching the bubble, and the South Bank faded to zero.

"It's so lovely to be in London," Kaia said, arriving back with my drink. **No! Go away!** "I'd forgotten how much I love this city." I glanced down. The bubble was still there. He was still writing. I tingled. Terror, delight. Terror, delight. I made myself smile at Kaia. She was wearing one of those rings that sits halfway up your finger. I'd bought one, years ago, and it had fallen down a public toilet on El Matador Beach.

"You know London, then?" I made myself ask.

The speech bubble was still there.

"I came here a couple of times on assignments," she replied. "I was a journalist, in another life."

She shuddered lightly and I waited, hoping she'd continue. I had literally nothing to say.

(**This!** This was one of those moments I'd talked about with Mrs. Rushby. Total loss of self. Of manners, sociability, control.)

Speech bubble: still there.

"But I realized I wasn't really enjoying my life." She paused, remembering the time when she didn't really enjoy her life. "So I drilled down to what I cared about, and that was nutrition, being outdoors, keeping my body peaceful and strong. I jumped out of the fast lane and did my yoga teacher training. It was one of the best things I ever did."

"Oh, great!" I said. "**Namaste** to that!"

Kaia took Reuben's hand underneath the table. "But then I suffered a major trauma two years ago and that's when the more profound change happened . . ."

Speech bubble: still there.

"And I realized, when I began to emerge from it all, that it wasn't enough to be true to myself and my needs. I had to look wider; I had to help others. Give freely of myself, if that doesn't sound too pious."

Her cheeks brightened. "Oh, my God, I sound **totally** pious," she laughed, and I remembered that this was no easier for her than it was for me.

Reuben looked at her as if the mother of Christ

sat on the bench next to him. "I don't think you sounded pious at all," he said. "Does she, Sarah?"

I put my phone down for a moment and stared at him. Was he seriously asking me to make his new girlfriend feel better about herself?

"So, long story short, I signed up as an associate at the Children's Hospital," she said hurriedly. She wanted to stop talking about herself now. "One of the fund-raisers. I do at least a day a week for them, often more. And that's me, really."

"I have a lot of time for the CHLA fund-raisers," I said, glad to at last have common ground. "Wonderful people, and very good friends of our charity. I guess that's how you two met, then?"

Kaia looked at Reuben, who nodded uncertainly. It's fine, I wanted to tell him. I'm jealous of your girlfriend, yes, but only because she seems to have got her act together. Not because I still want you, darling boy.

The awful thing about this, I thought, picking up my phone again (speech bubble: still there), was that I had probably fallen more profoundly for Eddie—whom I'd known seven days—than I had Reuben, to whom I'd been married seventeen years. It was me who should be feeling guilty, not Roo.

I turned my phone facedown on the table while I waited for Eddie's message to arrive, and a terrified euphoria blew over me. The wait was over. In a matter of minutes I'd know.

Reuben clearly had no idea what to add to this exchange, in spite of years in a job that had taught him to communicate in near-impossible circumstances. After a few unconvincing coughs he started talking about the fact that you couldn't taste chlorine in the tap water over here, or some other such nonsense.

My phone vibrated and I snatched at it. At last. **At last.**

But it was a text message from Dad.

> Darling, if you haven't left for Gloucestershire yet, don't. Your grandfather's been sacked by his brand-new carers. We've given up and are taking him down to ours to care for him ourselves. We'll put him in Hannah's old room. Please don't cancel your trip down to see us. We love you (and need you . . .). But if you could delay until tomorrow, we'd be very grateful. DAD x

I went straight back to my Messenger, oblivious to Reuben, Kaia, everyone.

There was no message. Eddie was still online but the speech bubble had disappeared.

I felt my face collapse. My heart.

I made myself look at Kaia, who was talking to me. "I saw two of your Clowndoctors in an oncology ward a couple of years ago," she was saying. **This couldn't be happening. Where is the message?**

"There was this little boy and he was so sick and sad and pissed about his chemo program and he shut down when your guys showed up. Just turned his face to the wall and pretended they weren't there."

"I explained that that often happens," Reuben said proudly. "It's why they work in pairs."

"So **clever**!" Kaia beamed. "They work with each other so the child can decide whether or not to join in. Right?"

"Right," Reuben said. "That way, the kids are in charge."

Oh, my God. Who was this tedious double act, and where was my message?

"So he turned away and your clowns started doing all these improvisations together, and he couldn't resist them. I mean, they had **me** in stitches! By the time they left the ward, he was laughing nonstop."

Grudgingly, I nodded. I'd seen it often enough.

Desperate for something—anything—to concentrate on that wasn't Eddie, I launched into a tale about the first time I'd seen Reuben working with kids after he'd trained as a Clowndoctor. Kaia watched me as I rambled on, her little brown chin resting on her little brown hand, the other holding Reuben's. I stopped eventually and looked at my phone, already picturing the physical shape of his reply, the length of the message, the gray oblong that held it.

But it was not there. It was not there, and Eddie was offline again.

"Can I get anyone a drink?" I asked, pulling my purse out of my bag. "Wine?" I looked at my watch. "It's quarter past twelve. Perfectly respectable."

I wrapped my hands around my torso as I waited at the bar, although whether it was to comfort myself or hold myself together I didn't know.

Twenty minutes later, by which point my solo glass of wine had begun to offer a faint numb, Kaia excused herself and went off to the toilet. I watched her slender legs move under her skirt and tried to imagine Kaia coming to pick Reuben up after work so they could go for dinner, or maybe an evening hike in Griffith Park. Kaia coming to our Christmas party or our summer barbecue; having lunch with Reuben's sweet, nervous parents at their house in Pasadena. Because all of that would be happening. (**A much better choice**, I imagined Roo's mum saying. She had never quite trusted that I wouldn't eventually return to England with her son.)

"She's lovely," I told Reuben.

"Thank you." He turned gratefully toward me. "Thank you for being so friendly. It means a lot."

"We needed each other," I said, after a pause, surprising us both. "And now we don't. You've met a nice girl and I'm happy for you, Roo. I mean it."

"Yeah," he said, and I could hear the joy deep in his heart. It was like Reuben had taken one of those long, slow breaths you had to do at the beginning of a yoga class, but he'd never gone back to his normal rhythm.

"Hey," Reuben began. He looked uncomfortable. "Hey, look, Sarah, I . . . I have to say, your e-mails yesterday were kind of out of character. You sounded . . . not very businesslike. And you sent those documents to our trustees without talking to any of us. Not to mention agreeing with a child that you'd send some of our clowns to her sister without even calling the hospital in question. I was at a loss."

Kaia was weaving her way back to our table. "I know," I said. "I had a bad day. It won't happen again."

He watched me. "Are you okay?"

"Fine. Just tired."

He nodded slowly. "Well, shout if you need me. We make mistakes when we don't follow protocol."

"I know. Hey, look, we need to talk about the hospice pitch."

"Sure," Reuben said. "Now?"

"We can't talk about it with Kaia here."

Reuben frowned. "Oh, she won't mind."

"I do. This is business, Roo."

"No," Reuben said gently. "No, it's charity. Not business. And Kaia gets it. She's a friend, not a foe, Sarah."

I made myself smile. He was right. Everyone except me was right these days.

Reuben and Kaia left forty minutes later. Reuben insisted on making a plan for our hospice pitch, in spite of what I'd said. And I'd gone along with it, because how could I not? Kaia had at least offered to go and sit outside while we talked. ("No, no!" Reuben said. "There's nothing secret about this.")

Kaia kissed me, and then gave me a hug. "So great to meet you," she said. "**So** great."

And I said ditto, because there really was nothing about this woman that wasn't nice.

After they'd left, I turned my phone off and my laptop on, and I worked. People came and went; tuna salads and chips with wobbling pyramids of mayonnaise; wine glasses smudged with workday lipstick and pints of hoppy ale. Outside, the sun was covered with gray sheets. Rain fell, wind blew, the sun returned. The South Bank steamed; umbrellas were shaken.

It was on day five of our affair that I'd looked at Eddie David and thought, I would spend the rest of my life with you. I would commit to it, right now, and know I wouldn't regret it.

The boiling weather had finally broken and a storm was rampaging across the countryside, flashing and bellowing, hammering on the roof of Eddie's barn. We were lying on his bed under a skylight, which he said he used mostly for stargazing and weather watching. Lying top to toe, Eddie massaging my foot absentmindedly as he stared up at the wild sky.

"I wonder what Lucy the sheep thinks of all this," he said. I laughed, imagining Lucy standing under a tree, baaing disconsolately.

"The storms we get in LA are crazy," I said. "Like Armageddon."

After a pause he said, "How do you feel about going back there?"

"Uncertain."

"Why?"

I propped my head up so I could see him properly. "Why do you think?"

Pleased, he tucked my foot under his head and said, "Well, you see, that's the thing. I'm not sure I'm willing to let you go back."

And I smiled back at him, and thought, **If you told me to stay, if you told me we could start a life together here, I'd stay. Even though I've known you only a few days, even though I swore I'd never come back. For you, I'd stay.**

It was nearly four by the time I packed up to leave. I switched my phone on, although by now I had no expectations. But there was a text message, from a number I didn't know.

stay away from eddie, it said.

No punctuation, no greeting, no capitals. Just, **stay away**.

I sat back down. Read it a few more times. It had been sent at exactly three o'clock.

After a few minutes I decided to call Jo.

"Come to mine," she said immediately. "Come straight to mine, babe. Rudi's at his granddad's. I'm going to give you a glass of wine and then we're going to call this person, this freak, and find out what's going on. Okay?"

The rain had closed in again. It raged at the Thames like a gray tantrum, pelting, hammering, screaming, just like the storm Eddie and I had watched from his bed. I waited for a few minutes before giving up and walking out, coatless, in the direction of Waterloo.

CHAPTER NINETEEN

Dear You,

You started writing to me earlier. What were you going to say? Why did you change your mind? Can you really not find it within yourself to talk to me?

I'll pick up where I left off.

A few months after turning seventeen, I was in a terrible car accident on the Cirencester Road. I lost my sister, that day, and I lost my life—or at least the life that I'd always known. Because after a few weeks I realized I couldn't live there anymore. Frampton Mansell. Gloucestershire. England, even. It was a very dark time.

I was broken. I called Tommy. He'd been in LA for two years. He said, "Get on the first plane you can," and I did. Quite literally: I flew the next day. Mum and Dad were so good about it. So extraordinarily unselfish, letting me go at a time like that. Would they have been so generous if they'd known what it would do to our family? I don't know. But regardless, they put my needs first, and the next morning I was at Heathrow.

Tommy's family lived on a residential street called South Bedford Drive that was as wide as the M4. Tommy's house was a strange taupe-colored affair that looked as if a Spanish bungalow had mated with a Georgian mansion. I stood in front of it on my first day, sick and dizzy with heat and jet lag, and wondered if I'd landed on the moon.

In fact, it turned out that I'd landed in Beverly Hills.

"They can't afford to live here," Tommy said grimly, when he showed me round. There was a pool! A swimming pool! With a deck with chairs and tables and vines and roses and tropical flowers hanging in pink clouds.

"The rent is crazy. I can't imagine how they'll keep it up, but Mum loves telling people back home that Saks is her corner shop."

Even though Tommy's mother had become barely recognizable, and even more preoccupied with things like clothes and treatments and lunches where she surely couldn't be eating anything, she was kind enough to see that I needed a break. She told me I could stay as long as I wanted, and told me where to get the exotic-sounding frozen yogurt Tommy had written about in his letters. "But don't eat too much," she said. "I can't have you get fat."

Beyond neatly mowed squares of their high-fenced garden stretched a city that stunned me. I'll never forget the first time I saw a road lined with palm trees reaching up into the sky; giant street names hanging off traffic lights; mile upon mile of squat little buildings, checkered with flowers, engineered for earthquakes. The never-ending whine of planes, the nail bars and rugged mountains and valet parking and clothes shops full of stunningly expensive and beautiful clothes. It amazed me. I spent weeks just staring. At the people, the festoons of fairy lights, the huge expanse of pale gold sand, and the Pacific, crashing away at Santa Monica every day. It was a miracle. It was Mars. And for that reason it was perfect.

I realized soon after arriving that Tommy's invitation for me to stay hadn't been purely philanthropic. He was lonely. True, he'd escaped the relentless savagery of his classmates, but nothing about his family, his relationship with himself, or his trust in humanity appeared to have changed for the better. Those early signs of body consciousness he'd had when he left England seemed now to have blossomed into something a lot darker. He ate nothing or everything, he exercised sometimes two or three times a day, and his bedroom was full of clothes from which he'd not even removed the labels. He looked embarrassed when I went in there, as if a part of him remembered who he'd been before all of this.

I asked him outright one day if he **was** actually gay. We were at the Farmers Market, queuing for tacos, and Tommy was already beginning to mumble some falsehood about not being hungry. I remember standing there, fanning my face with our parking lot ticket, and the question just kind of tumbling out of me.

Neither of us was expecting it. He stared at me for a few seconds, and then said, "No, Harrington. I am not gay. And what the hell does that have to do with tacos?"

From behind us there was a quiet eruption of laughter. Tommy cringed deeply into himself; I turned round to see a girl, maybe a couple of years older than me, laughing quite openly. "Sorry," she said, in a London accent. "But I couldn't help overhearing. You, mate"—she pointed at me, still laughing—"you need to work on your bedside manner."

Tommy agreed.

So did I.

An hour at a rickety table eating tacos led to a lifelong friendship. The girl, Jo, was working as a mobile beauty therapist and living in a

crummy apartment share nearby. Over the
next few months, before she ran out of money
and was forced to go back to England, she
bullied us back to a semblance of happiness
and functionality with which we could move
forward. She made us talk—something we
were failing at quite miserably—and she forced
us relentlessly out to parties, to the beach, to
free concerts. She's as spiky as a porcupine, Jo
Monk, but she's a woman of infinite kindness
and courage. I miss her terribly when I'm not in
England.

September came, and I had to go back to
England to finish my A levels. Only I couldn't
go. Whenever I phoned my parents and they
talked about my return, I'd start crying. Mum
would fall silent and eventually Dad would
have to pick up the extension outside the
downstairs loo and crack jokes. Mum did her
best to seem resilient—cheerful, even—but it
slipped out one day, as if she had turned her
back on her voice just for a moment: "I miss
you so much it hurts," she whispered. "I want
my family back." Self-loathing blocked my
throat and I couldn't even manage a reply.

In the end they agreed I should postpone my
A levels for a year to stay awhile longer. They
came to visit me, and although it was a relief to
see them, it was acutely painful that Hannah
wasn't there. They kept wanting to talk about

her, which I found almost unendurable. I was relieved when they left.

Then I met Reuben, and got a job, and decided it was time to become someone I could respect. I'll tell you about that next time.

Sarah

P.S. I'm going home to see my parents tomorrow. Granddad is staying with them for a bit. If you're in Gloucestershire and you're ready to talk, call me.

CHAPTER TWENTY

"Sarah!" Dad, who looked exhausted, hugged me tightly. "Thank God," he said. "Thank God you're here. Our still, small voice of calm."

He offered me some wine, which I refused. After my meeting on the South Bank yesterday with Kaia and Reuben, and the text message warning me off Eddie, I'd gone to Jo's and drunk far too much. My body had told me this morning that it would not tolerate an alcoholic drink for some time.

"Oh, Sarah." Mum hugged me. "I feel awful about the last few weeks. I really am so sorry." My mother spent a lot of time apologizing for her failings, in spite of having done nothing but love and look after me from the day I was born.

"Stop saying that. I had a lovely time. You saw me in Leicester. Was I not happy?"

"Happy enough, I suppose."

I still wasn't sure why I hadn't told them about Eddie. Perhaps because I was supposed to be home for the anniversary of the accident, not having sex with a handsome stranger. Or perhaps because, by

the time I had arrived in Leicester, I was beginning
to worry.

Or perhaps, I thought now, handing some flowers
to Mum, it was because a part of me already knew
it wouldn't work out. The same part of me that
had stood facing Reuben on our wedding day and
thought, **He'll be taken away from me eventually.
Just like Hannah.**

Mum put my flowers in one vase and then
swapped it for a different one. And then a different
one still. "Mind your own business," she said, when
she caught me watching her. "I'm a retiree now,
Sarah. I've earned the right to opinions on flower
arranging."

I smiled, quietly relieved. Last time I'd seen Mum,
she had seemed diminished somehow, squashed,
like a carton flattened for recycling. Which didn't
feel at all right, because, save for the odd lapse, she
had seemed so splendidly robust in the years following the accident. In fact, her fortitude was the only
thing that assuaged my guilt at having just cleared
off and left them in all that pain and chaos.

Today she—and Dad, for that matter—were how
I'd always held them in my mind's eye: kind, solid,
assured. **And mildly alcoholic**, I reminded myself,
as Mum poured herself some wine, even though we
were soon to leave for the pub. **Don't put them on
a pedestal. They've just dealt with things in a
different way.**

I glanced up at the ceiling and lowered my voice. "How's it been? How is he?"

"He's a rotten old bastard," Mum said squarely. "And I'm allowed to say that because he's my father and I love him and I know what a rough time he's had. But there's no denying it—he's a rotten old bastard."

"He is," Dad admitted. "We've been keeping tally of the number of complaints he's made today. So far we're at thirty-three, and it's only quarter to one. Why aren't you drinking?"

"I've a hangover."

Mum slumped. "Oh, I feel terrible when I'm mean about him," she said. "He's impossible to be with, Sarah, drives us mad. But underneath it all I feel very bad for him. He's been on his own so long now. His quality of life is awful, cooped up in that house on his own, nobody to talk to." My grandmother, a woman so round she had seemed almost spherical in the photographs, had died of a heart attack when she was forty-four. I had never met her.

"Well, at least he's got you two. I'm sure he appreciates the company, even if it might seem otherwise."

"He behaves as if he's been kidnapped by terrorists," Mum sighed. "He actually said this morning, when I gave him his pills, 'I can't believe you dragged me down to this godforsaken place.' I was very close to putting an end to his suffering."

Dad laughed. "You're an angel with him," he said,

and gave her a tender kiss. I looked away, mildly disgusted, very touched, and, actually, a little bit jealous. They were still so happy together, my parents. Dad had taken Mum out every day until she'd agreed to marry him; he'd telephoned her, written to her, sent her gifts. He'd taken her to concerts and let her sit at the sound desk with him. He had never left her hanging. He had never not called.

I asked if I should go up and say hello before we left for lunch at the pub.

"Luckily for you, he's asleep," Mum said. "But he'll definitely want to see you."

I raised an eyebrow.

"Inasmuch as he ever wants to see anyone."

We sat outside the Crown, even though it wasn't really warm enough. Gusts of wind riled my mother's hair into red flames, and Dad looked stunted, or perhaps drunk, because his side of the table was sloping down the hill. In the field rising steeply above the lane, a sheep had sunk down onto its knees to graze amid the pungent nettles. I laughed and then stopped laughing. I wondered if I would ever find sheep funny again.

"Tell me about this cello business," I prompted Dad. On the way up, Mum had reported that he'd been taking lessons.

"Aha! Well, I was having a few jars with Paul Wise last autumn, and he was saying he'd just read in the newspaper about how you can keep your brain sharp in old age by playing an instrument—"

"So he just drove to Bristol and bought a cello," Mum interrupted. "He was awful at first, Sarah. Terrible. Paul came and listened to him—"

"And the bastard just stood there and laughed," Dad finished off. "So I practiced like mad, and then found a teacher in Bisley, and I'm soon to take Grade Two. Paul will eat his words."

I raised my glass to propose a toast to Dad, just as a woodpecker drummed its rocky beak into the side of a tree. My hand sank back down to the table. The sound reminded me so strongly of Eddie, of our time together, that I found myself unable to speak.

The oily rolling returned to my stomach.

My parents talked about Granddad while I watched another family, sitting by a blaze of delphiniums further down the garden. The parents looked like mine: just beginning their transition into old age; grayer, more crumpled, but still firmly in their lives, not looking back on them. Their daughters were how I imagined Hannah and I would look if we could sit here today. The younger daughter seemed to be holding forth with some vehemence on some topic or other and I was mesmerized, imagining my own little sister as an adult. Adult Hannah would be full of opinions, I thought. She'd love a good polemic, never shy away from fights—the sort of woman who leads committees and is secretly feared by the other parents at school.

"Sarah?" Mum was looking at me. "Are you okay?"

"I'm fine," I said.

Then: "That family over there."

Mum and Dad looked. "Oh, I think the husband is one of our neighbor's friends," he said. "Patrick? Peter? Something with a 'P.'"

Mum didn't say anything. She knew what I was thinking.

"I just want **that**," I said quietly. "To be able to sit at this table with you two and Hannah. I would give everything I had if it meant we could all sit here. Talking, eating."

Mum's head dipped, and I sensed Dad had gone very still, as he always did when I talked about Hannah. "Well, we'd like that, too," my mother said. "More than we can say. But I think we've learned the hard way that it's better to focus on what we do have rather than what we don't."

A plate of cloud rolled over the sun and I shivered. It was typical of me to do this. To make my parents feel uncomfortable, remind them of how things could have been.

By six o'clock my heart was pounding and my thoughts had scattered like filaments from a dandelion clock. I told my parents, who were politely dismayed, that I was going for a run.

"New exercise regime," I smiled, hoping they would allow me this fiction.

Sickened by myself, I went upstairs to change. I couldn't decide what was worse: that this adrenalized state had become so familiar or that I couldn't find a solution beyond wearing myself out and lying to those who cared about me.

Remind me when you're back off to LA? Tommy texted just before I left.

> Leaving for Heathrow 6:15 a.m. on Tuesday. I'll be quiet as a mouse.

> OK. So you're staying with us on Monday night, right?

> If that's OK. I've got a conference in Richmond on the Monday; I should get to yours by about 7:30 p.m. But if not convenient, I can easily stay on Jo's sofa? I imagine you and Zoe have had it with me!

> No, it's fine. Zoe's in Manchester again. So you're not here Sunday night?

> Negative. Why? Are you entertaining another woman?

> Er, no.

Jolly good. See you Monday night, then, Tommy. Everything OK?

Everything's fine. So, Monday morning: will you go straight to the conference, or will you come here first?

I frowned. Tommy and Zoe had been remarkably generous with their spare room on this and every visit, giving me a key and telling me to use the flat as if it were my own. And apart from the odd time we'd made dinner for each other, I didn't think Tommy had ever asked about my comings and goings.

I was going to come to your flat first, but can go straight to Richmond if you'd prefer? I wrote.

No, Tommy replied. **It's fine. See you then. And don't you dare go hunting for Eddie while you're down there, OK? Don't look him up, don't go running past his front door, don't go and sit in that pub. Do you understand?**

I understand. Have a nice weekend entertaining your secret lady. xx

Watch it, he wrote. Then: **I mean it, Harrington. Don't even look the man up, do you hear?**

For a moment I wondered if Tommy was messaging me because **he** was meeting Eddie. I considered this possibility for a good few minutes before I realized how ridiculous it was.

Would I run as far as Sapperton, in the hope of seeing Eddie? The idea had been brewing for days. Although who knew if he was down here in Gloucestershire or up in London. Or in bloody outer space. And what would I do if I actually saw him?

But I knew that I would run to Sapperton, and I knew it would make me feel even worse, and I either couldn't or wouldn't stop myself.

The run was how I imagined a breakdown might feel. Eddie was everywhere I looked: watching me from tree branches, sitting on the old sluice, walking in the meadow that lay between the wandering branches of the river. And before long he was joined by Hannah, wearing the same clothes she'd worn that day, that awful day.

As I approached the tiny footbridge, I saw a woman walking toward me from the direction of Sapperton. She, at least, seemed real: a raincoat, hair tied back, walking shoes. Until she stopped suddenly and stared at me.

For reasons I couldn't quite understand, I stopped jogging and stared at her, too. Something about her was familiar, only I knew I'd never seen her before. She was too far away for me to be sure about her age, but from here she looked a good deal older than me.

Eddie's mother? Was that possible? I peered at her, but saw no obvious resemblance. Eddie was broad, round-faced, tall, whereas this woman was extremely thin and short, with a sharp chin. (And even if it **was** Eddie's mother, why would she stand in the middle of a footpath, staring at me? Eddie had said she was depressed, not mad.) Besides, she didn't know I even existed.

After another few seconds she turned round and started walking back in the direction she'd come. She walked fast, but her movements had the jerky irregularity of someone to whom movement does not come easily. I'd seen it enough times in children recovering from injury.

I stood there for a long time after she'd disappeared out of sight.

Had that been a face-off, or had the woman simply decided to finish her walk and go home? After all, there was no way of circling back from that section of the path: you either did a round trip of quite a few miles via Frampton Mansell or you turned round and went straight back to Sapperton.

I turned for home. Several times, I felt convinced that Eddie was walking along the footpath behind me. But the footpath was empty every time. Even the birds seemed silent.

I can't stand this, I thought, as I arrived at my parents' porch a few minutes later. **I can't stand it.** How did I end up here again? Scrabbling around this valley after someone I've already lost?

Next to the coat pegs by the front door was a framed photograph of Hannah and me in the field behind our house. I was sitting in a cardboard box,

Hannah next to it, a bunch of flowers in her small fist. Trails of mud and roots from the flowers dirtied her dungarees. She was scowling at the camera, scowling with a comic intensity that made my heart hurt. I stared at her, at my precious little Hannah, and loss thickened like glue in my chest.

"I miss you," I whispered, touching the cold glass of the frame. "I miss you so much."

I imagined her sticking her tongue out at me, and was crying by the time I came face-to-face with my grandfather at the top of the stairs.

I froze. "Oh! Granddad!"

He said nothing.

"I've just been for a run. I came to see you after lunch, but you were asleep, so I thought I'd . . ."

But I couldn't do it. I couldn't talk, not even to appease Granddad. I stood there in front of him, me in my running gear, he in a dressing gown that he'd been too weak to do up properly, beneath it the worn cotton of his old blue pajamas. The edges were piped in navy. My heart was broken. Granddad smelled of deep tiredness. I wept silently, my face crumpled around the flattened shape of my crying mouth. I'd lost Hannah, and now Eddie: I knew it, I couldn't pretend any longer, and here was my poor grandfather who'd been on his own for nearly fifty years, since Granny had had a heart attack and died in her chair with a ham sandwich in front of her, and now Granddad must be taking his daily exercise, because he had a walker in front of him, and neither of us knew what to say to each other. Neither of us had a clue.

"Come to my room," he said eventually.

It took Granddad a long time to get himself into the armchair Mum and Dad had installed for him. I used the time to try to clean up my face, then sat down on the edge of Hannah's old bed.

For a short while I thought he was actually planning to talk to me, to ask me what was the matter. But, of course, he was Granddad, and he did not. He saw my pain, wanted to help, but couldn't. So he sat there, looking out the window, and occasionally at a spot on the wall near my face, until I started to talk.

I told him about the family at the pub at lunchtime, and the sense of dread I felt being in this valley, even after all these years. "There isn't a day," I told him, "when I don't think about Hannah. When I don't long to see her again, even just for five minutes. Hug her, you know?"

Granddad nodded curtly. I noticed that he had pulled his bedsheets straight and managed to pat down his pillow prior to his walk along the landing. I was moved. A need for order, even amid the densest chaos, was something I understood.

"And then I thought something was changing, Granddad. I met a man, down here in Gloucestershire, while Mum and Dad were looking after you."

If I wasn't mistaken, there was the faintest elevation of an eyebrow.

"Go on, please," he said, after what felt like an age.

I paused. "I take it you know about my husband and me splitting up."

Again, a slow nod. "Although I had to drag it out of your mother," he said. "There's something about being above the age of eighty that convinces people you will die of shock if you are party to bad news." He paused. "I mean, who in your generation doesn't get a divorce these days? I'm surprised you people even bother marrying."

A blue tit whirled onto the feeder hanging outside the spare-room window, pecked at the nut hole and whirled away again. Kaleidoscopic disks of evening sun played on the window seat, where Hannah used to keep her toy hedgehog collection. The room was warm and silent.

"You were saying."

I was saying nothing, I nearly retorted, but there was something about his posture, his eyes, that told me he wanted to know. That he might actually care. And if I'd chosen to talk to him, I had to expect the odd grenade.

So I told him everything. From the moment I heard Eddie's laughter on the village green to my run along the canal just now, and all the desperate, shameful things I'd done since he disappeared.

"Luckily you were spared the indignities of online stalking, growing up when you did," I told him. "But it's not a nice experience. It never delivers what you're hoping for." It was too therapeutic, this business of talking to a silent person; I couldn't stop. "It never gives you control of the situation."

Granddad didn't say anything for a long time. "I don't condone your actions," he said. "They sound asinine and entirely self-defeating."

"Agreed."

"But I do understand, Sarah."

I glanced up; for once he was looking straight at me.

"I fell in love with a woman for whom I would have torn down buildings, if I could. I loved her until the day she died. I still love her, years later. Even now it is painful."

"Granny."

He looked away. "No."

A big cupboard of silence opened up between us. Downstairs, Mum and Dad were laughing; muffled noises gave way to the sound of Patsy Cline spilling out of Dad's speakers.

"Ruby Merryfield," Granddad said eventually. "She was the love of my life. Everyone told me I couldn't marry her, and so I didn't. She'd had a lover when she was younger, had had a child. It was placed in an adoptive family. It broke her heart. Nobody knew, other than my parents, because, of course, my father was her doctor. He forbade me from marrying her. I fought a spirited battle, Sarah, but in the end I had to give in because I was at medical school and I needed his support."

He made a quivering spire with his hands. "And so I stopped calling for her, and I married your grand-mother a year later, and we had a nice life together, Diana and I. But I thought about Ruby every day. I missed her. I wrote her letters I didn't dare send. And when I heard she'd died of influenza, I took myself off on a fishing trip for several days because I was ill with the grief. Over near Cannock. It was far too beautiful. I wished I'd gone somewhere ugly."

Granddad's eyes swam. "She had this laugh, like a little bird at first, only then it would broaden to something so unladylike. She saw the joy in life, wherever she went."

Granddad pressed the back of his hand, where the skin was pouchy and liver-spotted, into his eyes. Light was fading fast from the room.

"I should never have given up on her," he said.

The blue tit came back and we sat in silence, watching it.

"I don't entirely regret my decision," he went on. "As I said, I cared for Diana very much, and I mourned her when she died. And without her I could not have had your mother and her sister, al-though, God knows, your aunt has been a handful."

My aunt's latest husband was called Jazz.

"But if I had my time again, I would not have given up," Granddad said. "I don't believe that love is meant to be like an explosion. It is not meant to be dramatic, or ravenous, or any of the silly words ascribed it by writers and musicians. But I do believe that when you know, you know. And I knew, and I let it go without any real sort of a fight, and I will never forgive myself that."

He closed his eyes. "I need to go to bed now. And no, I do not need your help. Please could you shut the door on your way out? Thank you, Sarah."

CHAPTER TWENTY-ONE

Dear Eddie,

In the absence of a request to stop writing, I'm
going to continue.

It had been agreed that I would stay in LA
for another few months, even though this
would mean missing out on my final A-level
year. I didn't care: I couldn't go back.

I had a total of two friends, and I lived in
the "guest suite" of a house in Beverly Hills
that had a pool and a full-time housekeeper.
The only thing that reminded me even vaguely
of home was the flank of plane trees on either
side of South Bedford Drive. Only they weren't
really like home, because it had been a brutal
summer and they were charred like crispy
bacon by the time September was under way.

Tommy's mum arranged for me to clean
some of her friends' houses so I'd have a little
cash: it was my only option, without a visa.
I cleaned for the Steins, the Tysons, and the
Garwins, and on Wednesday afternoons I did

a weekly grocery shop for Mrs. Garcia, who used to beg me to become her kids' au pair. It bothered her a great deal that I said no. She couldn't fathom how I could get on so well with her kids and yet refuse to look after them, and I couldn't bring myself to tell her why.

I thought I'd reached my full height but started growing again, upward and outward. I had boobs and a waist and a bottom. I was turning into the shape I am now, I guess, and I was working out what sort of a woman I wanted to be. Strong, I'd decided. Strong, driven, and successful. I'd spent years being a wimp, a wallflower, a limp nobody.

One day in November Mrs. Garcia's daughter, Casey, broke her arm at preschool. The au pair Mrs. Garcia had eventually hired stayed with Casey's brother and I was asked to accompany the little girl to the hospital in a taxi. Mrs. Garcia was racing back from a conference in Orange County. She insisted I take her daughter to CHLA, even though it was miles away—she knew people there, she said; she wanted Casey to see a familiar face while she waited for her mom.

Poor Casey. She was so frightened by the pain; by the time we'd driven across town from Beverly Hills her teeth were chattering and she wouldn't talk to the doctors. I couldn't stand it. As soon as Mrs. Garcia arrived, I left the hospital and went to find a joke shop someone had mentioned, near the intersection of Vermont and Hollywood. I wanted to find something that would make Casey laugh. Before I got there, though, I was assaulted by a great explosion of kids coming out of a Mexican restaurant right on the corner. They had balloons and face paint and they looked to be a million miles from where Casey was right now.

Shortly after they were chased back inside by a harassed-looking mother, a clown came out of the restaurant and slumped against the wall. He looked shattered. He got out a packet of fags and took a Mexican beer wrapped in a paper bag out of one of his pockets. I laughed as he opened it up and took a long, grateful drink. He was a very funny sort of a clown, no face paint or wig, just a boy with a red nose and odd clothes. And an illegal beer.

"This isn't what it looks like," he said, when he saw me. "I'm not really drinking and smoking outside a kids' party." I told him not to worry and asked for directions to the joke shop. He pointed down Hollywood at a store covered in graffiti and murals. "Can I come with you?" the clown asked. "I'm traumatized. I trained with Philippe Gaulier in France. I'm meant to be a theater practitioner, not a kids' entertainer."

I asked what the difference was. Turned out it was quite considerable.

"I tell you what," I said to him, pausing on the steps of the joke shop. "If I promise not to tell on you for drinking and smoking outside a kids' party, will you do me a favor? A fairly big favor?"

So this poor bloke, who probably smelled of cigarettes and alcohol, followed me into the Children's Hospital and paid Casey a visit.

As we approached Casey's ER cubicle, I felt his energy change. "From this moment on I will be Franc Fromage. Don't use my regular name," he instructed, even though I didn't know what his "regular name" was.

Franc Fromage arrived at Casey's bedside and produced a ukulele. He sang a song to her arm, about it being broken, and even though Casey was still frightened and upset, she couldn't help but laugh. And then he asked her to help him make up the next verse, and she was concentrating so hard on that that she forgot where she was and how frightened she was. Soon after, she agreed to let the doctors set her arm.

Monsieur Fromage told me he'd enjoyed the visit very much. He got very overexcited and started using all sorts of theatrical and psychological terms I didn't understand. I was

rescued by a nurse asking if Franc Fromage
would come back, please, because all the other
kids wanted to meet the ukulele man with the
red nose.

When we finally left, he gave me his phone
number and—visibly terrified—told me I owed
him a drink. "My name is Reuben," he said
gravely. "Reuben Mackey."

So I called him and we went for a drink.
Reuben said he'd been reading about hospital
clowning since he'd met me and apparently it
was a real thing with a method and studies.
Some guy in New York had set up the first
charity in the eighties. I want to train with
him, he said. Use my skills to actually help
people, not just make them laugh.

Nothing happened that night. I think we
were both too shy. Besides, Tommy and Jo were
watching us from a table across the street "in
case he turns out to be one of them clowns that
murders people," as Jo put it.

Then Mrs. Garcia asked if I could get Franc
Fromage to come to the hospital again because
Casey was having her plaster cast removed. He
said okay, but only if I bought him another
drink.

He not only helped Casey get her plaster
off but he spent hours with the other kids
in orthopedics, too. He only stopped when

he realized his hands were trembling with
hunger. "Please come back!" one of the nurses
implored.

The problem was, he couldn't afford to work
for nothing. He was living in a tiny shared
apartment in Koreatown, he told me, couldn't
afford to earn a cent less.

That's when I said, "How about I raise the
money for you to do one day per month?" I
told him I worked for all these wealthy people
and how news of his time in the hospital had
spread fast.

And that's how it began. My relationship
with a clown and the birth of our company.
He went to New York to train with
psychotherapists, child psychologists, and
theater practitioners. Then he came back and
we got going. He visited the sick children and
I stayed in the background raising money
and organizing, which suited me perfectly. I
wanted to be involved—I wanted it more than
he knew—I just didn't want to be on the front
line.

I was good at it. Reuben was good at it.
People saw and heard about what we did and
they wanted us to visit their sick kids. We
hired three more people; Reuben trained them.
Before long we founded our first little training
academy. We got married, rented a flat in Los
Feliz, near the Children's Hospital. Years later

the hipsters moved in and Reuben was in his element.

As for me, I had a purpose, and a direction, and I had no time to think about the life I'd left. I had a man who needed me to be strong when he was weak, and vice versa. Our love was based on reciprocal need and strength, and it worked perfectly.

For a long time that kind of love was all I thought I needed. When I promised to love and honor him forever, I meant it. But, of course, I changed. As the years passed, I no longer needed him, and so our balance was fatally disrupted. We cared so much about each other, Eddie, but without that balance of need, the scales couldn't settle. My inability to give him a baby was the final straw. After the car accident I couldn't stand being near kids; couldn't bear the thought of a child suffering. The very idea of bringing a child into the world—a defenseless baby like my little sister had once been—created a storm of blind panic.

So I stuck to helping sick children from behind the scenes. It was bearable, and it was safe. It was the best I could manage, but it just wasn't enough for Reuben. He wanted to hold his own baby in his arms, he told me. He couldn't imagine a future in which that wasn't possible.

By the time he had the courage to end

things, I realized I had no idea what love should feel like. But when I met you, I finally knew what it should be. Our few days together weren't a fling for me, and I don't believe they were for you, either.

Please write to me.

Sarah

CHAPTER TWENTY-TWO

DRAFTS FOLDER

You're right, Sarah. It wasn't just a fling. And it wasn't just a week, either; it was a lifetime.

Everything you felt about you and me, I felt, too. But you should stop messaging me. I'm not who you think I am. Or perhaps I'm who you think I'm not.

God, what a mess. What a terrible mess.

Eddie

✓ DELETED, 00:12 A.M.

CHAPTER TWENTY-THREE

After a mere four days with my parents in Gloucestershire, I returned to London. I was to lunch in Richmond with Charles, our trustee; then I would speak at the palliative care conference he had helped organize. I would stay the night with Tommy, and begin my five-and-a-half-thousand-mile journey back to Los Angeles early the next morning.

I sat on the train up to London in quiet stillness, unable to tell if I was numb or simply resigned. I said the right things to Charles over lunch, and at the conference I spoke with precision but no passion. Charles, as I left, asked if I was all right. His concern brought me to the edge of tears, so I told him about my separation from Reuben.

"Please don't tell anyone," I begged. "We want to announce it properly at our next board meeting . . ."

"Of course," Charles had said quietly. "I'm so very sorry, Sarah."

I felt a terrible fraud.

• • •

Tomorrow, I promised myself, as I headed back to Central London on the train. Tomorrow I would regain control. Tomorrow I would get on a plane and I would fly back to LA, where I'd rediscover the numb of the sunshine, confidence, and my best self. Tomorrow.

My train pulled into Battersea Park Station and I rested my head against the greasy window, watching the scrum on the opposite platform. People were squeezing themselves onto a train before those on board had had a chance to get out. Shoulders were braced, mouths compressed, eyes were down. All of them looked angry.

I watched a man in a red-and-white football kit fight his way off the train, a suit folded over his arm. He walked toward the empty benches outside my own train, and I stared blankly as he folded his suit carefully into a satchel. After a while he straightened out and checked his watch, glanced briefly at me and then away, then hauled the satchel over his shoulder.

And then, as my own train began to pull away from the platform, I turned my head to follow his back as it walked off toward the exit steps, because I suddenly registered what it said on his football strip. **Old Robsonians. Est. 1996.**

In the hope of having another Google route to Eddie, I had tried many times to remember the name of his football team. Beyond the word "Old," though, nothing had materialized. My train began to accelerate and I closed my eyes, concentrating hard on the memory of Eddie's football trophies. **Old Robsonians**? Is that what they'd said?

I remembered Eddie's finger, sliding a snake of dust off the top of one of them. Yes! **Old Robsonians, The Elms, Battersea Monday.** I was certain of it!

I looked back out the window, even though the station had long since fallen away. Behind an old gasworks, the skeleton of a huge construction block was being fussed over by dizzying cranes.

That man plays in Eddie's football team.

Old Robinson footnalk, I typed, but Google knew what I was looking for. A website was offered. Pictures of men I didn't know. Links to fixtures; match reports; an article about their U.S. tour. (Is that where he'd been? The States?)

In the corner of the page, I scrolled through their Twitter feed: match results, banter, more pictures of men I didn't know. And then, a picture of a man I did know. It was dated a week ago. Eddie, in the background of a postmatch pub photo, drinking a pint and talking to a man in a suit. **Eddie.**

After staring at the photo for a long time, I selected "About Us."

Old Robsonians played on an AstroTurf pitch right by Battersea Park Railway Station on Monday nights. Their kickoff was at 8 P.M.

I checked my watch. It wasn't yet seven. Why had the other man been there so early?

At Vauxhall, I teetered at the door of the train, unsure as to what I should do. There was no guarantee that Eddie was in London, or playing tonight. And according to the website, the football pitch was on the grounds of a school: I either marched right up to the perimeter to brazenly confront him or I didn't go at all. It wasn't like I could casually stroll by.

The train doors rolled shut and I remained on board.

At Victoria, I got off and stood, paralyzed, on the crowded concourse. People bulleted and ricocheted off me; a woman told me outright not to "stand there like a fucking idiot." I didn't move. I scarcely even noticed: all I could think about was the possibility that Eddie, in less than an hour, might be playing football a few minutes from where I was standing.

CHAPTER TWENTY-FOUR

Dear You,

Today is July 11—your birthday! Thirty-two years since you forced your way out into the bright starkness of the world, stunned fists moving in the air like little tentacles.

Out you came, into the warm, blurred glow of love. "She's too small," I cried, when they let me visit you. I could feel your hopelessly fragile ribs around your tiny beating heart. "She's too small. How can she survive?"

But you did, Hedgehog. I remember now as then the fantastical brimming of love for which I was so wholly unprepared. I didn't mind Mum and Dad spending all their time with you. I wanted them to. I wanted your ribs to grow stronger, to strengthen and thicken around that tiny lamp of life in your chest. I wanted you to stay in hospital for months, not days. "She's fine," Mum and Dad told me, again and again. Dad made me a Banoffee pie because I was so afraid for you I cried. And yet you were fine. That heartbeat went on and on, through the day and through the night, on and on as seasons changed and you grew and grew.

Did you know it was your birthday today, Hedgehog? Has anyone told you? Did someone make you a cake, covered in chocolate stars, just how you liked it? Did anyone sing for you?

Well, if not, I did. Maybe you heard me. Maybe you're with me now, while I write this letter. Giggling about how much neater your handwriting is than mine, even though you're younger than me. Maybe you're outside, playing in your tree house, or reading girls' magazines in your den up on Broad Ride.

Maybe you're everywhere. I like that idea most. Up there in the pink-flushed clouds. Down here in the dampness of daybreak.

Wherever I go, I look for you. And wherever I am, I see you.

Me xxxxx

CHAPTER TWENTY-FIVE

On my last night in London I turned up at a six-a-side football game in Battersea in the hope of finding a man I'd met once, a man who'd never called.

What I did that night would lie way beyond the splintered edges of sanity. But as I stood on the concourse at Victoria Station earlier on, trying to reason with myself, I had realized that I wanted to see Eddie more than I cared about the consequences.

And now here I was, crammed into a hot corner of the 7:52 to London Bridge via Crystal Palace, first stop Battersea Park. Less than two minutes' walk from the station I would find an AstroTurf pitch, and on it—my stomach flipped like a February pancake—Eddie David. In a football kit, warming up for his eight-o'clock match. **Right now.** Passing to a teammate. Stretching his quads.

His body. His actual, physical body. I closed my eyes and crushed a surge of longing.

The train was slowing down already. The squeal of brakes, a pulsing wave of commuters forcing me down the steps, and then—suddenly, shockingly—I was standing on Battersea Park Road. Behind me, the amplified bark of ticket sellers' voices, an echoing busker's guitar. Above me, the heave and groan of the train viaducts and thickset white clouds like beaten meringues. And ahead of me, somewhere up an unpaved lane, Eddie David.

I stood there for some time, breathing slowly. Two further waves of passengers poured out around me. One man, wearing a red-and-white football shirt with "PAGLIERO" written in black on the back, sprinted up the lane toward the pitches, trying as he ran to send a text message and affix shin pads to his legs. His green satchel swung round and hit him in the face, but he carried on running.

That man knows Eddie, I thought. He's probably known him for years.

As the pitches slid into view, everything that I'd seen online was confirmed. The pitches were surrounded on all sides by high wire fences, train viaducts, buildings. There would be nowhere to hide. And yet here I was, all five foot nine of me, striding ever closer in my smart conference blouse.

This is the most appalling thing I will ever do.

But my legs kept on walking.

The players in the pitch closest to me were warming up. A referee jogged toward the center with a whistle in his mouth. Everything moved slowly, like an old VHS tape starting to jam. The air smelled of greasy rubber and exhaust fumes.

My legs kept on walking.

"Turn round and run," I instructed myself in a loud whisper. "Turn round and run, and we'll forget this ever happened."

My legs kept on walking.

It was at that moment I realized that, apart from the PAGLIERO man, there were no other players in the Old Robsonians' red-and-white strip. There was a team in blue and a team in orange on the pitch nearest me, and on the other one, black-and-white versus green.

PAGLIERO was putting his shin pads back in his bag. After a moment he straightened up, noticing me.

"Are you an Old Robsonian?" I asked him.

"I am. A very late one. Are you looking for someone?"

"Well, all of them, I guess."

PAGLIERO had the mischievous smile of a boy. "The game got moved to seven P.M. I forgot. They've already played."

"Oh."

He picked up his satchel. "But they'll be over there now, having some postmatch beers. Would you like to join us?" He gestured over to what looked like a shipping container.

I peered at it. It **was** a shipping container. How typically London. A craft ale taproom, probably, in a bloody windowless container. "Please do come and join us," he repeated. "We like visitors."

PAGLIERO looked too disorganized to be a rapist

or a murderer, so I fell into stride beside him, making small talk I couldn't even hear. I wasn't in charge of my own mind anymore, so this was all fine.

"Here you go," PAGLIERO said, holding open a door carved into the side of the container.

I was staring at the naked backside of an adult male for quite some time before I realized what was happening. Before I realized that I was staring at the naked backside of an adult male, with a towel round his neck and his back to the door, singing something with great enthusiasm and minimal musicianship. Other men, more fully clothed than this one, were sitting on benches, arguing about the match. Around them, a jungle of discarded football shirts read "SAUNDERS," "VAUGHAN," "WOODHOUSE," "MORLEY-SMITH," "ADAMS," "HUNTER."

Over by the door to what I realized now must be the showers, the naked adult male pulled on some boxer shorts.

"Oh, no," something deep inside me said, but it didn't make its way to my mouth. Behind me, in the direction of PAGLIERO, I heard a man laugh.

"Pags!" someone said. "You're an hour late." Then: "Oh. Hello."

I came back to life. "I'm so sorry," I whispered, turning to leave. PAGLIERO, laughing, moved to one side to let me out.

"Welcome!" someone else said, close behind me. I staggered outside, wondering how I would ever get over this. I had just walked into a changing room full of barely clothed men.

"Hello?" The man had followed me out. He, at least, was fully clothed.

He put on a pair of glasses, and from inside the container I heard the stunned silence lapse into laughter that I thought would never stop.

He shook his head in the direction of the door, as if to say, **Ignore them.**

"I'm Martin. Team captain and manager. You've just walked into our changing room, and while it's an unorthodox move, I sense that you might need some help."

"I do," I whispered, clutching my handbag to me. This must be the Martin who'd written on Eddie's Facebook page. "I need quite a lot of help, I think, but I'm not sure you can offer it."

"It could happen to anyone," Martin said kindly.

"It could not."

He thought about it. "No, I suppose you're right. We've never had a woman walk into our changing room, not in twenty years. But Old Robsonians is a modern team, embracing innovation and change. Showering after every match is one of our oldest principles, but there's no reason why we can't build new features into the practice—guests, maybe a live band, that sort of thing."

From inside the container drifted great shouts of laughter and male conversation. A ribbon of shower steam uncurled slowly into the evening air. Martin the team captain was laughing at me, although he did so with kindness.

I took a deep breath.

"It was a terrible, terrible mistake," I said. "I was looking for—" I stopped suddenly. In my horror, I had completely forgotten why I was there in the first place.

Dear Christ. I had walked into a changing room in the hope of seeing Eddie David.

I folded my arms tightly across my chest, as if trying to hold the shattered pieces of myself together. What would I have said? What would I actually have done? He could be in there, right now, toweling down after a shower, listening with the growing shock of realization as his teammates told him about the tall girl with the suntan who'd just marched into the changing room.

Sickness moved in my stomach. Something is wrong with me, I realized. Something is actually wrong with me. People don't do this.

"Looking for who? Someone in Old Robsonians? Or another team?"

"Old Robsonians, she said just now," PAGLIERO told him, stepping outside. Then: "Sorry, by the way. That was very bad of me. Although you made the boys' night. One of our founder members is visiting from Cincinnati—he thinks we hired you especially to welcome him back."

I stared at the ground. "It was a great joke," I whispered. "No need to apologize. And I got it wrong. I wasn't looking for anyone from Old Robsonians, I was . . ."

"Looking for someone from Old Robsonians," Martin said. "Who? Everyone's married! Well, apart from Wally, but he—" He stopped and stared sharply at me, and before he even said it, I knew what was coming. "Are you Sarah?" he asked quietly.

"Er . . . No?"

Two other men came out. "Is it true that—" one began, and then saw me. "Oh. It is."

"These gentlemen are Edwards and Fung-On," Martin said, although his eyes didn't leave my face. "I'm deciding which of them I think should be Player of the Night." Then: "I'll help you get back to the road," he said suddenly, marching me off toward the entrance lane.

"Bye!" called PAGLIERO, and Edwards and Fung-On, one of whom would be Player of the Night, gave a salute. I could hear their laughter as they went back into the container.

When they were gone, Martin stopped and faced me. "He's not here tonight," he said eventually. "He doesn't play for us every week. He's in the West Country most of the time."

"Who? Sorry, I . . ."

Martin looked sympathetic, but I could see he knew exactly who I was. And that he knew exactly why Eddie hadn't called.

"Is he in Gloucestershire, then?" I blurted. Hot tears of humiliation built in my eyes.

Martin nodded. "He—" He stopped abruptly, as if remembering his responsibility to his teammate. "I'm sorry," he said. "I shouldn't talk about Eddie."

"It's okay." I stood there, slumped with shame. I wanted to leave, but self-loathing and shock had immobilized my legs.

"Look, it's none of my business," he said slowly, running a hand over his face. "But Eddie's been a friend for years, and he . . . Stop trying to find him, okay? I'm sure you're very nice, and if it helps, I don't think you're mad, and neither does he, but . . . stop."

"He said that? He doesn't think I'm mad? What else did he say about me?" Tears rolled down my face and fell to the cooling concrete below. It defied belief that I was in this situation. Here, with this man. This total stranger, begging for scraps.

"You don't want to find him," Martin said eventually. "Please trust me. You do not want to find Eddie David."

And he turned round and walked back to the container, calling over his shoulder that it was nice to have met me, and he hoped what I'd seen in there hadn't scarred me for life.

A train hammered along the viaduct bordering the pitches and I shivered. I had to go home.

The problem was, I didn't know where home was anymore. I didn't really know anything, other than that I had to find Eddie David. No matter what this man said.

CHAPTER TWENTY-SIX

I pulled running shorts over my legs. It was 3:09 A.M., precisely seven hours since I'd stumbled away from the football pitch. My room was pungent with sleeplessness.

Sports bra, running top. My hands shook. Adrenaline was still collecting in fizzy pools around my body, dancing over the sickening exhaustion that must lie underneath. Tommy had barred the door when I'd emerged in my running gear after getting back from the football. He'd made me a hot drink and had then ordered me off to bed. "I don't even want to think about what happened at that football pitch," he'd told me severely, but within five minutes he'd cracked and knocked at my door, begging me to tell him what had happened at that football pitch.

"I'm sorry," he'd said softly, when I finished. "But well done for admitting something's gone . . . well, a bit wrong with you. That takes courage."

"The letters, Tommy, all those letters I sent him via Facebook. Calling his workshop, writing to his friend Alan. What was I **thinking**?"

"A silent phone brings out the very worst in us," he said. "All of us."

We sat together on my bed for a long time. Neither of us said much, but his presence calmed me sufficiently to try sleeping.

"I'm so sorry," I'd said, before he went off to his own bed. "I've become a burden on you again. You shouldn't have to spend your life rescuing me."

Tommy had smiled. "I didn't rescue you back then, and I'm not rescuing you now," he'd said. "I'm here for you, Harrington—you know I am—but I'm also certain you can sort this out. You're a survivor. One of life's cockroaches."

I'd just about managed a smile of my own.

Now, three hours later, I was trying again and again to knot my laces, but my hands wouldn't coordinate. Everything was wrong.

My airport taxi was at five. I had not slept and I wouldn't. There was plenty of time for a run, a shower, to gift wrap the little lemon tree I'd bought for Tommy and Zoe to say thank you. And I'd only go for a short jog; just enough to help me sleep on the plane.

I slid out of my bedroom door, grateful that Zoe was away. When Tommy went up to bed, that was where he stayed, but Zoe often got up very early to answer e-mails from Asia, wrapped in an elegant gray silk kimono. More than once she had caught me sneaking out for a run before the sun had risen.

Although this, I knew, glancing at my watch—3:13 A.M.—was not a run. This was a problem.

I glanced at myself in Zoe's big mirror in the hallway, framed by wood from a tree from her late parents' Berkshire garden. Zoe was right; I had lost weight. My arms looked stringy, and my face looked narrower, as if I'd taken out a plug and allowed some of it to drain.

I turned away, embarrassed to look at myself. Frightened, too. I had often wondered about the degree of consciousness held by the mentally ill as they began to deteriorate. How easily could they recognize a decline? How visible was the line between fact and fiction, before it disappeared completely?

Was I unwell?

I stopped in the kitchen for a quick drink of water. My leg muscles twitched impatiently. **Soon**, I told them. **Soon.**

In the kitchen doorway, I stopped dead. What? Zoe? But she was in—

"Jesus!" shouted the woman in the kitchen.

I froze. The woman was naked. Another naked stranger, little more than seven hours since I'd seen the last. Synthetic orange light from the streetlamp stippled her breasts and belly as she plunged about, trying to cover herself. A stream of expletives flew from her mouth.

I turned away, covering my eyes. And then I turned back, because a slender thread in my brain was be-

ginning to unravel: **This woman is not a stranger.**
"Stop looking at me," the woman snapped, although
less ferociously now, and I felt my face slacken with
disbelief as I finally recognized my oldest female
friend.

"Oh, my God," I said weakly.

"Oh, my God," Jo agreed, grabbing a Bluetooth
speaker from Zoe's work surface and holding it over
her pubic hair.

"Jo?" I whispered. "No. No, no. Tell me this isn't
what it looks like."

"It's not what it looks like," Jo muttered, swapping
the speaker for a cookery book and then giving up
completely. "I told you to stop looking at me," she
added, sinking down behind the kitchen island.

I stood, paralyzed, until an angry whisper rose up
from the other side of the kitchen. "Sarah, can you
please get me something to put on?" Wordlessly I
walked backward into the hallway, where I got a coat
off a hook. I handed it to her and slumped down on
one of Zoe's stools.

"What is happening?" I asked.

Jo stood up, pulling on what turned out to be an
enormous ski jacket. She merely huffed, rolling back
the cuffs so her hands could poke through.

"Would you like a pair of ski pants?" I asked
dazedly. "Some ski poles? A crash helmet? Jo, what
is this?"

"I could ask you the same question," she said,

frowning in distaste at the coat. "Wealthy arseholes," she added, presumably about anyone who liked to ski. "What are you doing here?"

"I'm staying here," I said. "As you well know. I'm going for a run and then I'm going to the airport."

"It's quarter past three in the morning!" Jo hissed. "Nobody goes running at that time!"

"You're naked in Tommy's kitchen!" I hissed back. "Don't start!"

Jo zipped up the coat. "Unbelievable," was all she could say.

I took a deep breath. "Jo, are you sleeping with Tommy? Are my two oldest friends having an affair? We'll deal with me shortly," I added, before she tried to interrupt.

"I was visiting," she said eventually. "Tommy said I could sleep on the sofa."

"Try again," I said. "Try again, Joanna Monk. Tommy went to bed at midnight, or so I thought. You weren't here then. But now you are, and you're naked, and I know how much you love your pajamas."

"Oh, shit," someone muttered. I looked up. Tommy was standing in the doorway, wrapped in his dressing gown. "I told you this was a bad idea," he said to Jo.

"I needed a drink! I don't drink from no bathroom taps, Tommy, you know that." Her voice was combative, which meant she was panicking. "And she should have been asleep anyway, not sneaking out for a run." She nodded her head at me.

I folded my elbows onto the kitchen island. "Right," I said. "I want to know exactly what is going on here. And how long it's been happening. And how this is justifiable when Tommy is in a long-term relationship." I paused. "Well, you too, Jo, although you'll forgive me for caring less about Shawn."

Tommy padded across the kitchen floor and sat at the top of the island, next to neither me nor Jo.

"Well, you see . . . ," he began, and then paused.

The pause became a silence, which hung in the air like fog. He looked at his hands. He picked at a hangnail. He lifted his hand to his mouth and nibbled at his thumb.

"I also want to know why I'm only finding out about this now," I added.

Jo suddenly sat down. "We're having sex," she said. Her voice was perhaps a little louder than was necessary.

Tommy flinched, but didn't deny it.

"And I'm not convinced you care all that much about Zoe, Sarah, but—for what it's worth—she's been sleeping with her client. The director of that company she represents, the one that makes them fitness watches. That's why she went to Hong Kong. He invited her. And Tommy's fine about it," she added firmly. "He came round to my flat the night she told him and we had too much to drink and . . . well."

Tommy looked at Jo, as if to say, **Really?** Then he shrugged and inclined his head, as if to confirm what she'd said. He was puce with embarrassment.

Another long silence.

"I'm sorry, but that's not good enough," I said. "What do you mean, 'We had too much to drink and . . . well'? Getting drunk and having sex are not interdependent, you know."

"Stop trying to catch me out with your long words," Jo muttered.

"Oh, behave yourself."

She sighed. "It was the night we all came here for dinner," she said, not quite meeting my eye. "That ramen you made, Sarah. You went to bed, all upset because of Eddie, and I went home. Then Zoe broke the news to Tommy and he stormed out of the flat, but after a few minutes he realized he had nowhere to go. So he called me, rather than storm right back inside. Got an Uber."

A smile I wasn't used to illuminated a corner of her face. She looked at him, perhaps torn between the need to respect his privacy and to say this out loud. To confirm the affair.

I looked at Tommy. "So you got in a taxi to Bow and, I mean, were you planning to . . ." I trailed off. I couldn't even say it.

"No," he said quickly. "Not at all. But that doesn't mean I regretted it," he added, when the smile slid from Jo's face.

"I see. So . . . is this a—a fling? Or a thing?" I asked.

There was a very long silence. Then: "Well, I love him," Jo said. "But I can't speak for Tommy."

Tommy looked up sharply. "I'm sorry?"

"You heard what I said," she snapped. She furiously zipped and unzipped one of the pockets on his ski jacket. "But that's by the by. The reason we didn't tell you, Sarah, is that we haven't told anyone. Zoe's told Tommy he can stay here as long as he needs to—until he finds somewhere to live. She's been staying with her fancy man at night so Tommy could tell you in his own time. He thinks she's being really generous; I think she just can't stand looking like the bad guy."

After a moment's thought, I smiled. This, at least, rang true.

"But she's not the issue here. It's Shawn." She stopped zipping. "He's the real problem."

"Why? What's he done?"

"It's what he could do," Tommy said, when he realized Jo was struggling. "She's worried he'll turn the whole custody thing into a nightmare if he finds out she's been seeing someone else. So she's going to split up with him, sort out custody, not mention me. Then we'll . . . well, we'll see what happens with us, I suppose."

Jo's face gave nothing away, but I saw it—even through my shock, I saw it. She really was in love with him. And she had been for a long time. She was petrified this was just a fling. A rebound. The poor woman could barely meet his eye. **We'll see what happens with us** was nowhere near enough for her.

Tommy, as if sensing the same, moved round the island and sat next to her. I saw her glance down as he placed his hand carefully on her leg, and something tender began to swell in my throat.

"He's a vindictive fucker," Jo said quietly. Shawn was safer territory than her feelings for Tommy. "I can't let him find out."

"Personally, I can't see how he'd ever get custody," Tommy said. "He's the worst he's ever been—not turning up to pick Rudi up from school, he's stoned most of the time, and he even left Rudi on his own in the flat a couple of weeks ago. Rudi nearly set fire to the place, trying to make his own tea. Jo's dad's got Rudi tonight." He glanced again at Jo, but she had closed down, as she always did when she'd exposed too much of herself.

Zoe's trendy wall clock rolled silently to 3:30 A.M.

"So that's that," Jo said, unable to bear the silence. She put her hands on the worktop, two raw little fists. "And I managed to bare my soul in the middle of it! Sorry," she said, half turning toward Tommy. "I really don't mind if it's just sex, babe. Forget the love thing. I was just being silly. OTT, you know me."

There was an uncomfortable silence.

"I should give you two some space," I said.

"Stay," Jo barked.

"Okay, thanks," Tommy said simultaneously.

I hovered, halfway out of my stool.

"I'm not very good at this," Jo said. Her face was the color of house bricks. "Shouldn't be left to my own devices. If you go, I'll only end up saying more stupid things."

I sat back down, sending Tommy an apologetic smile, but he was deep in thought, his eyebrows engaged in something that far exceeded my powers of interpretation. I looked away. Ran my gaze across Zoe's collection of cookbooks aimed at uptight women. At the picture of her and Tommy working out together in Kensington Gardens, back at the beginning of their relationship, when she couldn't keep her hands off him.

At the end of Zoe's road, a night bus whined up Holland Park Road. I wondered who this new man was. Where he lived. Zoe seemed impossibly wealthy to a pauper like me, but this man would blow her and her two-bedroomed flat in Holland Park out of the water. He'd be eye-wateringly rich and well connected. And—above all—right for Zoe. Right in a way Tommy never could have been, no matter how many times she forced him up the career ladder.

Eventually Tommy took a deep breath. He turned to Jo. "Look," he said quietly. "I do love you. I do love you, Jo. I just imagined telling you in . . . well, other circumstances."

Jo, who I suspected had stopped breathing, said

nothing. Tommy traced a finger along the edge of Zoe's kitchen island. "You're the only person I've never felt self-conscious with," he said. "The only person I can talk to about anything, always. I miss you when you leave a room. Even though you call me a 'privileged arsehole' too often. Even though you're the kind of infuriating woman who makes me say these things in front of Sarah."

Jo allowed a trace of a smile, but she still couldn't quite look at him.

"I thought I was happy," Tommy went on, "when I first moved in here. But I wasn't. I wasn't happy at all, and I haven't been for years. Even as recently as a month ago, I was able to convince myself that this"—he looked around Zoe's immaculate kitchen—"this was what I wanted. It's not. What I want is to be me. In my own skin, laughing, real. I laugh until I cry with you, several times a week. I've never done that with Zoe."

Jo remained silent.

"I mean, look at my career. It was never enough for her that I was a personal trainer. I'm quite certain she only subsidized my business because she wanted to tell people her partner ran a sports consultancy."

Jo picked at her coat, until Tommy leaned over and stopped her.

"Listen to me."

"Listening," Jo said gruffly.

After a moment Tommy laughed. "I can't believe we're having this conversation with Harrington in the room. This is . . . No offense, Harrington, but this is awful."

"No offense taken. And for what it's worth, I think it's lovely. If not a bit strange."

Jo hadn't yet relaxed. "Sorry," she mumbled. "It's scary for me. I've . . . I've got more to lose than you."

Tommy picked up one of her hands. "No, you haven't. I . . . Oh, for God's sake, will you **look** at me, you madwoman?"

Reluctantly, she looked.

"I'm **here**, Jo. In this. With you."

The adrenaline had wound down. Suddenly I was sitting in a room with my two oldest friends who were telling each other they were in love with each other, and suddenly it made perfect sense. I thought back to those months we all had together in California and wondered why I'd never thought about it before. Those two spent hours together, they went on trips, they surfed, they mixed hideous cocktails in Tommy's parents' garage. Perhaps I hadn't seen it because I'd been too deeply buried by grief and guilt. Or perhaps it was simply because I couldn't think of a less likely match than these two people. But love didn't work like that, as I'd come to realize. Here they were, sneaking around: clumsy, helpless, vulnerable. In love and unable to do anything other than be together, in spite of the risks.

"Well," I said slowly. I smiled, and my smile turned into a yawn. "This is going to take a while. But I'm happy."

Jo stared down at Tommy's hand, folded tightly around her own. "That's what I want, too," she said. "To be happy. That's all I care about these days."

My heart cramped. Jo never spoke like this.

I wasn't anywhere near warm enough, sitting in just my running shorts and vest, but in that second I wanted this moment to go on and on. I loved these two people. Loved that they loved each other in ways I'd never know. Loved that they'd been so desperate to see each other they'd smuggled Jo in here after I'd gone to bed.

"I'm going to have to go and finish my packing," I said. "I wish I could stay."

"Okay." Tommy yawned as I pushed back my stool. "Although . . . Sarah. I have to ask. Do we need to worry about you?"

"I . . ." My voice trailed off. "I have kind of scared myself a bit lately."

"Us too," Jo said. "You've been pretty weird, babe."

"I assume you know about the football?"

She nodded.

I raked my hands through my hair. "When I walked into that changing room, I had a horrible moment of realization. It was like I was finally back in my own skin. And I was scared."

Jo said, "Maybe you should go and talk to one of them therapists."

Ferapists. I smiled. "Maybe. There's no shortage of them in LA."

Tommy's eyebrows softened. "You've never done

anything unbalanced like this before," he said. "Remember that."

"But maybe that's because I didn't own a mobile phone when I met Reuben. Maybe it's because the Internet barely existed back then."

"No—you're not crazy, Sarah. If even half what you've told us is true, Eddie should have called you."

I walked round the kitchen island and hugged them both. My friends, the lovers. "Thank you, my dear Tommy, my dear Jo. Thank you for not deserting me."

"You're my closest friend," Tommy said. "Aside from Jo," he added quickly.

They were still there when I reappeared forty minutes later with my suitcase. Eating toast made of sliced white bread, the sort Zoe would never tolerate. They looked like they'd been together for years.

I parked my suitcase by the door. "Right, then."

Tommy stood up. "Hey, look, Harrington. One last thing before you go. I . . . well, I have to say, I'm still suspicious about Eddie."

"Oh, you and me both, Tommy. You and me both."

He paused. "I just . . . It just seems like an enormous coincidence that you met him in that place, at that time."

A bird tried its first woolly song in the tree outside Zoe's flat.

"What do you mean? Do you know something I don't?"

"Of course not! I just mean, think about what you were doing the day you met him. Marking the anniversary of the accident, walking along Broad Ride. I think you need to ask yourself why Eddie was there, too. On that day, of all days." His eyebrows had taken on a life of their own. "Has he got something to hide?"

"Of course he . . . No. No, Tommy."

I gave the idea a minute or two of my time and then dismissed it entirely. There was no way. No way on earth.

CHAPTER TWENTY-SEVEN

Dear Eddie,

I'm writing to say I'm sorry.

I ignored all of your signals and instead I bombarded you. I should never have written, and I should never have called you. And I certainly should never have turned up at your football match last night. (I'm guessing you've been told.) I cannot tell you how embarrassed I am. I know it won't make any difference to anything now, but the tiny speck of pride I still possess urges me to tell you I really don't behave like that normally.

For reasons I don't fully understand, our meeting and your subsequent silence seem to have brought up a lot of old feelings connected to the car accident I was in nineteen years ago. I think that's contributed to my insane behavior.

I'm at Heathrow, about to board a plane to LAX. The sun is shining and I am desperately sad that I'm leaving like this, knowing that

I will never see you again, but relieved to be going back there, where I have a busy job, friends, a shot at a new life as a single woman. I will work on whatever happened, and why I behaved the way I did around you. I will fix this. I will fix me.

Still, it would be remiss of me not to say that I found you cowardly and disrespectful for going silent on me like that, and I hope that you will think twice before doing that to another woman. But I accept that that's what you chose to do on this occasion, and I accept also that you must have had your reasons.

Finally, I wanted to say thank you. Those days we had together were among the brightest of my life. I will remember them for a very long time.

Take care, Eddie, and good-bye.

Sarah x

CHAPTER TWENTY-EIGHT

DRAFTS FOLDER

Please don't go. Don't leave.

I stopped writing there to call you, only I couldn't.

You're probably in the air now. I'm going outside to watch the sky.

Eddie

✓ DELETED, 10:26 A.M.

Part II

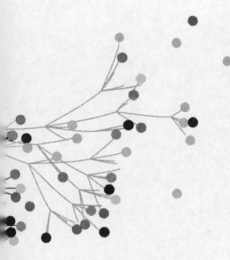

CHAPTER TWENTY-NINE

Welcome home!" Jenni shouted.

In all the years I'd been flying across the Atlantic I still hadn't mastered jet lag. The bursting pressure in my chest as I emerged into blinding sunshine and cementlike heat, the zigzags skirting my vision as I sat in a taxi on the 110. The first time I'd flown out here, in 1997, I'd been convinced for the first two days that I was very seriously unwell.

"I've missed you, Sarah Mackey." Jenni pulled me into a brisk hug. She smelled of baking.

"Oh, Jenni, I missed you too. Hello, Frap," I said, stroking Jenni's dog with a tired foot. Frap—short for Frappuccino, one of Jenni's vices—tried to cock his leg on me, like he always did, but I jumped sideways just in time.

"Oh, Frappy," Jenni sighed. "Why are you so determined to urinate on Sarah?"

I leaned forward and clasped her elbows. "Well?"

She couldn't quite meet my eye.

"The pregnancy test? Wasn't it today?"

"No, tomorrow." She turned away. "I'm super-nervous, so the less said about that, the better. Come in, get yourself on that couch."

I stepped into a haven of cooled, chocolate-scented air, and noticed that Jenni had bought another piece of artwork. This one was an abstract silhouette of a pregnant woman made up of thousands of tiny fingerprints. A coach she'd been seeing had recommended positive visualizations during the IVF process; this must be part of her response. The picture hung above the easy chair Javier used from 5:15 P.M. until he went to bed at 10:30 P.M. On the counter separating the living room from the kitchen, there was a two-layer chocolate cake, and a bottle of sparkling rosé in a bucket.

I smiled, exhausted and close to tears, as Jenni went into the kitchen and started throwing scoops of ice cream into the blender. "Jenni Carmichael, you are very kind and very naughty. We don't pay you enough to be buying champagne and cakes."

Jenni shrugged, as if to say, **How else would I welcome you home?**

She added more ingredients to the blender—few of which resembled food—and switched it on, yelling over the noise. "I had Javier go play some pool with his friends, so we could catch up," she bellowed. "And I couldn't have you come back here without a sugar binge. It'd be wrong."

I fell into her enormous couch, with its mallowy spread of cushions, and felt relief so sharp it was almost like a pain. I would be safe here. I would reflect, recalibrate, move on.

Jenni switched off the blender. "I went for bubblegum flavor."

"Jesus Christ. Really?"

Jenni laughed. "I'm not messing around today," was all she said.

A good couple of hours later, when we had drunk our thick shakes, eaten several slices of the gigantic cake, and binged our way through a large packet of pita chips, I lay back and belched. Jenni did the same, laughing. "I never burped before I met you," she admitted.

I poked her foot with mine, too bloated and heavy to move. "This has been a magnificent feast. Thank you."

"Oh, you're welcome," she smiled, rubbing her tummy. "Now, Sarah, I shouldn't have a drink, but you must try some pink fizz, okay?"

I eyed the bottle and felt a strong, physical sense of dread. "I can't," I said. "Thank you, darling, but I got a bit too drunk with Jo last week and I haven't been able to face booze since."

"Seriously?" Jenni looked shocked. "Not even a little glass?"

But I couldn't do it. Not even for her.

Then I told her everything. Even the awful bits at the football ground when, at the same moment that

I'd been confronted by a stranger's backside, I had also been confronted with the immutable fact that I had lost my mind. Jenni awwwed and tutted and sighed and even, when I showed her my final message to Eddie, welled up. She did not mock me for any of it. She did not even raise an eyebrow. She just nodded sympathetically, as if my actions had been entirely understandable.

"You can't let a shot at love slip through your fingers," she said. "You were right to try everything." She eyed me. "You did fall in love with him, didn't you?"

After a pause I nodded. "Although you shouldn't be able to fall in love after only—"

"Oh, quit it," Jenni said quietly. "Of course you can fall in love after a week."

"I suppose so." I picked at the hem of my top. "Anyway, I want to get back to what I know. I want to win that hospice pitch in Fresno; I want to get George Attwood on board in Santa Ana. It's time to move on."

"Really?'

"Really. There'll be no further attempts to reach Eddie. In fact, I'm going to remove him from my Facebook friends. Right now, with you as witness."

"Oh," Jenni said, unenthusiastically. "I suppose that's for the best. But it's so sad. I thought he was it, Sarah."

"Me too."

"To have met him on that date, in that place—it was just so perfect. It sent shivers down my spine."

I said nothing. I'd been trying to forget what Tommy had had to say on this matter. Jenni's explanation, on the other hand, was more comforting. A big, romantic coincidence; an incredible piece of timing. That worked for me.

I glanced over at her. "You okay?"

She sighed, nodded. "Just sad for you. And full of hormones."

I flopped back down next to her as I waited for Facebook to locate Eddie from within my friends list.

My stomach turned over.

"He's unfriended me," I whispered. I reloaded his profile, in case it told me a different story. It did not. **Add friend?** it asked.

"Oh, Sarah," Jenni murmured.

The freezing pain returned to my chest, as if it had never gone away. The bottomless longing, a well down which a pebble could fall forever.

"I . . ." I swallowed hard. "I guess that's that, then."

At that moment Frappuccino exploded into life as the front door opened and Javier strode in. "Hey, Sarah!" he said, offering the weird salute he always offered in place of a hug. Javier did physical only with Jenni and cars.

"Hey, Javier. How are you? Thank you so much

for giving us some time alone tonight." My body felt droopy and unformed.

"You're welcome," he told me, mooching off to the kitchen for a beer. Jenni kissed him and passed through to the bathroom.

"You been looking after my girl?" he asked. He sat down in his chair and opened the beer.

"Well, she's mostly been looking after me," I admitted. "You know what she's like. But I'll be here for her tomorrow, Javi. I can be here all day if she needs me."

Javier took a long swig of his beer, watching me with guarded eyes. "Tomorrow?"

I looked at him. Something wasn't right. "Er . . . yes," I said. "For the test result?"

Javier put his beer bottle down on the floor, and I knew, suddenly, what he was going to say.

"The test was today," he said shortly. "It didn't work. She's not pregnant."

Silence echoed between us.

"I guess she wanted you to be able to talk about your own . . . ah, problems . . . first," he said. "You know how she is."

"Oh . . . Oh, God," I whispered. "Javi. I'm so sorry. I . . . Oh, God, why did I believe her? I **knew** it was today."

I glanced at the kitchen door. "How's she been?"

He shrugged, but his face told me all I needed to know. He was lost. Out of his depth. For years, there had remained avenues of hope, and keeping

Jenni plugged into them had been Javier's job. It had shielded him from the lead weight of her fear, given him an active role. Now, there was nothing, and his wife—whom, for all his emotional limitations, he loved with every cell in his body—was in a deep well of grief. He no longer had a role, or any hope to offer.

"She has not said too much. Silence in the **clínica**. I don't think she is letting herself think about it. Not yet, anyhow. I thought she would tell you and then she would cry, let her emotions come, you know? That's why I went out. Normally when she can't talk to me, she talks to you."

"Oh, no. Oh, Javi, I am so sorry."

He swigged his beer and sank back into his chair, staring out of the window.

I looked over at the door. Still nothing. The clock on their kitchen wall ticked, bomblike.

Several minutes passed.

"She went to the bathroom on purpose," I said suddenly. "To hide. She knew you'd tell me. We should . . . we should go and get her." I got up, but Javier was already up. He strode across the kitchen floor, shoulders hunched.

I hovered uselessly in the kitchen as he knocked at the bathroom door. "Baby?" he called. "Baby, let me in . . ."

After a pause the door opened and I heard it: the desperate sound of his wife, my loyal friend, who'd postponed her own grief so she could look after mine, gasping for breath as tears and despair erupted savagely from within. "I can't bear it," she wept. "I can't bear it. Javi, I don't know what to do."

Then the unbearable sound of raw human misery, muffled only by the flimsy cotton of her husband's shirt.

CHAPTER THIRTY

When the hysterics had finally subsided, Jenni had sat on the couch between me and Javier and methodically binged her way through everything we hadn't already eaten. I'd ignored the scream of jet-lag tiredness and stayed with her until midnight, eating the odd sliver of cake to keep myself awake.

Now morning was here: the bright hot morning of which I'd dreamed, my first back in LA. During my final week in England I'd become certain that this first morning would bring with it renewal and hope: a sense of perspective I'd been unable to find in London or Gloucestershire. I would be happy. Purposeful.

In reality I was bloated and uncomfortable, and far too cold after a night with the air-conditioning at superfreezing. I curled up in Jenni's spare bed, too exhausted to get out and turn it down. I stared at myself in the mirror across the room. I looked puffy, white, unwell. Before even realizing what I was doing, I reached out to check my phone in case Eddie had replied to my farewell message. He hadn't, of course, and my heart ballooned with pain.

Add friend? Facebook asked, when I looked at his profile. Just to check. **Add friend?**

An hour later, still awaiting serenity, I left the house for a run. It wasn't yet eight, and Jenni and Javier— for once—were still in bed.

I knew that running wasn't kind, after a transatlantic flight and an evening of emotional tumult. Not to mention the sleepless night I'd had in London the night before, or that the thermometer on Jenni's deck was already scorching its way to a hundred degrees. But I couldn't sit still. Couldn't be with myself. I needed to move so fast that nothing could stick to me.

I had to run.

Three hundred yards down Glendale Avenue, I remembered why I didn't run in this city. I swayed on the corner of Temple, pretending to stretch out my quads so I could grab a lamppost. The heat was suffocating. I looked up at the sun, soupy and indistinct today behind a smear of marine haze, and shook my head. **I had to run!**

I tried again, but as the Hollywood Freeway loomed ahead, my legs gave way and I found myself sitting on the grass by a municipal tennis court, sick and dizzy. I pretended to readjust my shoelaces and admitted defeat.

Somewhere I could hear Jo's voice, telling me I was a fucking fruit loop, and did I have **any** respect for my body? And I agreed with her; I agreed whole-heartedly, remembering how sad and sorry I used to feel when I'd seen skinny women rasping up the hills of Griffith Park in the scorching heat.

I went back to Jenni's, showered, and ordered a cab. It didn't look like Jenni was going to make it to work anytime soon, and I couldn't sit there a moment longer.

During my journey to our offices in East Holly-wood, I planned next week's pitch to the directors of a hospice company in California. We were so used to having our services solicited by medical units nowadays, that I was a little out of practice at the art of sales. Vermont was all snagged up so I got out at Santa Monica and walked the last two blocks, rehearsing the pitch under my breath while sweat dripped, **plock, plock, plock**, down my back.

Then: Eddie?

A man in a taxi, waiting in the traffic jam on Vermont. Heading straight toward my office. Cropped hair, sunglasses, a T-shirt I was sure I recognized.

Eddie?

No. Impossible.

I started to walk toward the car. The man inside, who I would swear was Eddie David, was looking out at the confusing proliferation of street signs and checking his phone.

The traffic started to move at last, and honking started. I was in the middle of a six-lane road. Just as I was forced to turn away from the taxi, I saw the man take off his sunglasses and look at me. But before I could see his eyes, know for sure it was Eddie, I had to run or be run over.

Eddie?

Later that day, sent home by my colleagues ("We've got this, Sarah—go get some rest") but unable to sit still, I walked home. I stood at that same busy intersection for fifteen minutes, watching cars and taxis. An air ambulance landed on the roof of the Children's Hospital and I barely noticed.

It was him. I knew it was him.

CHAPTER THIRTY-ONE

Reuben and I flew in silence on a commuter plane to Fresno. Outside, the remains of a buttery sun melted over clouds; inside, civility hung between us on a fine thread. Tomorrow morning we would pitch to the board of directors of the hospice umbrella company, and Reuben was already angry with me.

On Monday morning he had arrived at the office with Kaia and taken us all through to the meeting room. He hadn't quite been able to look me in the eye.

"So, I have some really great news," he began.

"Oh, great!" Jenni said. She didn't quite sound like herself, but she was trying.

"While we were in London last week, Kaia sent some e-mails to an old friend of hers, a guy called Jim Burundo, who runs a bunch of private special-needs schools in LA. Kaia told him all about our work, sent him some video clips, and he got back to her to ask if we'll start regular Clowndoctor visits!"

There was a short silence.

"Oh," I said eventually. "Fantastic. But . . .

Reuben, we don't have enough practitioners to take on a commitment like that at the moment."

And Jenni had added, "Reuben, honey, we'd need to cost this up and get me a fund-raising target. I need—"

Reuben held up his hands to interrupt. "They're self-funding," he'd said proudly. "Paying one hundred percent of our costs. We can take on new Clowndoctors and train them and Jim's company'll pay everything."

I paused. "But we still need to go and visit the school, Roo. And set up meetings. And a million other things besides. We can't just—"

Reuben interrupted me with a smile that contained—shockingly—a warning. "Kaia has done a wonderful thing," he said carefully. "You should be pleased! We're expanding again!"

Jenni seemed too worn down to intervene.

Kaia tentatively stuck her hand up, as if in class. "I really didn't expect Jim to say yes on the spot," she said quietly. "I hope I haven't made things complicated."

"I'm going to schedule some meetings so we can plan it out," Reuben said. "But for now I think we have a big 'thank-you' to say to Kaia."

And with that he had started clapping.

We all joined in. **My life**, I thought. **Jesus Christ, my life.**

• • •

The first meeting had taken place two days later. And even though it did look like everything would work out, even though, yes, Jim's people would fund everything, including training—**Sure, just tell us what it is you need from us**—I was on edge. It was all happening too fast. But when I tried to broach this with Reuben this morning, he'd actually snapped at me. Told me to be less corporate, more grateful.

I snuck a sideways glance at him as the plane began to bank into Fresno. He had fallen asleep, his face baggy and unguarded. I knew that face so well. Those long, midnight-black eyelashes; the perfect eyebrows; the veins in the deep valleys of his eye sockets. I looked at this familiar face and my stomach moved uneasily. **I was meant to be back to normal by now**, I thought, as the plane turned in the air and the low, golden sun stroked geometric shapes across Reuben's face. **I was meant to feel fine.**

Later on, after we'd had dinner in a steak house next to our hotel, I went and sat outside by the small, probably never used pool. It was surrounded by a high metal fence, and its few lounge chairs were covered in mildew.

For the first time I allowed myself to consider properly what Tommy had said about Eddie last week. What it might mean that Eddie and I had met in that place, at that time, on that day. Whether he had something to hide. It had felt like an absurd theory at first: Eddie had just gone out that morning because he'd needed a break from his mother, and had been delayed on the village green because he'd met a sheep. To read any more into our meeting would be wrong.

But the problem was, I was beginning—at last—to get a handle on the thoughts that had been whispering at the peripheries of my consciousness these last few weeks. They were beginning to form a pattern. And I didn't like what I saw.

I went inside as the first silver forks of lightning reached down from the sky, unable to shake the sense that a crisis was looming.

The next morning our meeting was preceded by a tour of the hospice.

Like anyone, I supposed, I found hospices hard—after all, few places in life treated death with such certainty. But I wore my best impassive face; kept the lurch of fear deep inside myself; made sure to breathe slowly. And I was doing quite well at it, I thought, until we walked into the TV lounge and I saw a girl in a chair near the window.

I stared at her.

"**Ruth?**" She was wrapped in a soft blanket, waxy pale and horribly slight.

Ruth looked up, and after what felt like an agonizing pause, she smiled. "Oh, my God," she said. "This I did not expect."

"Ruth!" Reuben bounded over to hug her.

"Careful," Ruth said quietly. "Apparently my bones are brittle. You don't want to snap me in half or anything. You know how fond Mom is of a lawsuit."

Reuben hugged her gently; then I joined in.

Ruth had been one of our first patients, back in the day when it was just Reuben and me and we'd barely heard of Clowndoctors. She had been a tiny baby, in and out of surgery, and we'd always known that her life expectancy—if she survived at all—was very limited.

But my God, that girl had fought. And so too had her single mother, who had raised the money to go to the Children's Hospital LA for her neonatal care because a doctor there was a world specialist in Ruth's rare genetic condition. Their we-will-not-take-no-for-an-answer attitude had repeatedly compelled Reuben and me to push on with our own work.

I did not make a habit of meeting the kids. I found it far too painful. But there was something about Ruth I couldn't resist. Even when my job had ceased to involve hospital visits, I still went to see her, because I couldn't not.

Now here she was, aged fifteen and a half, wrapped in a blue fleece blanket with a moon print on it, an IV stand next to her armchair. Tiny and scrappy; her thin hair brittle. For a moment I stood still as shock curled around my throat.

"Well. This is a nice surprise," I said, sitting down next to her.

"What, to find me looking like a dead chicken in a hospice?" she asked. Her voice was thin. "How do you like my hands? See? Like chicken feet. Oh, come **on**," she said, when I tried to disagree. "You're not going to try to tell me I look like a hot babe, are you? Because if you are, go away." She smiled through chapped lips and I felt a savage tearing in my heart.

"You came back home, then," Reuben said. "To sunny Fresno."

"Yeah. I felt that the least I could do would be to check out somewhere close to home," she said. "Poor Mom's exhausted."

And without warning, she started to cry. She cried silently, as if she no longer had the energy to produce noise or tears.

"This sucks," she said. "And where are your guys? Where's a red nose when you need one?"

"That's what we're here to talk about," Reuben said, blotting her tears with a tissue. "But even if it doesn't go ahead, we'll try to have a Clowndoc come visit you. As long as you don't think you're too old."

"I don't," she said weakly. "Your people have never talked to me like I'm a kid. Last time I saw Doctor Zee, he said he was going to help me write a poem for my wake. He's a great wordsmith when he's not being a dick. Can you send him?"

"We'll make it the first thing we talk about in our meeting," I told her. "I'm sure Zee'll be up for visiting."

"I love those guys," Ruth said. She leaned back against the chair, the effort of talking to us leaching energy fast from her body. "They've been the only constant, all these years. The only people who are bigger assholes than me. No offense," she said in Reuben's direction. "I know you started out as a clown."

He smiled.

"Do you want us to help get you back to your room?" I asked Ruth. I tucked the blanket more tightly around her. There was a hard swelling in my throat. How was this possible? Funny, smart Ruth, with her ginger ponytail and those parsley-green eyes. Why was her life ending just as it was beginning? Why wasn't there anything anyone could do?

"Yes," she whispered. "I need a nap. Damn you, making me cry."

As we left her room a few minutes later, I brushed away an angry tear and Reuben took my hand. "I know," he said. "I know."

After our presentation to the board we broke to a sunny terrace for coffee. The hospice's VP of Care Services took me to one side to ask further questions.

I should have seen it coming; I should have known from the questions he'd asked earlier. We often came across people like this man, who couldn't see past the red noses, refused to differentiate our practitioners from party clowns.

"The thing is," the man was saying, with his pebbly glasses and wobbly chin and thunderous hauteur, "my team have years of training among them. I'm not sure I'm comfortable with them having to work around . . . well, clowns."

The passion that had driven our presentation had now dissipated. I felt an overwhelming need to escape.

"Your staff will always be in charge of the children's medical care," I made myself recite. I watched a bird in the tree above him. "Just look at our practitioners as you would any other visiting entertainer. The only difference is that they've been through months of specialist training."

He frowned into his coffee and said that his own staff were also highly trained, actually, but they didn't need to wear silly clothes or carry musical instruments. And suddenly—even though years in this job had taught me never, **ever** to take on people like this man—I found myself doing just that.

"You can focus on the playful side of what they do, if you want," I said. "But we've had countless doctors and nurses tell us they've learned helpful tools from our practitioners."

The man started. "Oh!" he said. The sun flashed in his glasses. "So you're telling me our staff could learn something from a bunch of out-of-work actors?"

Reuben, standing with the main group, turned round.

"That's precisely what I'm not saying," I said. I had him eye to eye as if we were in some kind of duel. What was I **doing**? "All I'm saying—as you'd know, if you had actually listened—is that feedback from medical professionals is resoundingly positive. But these professionals have had some level of humility."

"**Mrs. Mackey**. Did you just say what I think you did?"

Reuben joined us very quickly. "Can I help with anything?" he asked.

"I don't think so," the man said. "Your business partner was just telling me that my care staff could learn a thing or two from your clowns. Including humility, if you can believe it. So I'm just taking a moment to let that one sink in."

"Mr. Schreuder—" Reuben began, but he was cut off.

"I have a team to manage," Pebble Glasses said. "Good day."

The bird above him took off and flew down the street. I watched, wishing I could go with it.

"What the hell is going on?" Reuben demanded, as soon as we got into the taxi.

"Sorry."

"**Sorry?**" Reuben was furious. "You might have just cost us that entire contract. Which would be fine, Sarah, if it were just about us, or money, but it's not. It's about Ruth. And all the other kids in there, and the four other hospices they own."

From the front of the taxi I could hear snatches of a Latin American voice and **cumbia** music. I took a few slow breaths. If I were Reuben, I'd be furious, too.

"For chrissakes, Sarah!" Rueben exploded. "What's **up**?"

The taxi driver had finished his phone call and was listening to us with interest. He didn't get a great deal of satisfaction, however, because I had nothing to say.

After a long pause Reuben spoke. "Is it about me and Kaia?" he asked. He was staring fixedly at the spread of traffic on the other side of the highway. "Because if it is, we really need to talk it out. I—"

"It's not about Kaia," I said. "Although if I'm honest, I think she needs to back off."

"Then what? You've been off-key a while. Sarah, we were married seventeen years," Reuben said. "I still know you."

"No, you don't."

A mother and her two kids crossed the road ahead of us at the lights. One of them was kicking his legs in a stroller; his sister was dancing ahead of them with a shiny little party trumpet, toot-toot-tooting for all she was worth. Hannah had had one of those.

Sometimes she'd blast it in my ear if she woke up before me, and I'd scream my head off. And she would be in hysterics, running around with her trumpet, hooting and tooting and laughing.

As the lights changed and we pulled forward, I realized I was crying.

I stood in the dirt-flecked window of the gate later on, watching planes taxi through an evening the color of rust. My cell phone rang out three times before I realized it was mine.

"Jenni?"

"Oh, Sarah, I'm glad you picked up."

"Are you okay?"

"Pass. But look, the strangest thing happened just now."

I waited.

Reuben waved at me. The last few passengers were disappearing out of the gate area.

"I just saw Eddie, Sarah. In our building."

"Sarah!" Reuben called. "Come on!"

I signaled to him to wait, holding my hand in the air as if waiting to be counted.

"I've looked at his photo so many times," Jenni was saying. "There was no mistaking him. He was talking to Carmen at reception, but by the time I went out there, he'd left."

"Oh."

My arm dangled stupidly in the air, all the blood running out.

"He asked Carmen if you were in, then left without leaving a message."

"Oh."

"It was him, Sarah. It was definitely him. I looked at a photo right afterward. And Carmen said he had an English accent."

"Jenni, are you sure? Are you one hundred percent sure?"

"One hundred percent."

"Right."

"Sarah? What the hell's going on?" Reuben sounded angry again.

"I have to go," I said heavily. "I have to get on a plane."

CHAPTER THIRTY-TWO

Dear Eddie,

I promised you that the last letter I wrote would really be my last.

But the thing is, I'm beginning to wonder who you actually are. My friend Tommy recently asked if I thought you might have had something to do with the accident. I dismissed the idea out of hand, only now I'm not so sure.

Was it you who came to my office today? Was it you I saw at a traffic light last week? And if it was, why? What are you doing?

Eddie, do you know exactly who I am? Why I never came back to England?

Are you the person I'm afraid you might be?

The chances are, you'll read this and think, **What is this girl talking about? Why won't she leave me alone? Is she out of her mind?**

But what if that's not what you're thinking?

What if you know exactly what I'm talking about?

I just keep wondering, Eddie. I just keep wondering.

Sarah

CHAPTER THIRTY-THREE

Extract from the **Stroud News & Journal,**
June 11, 1997

Police have arrested a man in connection
with the fatal accident on the A419 near
Frampton Mansell earlier this month. Senior
Investigating Officer PC John Metherell
confirmed last night that a nineteen-year-old
man from Stroud had been taken into custody on suspicion of causing death by dangerous driving.

The crash, which has left a local family
devastated, has led to calls for better speed
control on this remote stretch of road. Frus-
tration has also been expressed at the police's
failure to make any arrests until now.

Since the accident Gloucestershire Con-
stabulary have been searching for a man—
described at the time as male, in his late teens
or early twenties—who escaped the scene of
the crime via fields or local footpaths. New

information received by the force on Monday has led to his successful detection and arrest.

The **SNJ** was unable to obtain confirmation before going to print that the suspect had been charged.

CHAPTER THIRTY-FOUR

I lay in Jenni's spare bed, listening to Javier loading his truck outside. On his radio a man spoke in rapid Spanish about the wildfire roaring across the dry hills of California. **El fuego avanca rápidamente hacia nosotros**, he said. **The fire is coming at us fast.** When he said the word "fire" his voice slowed right down, caressing each syllable like a new flame licking through paper. **Fu-e-go.**

Jenni was playing Diana Ross in the shower, although she wasn't singing along. The boiler was groaning. Next door's cat was making childlike wails, which meant Frappuccino was out in the yard.

I rolled over onto my back and rubbed my belly.

There was a man out there, somewhere, a nameless man I'd been thinking about for nineteen years. I didn't know his face or his voice, had nothing to go on beyond his surname, but I'd always known I'd recognize him when he found me. I would look him in the eye and I'd just know.

Which was why Eddie David couldn't be that man, I told myself. Despite the fact that his surname was wrong, I'd have sensed who he was the moment I met him. I'd have known.

The fire is coming at us fast.

Without warning I got up and ran to the toilet and threw up.

"A school-night hangover!" Kaia held a smile in those pleasant eyes of hers, so I'd know she wasn't judging me. "You're making me feel old, Sarah."

I crouched in front of our little fridge, crammed with salads and wraps, and closed my eyes. I couldn't eat my lunch. I couldn't face even finding it. "You shouldn't be impressed," I said. "You should judge me. I deserve it." I pulled myself up.

"We've all been there," Kaia said. She was huddled over something by the kettle, as if to shield it from my view. I peered miserably over her shoulder and saw, as expected, a perky salad.

I wish she weren't so good at handling me, I thought. **Or so bloody thoughtful.** She was only hiding that salad so I wouldn't feel bad about myself. Above all I wished she weren't here in our office. Yesterday her excuse for coming had been that she had some insight to share from a recent fund-raisers' meeting at the Children's Hospital, but today there had been no explanation. She'd just wandered in at ten and sat at a computer. Even Jenni was annoyed.

I went back to my desk with a glass of water in one hand and a tremor in the other. Reuben and Kaia went out onto our little roof terrace for lunch.

I tried to read my e-mails, but once again the words were shapeless and floppy. I tried to drink the water, but my stomach wasn't having it. **Ice!** it told me. **The water has to be iced!** I dragged myself back to the kitchen, only to find the ice tray in the freezer empty. I sat back down at my desk and watched my husband and his girlfriend canoodling outside. Kaia was sitting in the crook of Reuben's arm.

"I can't do this," someone said.

Me, I realized, after a pause. I had said it.

I almost laughed. Here I was, shaking, nauseous, dizzy, now talking to myself at my desk. What next? Animal sounds? A nude streak?

Then: "I can't," I heard myself say. My voice was coming from a part of me I couldn't control. "I can't do it. Any of it."

I escorted myself quickly into our meeting room. **Stop this**, I told myself, closing the door behind me. **Stop this immediately.** I wandered around the table, pretending to text someone; looked at them again. Kaia kissed Reuben's forehead. A stray cat watched them from the roof of a neighboring Botox clinic. Behind them rose the straggle of high-rise buildings over in Downtown.

"I can't do this."

Stop it!

Anyone would feel unsettled watching her ex-husband fall in love again, I reasoned. It was okay to feel upset.

Only it wasn't about Reuben and Kaia.

The fire is coming at us fast.

I tried to stop the words worming their way to my mouth but hadn't the strength. "I want to go home," I said.

The meeting room hummed quietly.

"Stop it," I whispered. Hot tears prickled. "Stop it. This is your home."

No, it's not. This was never more than a hiding place.

But I love this city! I love it!

That doesn't make it home.

Jenni slid through the door. "Sarah," she said. "Sarah, what's up? You're talking to yourself."

"I know."

"Is it about Reuben? I can ask Kaia to leave, if you want. They shouldn't behave like that."

I took a long breath. But while I waited for the right words, Jenni marched out of the room. I stared stupidly at her back, realizing only too late what she was about to do.

Kaia and Reuben looked up. Jenni said something; they smiled, nodded. Reuben was whistling as he came through the door, but there was something about his face that told me he knew what was coming.

No, I thought weakly. **Not this. This is not the problem.** But Jenni had already kicked off. She stood squarely at the top of the table, talking in a voice I had heard three, maybe four times in our entire history.

"Kaia, we're very grateful you've been helping us out, but I think we need to clarify exactly which projects you're helping with, and whether or not there's an unmanageable workload somewhere in our team. Because if there is, we'll need to take a look at that. It's not appropriate for you to be here, helping on a casual basis. Nobody signed off on it."

Silence. Reuben's eyes rolled over to mine, wide with shock.

Kaia's face had paled. "Sure," she began, although I knew she had no idea what to say next. "I . . . well, I've just been trying to help with a few things that Reuben needed off his desk . . . And Sarah's deputy, Kate, seemed to . . ." She fiddled with the ring that sat halfway up her finger and I realized her hands were shaking.

This is neither the problem nor the solution, I thought. I was so tired. So desperately tired.

"I'm sorry," Kaia said after a pause. "I didn't want to be inappropriate. I realize I've probably been here a bit too often . . ." Her eyes filled with tears.

Instinctively, I stepped forward, but Jenni stopped me. "I've got this," she said, passing Kaia a tissue. She didn't put her arm around her. I watched in horror and fascination as my friend directed all of her rage and disappointment at the woman crying at our meeting table.

Reuben was paralyzed.

"I . . . lost a . . . It just really helps me to come here . . ." Kaia was backing off now; an animal half run over. "I'm sorry. It just helps me. I'll stop coming. I . . ." She moved toward the door.

And suddenly I knew. "Kaia," I said quietly. "Hang on a second."

She hovered.

"Look, that story you told me, the day I met you," I said, and her face slackened, became all loose and billowy somehow, like a tent with its poles removed. "The story about the boy on the oncology ward. Who our clowns cheered up." The tent collapsed completely and there it was: a human being razed to the bone. "Was he your son?" I asked.

Reuben stared at me. Kaia took a slow, potholed breath and nodded.

"Phoenix," she said. "He was my boy, yes."

I closed my eyes. This poor woman.

"How did you know?" Reuben asked, stunned.

When I'd opened our mail this morning, I'd found a letter from a couple called Brett and Louise West. Four months after losing their son, they had finally managed to put pen to paper; said we were their first letter. **Thank you so much . . . It vastly improved his last few weeks . . . Can we help your organization at all? . . . Would love to come and volunteer . . . Would be great to give something back . . . Make ourselves useful . . .**

It had made me wonder again about Kaia, and why she was here. I wasn't convinced it was just because of Reuben.

A few days earlier we had had a call to say that a

child we'd been working with for months was in re-mission and ready to go home. Kaia, who had never met the child, had broken down in tears. "A second chance," I'd heard her saying to my deputy, Kate, who'd announced the news. "A second chance at life. Oh, that is a blessed thing."

And it was a blessed thing. We'd all cheered. But I had watched Kaia, long after everyone had gone back to work, and I'd wondered. Wondered if maybe there had been someone in her life who had not been given a second chance.

And as I watched her trying hopelessly to explain herself to Jenni just now, it seemed obvious that the little boy she'd told me about the day we met had been her own. She had lost her son, and with him an irreplaceable part of herself. And at some point, when she was able to get out of bed, to breathe, she had arrived in the nonprofit sector—just like the two parents who had written to us today; like me, and so many others—because it felt like the only conceivable way of forging good from bad. Of keep-ing going.

"I'm so sorry," I said.

She nodded. "Me too. And I apologize for having been here too much. My partner and I split up last year; we couldn't get past it. So it's been . . . lonely. Not that that's your problem, but it . . . it just kind of helps, being here."

I closed my eyes. I was so bloody tired. "I get it."

• • •

I watched them leave. Jenni was slumped at the end of the table.

I walked over and put a hand on her shoulder. "Stop it," I said quietly. "You weren't to know."

Jenni just shook her head.

"Look, Jen, I'm touched that you were willing to stick up for me, and for the team, the way you did. You were polite; you were nice; you handed her a tissue. What more could you have done?"

"I could have said nothing," she said. Her voice was gluey with guilt. "I could have just let her be."

I rubbed her shoulders, staring out the window. One of my legs started shaking and I sat down next to her.

"The worst of it is, we're in the same boat, me and Kaia," Jenni said dully. "There's a part of both of us missing. Although she actually **had** a child, Sarah, and he was taken away from her, and . . . Oh, my God, can you even imagine?"

When eventually she recovered, I told her I needed to go. "I think I need to go to the walk-in clinic. I'm not . . . I'm not functioning very well at the moment, am I?"

"No," Jenni said squarely, and I almost smiled. "But how's the doctor supposed to help? You're not going to ask for medication, are you?"

I paused. "No," I said. "I just need to . . . talk."

She frowned. "You know you can talk to me, right?"

"I do. And thank you again," I said. "For earlier. Your heart was in the right place."

Jenni sighed. "Oh, I know. I'm going to bake her the biggest cake. Out of vegetables, or green powders, or something. It'll be great."

A few moments later the door to our building clicked behind me. I felt the muffled punch of a boiling July lunchtime, steadied myself against the doorframe. I wanted to sleep, only I couldn't stand the silence of Jenni and Javier's. I wanted to sit in cooled air, only I couldn't go back to work. I wanted—

I froze.

Eddie. I wanted Eddie. But deep inside my brain, something had to be misfiring, because he was there.

There.

Right across Vermont Avenue. Waiting for the traffic lights to change. Looking straight at me.

No!

Yes.

I stood stock still. I stared at him. A long, red Metro bus snaked along between us for what felt like hours. Then it was gone and he was still there. Still looking right at me.

I felt numb as I looked at him. There was a strange quiet, suddenly, out of step with the thunder of traffic passing between us. The lights changed and a white pedestrian light invited me to walk toward him, but I didn't, because he was walking toward me, and he was still looking right at me. He was wearing shorts, the same shorts he'd been wearing the day we met. The same flip-flops. They smacked across the boiling road, and above them swung the same arms that had wrapped me like a present while I slept.

Eddie was coming. Across the world, across the road.

Until he turned round suddenly and retreated to the other side. The pedestrian sign held up a red hand, counted down three, two, one, and the traffic resumed. Eddie looked at me over his shoulder, then he made off down the street.

By the time the lights changed again and I was able to run across the road, he had disappeared down Lexington Avenue. I stood on the corner of Lexington and Vermont, stunned by the enormity of my feelings. Even now, after weeks of humiliation.

Nothing had changed. I was still in love with Eddie David. Only now I knew—I could no longer deny it—exactly who he was.

I set off toward the walk-in clinic.

The sun was sinking low over the west of the city. Below me, silvery roads ran dead straight to the horizon, lost in trembling haze and smog. Helicopters shared the sky with birds of prey riding thermal currents; hikers beetled up and down the paths carved into the hillside like scars.

I'd been up here two hours. More, probably. Alone

on my favorite bench near the observatory in Griffith Park. The tourists had mostly left, anxious to get away before darkness fell. A few remained, anxious to photograph a perfect sunset. And among them I had sat quietly, trying to forget what the doctor had said earlier, concentrating instead on my week with Eddie. Waiting for the clue to reveal itself to me. I hadn't found it yet, but I was close. It was amazing what you could find, once you knew what you were looking for.

I'd combed my way through almost to the end and now, as the sun bled all over the unseen Pacific, I was thinking about our final morning together. The brightness outside, the sense of loss as we said good-bye, the excitement at what was to come. He was leaning against the newel post on his stairs. The window was open and I could smell the fusty sweetness of the hawthorn blossom, the clean tang of warming grass. My eyes were closed. He was kissing me, a hand in the small of my back. He rested his nose against mine, eyes closed, and we talked. He gave me a flower, took my numbers, added me on Facebook, gave me Mouse for safekeeping. He said, **I think I might have fallen in love with you. Is that too much?**

No, I'd said. **It's perfect.** And then I left.

I imagined him turning away when I'd gone, climbing the remaining steps. Picking up the tea he'd left at the top. Maybe pausing to take a sip. He still had his phone in one hand, because we'd just exchanged details. Perhaps he sat on a chair by the window and took a look at my Facebook profile. He'd scroll down, maybe, and—

I reached for my phone.

I felt oddly calm as I searched my own Facebook page. And there, of course, it was. A friendly message from Tommy Stenham, on June 1, 2016.

Welcome home, Harrington! Hope you had a good flight. Can't wait to see you.

I put my shoes back on. I walked back toward the observatory and ordered an Uber. While I waited for it to arrive, I got out my phone and started writing. I had my answer.

CHAPTER THIRTY-FIVE

Eddie,

I know who you are.

For years I used to dream about meeting you. The dreams took place in the darkest edges of my mind and in them you never really had a face or a voice. But you were always there, and it was always awful.

Then you were there, really there, that day in June, sitting on the green at Sapperton with a sheep. You were smiling at me, buying me drinks, and you were lovely. And I didn't have a clue.

The world tastes like it did the summer I turned seventeen. Like bile in my throat.

We need to talk. Face-to-face. Below is my American cell number. Please call it. We can arrange to meet.

Sarah

CHAPTER THIRTY-SIX

Sarah Mackey," Jenni said. "Where have you been? I've been calling you."

I slid off my leather sandals and perched on the edge of a barstool. "Sorry. I left my phone on silent. Are you okay?"

Jenni ducked my question, padding off to get us some water. "I can fix you a soft drink if you prefer," she said, handing me a glass. Her eyes were bloodshot and I could tell she'd been in bed since she'd got back from work.

Promptly, I burst into tears.

"What's happening?" Jenni came back over. She smelled of coconut shampoo and marshmallow skin. "Sarah . . ?"

How could I explain this squalid, sorry mess to a woman who'd just lost her last, cherished hope of a family? It was unthinkable. She would listen to me, and she would be horrified. And then crushed, because there would be nothing—absolutely nothing— she could do to solve it for me.

"Tell me," Jenni said sternly.

"It was all fine at the doctor's," I lied, after a long

interval. I blew my nose. "Fine. There are blood tests to come, but everything's okay."

"Okay . . ."

"But . . . I—"

My phone started ringing.

"It's Eddie," I said, diving blindly around the room for my phone.

"What?" Jenni, suddenly capable of lightning reflexes, plucked it out of my bag and hurled it at me. "Is that him?" she asked. "Is that Eddie?"

And my chest drummed with pain, because it was, and the situation was unbearable. I could never be with him. I had found him at last, and we had no future.

"Eddie?" I said.

There was a pause, and then there was his voice, saying hello. Just like I had dreamed it would, only this time it was real. Familiar and strange, perfect and heartbreaking. **His voice.**

My own held just long enough for me to say yes, I could meet him tomorrow morning, and yes, Santa Monica Beach was fine; I'd meet him by the bike-rental place just south of the pier at ten.

"I was beginning to think it was a lie that LA's on the ocean," he said. He sounded tired. "I've been driving around for days and haven't seen it once."

And then the call was over and I curled myself into the corner of Jenni's couch and cried like a child.

CHAPTER THIRTY-SEVEN

Dear You,

Hello, Hedgehog.

Nearly two weeks have passed since you should have celebrated your birthday, but I still think about you every day. Not just birthdays.

Sometimes I like to imagine what you would be doing if you were still here. Today I imagined you living in Cornwall; a young, broke artist with paint in her hair. In this version, you study Fine Art at Falmouth and then take over a derelict building high on a hill with your arty friends. You like headscarves and you're probably vegetarian, and you're busy getting Arts Council grants, organizing exhibitions, teaching painting to kids. You're electrifying.

Then comes the pendulum swing of grief and I remember you're not in that crazy house on a hill. You're scattered in a peaceful corner of Gloucestershire, a quiet hum of memory where once was my sunbeam of a sister.

I wonder if you know about what I'm doing tomorrow morning. I wonder if you know who I'm meeting on the beach. And if you do, I wonder if you will forgive me.

Because I can't not go, little Hedgehog. I have to know how you were on the day you died: what you were doing, what you were saying, what you were eating, even. When I had to identify your body, I was pooled in the corner like something melted. It took me hours to get up and drive home. But when I got there, I found a half piece of toast by the sink. Cold and rigid, with the indentation of your little teeth on a corner. Like you'd considered the idea of a final mouthful but then skipped off to do something else.

What else did you eat that day? Did you sing a song? Did you change your clothes? Were you happy, Hedgehog?

I have to ask these questions. And I have to figure out why, in spite of everything, I am still in love with the very person who took you away from us all.

I feel like I'm letting you down so desperately by going tomorrow. I hope you can understand why I am.

I love you.

Me xxxx

CHAPTER THIRTY-EIGHT

I watched a group of kids playing volleyball while I waited for Eddie. I wondered if he would even turn up, and wondered if it would be easier, better, if he didn't.

The tide was far out, the beach quiet. A light carpet of cloud hovered between Santa Monica and the fierce sun. The air smelled of something fuggy and sweet—melting sugar, perhaps, or cooking doughnuts—a childhood smell; it lit up an old corner of memory. Long holidays in Devon. Scratchy sand, salty limbs, slippery rocks. The delicate patter of rain on our tent. Whispering late into the night with my little sister, whose presence in my life I had never then thought to question.

I checked my watch.

Over on the volleyball court, the kids finished their game and started packing up. The boardwalk rumbled as a lone Rollerblader panted past. I ran damp fingers through my hair. Swallowed, yawned, clenched and unclenched my fists.

• • •

Eddie's voice, when it came, was from somewhere behind me. "Sarah?"

I paused before turning to face him, this man who had lived in my head so many years.

But when I did look at him, I saw only Eddie David. And I felt only the things I'd felt before I'd realized who he was: the love, the longing, the hunger. The **whump!** as my body ignited like a boiler.

"Hello," I said.

Eddie didn't reply. He looked me straight in the eye, and I remembered the day I met him. How I'd thought to myself that his eyes were the color of foreign oceans: full of warmth and good intentions. Today they were cold, almost blank.

I shifted my weight from one foot to the other. "Thanks for coming."

A tiny twitch of his shoulders. "I've been trying to come and talk to you for the last two weeks. Been staying with my mate Nathan. But I . . ." He trailed off, shrugged.

"Of course. I understand."

A family on yellow rented bikes pedaled along the boardwalk between us and he stepped back, watching me.

We walked down the beach and sat on the sand where it sloped to the water. For a long time we watched the Pacific crashing in on itself; sheets of silver foam on a relentless journey to nowhere. Eddie had his arms looped around his knees. He took off one of his flip-flops and splayed his toes in the sand.

The shock of longing almost winded me.

"I don't know how to do this, Sarah," he said eventually. His eyes were glassy. "I don't know what to say. You . . ." He spread his hands wide, looked helpless.

Once upon a time Eddie had a sister, a sweet girl called Alex. She had blond, tangly hair. She sang a lot. She had large blue eyes, full of life and plans, and she loved fruity sweets. She had been my sister's best friend.

My stomach clenched as I held her in my mind's eye, waiting for what I knew was coming.

"You killed my sister," Eddie said. He took in a sharp breath and I closed my eyes.

Last time I had heard those words, it had been through the big Panasonic answering machine next to Mum and Dad's phone. It was one, maybe two weeks after the accident and Hannah had finally been discharged from hospital. She had refused to get into the car with me; refused even to go home. There had been a scene, and eventually a patient transport bus had been found to take her and Mum home, while Dad and I drove.

When we got in, there had been a red flashing light—a sight I'd grown to dread—and a message from Alex's mother, who by then was in a psychiatric hospital. Her voice had been like smashed porcelain. **Your daughter won't get away with this. She**

can't. Sarah killed my baby. She killed my Alex, and she's going to prison, I'll make sure of it. She doesn't deserve to be free. She doesn't get to be free when Alex is . . . is . . .

She's going to make sure you go to prison, Hannah had echoed, scowling tearfully at me. Cuts and bruises were flung like pebbledash across her body. **You killed my best friend. You don't deserve to be here if she isn't.** She started to cry. **I hate you, Sarah. I** hate **you!** And that had been the last thing she had ever said to me. Nineteen years had passed; nineteen years, six weeks, two days, and she hadn't spoken a single word to me, no matter how hard I'd tried, no matter how many interventions our parents had staged.

"I'm so sorry, Eddie," I whispered. I rubbed my ankles with shaking hands. "If it helps in any way, I have never forgiven myself. Hannah never forgave me either."

"Oh yes, Hannah." He looked at me, then immediately away, as if I disgusted him. "You told me you lost your sister."

"Well . . . I did." I traced a wobbly line through the sand. "Hannah stopped speaking to me. She cut me out of her life, permanently. So I don't feel like I have a sister. Not really."

He looked briefly at the line I'd drawn in the sand. "Hannah never spoke to you again?"

"Never. And God knows, I've tried."

He went silent for a while. "I can't say I'm as surprised as I should be. She's stayed in regular touch with my mother. You can imagine the conversations." His voice was flinty. "But that's by the by. The fact remains, you have a sister. Even if she wants nothing to do with you, you have a sister."

I paused. Wished I could bolt. **I am the woman he can hardly look in the eye. I am the woman he probably wished dead all these years.**

"I am so sorry your sister was best friends with mine, Eddie. I'm so sorry I took them out of the house that day. I'm so sorry my reactions weren't the right ones when he . . . when that man . . ." I took a swallow. "I can't believe you're Alex's brother."

Eddie flinched. Then: "I want you to tell me everything," he said, and I heard the effort it was taking to keep his voice neutral.

"I . . . Are you sure?"

His body—his strong, warm, lovely body, of which I'd dreamed so many times, gave a sort of twist of assent.

So I did.

I tried so hard to keep my place in Mandy and Claire's friendship group that summer—so miserably, exhaustingly hard. In the weeks following our GCSE exams they met up every day, but they invited me to join them only a handful of times. "**God**, Sarah, stop reading into it," Mandy said, when I found the courage to confront her.

We were teenage girls. Of course I read into it.

During their time in each other's pockets they'd developed a new code of behavior they were unwilling to share with me, so my first few weeks in year twelve were a minefield. I said the wrong things, talked about the wrong people, and wore the wrong clothes, realizing only when I caught the edge of an eye roll that they'd moved on.

On the day of my seventeenth birthday I came into school and found that they'd stopped sitting in our corner of the sixth-form common room and had moved somewhere else. I had no idea if I was invited.

During the spring term Mandy started going out with someone from Stroud, the town where we went to school. Greggsy, his name was. He was twenty, and therefore a catch: no matter that he had a nasty, weasellike face, or a questionable relationship with the law. Claire was sick with envy and spent all her time trailing around after them. I began to lose hope, certain that this would be the final straw for me. Girls who went out with older men were of a higher caliber. They were sexual, successful, self-contained; untouched by the pimpled anxieties of the sixth form.

Mandy might take Claire before she pulled up the ladder behind her, I thought, but she certainly wouldn't take me.

But one day in March Mandy said quite casually that Bradley Stewart had been asking about me. Bradley Stewart was Greggsy's cousin. He drove an

Astra. He was one of the best-looking boys in that nasty group, and I was pathetically pleased.

"Oh?" I said, not looking up from the Diet Coke label I was peeling. It was important I played this right: Mandy would use my words to shame me at a later date, if I seemed too keen. "I suppose he's all right."

"I'll hook you up," she announced breezily. Claire, with whom Mandy had fallen out earlier, was fuming, and I realized this opportunity would never have presented itself if they hadn't fought.

We didn't go on a date, because nobody went on dates back then. We just met up on the pedestrian street outside the Pelican, with all the other teenage drinkers. We drank bottles of Hooch and Smirnoff Ice, and tried to be sharp and funny. Bradley, with his black hair and black trainers and his piercing eyes, somehow persuaded me off to the multistory car park on the London Road "for a drink." He steered me into a wall and started kissing me. He put his hands up my top, and I let him, even though he was rough and impatient. He put his hands down my jeans, and I let him. I didn't want to, but I had had almost no experience with boys and a chance like this wasn't going to come my way anytime soon. He tried to have sex with me; I said no. He asked for a blow job, settling eventually for a nervous hand job. I didn't enjoy it, but he did, and that was enough for me.

Then he didn't call, and I was crushed. I stared at Mum and Dad's phone for days, eventually giving in and trying his number when I couldn't bear it any longer. Nobody answered. I even got the bus to his house, near Stroud. I walked past his front door three times in thirty minutes, rain soaked, hopeful, and hopeless.

"You should have slept with him," Mandy advised. "He thought you must be seeing someone else. That or you're frigid."

Claire, back in favor, laughed.

I could feel it slipping away already, that tiny flash of value I'd held since Bradley had taken me off to the Brunel multistory. So I told Mandy to tell him I was ready to put out (her words) and he called me.

We became a couple, of sorts. I convinced myself that it was love and never imagined that I might deserve better. Nor would I have wanted someone better: I was part of a gang now; I belonged everywhere. I existed on that higher platform with Mandy and there was no way I was going back down.

Bradley often told me about other girls who fancied him and my teenage heart would freeze with terror. He went days without calling me, never walked me to the bus stop, and often insisted on going without me to the Maltings, a nasty meat market of a club, so that he could "be himself." More than once he decided this while we were in the queue, knowing I had nowhere to stay if I couldn't stay at his.

The day I passed my driving test, he failed even to congratulate me. He merely suggested I drive over to his house for sex.

"Sounds like a top bloke," Eddie said.

I shrugged.

He looked at me briefly, and I was reminded of our first morning together, when we'd sat facing each other across his breakfast bar. Me, him; the smell of bread and hope. Then he looked away, as if he couldn't bear to look at me. "Do you mind if we just get to the point?" he asked quietly. "I understand why you're telling me this stuff, but I—I just need to know."

"I'm sorry. Of course." I grappled with rising chords of panic. It was years since I'd talked out loud about what had happened that day. "I . . . Why don't we go for a walk? It's getting too hot to sit still."

After a moment Eddie got up.

We walked up past a pastel-blue lifeguard's hut and onto the boardwalk, which snaked south all the way to Venice. Bikes and Rollerbladers whisked past us; gulls cartwheeled above. The morning's brief cloud cover had been burned away and the air now shimmered with heat.

It was summer, a Monday afternoon in June. Mum and Dad had gone to Cheltenham for something and had left me in charge of Hannah after school. Hannah had Alex over. After an hour pretending to do their homework, they'd told me they were so **bored** they might seriously **die** and instructed me to drive them to Stroud for a Burger Star. I'd said no. Eventually we'd compromised with a hanging-out-eating-sweets session on Broad Ride. They'd made a den up there a few years ago, when building and maintaining a den was still an acceptable way to spend a day. Now, long past that sort of thing, they liked to go up there to listen to music and read magazines.

I was sitting on a rug a little distance from them, reading one of my A-level texts. I had no interest in their whispered conversation about some boy in their class, but they were twelve years old and I wasn't letting them out of my sight. Hannah was too much of a show-off to be responsible for her own safety. She didn't understand the slimness of life; the consequences of a twelve-year-old's bravado.

It was a warm day, the sky carrying thin twists of cloud, and I felt about as peaceful as I was capable of feeling back then. Until I heard the sound of a car, thumping and buzzing with overamplified music. I looked up and my heart lifted and sank. Bradley had called earlier, wanting me to drive over to pick him up. His car wouldn't start, he'd said, could I come and get him? Maybe lend him some money to fix it?

No, I'd said to both. I was looking after two twelve-year-old girls; plus he already owed me seventy pounds. "Borrowed Greggsy's new car," he said now, ambling toward me with a rare smile. "Seeing as you were too lame to help me out." He looked at Hannah and Alex with interest. "All right, girls?"

"Hi," they said, goggling at him.

"Since when did Greggsy drive a car like that?" I asked. It was a BMW. Souped up, just how Bradley and Greggsy liked their cars, but a Beamer all the same.

"He came into a bit of money." Bradley tapped his nose.

Hannah looked excited. "Did it fall off the back of a lorry?"

Bradley laughed. "No, mate. It's legit."

He couldn't sit still for very long. After about ten minutes on the blanket he suggested we go "for a race" in our cars.

"No way," I said. "Not with the girls." I'd been in a race with him once before: Bradley versus Greggsy back and forth on the Ebley bypass late at night. It had been the most frightening twenty minutes of my life. When it had come to an end, in the new Sainsbury's car park, my head had flopped down onto my chest and I had cried. They'd laughed at me. Mandy, too, even though she'd been just as scared.

Hannah and Alex, however, teetering on the wobbly diving board into adolescence, thought it was a great idea. "Yeah, let's go for a race," they said, as if it were a little sports car Dad had lent me, not a banger with a one-liter engine and a head gasket whose days were numbered.

They went on and on, Hannah and Alex, Bradley

riding on their coattails. **It's not the M-fucking-five, Sare. It's just a shit little road going no-where.** Alex kept flicking her blond hair over her shoulder and Hannah copied her, only she was less convincing.

My need to protect Hannah had not dwindled as the years had passed. If anything, it had strengthened as she'd transitioned from fearless child to swaggering girl. So I refused. Again and again. Bradley got more irritable; I got more stressed. Neither of us was used to me saying no.

But then the matter was taken out of my hands. Hannah, giggling, ran over to Bradley's passenger door and got inside. Bradley ran round to the driver's seat, quick as a wink. I started shouting at them, but nobody heard me because the car Bradley had borrowed had a dual exhaust and he was roaring the engine. He shot off toward Frampton and my stomach spilled out through my legs.

"Hannah!" I shouted. I ran toward my own car, Alex behind me.

"Shit!" she breathed. She sounded impressed and frightened. "They've gone!"

I made her do up her seat belt. I told her she shouldn't be swearing. I prayed.

"And off we went," I said, coming to a halt on the boardwalk.

Eddie turned away from me and stared out to sea, hands jammed in his pockets.

"You were on the village green because you'd just been walking along Broad Ride," I said. "Weren't you? The day we met. You were there for exactly the same reason as me."

He nodded.

"It was the first time I'd been up there on the anniversary of her death." His voice was tight, bound securely to prevent collapse. "Normally I'd spend it with Mum, who'd just go through old photo albums and cry. But that day I just . . . I just couldn't do it. I wanted to be out there, in the sunshine, thinking good things about my little sister."

Me. I'd done this. Me and my weakness, my monstrous stupidity.

"I walk along there every year on June second," I told him. I wanted to fold myself around him, absorb his pain somehow. "I go there, rather than up to the main road, because Broad Ride was their kingdom that afternoon. They had nail varnish and magazines and not a care in the world. That's the bit I fly back to remember."

Eddie looked briefly at me. "What magazines? Do you remember? What nail varnish? What were they eating?"

"It was **Mizz**," I said quietly. Of course I remembered. That day had been playing out in my head my entire adult life. "They'd borrowed my nail varnish. I'd got it free with a magazine; it was called Sugar Bliss. We had Linda McCartney sausage rolls, because they were both having a vegetarian phase.

Cheese-and-onion crisps and a tub of fruit salad. Only Alex had smuggled in some sweets."

I remembered it as if it were yesterday; the wasps hovering over the fruit, Hannah's new sunglasses, the swaying shades of green.

"Skittles," Eddie said. "I bet she brought Skittles. They were her favorite."

"That's right." I couldn't look at him. "Skittles."

I caught up with them at the main road. Bradley was trying to turn right, toward Stroud, but a succession of cars stuck behind a tractor had held him up.

Stay calm, I told myself, as I got out of the car and jogged up to his passenger door. **Just get her out and treat this all as a joke. He'll be okay if—**

Bradley spotted me and quickly turned left instead, engine roaring. I ran back to my car.

"You can speed up if you want," Alex said. Already Bradley's car was nearly out of sight. "You can floor it. I don't mind."

"No. He'll slow down and wait for me so he can race me. I know what he's like." Blood pounded in my ears. Please, God, let nothing happen to her. Let nothing happen to my little sister. I looked at my speedometer. Fifty-five miles per hour. I slowed down. Then I sped up. I couldn't stand it.

Alex turned on my stereo. It was a group of American kids, Hanson, singing a silly earworm song called "MMMBop." Nineteen years on I still couldn't bear to hear it.

After a horrifyingly short time, Bradley was racing back toward us on the other side of the road at sixty, maybe seventy miles per hour. "Slow down!" I yelled, flashing him. He must have U-turned in the road up ahead.

"Chill!" Alex said. She flicked her hair nervously. "Hannah's fine!"

Bradley shot past, beeping, and then screeched the car round onto our side of the road. "Handbrake turn," Alex marveled. I came almost to a stop, watching them in my rearview mirror. I barely breathed until they had straightened out and were driving behind us again. I could see her there, in his front seat, a whole head shorter than him. A little girl, for Christ's sake.

She stared straight ahead. Hannah was only that still when she was afraid.

"How do you know what a handbrake turn is?" I heard myself ask. I was driving slowly, my hazard lights on. **Please stop. Give me my sister back.** I wound down the window and pointed frantically toward the verge.

"My brother told me," Alex said. "He's at university."

For a moment I felt angry that her brother—some **idiot**—thought it was clever to teach his little sister about handbrake turns. But then Bradley dipped back so he could roar up behind us, screeching on his brakes at the last minute. I gasped. He did it again. And again, and again. I tried several times to

stop, but each time I did, he tried to overtake me.
So I continued driving, just like he wanted me to. I
couldn't let him fire off ahead with my sister again.

He carried on like that until we started to approach the dip in the road, not far from the Sapperton junction and the woods. But by then he must
have become bored, because he didn't stop when he
revved up into the back of my car; he hit it. Gently,
but still hard enough to make me panic. I'd only
had a license three weeks.

"Shit," Alex said, only more quietly than before.
She was still trying to look excited, but it was obvious she was afraid. Her slender fingers were closed
tight around the old gray webbing of the seat belt.

We descended into the dip, Bradley flashing and
beeping on my tail. He was laughing. And then—
even though we were heading down into a blind
bend—he pulled out to overtake.

Everything seemed to hang like a droplet on a tap,
ready to fall and smash.

A car came round the bend on the other side, just
as I knew it would.

Bradley was nearly level with me. There was no
way they could avoid crashing.

My sister. Hannah.

My emergency-response system took over at that
point, I told the police afterward. I knew that because
what happened next was not a matter of choice; it
was simply what happened. My brain instructed my
arms to swerve the car left, and the car swerved left.

If you lose control of your car, never aim for a tree, Dad had told me when he taught me to drive. Always aim for a wall or a fence. They'll give way. A tree won't.

And the tree did not give way, when the passenger side of the car—the side containing sweet little Alex Wallace with her blond flicky hair and her Skittles and her blobby nail varnish—slammed into it.

The tree didn't give way, but Alex did.

I forced myself to look at Eddie, but he was still facing away from me, looking out to sea. The shining globe of a tear tracked slowly down his face and he brushed it away, pinching the top of his nose. But after a few seconds he let his hand fall, and with it tears. He stood and cried, this big, kind man, and I felt it more strongly than I had done in years. That loathing of myself, that desperation to do something, change things, and the subsequent despair that I could not. Time had marched on, leaving Alex behind. Leaving Eddie in small pieces, my sister unable to forgive me.

"I spent years wondering what I'd do if I met you," Eddie said eventually. He wiped at his eyes with his forearms, turned to face me. "I hated you. I couldn't believe that scumbag went to jail and you didn't."

I nodded, because I hated myself, too.

"I asked why they weren't punishing me," I said uselessly. "But they kept on saying I didn't do anything illegal. I wasn't driving recklessly.'

"I remember. Our family liaison officer had to explain it to us." Eddie's voice was flat. "It made no sense to my mother."

I closed my eyes, because I knew what he was going to say next.

"All I know is that you chose to save your sister, and because of that, mine died."

I wrapped my arms around myself. "That wasn't the choice I made," I whispered. Tears blocked my airways. "That was not the conscious choice that I made, Eddie."

He sighed. "Maybe not. But it's what happened."

The police came to the hospital. The BMW had been stolen, they said.

Why had I accepted what he'd told me? Why had I ever listened to **anything** he had said? A sick panic washed over me at the thought of all I'd given this man. My virginity. My heart. My self-respect. And now the life of a young girl. My sister's best friend.

A witness had seen the driver running across fields, away from the accident. Who was he?

"Who was he?" Dad repeated, confused. He was sitting by my bed, holding my hand. Mum was on the other side, a human shield between the police and her daughter. "Who was he, Sarah?"

"My boyfriend. Bradley."

"Your what?" Dad was even more perplexed. "You had a boyfriend? But how long for? Why didn't you tell us?"

And I turned my head and cried into the pillow, because it was so obvious now. So obvious that Bradley was a vile human being—had always been a vile human being—and so obvious that, deep down, under those tightly folded layers of adolescent insecurity, I'd known.

My actions might have saved my little sister from death, but they failed to protect her from harm. Bradley had swerved into the space I'd created, ramming Hannah's side of the stolen car into the back of mine. Hannah had two surgeries in two days. She was in the ward on the floor above mine, concussed, badly injured, and for the first time in her twelve years, silent.

Bradley, whose name I gave to the police, was nowhere to be found. "Try Greggsy's," I told them, and he was arrested soon after.

After I was discharged, I sat by Hannah's bed every day for two weeks until she was free to go. I didn't go to school; I barely went home. I remembered almost nothing, other than the quiet beep of machines and the hum of a busy pediatrics ward. The fear when one of Hannah's machines made a strange noise; the guilt like a blowtorch to my chest. Mostly she slept; sometimes she cried and told me she hated me.

The police insisted there were no charges to bring against me, no matter how determined Alex's family was to see me punished. The guilt grew stronger. I testified against Bradley at Gloucester Crown Court and was reprimanded because I begged the judge to try me, too.

I didn't know Alex's family. Mum and Dad had almost always ferried her to and from playdates at our house because—as Mum put it—"Alex's mother struggles sometimes." She had since had a full mental breakdown, they said in court. Not only that but she had been single since Alex was young, so her son had had to drop out of university to look after her. Neither of them made it to court.

Someone in the jury looked at me then. A woman, probably Mum's age, who could imagine what it must be like to lose a child. She looked straight at me and her face said, **That's your fault, too, you little bitch. That's your fault, too.**

Carole Wallace managed to call us three times before the psychiatric nurses realized she wasn't calling her son and revoked her telephone access. I was a murderer, she said, once to Dad, twice to our answerphone. Our neighbors stopped inviting Mum and Dad round for dinner, or talking when they came past. They didn't blame me, I don't think; they simply had no idea what to say to any of us. "Sometimes the elephant is just too big for the room," Dad said.

Hannah refused to sit at a table with me. People stared at my parents in the supermarket. Alex's photo continued to appear in the local press. I went back to school, but within hours I knew I was finished there. People were whispering. Claire said I should have been done for manslaughter. Mandy was not talking to me at all, because I'd sent the police after Greggsy's cousin. Even some of the teachers couldn't quite look me in the eye.

That night Mum and Dad sat me down and told me they were putting the house on the market. How would I feel about moving to Leicestershire? Mum had grown up in Leicestershire. "We could all do with a fresh start, couldn't we?" she asked. Her face was translucent with worry and exhaustion. "I'm sure we'd be able to find somewhere for you to carry on your A levels."

Mum was a teacher. She knew that was impossible. It was only then that I realized quite how desperate she was.

I went upstairs and called Tommy, and flew to LA the very next day.

I went so that Alex's family could grieve in peace, without the risk of ever having to run into me. I went so that my parents wouldn't have to move halfway across the country, so they'd have a chance at starting over without the titanic shadow of their daughter looming over everything. I went to find sanctuary in a place where nobody would know what I'd done, where I wouldn't be "that girl."

But most of all I went to LA to become the sort of woman I wished I had been the day I'd met Bradley. Strong, sure of myself, afraid of nobody. Never, ever, **ever** afraid to say no.

• • •

Eddie and I were drawing close to Venice now, the boardwalk snaking past shops and stalls peddling cheap gifts and henna tattoos. Music boomed out of a speaker somewhere; homeless people slept under palm trees. I gave a few dollars to a man with a rucksack full of patches. Eddie watched me with a blank face. "I need to sit down," he said. "I need to eat something."

We sat outside a bar, where we were the focus of a madwoman with a parrot and a roaming accordionist. Eddie had no answers to the madwoman's questions and just gazed blankly at the busker as he swayed around us.

"I can take you to Abbot Kinney, if you like," I said. "It's another street, nearby. More upmarket if this is too crazy for you."

Reuben loved Abbot Kinney.

"No, thanks," Eddie said. For a moment he looked like he might smile. "Since when was I upmarket?"

I shrugged, suddenly embarrassed. "I never really got to find out."

He glanced sideways at me and I saw what might be a pocket of warmth. "I think we got a pretty good measure of each other."

I love you, I thought. I love you, Eddie, and I don't know what to do.

His muffin arrived. I imagined my life, stretching out ahead of me without Eddie David, and felt light-headed with panic. And then I imagined him, all those years ago, envisaging a life stretching out ahead of him without his sister.

He ate his muffin in silence.

"My charity," I said eventually. "My charity was set up for Alex."

"I did wonder."

"For Alex and for Hannah." I picked at a hang-nail. "Hannah has kids of her own now. I've seen pictures. I sent them presents every birthday at first, but in the end she sent a message through Mum asking me to stop. It kills Mum and Dad. They tried everything to bring us back together. They just thought she'd climb down, eventually. Perhaps she would have done, if I was still in England . . . I don't know. She was such a stubborn child. I guess that's the sort of adult she became, too."

Eddie looked down the beach. "You shouldn't underestimate the impact that my mother will have had on her. She never stopped hating you. At times it's the only thing that's got her through."

I tried not to imagine Eddie's mother's house, the walls holding old anger like nicotine stains. I tried not to imagine my sister there with Carole Wallace; the words they'd use; the tea they'd drink. Although, oddly, there was comfort to be found in that picture, too. In the possibility that my sister's wholesale rejection of me could perhaps have been helped along by someone else.

"Do you think that's partly why?" I asked, turning back to him. My desperation was palpable. "Do you think your mum might have been egging her on, all these years?"

Eddie shrugged. "I don't know your sister very well. But I know my mother. I'd probably have reacted differently to you if I hadn't been listening to Mum for nineteen years."

He looked as if he might say something else, but then closed his mouth.

"I've struggled to be anywhere near children since it happened," I said. "I refused childminding jobs, wouldn't babysit, went on ward visits with Reuben only when there was no other option."

I paused. "I even refused to have a baby with him. He made me go to therapy, but nothing would change my mind. When I saw a child—any child—I saw your sister. So I steer clear. It's easier that way."

Eddie ate the final piece of his muffin and rested his forehead in his hand. He said, "I wish you'd used your family name when we met. I wish you'd said, 'I'm Sarah Harrington.'"

I yanked the hangnail off, leaving a soft strip of stinging pink. "I'm not reverting to Harrington, not even after the divorce. I don't want to be Sarah Harrington ever again."

Eddie was squashing the final crumbs from his plate onto a finger. "It would have saved us a lot of heartache."

I nodded.

"And your parents were meant to have moved to Leicester. There was a SOLD sign at the end of their track for weeks."

"I know. But I moved to LA, and I was the problem. Their buyer fell through and they decided to stay. I think by then it was pretty clear I wasn't coming back."

A long silence fell.

"Could I ask why you call yourself Eddie David?" I asked, when it became unbearable. "Surely your name's Eddie Wallace?"

"David's my middle name. I started using it after the accident. For a while everyone recognized my name and there'd be all this . . . I don't know . . . kind of suffocating sympathy, I suppose, when people realized who I was. It was easier to be Eddie David. Nobody knew him. Just like nobody knew Sarah Mackey."

After a while he turned to look at me, but his gaze was pulled away again, like water running back to the sea. "I'd give anything to have worked out who you were before it was too late," he said. "I just—I just can't believe we never made the connection." He scratched his head. "You know they let him out after five years?"

I nodded. "He moved to Portsmouth, I heard."

Eddie said nothing.

"It was my Facebook, wasn't it?" I said. "You saw a post from Tommy. He called me Harrington."

"I saw it about twenty seconds after you left. And

for the first minute or so, before the shock set in properly, I just thought, **No. Pretend you haven't seen that. Make it go away, because I can't not be with her. It's only been a week, but she's . . .**" He flushed. "**She's everything**," he finished off. "That's what I was thinking."

We sat in silence for a long time. My heart was racing. Eddie's cheeks were faintly red.

Then he told me about his mother, about her depression, how it had exploded after Alex's death and deteriorated into a complex mental health cocktail from which she had never really emerged. He told me she had moved to Sapperton when she'd come out of the worst of the breakdown, because she wanted to be "closer" to her dead daughter. Recognizing that she was too vulnerable to survive alone, Eddie had abandoned any hopes of returning to university and moved in with her for a while. He persuaded Frank, the sheep farmer, to rent him a crumbling cow barn on the edge of Siccaridge Wood, which he slowly turned into a workshop and then, once she was able to live on her own, a home of his own.

"Dad funded it," he said. "Cash was his solution to everything, after he left us. He couldn't bring himself to call, once Alex's funeral was over, or to come and visit, but he was fine sending money. So I decided to be fine about spending it."

He told me about the day he'd discovered who I was. How the trees outside his barn had seemed to collapse in on him as he reframed me as Sarah Harrington, the girl who'd killed his sister. How he'd canceled his holiday to Spain. Put his commissions on hold. How he'd gone to check on his mother one day and found her zonked out on medication, and the guilt he had felt as he had watched her sleep.

"It would be catastrophic if she found out about me and you," he said quietly. "Although it felt pretty catastrophic even without her knowing. I fell into quite a hole. I didn't look at Facebook, or e-mails, or anything. Just kind of cut myself off. Took a lot of walks. Did a lot of thinking and talking to myself."

He cracked his knuckles. "Until my mate Alan turned up to check if I was dead, and told me you'd been in touch."

Then he sighed. "I should have replied to you," he said. "I'm sorry I didn't. You were right—that's no way to treat anyone. I started to write to you, again and again, but I just didn't trust myself to talk to you."

I tried not to imagine what he might have said.

"But I loved your life story. Your messages. I craved them when they didn't come. I read them over and over."

I swallowed, trying not to attach meaning to this. "Did you ever call me?" I asked tentatively.

He shook his head.

"Are you sure? I had . . . I had some dropped calls.

And, well, a message, telling me to stay away from you."

He looked puzzled. "Oh. You wrote to me about that, didn't you? In one of those letters? I'm sorry—I didn't really pay it much attention. I think I just assumed you'd made it up."

I winced.

"Did you hear from them again?"

"No. But I did think . . . Look, I did wonder if it might be your mother. Is there any way she could have found out about you and me? I saw a woman, on the canal path between my parents' house and your barn . . . And when I went to Tommy's sports thing at my old school, I saw someone wearing the same coat. I mean, I can't be certain it was the same person, but I'm pretty sure it was. She wasn't doing anything particularly strange, but both times I felt like I was being, well, stared at. And maybe in a hostile way."

Eddie folded his arms. "That's very odd," he said slowly. "But there's absolutely no **way** it was Mum. She hasn't the faintest clue about you. And anyway, she . . ." He trailed off. "She's just not capable of that sort of thing. Crank calling, following people— that's just way beyond her capabilities. She'd get superstressed even thinking about doing something like that. In fact, she'd fall apart."

"And there's nobody else it could have been?"

Eddie looked utterly confused. "No," he said, and

I believed him. "The only person I told was my best mate, Alan, and his wife, Gia. Oh, and Martin from football, because he also saw your post on my Facebook page. But all of them I told in confidence."

He leaned forward, his face knotted with concentration. He must have failed to get anywhere, though, because after a few minutes he shrugged and straightened up. "I really don't know," he said. "But it wasn't Mum. Of that you can be certain."

"Okay." I slid off a flip-flop and tucked one foot up on my chair. Eddie was looking miserable again. He pressed a finger down onto the rim of his plate so it reared up like a flying saucer. He wheeled it left and right.

"Why are you here, Eddie?" I asked, eventually. "Why did you come?"

He looked at me then. Looked at me fully, and my stomach pulled up into my throat.

"I came because you messaged me saying you were going back to LA and I panicked. I was still angry, but I just couldn't let you walk out of my life. Not until I'd spoken to you. Heard what you had to say. I knew Mum's view couldn't be the only view."

"I see."

"I booked a flight and e-mailed my mate Nathan to ask if I could crash at his place. Called my aunt and asked her to come and stay with Mum. It was like watching myself in the third person, really. I knew I shouldn't come, but I couldn't stop myself.

And I couldn't stop you, either: you were already on the plane when you e-mailed me."

But when he got here, he found himself paralyzed. Three times he came to confront me; three times guilt over his sister sent him running back into the obscurity of the city. I slumped in my chair. Even talking to me felt like a betrayal.

"Why didn't you tell me about your past?" he asked, when I signaled for the bill. "You told me so much about yourself. Why didn't you ever mention what happened?"

I pulled some cash out of my wallet. "I just don't tell people, full stop. The last person I told was my friend Jenni, and that was seventeen years ago. If we . . . Had we . . ." I cleared my throat. "If we had turned into a Thing, I would have told you. I nearly did, in fact, on the last night. But other things got in the way."

Eddie looked thoughtful. "Whereas I'm used to telling people. I often have to, because of Mum being so up and down. But that week with you just felt so different to anything else. I wasn't Eddie, Carole's son, the bloke who lost his sister and has to spend far too much time running around after his mum. I was me." He slid his phone back in his pocket. "For the first time in years, I didn't think about the past. At all. Plus Mum had her sister with her, because I was about to go off to Spain, so I didn't even need to think about her."

He stood up, giving me an odd smile. "Which is ironic, really, given who I was with."

I left a couple of dollars on the table and we walked down to the water's edge. Wavelets furled silkily around our feet, drawing back into the boundless blue swell of the Pacific. The horizon boiled and shimmered, indistinct.

I slipped my hand into my pocket. Mouse. I ran a thumb over her, one final time, before offering her over to Eddie on the palm of my hand.

He stared at her for a long time. "I made her for Alex," he said. "For her second birthday. Mouse was the first decent thing I made out of wood."

With tenderness, he picked her up, holding her in front of his face, as if learning her shape once again. I imagined him chiseling away at this tiny lump of wood, maybe in his father's garage, or simply at a kitchen table, and my heart broke. A round-faced little boy making a toy mouse for his baby sister.

"Alex thought Mouse was a hedgehog, when she was a toddler. Only she couldn't say "hedgehog" back then, it came out as 'Ej-oj.' Made me laugh. I started calling her Hedgehog; it never quite wore off." He fitted her back onto his key ring and put it back in his pocket.

I had run out of delaying tactics. The sea shifted in and out. Neither of us said anything.

We watched herring gulls and sandpipers circling above a family picnic, and a wave tumbled in on us, faster than we could move back. His shorts got wet.

My skirt got wet. We laughed, he lost his footing and nearly fell, and for a second I could smell him: his skin, his clean hair, his Eddie smell.

"I'm going to fly back tomorrow," he said, eventually. "I'm glad we've had this conversation, but I'm not sure there's anything else we can say. Or do, for that matter."

No, I thought hopelessly. No! You can't walk away from us! It's here! Our thing! It's right here in the air between us!

But nothing came out of my mouth, because it wasn't my decision to make. I had driven a car carrying Alex into a tree and she had died, right there beside me. Time would not change that. Nothing would change that.

He picked up my hands and uncurled my clenched fists. My nails left sad white crescents in my palms. "We could never go back to what we had the first time round," he said, smoothing his thumb across the nail marks, like a father rubbing a child's cut knee. "It's done. You do understand that, Sarah, don't you?"

I nodded and made a face that suggested agreement, or perhaps resignation. He dropped my hands and looked off at the sea for a while. Then, without any warning at all, he bent down and kissed me.

It took me a while to believe it was happening. That his face was pressed against mine, his mouth, his warmth, his breath, just like I'd imagined a hundred times over. For a few seconds I was perfectly still. But then I started kissing him back, elated, and he wrapped his arms tightly around me, like he had the first time. He kissed me harder, and I kissed him back, and the wheeling gulls and shrieking children were gone.

But as I began to let go completely, he stopped, resting his chin on my head. I could hear his breath, fast and unsteady.

Then: "Good-bye, Sarah," he said. "Take good care of yourself."

His arms released me and he was gone.

I watched him walk away, my hands dangling by my sides. Farther and farther away he walked. Farther and farther away.

It wasn't until he was back up on the boardwalk that I said out loud the thing I'd been unable to say before now, not even to myself.

"I'm pregnant, Eddie," I said, and my words were carried away by the wind, just like I wanted them to be.

CHAPTER THIRTY-NINE

I laid a hand on my belly. **I am pregnant. I am carrying a baby.**

Jenni was telling Javier about a Slovenian genetics researcher she'd met in the waiting room at the acupuncture clinic yesterday. Javier was listening attentively to his wife while keeping a keen ear on the lady dispensing orders at the counter. The last number she'd called had been eighty-four. Our ticket, curled between Javier's fingers, said eighty-seven.

I imagined cells multiplying, all those weeks ago. Sarah cells, Eddie cells. Sarah-and-Eddie cells, splitting into more Sarah-and-Eddie cells. The Internet said it would be the size of a strawberry by now. There was a computer-generated picture on the page, and it looked like a tiny child. I'd stared at that picture for what seemed like hours, and felt things I had never felt before, things to which I couldn't even put a name.

I am nine weeks pregnant.

But we'd been careful! Each and every time! And how could I be pregnant when I was three pounds lighter?

"You told me yourself you've struggled to eat," the doctor had said patiently. "Weight loss is not uncommon with morning sickness."

Nausea. Fatigue. Tumbling hormones, food aversions, a brain packed with thick fog. The real surprise, I supposed, was not so much that I was pregnant but that I had failed to spot so many obvious markers.

A parcel had arrived for me this morning. I'd been lying in bed, filling in the paperwork for my scan, and had felt so dislocated from reality that for a moment I had wondered quite seriously if it might be Eddie. Eddie, curled up inside a box, ready to spring out, shouting, "I've changed my mind! Of course I want to be with you—the woman who killed my little sister! Let's start a family!"

Instead I had unwrapped a toy sheep, with little leather hooves and a wool coat, and a note round its neck saying—in Eddie's handwriting—**LUCY**. There had been a letter, too, in an envelope that smelled oddly of sherbet. I took it outside.

On Jenni's deck, I curled myself into a chair and stared at the dirty jumble of air-conditioning units and satellite dishes stretching out below me. I ran my fingertips along the tiny indentations that Eddie's pen had left where he'd written my name. I knew what this letter would be. It would be the final punctuation mark to a relationship that had ended nineteen years before it had even begun, but I wanted a few more minutes before I saw that final full stop. A few more minutes of precious, poisonous denial.

I watched a cat for a while. The cat had watched me. I'd breathed the slow, steady breaths of someone who knows the drama is over, who knows herself to be truly beaten. When the cat had marched off disdainfully, tail in the air, I'd slid my thumb into the gap at the top of the envelope.

Dear Sarah,

Thanks for your honesty yesterday. It was very comforting to know that Alex was happy that day.

I want to say everything's fine, but it's not, nor can it be. For that reason I think it best we don't stay in touch—it would be too confusing to be friends. I do wish you well, though, Sarah Harrington, and will always remember the time we had together. It meant everything to me.

What a terrible coincidence, eh? Of all the people in the world.

Anyway, I wanted to send a little something to make you smile. I know how rough this whole thing has been for you, too.

Be happy, Sarah, and take care,

Eddie

I read the note three times before folding it back into its envelope.

Be happy, Sarah, and take care.

I'd leaned my head back against the outside of Jenni's bungalow and stared at the sky. It was milky and expectant up there, smudged with clouds the color of Turkish delight. A sweep of birds passed high above, and, beyond them, a plane on its ascent.

I hadn't told Jenni about the baby. I couldn't bear it; couldn't bring myself to tell her that I'd got pregnant while using birth control, when for more than ten years she had put every scrap of her emotional, physical, and financial resources into creating a family of her own.

I'd stared at my abdomen, trying to imagine the tiny beginnings of a person in there, and felt an odd sensation in my heart, like my chest was being compressed. Was that pleasure? Or panic? It had its own heart now, the doctor told me. In spite of the poor nutrition, the wine, and the stress I'd fed it. It had its own tiny heart that was beating twice as fast as my own, and I would see it on a scan tomorrow afternoon.

I stared at the sky. Was he up there already? Still waiting at the gate to board? I half rose out of my chair. I had to go to the airport. Find him. Stop him. For the sake of this baby I had to talk him round, convince him that I—

What? That I wasn't Sarah Harrington? That I hadn't driven his sister into a tree that day?

I'd sat there, drumming my fingers on my thighs, until Javier had let Frappuccino out into the yard and the dog peed on my leg. I'd started laughing, and then crying, wondering how I could possibly have a baby when I'd spent my whole adult life avoiding children. Wondering how I could bring **anyone** into the world, knowing the father wanted nothing to do with me. Yet somehow knowing that it was already too late to turn back. That I wanted this baby in ways I didn't even understand.

I continued in this vein for hours. Jenni, when she finally got out of bed, tried to look after me, but she had nothing left to give. We spent two hours sitting together in grim silence.

When Javier was unable to bear the emotional potency a moment longer, he offered to drive us all up to Neptune's Net in Malibu—a bikers' café—for fried fish. It was his solution to all serious problems. He had hunched over the wheel as he'd motored up the coast, although whether to speed us on toward the comfort of food or to protect himself from all the messy feelings surrounding him, I didn't know.

And now here we were, jammed like sardines into a booth. The restaurant was packed. Every table was full, and the entrance was packed with people waiting for a seat. We, the seated, ignored them. They, the standing, stared determinedly at us. Music was drowned out by the deafening roar of conversation, Harley-Davidsons revving outside, and the furious sizzle of that morning's catch hitting boiling oil. It was a big, long motorbike ride away from calm, but, in some small way, it was working.

"Eighty-seven!" called the lady at the counter, and Javier sprang up, shouting, in a voice hoarse with relief, "**Sí! Sí!**"

Jenni seldom acknowledged her husband's limited emotional capacity, but today, just for me, she allowed herself a quick eye roll. Then she fixed me with one of her looks and asked me what I was going to do about Eddie.

"Nothing," I said. "There's nothing I can do, Jenni. You know it. I know it. Even Javier knows it."

Javier silently placed a seafood basket between us, handing Jenni a Sprite and me a Mountain Dew. Then, letting out a quiet but perfectly audible sigh of relief, he turned to his own pile of shrimp tacos, pale-battered calamari, and cheesy chili fries, knowing it would be some time before he might be expected to contribute.

"He really left **no** doors open? Not even a glimmer of hope?"

"Not so much as a dust mote," I said. "Look, Jenni, I'm going to say this one last time. Imagine it was your sister, Nancy. Imagine that a man drove lovely Nancy into a tree. Would you contemplate a relationship with him? Would you **really**?"

Jenni put down her cutlery, defeated.

"Ninety-four!" yelled the woman at the counter.

I speared a scallop.

Then: **Should I be eating this?** I wondered suddenly. I was sure I'd seen pregnant friends avoiding shellfish. I looked at the meal in front of me. Seafood, shellfish, and a large glass of Mountain Dew. Wasn't caffeine banned, too?

Yet again, the tectonic plates of my life shifted underneath me. **I am nine weeks pregnant.**

"Here," Jenni said heavily. "Take some scallops before I eat it all, Sarah. I'm sensing another binge coming on."

I declined.

"But you **love** scallops."

"I know . . . I'm not feeling the love today, though."

"Seriously? Well, at least have some of this blue-cheese dip for your fries. I think it's actually real cheese. It's good."

"Oh, I'm fine with ketchup. You have it."

Jenni laughed. "Sarah Mackey, you detest ketchup. No scallops, no blue cheese—anyone'd think you were pregnant. Look, please don't try to starve yourself, honey. It won't help anything, and besides, life is totally miserable without food."

I laughed, a little too loudly. Picked up a scallop to prove that I was fine, and certainly not pregnant, but I couldn't do it. I couldn't make myself eat the stupid thing. I had a baby the size of a strawberry growing in me, a baby I'd neither planned nor asked for, but still I couldn't eat the scallop. The edge of a frown crossed Jenni's face.

"Best to just ignore me," I said, in a voice stiff with forced jollity. Javier glanced up. "I've got a funny appetite today."

"That'd be the ultimate irony, wouldn't it?" Jenni said. "You being pregnant."

"Ha! Can you imagine?"

Jenni went back to her food, but after a few seconds she looked at me again. "I mean, you're not, are you?"

"Of course I'm . . ."

I couldn't do it. I couldn't lie to her. So I shut my mouth.

Jenni lowered her fork to the table. "Sarah? You're not pregnant, are you?"

My face burned. I looked down, around, anywhere but at Jenni.

"That's not why you . . . That's not why you've been ill? The doctor . . . ?"

Javier stared at me. **Don't you dare**, his face said. **Don't you dare.**

Jenni watched me, and her eyes began to swim with tears. "Why aren't you saying anything? Why aren't you answering me?"

I closed my eyes. "Jenni," I said. "Oh God, Jenni, I . . ."

Her hand rose to her mouth. She stared at me in disbelief, and her tears bulged and broke. "No, you're not . . . You couldn't be pr— Oh, Jesus. Sarah."

Javier wrapped a protective arm around his wife's shoulders. After a deep breath he looked up at me, and his face wore the first tangible emotion I'd seen in fifteen years: fury.

"Jenni," I said quietly. "Listen, darling. When I

went to the doctor's, she said . . . She did some tests, and she said . . . Jenni, I am so sorry . . ."

"You're having a baby."

"I . . . Yes. I can't even begin to tell you how sorry I am."

Into the perfect silence of our table, my phone started ringing.

"Eddie?" Jenni whispered, because even when her friend smashed her round the face, she couldn't give up.

"I . . . I don't know. I deleted his number. But it's a UK mobile."

"Take it," she said flatly. "Just take it. He's the father of your child, after all."

As I reached the crowded doorway, phone in hand, it came to me that I should turn round to see Jenni's face, one last time. **One last time before what?**

I turned, not fully understanding why, but a barrellike woman was craning herself into one of the fixed seats and Jenni was obscured.

So I carried on, threading my way through the diners on the outside terrace. I walked through the bikers, the bikes, down toward the highway. I wondered if Jenni would ever get over this. If our friendship would survive.

Wearily, I answered the call.

There was a delay of a few seconds while a voice whizzed through cables deep under the Atlantic.

Then: "Sarah?"

"Yes."

After a moment the voice said, "It's Hannah."

"Hannah?"

"Yes. Er . . . Hannah Harrington."

I put out a hand to steady myself, only there was nothing there. So I held on to the phone with both hands, because it was the only solid thing I had.

"Hannah?"

"Yes."

"My sister Hannah?"

"Yes."

A moment's silence.

"I appreciate this might be a bit of a shock."

"Your voice," I whispered. "Your voice." I held more tightly on to the phone. She started to say something but her voice was drowned out by a salvo of motorbikes swarming into the car park, all fitted out with powerful engines.

"Sorry?" I said. "What was that? Hannah?"

"Can you hear me now?" I heard her say. "I'm kind of bellowing . . ." The bikers, all parked, were now sitting, revving, for no reason. Unreasonable fury rose in my chest. "Shut **up**!" I shouted. "Please, stop it!"

On the other side of the road, a peaceful-looking path led haphazardly toward the distant sea. **I have to get across the road**, I thought desperately, as vehicles roared along the highway in front of me, and motorbikes revved behind. **I have to get across the road, right now.**

"Are you still there?" I heard her say.

"Yes! Can you hear me?"

"Just about. What the hell's going on there?"

I knew what Hannah looked like: Mum and Dad used to send me photos, until it had become too painful for me to see them. It was almost impossible to imagine that the woman from the pictures was the woman talking to me now. The woman with the curly-haired husband, the two children, and the dog. My little sister.

"Look, Hannah, let me cross the road. I'm at a bikers' café; there's a lot of noise, but it'll be quiet over there . . ."

"Are you a **biker**?" There was just a corner of a smile in her voice.

"No, I'm not. I— Hang on, let me just get across to the other side. **Please** stay on the line . . ." There was a gap in the southbound traffic. For no earthly reason, I didn't turn to check the northbound lane. I just ran. Toward the sea, toward Hannah.

I heard nothing; I saw nothing. Not the deadly lumber of a truck traveling at high speed. Not the screech of brakes, not the panicked yells from the terrace. I didn't hear my own voice, forced out of me in a guttural scream, then falling sharply into silence, like an ambulance turning its siren off because there was no longer any point, and I didn't hear the wail that came out of Jenni's mouth as she pummeled her way out of the restaurant.

I didn't hear a thing.

Part III

Part III

CHAPTER FORTY

Eddie

Dear You,

It's 3:37 A.M., nearly eighteen hours since I touched down at Heathrow.

Nobody was waiting for me, of course, because the only person who knew I was coming back today was Mum. I feigned indifference as I scanned the sea of welcome cards that didn't say my name. I whistled a bit of Bowie.

I called Mum on my way to the Long Stay car park. For reasons as yet unclear, she seems to have found my absence particularly hard this time. Maybe it was the distance that threw her. It certainly isn't the first time I've gone away for two weeks. Anyway, she told me she'd been up all night worrying about my plane crashing. "It's been awful," she told me. "I'm so tired I can hardly speak." But she must then have made an immediate recovery because she

went on to spend ten minutes telling me about
the things her sister failed to do in my absence.
"She still hasn't taken the recycling away. It's
just sitting there by the front gate! I can't bear
to look out of the window. Eddie, do you think
you could pop over on your way home?"

Poor Aunty Margaret.

Mum came close to a panic attack when
Margaret tried to take her for her psychiatrist's
appointment apparently, so I've got to take her
next week. She said she just couldn't cope with
cars, hospitals, people. Not without me. The
conversation was plowed with deep furrows of
guilt. Mine, for having just buggered off—even
though Mum's always telling me I've got to
lead my own life—and hers, because she knows
this is what happens when I do.

I picked up the Land Rover and drove back
down the M4. Back to Gloucestershire, to
Sapperton, to this life. I listened to the radio for
a while, because it stopped me thinking about
Sarah. I came off at Membury Services for a
cheese sandwich.

Then something weird happened as I
headed down the Cirencester Road: I didn't
slow down for the Sapperton junction. I didn't
even indicate; I just shot on past. I carried on
to the Frampton turnoff, but I didn't come
off there, either. I found myself driving to
Minchinhampton Common. I parked at the

reservoir and got an ice cream and walked
round Amberley, and then dropped into the
Black Horse. I had an orange Henry, then sat
there for about two hours, just staring across
the Woodchester Valley.

I'm not sure what was going on in my head.
Everything felt oddly detached, as if I were
watching CCTV footage of myself. All I knew
was that I couldn't go to Mum's.

By this point she'd texted and called me
several times, worried I'd crashed on the
motorway. So I told her I was fine, had just got
held up sorting something out, but that was
more because I didn't know what I was doing
than because I was hiding something specific.
At about four I was back at Tom Long's Post,
and that's when it got really worrying, because
rather than turning right toward Sapperton, I
found myself turning left toward Stroud.

I went for a pint at the Golden Fleece and
then popped in on Alan and his wife, Gia.
They were lovely. So kind and supportive. Let
me share Lily's tea and told me I'd done the
right thing, walking away from Sarah. They
had no idea I was hiding from my own mother.

Lily refused to go to bed. She sat on my knee
and drew mermaids. Since meeting Sarah, I've
felt a strange breathlessness when I hang out
with Lily, a pressing sadness mingled with the
love and affection I feel for my best friend's

little girl. Sarah broke some kind of a seal in
me, I think. After years of disregarding the
idea, I began to be able to imagine myself with
a child of my own. Lily drew an ink mermaid
on my hand and I felt a deep trench open up
inside me, like a fissure in the ocean floor.

I texted Mum and said something had come
up with Alan and that I wasn't going to make
it tonight. **I'll be over in the morning**, I
promised. She wasn't happy, but she took it. It's
not as if I make a habit of standing her up.

Relief, despair, when I finally unlocked
my door. I love that barn more than I ever
imagined loving bricks and mortar, but it's also
a grim reminder of the facts of my life. To the
outsider, my barn says, The Good Life. Glasses
of crisp Picpoul as the sun sets over the trees!
Dinner made of foraged organic vegetables
while the birds roost! Crystal-clear Cotswold
water, pulled fresh from the earth!

They have no idea how trapped I am. Even
if I told them what it's like with Mum, they
wouldn't believe me.

Later on I gave the workshop a bit of a tidy
and organized the whiteboard for tomorrow.
I didn't make dinner. When I walked into
the kitchen, I was assaulted by memories of
Sarah and me in that same space, cooking and
talking and laughing, our minds galloping

wildly into the future. And of course then I couldn't face cooking alone, in silence. So I ate some Bombay mix and went to bed. Letting Sarah go was the right thing to do, I reminded myself, while I was brushing my teeth. I noticed I had a minor suntan.

Then I lay under my skylight, stars winching slowly across the sky, congratulating myself on my fortitude, my determination, my willpower. Well done, mate. It wasn't easy but you had to do it.

Only, the longer I waited for sleep, the less I believed that.

For a while I got up and tried to watch television. Take my mind off things. But all I got was a news report about a terrible pileup on the M25, multiple fatalities and severe injuries, and before I knew it, there was a voice in my head asking me how I would feel if Sarah died. (Really helpful.) What if you had a call to say she'd been in a motorway pileup? it asked. Caught in a cartel shoot-out? Run over by a truck? Would you still feel like you'd done the right thing?

I turned off the telly and went back to bed, but the idea was there by then. Like a rusty hook in my consciousness. Pulling and dragging. If Sarah died, would you still think you'd done the right thing?

And that's the problem, Alex, because—if I'm honest with myself—I would not. If Sarah died, I would regret it for the rest of my life.

I've lived well these last two decades. Fought my way out of grief and into life. But I've allowed Mum to be more important than me, all that time, because I've felt I had no choice. What decent human being wouldn't look after his mother if she needed help? But something changed when I walked away from Sarah on the beach. Choosing Mum didn't feel right. And it still doesn't.

It's 3:58 A.M. Am literally praying for sleep.

Me x

CHAPTER FORTY-ONE

That man. He keeps staring at me."

I look at Mum, pressed back into her seat, her neck thrust forward like a turtle. Then I look at the man, who's vast, poor sod, absolutely enormous, spilling over three chairs and chain-drinking Diet Coke from a two-liter bottle. Above his head, a bluebottle bats at the window, again and again, like a child telling the same joke because it made someone laugh half an hour ago.

I watch the man for a while, but he doesn't look at Mum. He's reading an NHS leaflet entitled "Let's Talk."

"He's not staring at you," I whisper. "But we can go and sit over there if you'd prefer."

I point at a row of green chairs, facing away from this perfectly innocent man, but I know she won't go for it. At the end of the row, there's a mother with her baby asleep in a buggy, and Mum can't cope with children these days. Last month she locked herself in the toilet at her GP practice because a toddler was handing her Duplo bricks in the waiting room.

"I think I'll stay here," she says eventually. "Sorry,

Eddie, I don't want to make a fuss, but will you keep an eye on him?"

I nod, closing my eyes. It's too warm in here. Nothing to do with the sunshine outside; it's that flabby medical-waiting-room heat, fired by anxious breath and underused bodies.

"Are you missing the beach?" Mum says. She has on that tone she uses when she's worried she's annoyed me. Lighter than normal, full of overinflection. "Santa Monica?"

"Ha! No, not really. Did I tell you about it?"

She nods, her eyes skittering over to the Diet Coke man before returning to my face. "It sounded lovely," she adds, and I wonder what jet-lagged lie I told her about my day on that beach. I can't stand lying to her. It's hard not to take the view that life has betrayed my mother, so it feels extra sickening when I do the same. No matter that I do it for her own good.

Mum turns away and my thoughts return to the funeral procession I saw earlier, heading down past the green toward Frampton Mansell. The hearse had been full of wildflowers, bunches and sprays of them, toppling down over the sides of the wooden box as if on the banks of a stream. It was followed by three empty black cars. **Must be a young person**, I thought. The aged seldom had so many mourners. I wondered who they were off to collect. Which broken, desperate family was gathered in a house somewhere nearby, draining their coffees, adjusting their uncomfortable black clothes, and wondering, over and over again, **How can this be happening to us?**

I'd glanced sideways at Mum as the procession passed, hoping it wouldn't throw her off-balance.

I found her with an ugly expression on her face. "Looks like they're heading for Frampton Mansell," she observed, sounding oddly pleased. Spiteful, even. "Let's hope it's that girl who's died. Sarah." Then she looked at me, as if expecting me to agree.

I couldn't say anything for several minutes. I just breathed through my mouth—a sort of Eddie Emergency Response that I remember well from the weeks following Alex's death. I felt sick. Physically sick, a banding round my chest. I tried with every resource I had to bury what she'd just said, but I couldn't.

No wonder Sarah moved to the other side of the world, I thought weakly. How could she ever have survived here?

The bluebottle at the window falls silent for a moment, and I think, now, about how strongly Sarah would approve of wildflowers on a coffin. She brought bunches of them into my house during our week together. Filled almost every mug I own. "Is there anything more beautiful?" she asked, smiling down at them.

You, I thought. You're the most beautiful thing that has ever come into this house.

Save for my mate Baz, who works for the Natural History Unit in Bristol, Sarah's the first person I've met under sixty who knows much about wildlife. I remember her voice rising in excitement when I quizzed her on birds from that Collins Gem book. **Nuthatch! Stonechat!** Then her laughter, wonderfully dirty and full of life.

God, it hurts. It hurts in ways I never imagined.

I turn to look at Mum, to reinforce to myself that Sarah **is** the very last woman on earth with whom I could have a relationship. **This is your mother**, I tell myself. **Your mother, a mental health services user for nearly two decades. A woman who can't remember the textures of life, the rhythm of the world, because she's become so isolated. She needs you.**

Mum's pretending to rest her head in her hands, as if dead tired, but she's just watching the guy with the Diet Coke through splayed fingers.

"Mum," I whisper. "It's okay."

I'm not sure she even hears me.

When I went over to Alan's the other night, he said I should join Tinder. I said okay, because that's what he wanted me to say, and then had to go to the loo, as if to flush away, turdlike, the horror I felt. **Tinder?** Nobody warns you that life continues to be complicated after you've Done the Right Thing. That there is no reward, beyond some intangible sense of moral fortitude. I've been back eleven days now, and if anything, I feel worse than I did when I left Sarah standing on the beach.

Tinder! I mean, for fuck's sake!

"Where's Arun?" Mum whispers. "We've been waiting ages."

I check my watch. We've been waiting ten minutes.

"Do you think he's off sick, Eddie?" she asks. "Do you think he's left?" Her face clouds at the thought.

"No." I tuck her hand into my elbow. "I think he's just running late. Don't worry."

Mum's psychiatrist, Arun, is one of only two non-family members she can talk to without reaching overwhelm. The other is Derek, her community psychiatric nurse, who handles Mum better than any of us. She does have the odd visitor from elsewhere— the local vicar, Frances, pops in when she can, because these days Mum finds it too stressful to go to church with "all those people." And indeed Hannah Harrington, Sarah's sister, used to visit every now and then, although Mum hasn't mentioned her in a long time, so I wonder if those visits have dried up. But neither Hannah nor the vicar ever stayed for long. After about half an hour Mum would be up and cleaning, glancing anxiously at the clock as if she had somewhere to be.

Arun's ability to get through to Mum is partly because he's a really nice man, and great at his job, but partly because she has, I think, got a shy little crush on him. And of course he hasn't left. Nor is he off sick. They'd have canceled us if he were, probably sent out the community psychiatrist. But the idea has lodged itself in her head now, just like those infuriating thoughts about Sarah have lodged themselves in mine.

What if Sarah died? Would you still think you'd done the right thing? The question continues to seep into everything, like rising damp. Where has it come from? Why won't it go away?

Sarah is fine, I tell myself sternly. She would almost certainly be asleep now, thousands of miles away in her friend's little bungalow. Breathing in and out. Limbs soft, face quiet.

When I realize I'm imagining lying next to her, sliding a sleepy arm around her waist, I get up. "I'll go and check how much longer," I tell Mum.

The lady at reception knows I'm not asking for myself. SUE, her security pass says. "You'll be seen next," she says extra loud, so Mum can hear. There's a picture behind her of her family. A pleasant-looking man, two children, one wearing a lion costume. I wonder if Sue looks at families like mine and thinks, **Thank God I'm not in their shoes!** That's pretty much what my last girlfriend, Gemma, said when we split up. She ended things after three months because she couldn't handle me running off to deal with a Mum-related emergency once a week.

I felt bad about Gemma for a while—she was the third girlfriend in six years worn down by Mum's demands—but I bumped into her in Bristol a few months ago, holding hands with a bloke who called himself Tay and told me he did street art. He had a man bun. And I'd realized, as Gemma and I exchanged bland pleasantries on the pavement, that neither of us had ever been all that mad about each other anyway.

Mad about each other—like Sarah and me—that's how you have to feel. That's how good it's got to be.

When I sit back down, Mum's checking her hair in a pocket mirror. Her hairstyle has the contours of a rugby ball today. "It's a beehive," she says. "I used to have one in the sixties." She peers at it. "Do you think it's over the top?"

"Not at all, Mum. It's lovely."

In truth, the beehive is (a) hollow and (b) leaning to the right like the **Torre de Pisa**, but I know she's done it for Arun.

She puts her mirror away and starts doing something with her phone. After a few seconds I realize she's pretending to message someone so she can take sneaky photos of the poor guy in the corner, presumably to be used in evidence when he has brutally murdered her. If Arun Sopori doesn't come out soon, with his beautiful Kashmiri features and his warm smile, today is going to go very badly indeed. And I really need to get back to work.

Then: "Hello, Carole," says Derek's voice. He ambles in—Derek never strides—and shakes my hand, taking a seat on the other side of Mum. "How are you doing today?" He stretches his legs out in front of him and I feel her begin to relax as she tells him she's had better days, if she's honest.

"Storming hairstyle you've got there," he tells her, when she's finished.

"You think so?" She's smiling already.

"I absolutely do, Carole. Storming."

Thank God for Derek! Week in, week out he visits her. He's like a magician, I sometimes think—he can spot things nobody else can see; he can make her talk when no one else can get through. He's never once lost his cool, no matter how unwell she's gotten.

"Does your mother have a specific diagnosis?" Sarah asked one day. I'd just mowed the lawn of my clearing because I was hoping to lure her back to England with the smell of cut grass. When I'd finished, we'd sat down with some cold ginger cordial, and she'd sniffed the air happily. Then she'd just turned to me and asked that about Mum—straight out, no pussyfooting around, and I'd liked her even more.

Still, I hadn't wanted to answer, at first. I'd wanted to be the man with a Cotswold stone barn who bakes bread and makes ginger cordial and leads an extremely appealing life, not the man who has to field several phone calls a day from his mother. But it was a reasonable question, and it deserved a reasonable answer.

So I prepared myself to reel off the list of diagnoses she'd been given over the years—the chronic depression; the generalized anxiety disorder; the cluster-C personality disorder that hovered somewhere between anxious and dependent and obsessive-compulsive; the PTSD; the psychotic depression that **might** be bipolar—but when I opened my mouth, a great weariness washed over me. Somewhere along the line I had given up on labels. Labels gave me hope of recovery, or at least improvement, and Mum had been sick for nearly twenty years.

"She just struggles," I'd said eventually. "If my aunt wasn't with her this week, I imagine I'd have had to answer the phone quite a bit. Probably go and see her at some point."

I wish, now, I'd told her more. But what would that have achieved, other than to end our time together? We'd have worked out who each other was in minutes, and then I'd never have known what it felt like to be that happy. That **certain.**

"Mrs. Wallace." I look up; Mum's hands fly to her beehive/rugby ball. Then she tucks herself into my side, suddenly shy, as Derek and I lead her over to Arun and the open door.

CHAPTER FORTY-TWO

Several hours later I'm free.

I walk through an evening softened by misting rain, humming some tune or other. Mostly, I'm on footpaths, but from time to time I take a lane. Damp earth, damp tarmac, damp leaves. Damp Eddie. From time to time droplets fall from the edge of my hood.

I kick a stone along in front of me and think about the session with Mum today. Based on Derek's recent reports, Arun wants to tweak her medication, which I think is a good idea. It hadn't escaped my notice that she was sliding into paranoia—at first I'd thought it was perhaps just a temporary reaction to my absence, but Derek said he'd noticed warning signs before I'd gone away.

I learned many years ago that miracles don't happen, so I'm not expecting a monumental change, but with a bit of luck Arun's new cocktail will arrest a downward spiral and avert a crisis, and that's more than good enough for me. No matter how fantastic her mental health team are, how brilliant the research, how efficacious the treatments, they can't transplant Mum's brain.

The best thing was that she came away from the meeting in relatively good spirits: so good, in fact, that I persuaded her to go for tea and cake in Cheltenham. She had a large slice of flapjack and only suspected one man of plotting to murder her. She even managed to laugh at herself.

When I dropped her off so I could get back to the workshop, she told me I was the best and handsomest man on earth and that she was more proud of me than she could ever say.

So that was nice.

Later, Derek called me. "How are you doing?" he asked.

I told him: "Fine."

"Sure?"

He said that I had looked exhausted. "Remember, I'm always here if you're struggling, Eddie."

Half an hour later I reach Bisley and the heavens open. "Pleasant," I remark to a crow on a post. It flies off, presumably to somewhere nicer, and I feel a touch of envy. Mum might be heading out of danger, for now, but nothing about my life has changed. I'm not free, and I can't have Sarah. And nothing Derek can do for me—no strings he can pull within the mental health services—can change that.

• • •

"Right, Ed," says Alan, a few minutes later. He offers me the most severe expression he has, which is not at all severe. "I'm afraid this isn't good enough." Alan is one of the gentlest, warmest people I've ever met. Tonight he smells of strawberries and sourness, and his jumper is covered in pink stains. Lily had a tantrum involving strawberry yogurt when he told her he couldn't read her bedtime story.

I grin at him, although I can't remember a time I felt less jolly. "I know. Just give me another week or two to get over the business with . . ."

I can't say her name.

". . . with . . . the lady . . . and then I'll be on it."

The **lady**?

Alan is kind enough not to laugh.

I've been summoned to the pub to discuss my fortieth birthday, which is less than four weeks away. So far, I've organized nothing and Alan says he's "concerned." **I think I should check up on you,** he messaged yesterday. **Get some plans brewing & make sure you're not growing a beard.**

He's chosen the Bear in Bisley for the intervention. It's a lovely old pub, and it reminds us both of the glory days of our youth, but it's convenient for neither of us. We'll have to share an expensive taxi later, and Alan'll have to somehow pick up his car tomorrow. But he's moving to the village soon, and wants to check out the beer situation, and I was very happy to walk here after a day of hospitals and kitchen building.

Hannah Harrington lives only a few doors from here. I bumped into her in Stroud a couple of years back, in the health food shop of all places. I was buying something not particularly healthy, like banana chips, but she was carrying armfuls of oat bran and all sorts of other things that have become curiously indispensable to middle-class people. It was perhaps the fourth or fifth time I'd seen her since Alex died, and—as ever—I was struck by the remarkable similarities between twelve-year-old Hannah and grown-up Hannah.

I wondered how much my sister would have changed, if she'd lived.

Hannah had told me that she and her husband had had an offer accepted on a house in Bisley. We'd discussed house prices and builders, and then gone our separate ways. I wish she'd told me that Sarah had moved to America. I wish she'd said, "Hey, remember my evil big sister? She buggered off abroad, years ago, so you and Carole need never worry about bumping into her again!"

Alan puts a pint in front of me and sits down.

"Thinking about the lady?" he asks.

"Yes. Stop me."

He karate chops my forearm and says, "Stop it, Ed. Right now."

Then he looks at me, and I see in his eyes the

ghoulish fascination of the long-term married. "What were you thinking? Was anyone naked?"

I smile. "No."

"What, then?"

"Just stuff about how avoidable it all was. How I'd have been able to work it out in seconds, if only I'd known that she moved to America."

Alan looks thoughtful. He takes a good draw on his pint, and I notice that the yoghurty stains extend down his shorts. There's even a splodge of pink in his leg hair.

"Even if you had worked it out, though, you might not have stopped yourself," he says. "You told me you fell for her almost straightaway."

I think back to those first few minutes in Sarah's company. How smart and funny she'd been, how pretty. How I'd dragged on the joke about the sheep for far too long because I'd wanted to keep her talking.

"But I did stop myself. The moment I realized. And by then I was pretty far gone. Listen, you knob, I asked you to stop me thinking about her."

He chuckles. "Yes, Sorry."

Alan is the person people think I am. Easy in his own skin, troubled by little. The sort of man who's always on the edge of laughter, even when he's just missed a train (which he does frequently) or lost his wallet (ditto). We became friends the day I noticed him launching an exploratory finger up his nostril during our welcome speech at secondary school, and instead of blushing, he had grinned and carried right on. Later he had challenged me to a game of shithead and didn't mind in the slightest when I thrashed him.

We didn't discuss becoming best friends because we were too busy kicking footballs and pretending not to notice any of the girls, but best friends we became. Partners in crime; frequently in trouble. We were even suspended from school once, for concocting a vomitlike substance and throwing it out of the toilet windows where the rebellious teachers smoked, the ones who wore leather jackets and didn't have their hair cut often enough. I thought Mum would actually kill me, but when we got into the car, she started laughing. She often laughed, back then. "You're only boys," she said.

Nearly thirty years on, Alan and I probably seem unchanged.

Only I'm not the same as Alan anymore. That boyish, uncomplicated Eddie was almost certainly lost the first time I found Mum unconscious, puddled in vomit and surrounded by pill bottles. And if he wasn't lost then, he would have been extinguished maybe the second time, or the third, when I found her in the bath with newly cut wrists leaking red trails into the water. And if those first three attempts didn't finish me off, the fourth attempt would have done, years after she'd been discharged from the psychiatric hospital, long after I thought I was done with ambulance journeys and the Mental

Health Act and late nights fumbling for change by the hospital drinks dispenser.

Don't get me wrong: these last two decades haven't been all bad, not by any means. I've plenty of friends, a decent social life (for a barn-dwelling hermit), and I've even had girlfriends. I do a job I love, and I live in a beautiful place, and when I need to go away, I've a very patient aunt who comes to stay with Mum.

But then I met Sarah, and I remembered how life could feel. The lightness, the ease, the laughter. Life sung in a major key.

I've often wondered if I presented her with a counterfeit version of Eddie David during our week together. A happier, freer version. But I don't think that's what happened. I think she just got to see a version of me I'd long forgotten; a version that only she seemed able to revive.

"It's rough, Ed," Alan sighs, leaning forward to scrape off the yogurt spot on his leg. "I'm sorry."

Firmly, I tell him I'll get over it.

I take a long sip of beer and settle back in my chair, ready to talk about the problems Lily's been having at primary school, or the baffling news that our friend Tim has been cuckolded by his pregnant wife.

But Alan's not done with me. "Are you sure?" he asks. "Forgive me, Ed, but you don't look like you're getting over it. You look bloody awful."

He catches me unawares. "Yes, I'm sure," I say, although it sounds more like a question than a statement. "But regardless, what choice do I have? Me getting together with Sarah would finish Mum off. And I mean that quite literally."

Alan winces. "I know. I don't disagree. But that's not what I asked. I asked you if you were sure you were getting over it."

He looks straight at me, and I feel it. Right under my skin. Years and years of it, pressing desperately outward, contained only by thin dermal layers.

"No," I say, after a pause. "I'm not."

He nods. He knows.

"I'm on the edge. I'm on the fucking edge, and I don't know what to do."

I turn my pint round and round in circles, fighting the heat that's pushing at my eyes. "Not sleeping. Can't concentrate. All I can think about is Sarah. I just feel . . . well, desperate, knowing I've cut off any possibility of anything. And since LA, looking after Mum has started feeling impossible. I keep catching myself thinking, **I can't do this anymore.** But that's not an option, Alan, because what the hell is she supposed to do if I just flip out and run off? I . . . Fuck."

"Fuck," Alan agrees quietly.

I don't trust myself to speak.

Alan takes a sip of his pint. "I do often wonder if you need to get some extra help with your mum, Ed. Gia was telling me about some friend who's been caring for her husband for fifteen years. Awful story—he fell off his bike and now he's completely paralyzed . . . Anyway, this woman had a break-down last month. Just hit a wall. Couldn't do an-other minute. And it's not as if she's fallen out of love with him. She adores him."

He pauses, takes another sip. "Made me think about you, mate. I mean, it must be wearing you down in a serious way."

I make a noncommittal sound, because I don't want to have this conversation. Gemma was the last one who tried it—tried telling me that I would even-tually go under if I couldn't find a way of carving out more freedom for myself. I chose to take it as a criticism of my mother and we had a fight, but I knew, deep down, that she was probably right.

"There's nobody who can do what I do, though," I say now. "It's not like she needs someone to wash her, or make her food—she just needs a person she trusts at the end of the phone, or to come round if she goes into overwhelm. I take her shopping, I sort stuff out, I talk to her. I'm her buddy. Not her carer."

Alan nods, but I don't think he sees it in the same way. "Just think about it," he says. "But as for Sarah . . . You did the right thing, Ed. You did the **only** thing."

"Mmmm."

"Think about Romeo and Juliet. Or Tony and Maria."

Alan's love of musical theater delights me nor-mally, but I'm not in the mood for **West Side Story** tonight.

"They knew it was wrong to get together," he persists, "but they went for it anyway and then ended up dead. You've been a lot smarter than that. You've resisted, which takes much more courage."

"Well, that's great to know, Alan. Thank you. But the real problem is that I have to stop loving her and I don't know how."

Alan looks thoughtful. "I've often wondered how that works. Making yourself fall out of love with someone," he says. "What do you actually **do**? Why haven't Haynes published a manual on it?" His hayrick hair sticks crazily out from the sides of his head as he ponders the question. Alan's never had to stop loving anyone. He and Gia have been married for nine years, together for nineteen. Before her there was only Shelley, whose heart Alan (very guiltily) broke, and a small handful of girls from school with whom he was mostly just trying to subdue his never-ending teenage erection.

How **do** you just stop loving someone? The love I felt for Sarah wasn't just a version of something that already lived in me; it was something I built from scratch, something I grew. By the time we said good-bye, it was as tangible as she was.

How do I just kill it? Even if I let time wear it down, there would still be fragments scattered all around inside me. The unexpected earthiness of her laugh, the fan of her hair on a pillow. The sound of a sheep's baa, the sight of Mouse in her slim fingers.

"I have no idea how you stop loving someone," I

say eventually. Alan's watching me again. "I guess you just sit and wait for . . . I don't know. The intensity to fade? Right now, though, I feel like a pressure cooker."

"Maybe that's why so many poets have written about heartbreak. Helps them let off steam. Like bloodletting. Rapid discharge of overwhelming feelings."

"Right," I sigh. "Rapid discharge sounds good. Release."

There's a pause, and then a snort, and then we both start laughing. "If you want to take yourself off home for a bit of rapid release, I won't mind," Alan says.

He gets up and goes to the bar. I look at his ankles and smile. He is of normal build, Alan, but he has ankles so slender you can get a hand round them. He gets really cross when I do that.

The wine fridge hums. In a distant kitchen, someone is scraping plates.

I look at my watch: 8:40 P.M. I wonder what Sarah's having for lunch, and I can't stand it.

Alan returns with our pints and sits down, rubbing his hands with glee at the thought of the steaks he's just ordered, and I want more than anything to be him at this moment. To be Alan Glover, smelling lightly of yogurt, secure in his life, responsible only for the well-being of his lovely little girl.

"Just going to the loo," I tell him.

• • •

On my way back to the table, I notice that a couple has taken residence at a table in the corner. They're dressed in black and I can tell, straightaway, that something about them isn't quite right. They aren't talking, although the woman is holding on to the man as if they were in a strong wind.

At the same moment I realize the woman is crying, I realize I know her. I slow down, so I can get a good look at her, and after a few seconds I recognize Hannah Harrington. Sarah's sister. Less than two yards from me, curled into the side of a man I take to be her husband. Her face is red, disfigured with sadness, but I can see **her**. A shadow of Sarah. Just like she was on the beach when I left her—stunned, miserable, utterly silent.

Hannah doesn't spot me and I move quietly back to our table. I tell Alan about the funeral cars I saw heading to Sarah's village earlier on. Then, because my stomach is churning, I blurt out that if Hannah's crying, it must surely be someone Sarah's family knows very well. "Sarah could have flown back for the funeral," I whisper, and my voice has tipped just a bit too far toward madness. "She could be a few miles away from here, Alan!"

Alan looks alarmed. "Don't go looking for her," he says eventually.

Our steaks arrive soon after, and he ends up eating mine.

A little later on I get up to buy a round and see that Hannah and her husband have gone. I can't stop thinking about who might have died. For a terrible moment I even consider the possibility that it could have been Sarah herself.

It's irrational, of course, but as the evening passes I struggle to let it go. It fits far too comfortably with those intrusive thoughts I had when I got back from LA. That voice, asking if I'd still feel like I'd done the right thing if Sarah died.

I get embarrassingly drunk, and at some point I thump my fist on the table at the general hopelessness of things.

I am not the sort of man to thump a table. When Alan says he reckons he'll come back to mine to drink whisky and watch the Olympics, I don't argue. I'm not sure I'd leave me to my own devices if I were him, either.

CHAPTER FORTY-THREE

Dear You,

Enough: I have to let go of Sarah. Not
just tell myself to do it and then spend all
my time thinking about her—I have to stop
the thoughts as soon as they've begun. Because
they're not just unhelpful, they're dangerous.
Once they're out of the starting gates, they
spread faster than a virus and I find it almost
impossible to control them—and when I look
at Mum, I see how far they could take me.

So this is it, Hedgehog. It's time to exercise
that power of choice I like to bang on about.

Thank you for being my witness. As ever.

Me x

I reread the letter before reaching for an envelope,
as if trying to hold on to Sarah for a few moments
more. Early morning sun falls steeply through the
window, across the forest of detritus that lives on my
desk: dusty catalogs, invoices, a ruler, endless pencils

and offcuts, cold cups of tea. Through these obstacles a narrow finger of light makes it through to the rectangle of purple paper on which I've just written. It points at the letter, seems almost to trace along the words as the trees move outside. Then a cloud passes, gobbles it up, and the letter lies once again in the thin gray of morning.

I pull out a purple envelope, just as a creak overhead announces Alan's awakening. A muffled voice: "Ed? Oi, Ed!"

He fell asleep on the sofa while writing a text to Gia about the state of my mental health. **I need to keep an eye on him**, he'd written, before passing out. I finished the message and sent it to Gia, so she wouldn't worry. **He lost it in the pub**, I wrote. **Best that I stay over.** Gia is extraordinarily tolerant when it comes to Alan and me.

Alan snored from time to time. Team GB won bronze in the men's synchronized diving. I sat on the sofa, trying not to think about Sarah.

Sounds of hungover padding above my head. Alan'll be poking around in the kitchen now, like a hungry bear, sniffing out tasty things he can stick his paw into. He'll want a large cup of tea, at least four pieces of toast, and then a lift to work. Probably some clothes, too, because his are covered in strawberry yogurt.

I'll gladly provide these things, because Alan is a real friend. He knew I needed the company last night. He knew I'd be miserable about Sarah, and he also knew, somehow, that I'm not in a good place with Mum. The least I can do is make him toast.

I turn back to my letter, sliding it into a purple envelope and writing Alex's name on the front. Quietly, so that Alan won't hear me, I cross over to the drawers under my workbench. I open the one marked CHISELS.

Inside, there's a soft sea of purple paper. A sad treasure chest; my dark secret. The drawer's filling up again: some of the letters at the back are in danger of falling into the drawer below, where I really do keep chisels. Carefully, I slide them toward the front. It's stupid, really, but I hate the thought of any of them getting lost. Or bent, or crushed, or hurt in any way.

I breathe slowly, staring down at them.

I don't write all the time—maybe once a fortnight, less if I'm really busy—but this is still the third drawer I've filled in the past two decades. I scoop my hand in among them now, tender and ashamed. **What's wrong with him?** I imagine people saying. **Still hanging on to a dead girl? He should get help.**

It was a lady called Jeanne Burrows, a bereavement counselor, who suggested I write to my dead sister. I couldn't stand the thought of never being able to talk to her; it made me dizzy with panic. **Write her a letter**, Jeanne had suggested. **Tell her how you're feeling, how you miss her. Say the things you'd have said if you'd known what was coming.**

In those silent hours spent driving between the Crown Court, the psychiatric hospital, and my empty childhood home, I found comfort in those letters. I had friends, of course: I even had a new girlfriend back up in Birmingham, where I'd just finished my first year as an undergrad. Mum's sister, Margaret, phoned daily, and Dad came down from Cumbria to help organize his daughter's funeral. But nobody really knew what to do with me, nobody really knew what to say. My friends were well meaning but useless, and my girlfriend escaped as soon as she decently could. Dad deferred his own grief by spending most of the time on the phone to his wife.

I wrote the first letter in my empty room at halls, the day I drove up there to clear my stuff out. Mum was being treated in a secure unit at the time. There was no way I'd be going back for my second year.

But I slept, after writing that letter. I slept all night, and although I cried when I saw the purple envelope the next morning, I felt less . . . stuffed. As if I'd made a small puncture, allowed some of the pressure to escape. I wrote another letter that night, when I had unpacked back in Gloucestershire, and I never really stopped.

I've booked in to see Jeanne in a couple of days. She's still practicing out of her house on Rodborough Avenue. Her voice sounds exactly the same, and she didn't just remember me, she said she was **delighted** to hear from me. I said I wanted to see her because my involvement with Sarah Harrington had reopened some "old wounds," but I don't know if that's quite it. I just feel—have felt since I got back—like everything is wrong. Like I've arrived back in the wrong life, the wrong bed, the wrong shoes.

What's really alarming is the sense that everything's been this wrong, without my fully realizing it, for nearly twenty years.

I turn to look at my workshop, my safe house, my retreat. The place where I've hammered and sawed through fury and despair. Drunk hundreds of thousands of cups of tea, sung along to the radio, pulled out a raft of splinters, had the odd drunken bonk. I don't know what I would have done if I hadn't had this.

And it's Mum I have to thank for it, really. Dad, whose fault it was that I'd become fascinated with wood in the first place, was dead against me doing this for a living. During the ten years between him running off with Victoria Shitface (this was the name Alan made up for her at the time: it's never really lost traction) and Alex dying, Dad continued to interfere with my life and decisions as if he were still sitting at the head of our table. He went mad when I said I was considering a furniture-making foundation course instead of A levels. "You've an academic brain," he shouted down the phone. "Don't you dare waste it! You'll destroy your career prospects!"

In those days Mum was still capable of engaging with conflict. "So what if he doesn't want to be a bloody accountant?" she'd said, grabbing the phone from me. Her voice shook with anger. "Have you ever actually **looked** at what he makes, Neil? Probably not, given how rarely you come down here. But let me tell you, our son has an exceptional talent. So **get off his back**."

She bought me my first No. 7 jointer, a fine old Stanley. I still use it today. And so it's always her I'm grateful to, when I consider what I've got.

"**Bonjour**," Alan says, his voice a little woolly. He's standing at the bottom of the stairs, wearing pants and one sock. "I need tea, and toast, and a lift, Eddie. Can you help?"

An hour later we pull up at his house, right at the top of Stroud. I keep the engine running while he runs inside to find a suitable work outfit (he flatly rejected everything I own) and gaze down at the old cemetery falling away below me, a chessboard of loss and love. There's nobody there, save for a cat picking its way along a row of limey gravestones.

I smile. Typical cat. Why walk respectfully on the grass when you could walk disrespectfully on a human grave?

A church bell starts ringing somewhere—it must be nine o'clock—and I'm reminded suddenly of that funeral procession yesterday. The hearse, polished and quiet and disconcerting in every way. The careful set of the driver's face, the cascades of wildflowers trailing down the coffin, that heady fear that comes with any reminder of human mortality. I cross my arms across my chest, feeling suddenly queasy.

Who died? Who was it?

But then I remember the promise I made to my sister, a mere ninety minutes ago. No more thoughts of Sarah. Not now, not ever. And I draw a screen across that part of my mind, forcing instead a plan for the working day ahead. Number one: a bacon sandwich from the roadside café at Aston Down.

"Meow!" I call to the cat, but it's busy plotting the death of some poor shrew.

CHAPTER FORTY-FOUR

Six Weeks Later

Autumn is here. I can smell it in the air, rough and unprocessed and—I've always thought—oddly apologetic. As if it feels slightly embarrassed, dismantling the heady dreams of summer to make way for another cruel slog.

Although personally, I've never minded winter. There's something exquisitely unworldly about this valley when frost spikes the ground and the trees fling long shadows across the bare earth. I love the sight of smoke twisting out of a lone chimney, the fairy-tale pinch of light in a remote window. I love how my friends brazenly invite themselves over so they can sit in front of my fire and eat the hearty stews they seem to think I cook all the time just because I live in a rural barn.

Strangely, Mum always seems a little happier in the winter, too. I think that's because it's more acceptable to stay indoors once the temperatures drop. Summer is fraught with the expectation of increased socializing and outdoor activity, whereas in the winter her small existence needs little explanation or defense.

But today it's only September and I'm still in shorts as I march up the composty hillside of Siccaridge Wood. Shorts and a jumper I still can't bring myself to wash and debobble, because the last person to wear it was Sarah.

I walk a little bit faster. A mild burn spreads through my calf muscles as I stump on up the hill, too fast to let my feet sink into the layered mulch. I start singing Merry Clayton's part from "Gimme Shelter." The only people who can hear me singing about rape and murder being just a shot away are the birds, who probably thought I was mad already.

My voice reaches the final section of the song, where Clayton is basically screaming, and I start laughing. Life is not feeling all that tranquil right now, but refusing to think about—well, about unhelpful things—definitely gives me a breather.

The problem is, Jeanne Burrows is not really on board with my plan to block all thoughts of Sarah from my mind. My sessions with her make me feel so much better, so much less alone, and yet she is breaking my balls every week. I didn't imagine you could break someone's balls in a deeply kind, gentle, respectful way, but Jeanne seems to be doing just that.

Today's session, however, was unprecedented.

Just as I reached the end of Rodborough Avenue, where Jeanne lives, I saw none other than Hannah

Harrington reversing out of Jeanne's parking spot. She was concentrating on not hitting a neighbor's car, so she didn't notice me, but I got a good look at her. She looked not dissimilar to the last time I saw her: tearstained, tired, lost.

Of course, I wondered immediately why Hannah was seeing Jeanne, and before I knew it the old fear engine had fired up again. What if it was one of Sarah's parents who died? Sarah would be distraught. She told me in those letters how guilty she'd felt, all these years, insisting on living thousands of miles away. I decided it was my duty to help her.

"I want to call Sarah Harrington," I announced to Jeanne on arrival. "Can I do that here, with you?"

"Come and sit down," she said calmly. **Oh brilliant**, I imagined her thinking. **Here we go.**

Within a few minutes I had calmed down and accepted that I had no business calling Sarah Harrington, but it did inevitably lead to a conversation about her. Jeanne asked again if I felt that blocking all thoughts of Sarah was helping me let her go.

"Yes," I said stubbornly. Then: "Maybe." Then: "No."

We talked about the process of letting go. I told her I was fed up with being so bad at it, but that I didn't know what else to do. "I just want to be happy," I muttered. "I want to be free."

Jeanne laughed when I complained that there was not a manual for stopping loving someone. I admitted that that was actually Alan's joke, and then she threw me a neutral look and said, "While we're talking about setting ourselves free, Eddie, I wonder how you feel about that in relation to your mother? How do you feel when you imagine freedom from your duties to her?"

I was so shocked I had to ask her to repeat herself.

"How does the idea of lessening some of that burden feel?" Her tone was friendly. "That's how you described it last week. Let me see . . ." She peered at her notes. "A 'nightmarish burden,' you said."

My face blew warm. I pulled at a loose thread on her sofa, unable to look her in the eye. How dare she bring that up?

"Eddie, I want to remind you that there is no shame—none at all—in finding it hard. Family carers might feel great love and loyalty toward their relative, but they also experience resentment, despair, loneliness, and a whole range of other emotions about which they would not want the patient to know. Sometimes they reach a point where they need to take a break. Or even completely rethink the care arrangement."

I stared at the floor. **Back right off!** I wanted to shout. **This is my mother you're talking about!** Only nothing came out of my mouth.

"What are you thinking?" Jeanne asked.

I don't get angry very often—I've had to learn not to, for Mum's sake—but suddenly I was furious. Far too angry to appreciate what she was trying to do for me. To be grateful that she had waited weeks before bringing it up. I wanted to pick up the vase of peachy snapdragons on her mantelpiece and throw it at the wall.

"You have no idea," I said, to a counselor of thirty-seven years' experience.

If Jeanne was shocked, she didn't let it show.

"How dare you?" I went on, voice rising. "How dare you suggest I just run off and abandon her? My mother tried to kill herself four times! Her kitchen looks like a fucking hospital dispensary! She's the most vulnerable person I know, Jeanne, and she's my **mother**. Do you have a mother? Do you care about her?"

It took nearly half an hour for me to apologize and calm down. Jeanne asked kind and respectful questions, and I responded with curt monosyllables, but she kept going. Nudging me, with those clever bloody questions, closer and closer toward an acknowledgment that I was dangerously near to breaking point with Mum. With life. Nudging me toward a grudging acceptance that it might be my own grief that had stopped me admitting this.

Jeanne seemed convinced that Derek could help find a solution. "It's his job," she kept saying. "He's a community psychiatric nurse, Eddie, he's there for both of you."

And I kept replying that there was no way I could hand my mother over to Derek. However wonderful he was. "I'm the only person she wants to call when she needs help," I said. "There's nobody else she'd trust."

"You don't know that for certain."

"But I do! If I told her she couldn't call me—even if I said she couldn't call me as **often**—she'd either take no notice and carry on as before, or she'd become dangerously ill. You know her history. You know I'm not just being pessimistic."

By the time our hour was up, we had made no real progress, but I had promised I'd continue next week without any tantrums.

Jeanne laughed. She said I was doing really well.

I reach the top of the hill, finally, arriving underneath the beech tree I've come to check. (It's meters from the mystery welly.) Back in June, when I was tramping the countryside, thinking angry and confused thoughts about Sarah, I noticed it was suffering dieback—only it's looking much worse now. I'm guessing some sort of beetle, as there's no obvious pathogen in the bark, but it's definitely a goner. I rest a hand on the trunk, saddened to imagine this magnificent beast felled by a snarling chain saw.

"Sorry," I tell it, because it feels wrong to say nothing. "And thank you. For the oxygen. And everything."

I check the surrounding trees (the welly is still there) and then walk back down the hill, hands in pockets. My brain keeps trying to slide me back in the direction of Sarah, and her sister's visit to a grief counseler, but I resist. I make myself think about the tree instead. The tree is a problem I know how to solve. I'll call Gloucestershire Wildlife Trust tomorrow, see if they'd like some help bringing it down.

By the time I get back to my barn, I'm feeling quite normal again.

Then I step inside and find my mother standing by my drawer of purple letters. My secret drawer of purple letters, which nobody on earth other than Jeanne knows about. And I realize that Mum is reading—**she is reading quite calmly**—one of my letters to Alex. She holds it in one hand, an ugly expression on her face.

I have to take a moment to be certain this is really happening. To be certain that my mother—my dear mother—is committing a breach of privacy on this level. But at that moment Mum turns the letter over, so she can read the back of the page, and I know there's no doubt.

Disbelief melds slowly into fury.

"Mum?" I say. My hand is clamped to the doorframe like a bench vice.

In one movement she slides the letter behind her and turns to me.

I reread in my head the text message I sent her before going out: **I'm going for a walk. Just to warn you, I'll be leaving my phone, for a bit of peace. But I'll be back in a couple of hours.**

I always deliberately overestimate the time it'll take me to do something. She panics otherwise.

"Hi, darling!" It's that voice again, the one she does when she's pushed me too far. Only today it's even higher. "You were very quick."

"What are you doing?"

"I . . ."

There is a thick, panicked silence as she weighs up her options. Everything is still. Even the trees outside seem to have paused, as if waiting for confirmation of treachery. But she can't do it. She can't tell me the truth. "I could hear something," she says, and her voice is so full of inflection she could be on children's television. "It sounded like a mouse. Have you had trouble with mice recently, Eddie? It was near here. I've just been poking around . . . I've opened a few drawers. I hope you don't mind . . ."

She continues in this vein until I shout— No, I actually bellow, "HOW LONG HAVE YOU BEEN READING MY LETTERS?"

There is a bottom-of-the-sea silence.

"I did find some letters, just a second before you arrived," she says eventually. "I haven't read them, though. I took a look at one and thought, **Oh, this has nothing to do with me**, so I was just putting it back when—"

"**Don't lie to me!** How long have you been reading my letters?"

Mum's hand flies to her face, and she starts to take

off her glasses, but then changes her mind, leaving them skewed across her nose like a child's seesaw. I look at her and I don't see my mother. Only rage, a giant hotplate of fury.

"How long have you been reading my letters?" I ask, for the third time. I don't think I have ever spoken to her in this tone. "And don't lie," I say. "Not again. Seriously, Mum, do not lie to me."

I'm wholly unprepared for what comes next. I'm expecting weeping, my mother slumped on the floor begging forgiveness, when suddenly she turns, sweeping the letter into the air as if it were a parking ticket or some other insult to her existence. It zigzags slowly toward the floor. "Like you've lied to me?" she says. "Like you lied to me about wanting to go to LA for a 'holiday'? About wanting to see your friend Nathan, do a bit of surfing? Like you lied to me about Alan having an 'emergency' the day you got back?"

With a deliberateness I find mesmerizing, she moves forward and plants her hand on the bench that runs down the center of this part of the workshop. "Like you lied to me about that . . . that **girl**?" She stares wildly at me, as if searching for her son in the face of a serial killer. "How could you? How could you have **slept** with her, Eddie? **How could you betray your sister like that?**"

She must have been reading my letters for months. No wonder she's been so paranoid and clingy since I got back from LA. And no wonder she tried everything in her power to stop me going over there in the first place. Usually when I tell her I'm planning a trip, she looks pleased, because it allows her to convince herself I'm still having a life. This time she behaved as if I were emigrating to Australia.

"That girl," she adds, shuddering. She looks like she's talking about a rapist or a pedophile, not Sarah Harrington. Although I guess that to Mum there's no moral distinction. "I meant what I said that day. I hope it was her in that hearse."

"Jesus **Christ**, Mum!" I breathe. My voice is soft with wonder. "After all you've been through, you wish the same pain on someone else? Are you for real?"

She makes a dismissive noise with her mouth. My mind leaps in all directions, finding clues everywhere. This is why she's started to become ill again. She has known about Sarah for months.

"Was it you who called her?" I ask quietly. "On the phone? Was it you who sent her that threatening message? Is that why you wanted to get a new phone back in July?"

I've started getting those marketing calls, she'd said. They're really stressing me out, Eddie. I need a new phone number.

"Yes. It was me who called her. And I don't regret it." She's wearing a pink jumper. For some reason the pink makes this ugliness all the more shocking.

"And did you turn up at her old school that day? Did you lurk about on the canal path near her parents' house when she came down to visit?"

"Yes." She's almost **shouting**! "Somebody had to do something. I could not have her infect you. You're all I have left!"

"Somebody had to do something," she repeats, when I fail to reply. "And you obviously weren't going to. Moping around like that, telling your poor sister how much you **loved** the woman who killed her . . ." She trails off. She's hissing again. I stop hearing the words. All I can think is, **Do you have any idea what I have gone through to keep you safe from this? How lonely I've been? Do you have any idea what I have sacrificed for the sake of your sanity?**

It comes to me at some point that she has stopped talking. Her eyes are wide and glassy with tears.

"How did you get Sarah's phone number?" I hear myself asking, although I know the answer. "How did you know she was at her old school that day? Have you been looking at my phone, too?"

She tells me yes. "And it's your fault, Eddie, so don't you get angry with me. I had to intervene, somehow. I had to try to protect Alex from . . . from **this**."

A tear escapes her eye, but her voice remains firm. "It's your fault," she repeats. "You who loves to talk about choice! You had a choice, and you chose that woman. That **girl**."

I shake my head, sickened. Her hatred is as livid and vital as it was in the weeks following Alex's death, intact after all these years.

"It's your fault," she repeats once more. "And I will not apologize."

And with that I feel a rupture in my skin—those layers, so thin and strained, so many years, just give way and it all hemorrhages out. The resentment, anger, loneliness, anxiety, fear, whatever—you name it, it's all storming out like a burst water main. I know in that moment that I cannot carry on like this. I'm done.

I lean against the door, exhausted. And when my voice comes out, it's oddly level, as if I'm reading the shipping forecast.

"No," I say blankly. (**Bay of Biscay: good.**) "No, Mum, you're not blaming me. I am not responsible for your actions. I am not responsible for how you feel, or what you think. It all comes from you. None of it is mine. You chose to read my letters. You chose to harass Sarah. You chose to turn what's happened to me in the last few months—which, for the record, has been hell—into some sort of grand betrayal. You did that all on your own; I didn't do a thing."

She starts to cry in earnest, although she still looks furious.

"I am not responsible for your illness, Mum. Nor is Sarah. I have done my best for you—my very best—while you've invaded the only tiny bit of privacy I thought I had left."

She shakes her head.

"Yes, I met Sarah, and yes, I fell for her. But I gave her up the moment—the **second**—I found out. And everything I've done since then has been in your best interests. Not mine, **yours**. And you're still blaming me?"

I watch her consider her response. She's starting to panic. It's not that she's listened to what I've said, or thought about it, or (God forbid) realized that I might have a point; it's more that she's used to me having given way by this stage, and it's beginning to dawn on her that I won't.

So she does what I knew she'd do, eventually: she recasts herself as victim.

"Okay," she says, and the tears begin to stream down her face. "Okay, Eddie, it's my fault. It's my fault that I have this awful, miserable life, that I'm trapped in my house, taking all that horrid medication. It's all my fault."

She watches my face, but I don't move a muscle. "You tell yourself whatever you like, Eddie, but really you have no idea how hard my life is."

Given that I've been looking after her for nineteen years, I think this is a little unfair.

We stand like two pawns in a chessboard face-off. Mum breaks eye contact first, doubtless to make me feel like the aggressor. She looks wretchedly down at the bench, tears squeezing and dripping into the deep ruts and saw marks below.

"Don't leave me, Eddie," she says eventually, like I

knew she would. "I'm sorry I did what I did. I'm just devastated about you and . . . her. It's destroyed me."

I close my eyes.

"Don't leave me, Eddie," she repeats.

I move round the bench and hug her. A tiny sparrow of a human being, so easily crushed. I hold her, rigid, and think of my ex-girlfriend Gemma. This was the moment she could never truly understand. The moment when, even after Mum had pushed me to the outer edge of my capabilities, it was still **my** job to comfort her, to tell her everything was okay. The capitulation was totally inexplicable to Gemma. But I suppose that, like most people, she's never had the experience of being responsible for someone else's mental well-being. She's never lost her sister, and then, nearly, her mother.

This time, though, it's different. I'm hugging Mum because I have to, but inside, the landscape has already changed.

It's raining by the time I get her into the Land Rover and drive her home. The sky is stuffed with gray clouds, swarming quickly over each other like angry thoughts. I apologize silently to Sarah. Wherever she is. **I don't wish you dead**, I tell her. **I wish you only happiness.**

In Mum's house, I give the heating a boost and make her some toast before she goes to bed. I give her a sleeping pill and hold her hand until she's asleep. I have never had the experience of watching my own child sleep, but I imagine it's a similar feeling. She looks, somehow, both lost and peaceful as she lies there, curled against my hand like a safety blanket, twitching occasionally, her breath barely audible.

Then I step outside and call Derek, and I leave a message on his answerphone, saying, in a very matter-of-fact way, that I have hit a wall and need his help.

On returning home, I watch three episodes of some Netflix series and—exhausted but unable to sleep—spend most of the rest of the night on my garden bench, wrapped in my duvet, having a one-way conversation with Steve the squirrel.

CHAPTER FORTY-FIVE

December—Three Months Later

Dear You,

Well, ho, ho, ho! Merry bloody Christmas.

I'll be thankful for the end of this year.

This is my first letter to you in more than three months. I guess I've had a lot to think about. I've also been very busy trying to effect change with Mum without her realizing. That's been Derek's plan: liberate Eddie by stealth. He's been magnificent, of course.

He set up a meeting with Frances, the vicar who's been visiting Mum for years. She said there are a few people locally who are happy to visit isolated parishioners. Derek said that the idea was to establish a friendship between Mum and a volunteer—however long it took—so that eventually she'd trust them enough to want them to take her shopping, or to the odd medical appointment. Someone other than me she could call, someone to open her world up, just a chink.

So a chap called Felix is visiting Mum, alongside Frances, once a week. Felix is a Gulf War veteran. Lost his arm out there. Then his wife left, because she couldn't cope, and then he lost his son in Iraq in 2006. So Felix knows about pain and loss. And yet, you know what, Hedgehog? He's so jolly! I've only met him twice, but he seems like the most positive chap. Listening to him and Mum is quite something—her response to just about everything is negative, whereas his is unfailingly upbeat. Sometimes when he's talking, I can see her thinking, **Is he completely mad?**

"Give her another few weeks," Derek said to me the other day. "I don't think she's far off going out of the house with him."

Derek even persuaded her to spend Christmas with her sister so I could have a break.

So . . . slowly but surely, I'm getting a bit more space. A bit more oxygen. I get glimpses of myself, from time to time—how I was before all of this. How I was during that week with Sarah. How I was when I was young. And they feel good.

Anyway! Here I am, on Christmas Day, in

Alan's new spare room in Bisley. It's 5:45 A.M.
and Lily's already up, pounding on Alan and
Gia's door. I went mad and bought her a whole
stocking's worth of presents. Alan says I'm a
selfish turd and that I've shown him up.

For now, though, I'm looking out of the
still-to-be-curtained window at a gunmetal sky
and I'm thinking about you. My dearest, most
precious Alex.

I have no idea if you're there. If you've stood
at my shoulder all these years, reading the
words I've written to you, or if you've been
no more than a vibration of spent energy.
Whatever you've been, though, I hope you have
somehow known how dearly loved you were,
how desperately missed.

Without you, or these letters, I don't know
if I'd have made it. In death you were as in
life: kind, colorful, warm, a friend. I felt you,
through these purple pages. Your vitality
and silliness, your nosiness, your goodness,
your innocence, your sweetness. You kept me
putting one foot in front of the other. You
helped me breathe when life was strangling me.

But the time has come for me to go it alone,
as Jeanne says. To stand on my own two feet.
And so, my little Hedgehog, this is to be our
last letter.

I am going to be okay. Jeanne is certain of

it, and—actually—I am, too. I have to be, really; I see every day in our mother what the alternative looks like.

I am even going to give in to Alan's insistence that I start dating. I don't really want to, but I accept that I have to at least give myself the chance of loving someone else.

Because that's the thing: Mum can't change, but I can. And I will. I will march on through winter, I will finish my commissions, and I'll take on more. I'm going to start offering summer workshops for young people. I'm going to do this stupid Tinder thing. I'm going to get fit, too, and get better at stonemasonry, and be a stupendous godfather to Lily. And I'm going to do all of this with a smile on my face, because that's the person people think I am, and that's the person I want to be again.

That's my promise, Hedgehog. To you, and to myself.

I will never forget you, Alex Hayley Wallace. Not for a day. I will love you until the end of my life. I will always miss you, and I will always be your big brother.

Thank you for being there. In life and in death.

Thank you, and good-bye, my darling Hedgehog.

Me xxxxxxxxxxx

CHAPTER FORTY-SIX

Early March—Three Months Later

The day my life changes forever, I'm gearing up for my first Tinder date. I feel quite stupid with nerves. (It doesn't help that Alan is texting me on the hour, every hour, to check I'm not backing out.) She is called Heather, and she has nice hair, and she seems smart and funny. But I still don't want to go. I actually caught myself earlier, wondering if I could hammer a nail through my hand so I'd have the excuse of an afternoon in the emergency room.

I have not admitted this to Alan.

It's also Mum's sixty-seventh, so I've taken her for lunch in Stroud. We're in Withy's Yard, which has always been a safe place for her—presumably because it's hidden up an old stone alleyway, visible to almost nobody—and today she's full of chat. Felix took her shopping yesterday, and he's better at it than I am. His only downfall is that he can't carry as many shopping bags because he has only one arm.

In all honesty I'm only half listening, because I'm

busy imagining tonight's terrible silences and oddly pitched laughs—so it takes me a little while to realize Mum's stopped talking.

I look up. She's frozen, staring off to her right, soupspoon hovering inches from the bowl. I follow her line of vision.

I don't recognize them, at first. They just look like two middle-aged people eating salads. She's wearing a checked shirt and is talking on a mobile phone. He is wearing a cord jacket, and he's watching her. Like Mum, both of them appear to have stopped eating. I feel a vague shift of recognition, looking at the man's profile, but nothing more.

But as I glance back at Mum, I know exactly who they are. The only people who could have this sort of effect on her. Her spoon has been dropped into the soup now; its handle is slowly disappearing like the stern of a sinking ship.

I look back at Sarah Harrington's parents. I do recognize them. Of course I do; they often came to pick up Alex for playdates, or to drop little Hannah off for the afternoon. I remember them always being friendly. So much so that I sometimes wanted to go and play in Frampton Mansell, too. They seemed so solid together; a proper family, whereas mine was made up of a father hundreds of miles away with a new baby on the way, and a mother crippled by bitterness and depression.

I have two distinct thoughts: First, what am I going to do with Mum? She cannot be here, two tables away from Michael and Patsy Harrington. And second, if it's not Michael or Patsy Harrington who died last year, **who was it?**

I distinctly hear the woman saying, "We're on our way." And then they're both up and gone, not pausing even to straighten up their chairs or apologize to the lady behind the café counter. Sarah's mother is pulling on her coat as she hurries down the alleyway toward the High Street. Mum and I sit still for a few moments, silent amid the hum of conversation and clinking cutlery. It's not until the milk steamer starts screeching that we look at each other.

In the end we go to the farm shop on the Cirencester Road to get some nice soup to have at Mum's: after the Harringtons left, she said that her birthday lunch was ruined and she wouldn't eat any more.

The extent of our conversation about them has so far been this:

Me: "Are you okay?"

Mum: "I don't want to talk about it."

I haven't pushed her. But I can't think about anything else. **Sarah's parents.** The people who made her. Where were they off to? What was wrong? It didn't look like a good-news sort of call.

Sarah looks like her mother. Although, actually, she looks like her father, too. I could have stared at their faces for hours, scouring them for tiny details of her.

We get back to Mum's and I heat the soup, put

some beautiful-smelling sourdough under the grill, but I know she's not going to eat. She seems angry at me, although I'm not sure why. Was I meant to go over and punch Sarah's parents for having created her? I stand in Mum's kitchen feeling hollow and uneasy, wondering again who died last August. At the end of her garden, under the plum tree, there's a little pool of gold where celandines jut bravely through patchy grass. I remember those wildflowers on the coffin and have to have very stern words with myself about the direction these thoughts are taking.

As predicted, Mum won't eat. "They've ruined my day," she repeats. "I've no appetite now."

"Okay," I say. "Well, I'm going to eat mine. You can always heat yours up again if you want it later."

"I'd get food poisoning. You can't reheat twice."

I'm about to say, "Mum, it's tomato soup!" but I desist. It's pointless.

So, solo spoon chinking against china, I eat my soup, soaking in big chunks of buttered sourdough. I finish, wash up, offer Mum her present, which she says she'll open later, and eventually get my coat.

"I can stay and talk if you want," I say. Mum is burrowed into the corner of her sofa like a cat.

"I'm fine," she says stiffly. "Thanks for coming."

I go over and kiss her. "Bye, Mum. Happy birthday."

I pause by the door. "Love you."

I'm at the front door when she calls, "Eddie?"

"Yeah?"

I go back in, and this is the moment that will change everything, although I don't know it yet.

"There's something you should know," she says. No eye contact.

I sit warily on the chair opposite her. Over her shoulder is a photo of Alex on a swing, shortly after she started primary school. She's screaming with happiness as she flies toward the photographer. Totally ecstatic. Over the years I have wondered if perhaps Mum got pregnant deliberately, to try to stop our father leaving—the affair with Victoria Shitface had been going on for a long time apparently—but whenever I look at that picture, I remember that it doesn't matter. Alex brought nothing but joy to our lives, with or without Dad.

"Seeing the Harringtons earlier has ruined my day," Mum repeats after a pause. She bites a fingernail.

"I know," I say tiredly. "You said earlier."

She looks around her, runs a hand along the edge of her side table, checking for dust. "I don't know how they can forgive that daughter of theirs . . ."

I stand up, ready to leave again, but something in her face makes me sink back down onto the arm of the chair. She knows something.

"Mum, what was it you wanted to tell me?"

"Hannah's turned out well, at least," Mum says, ignoring me. "She still visits me, you know. She still cares, even if the parents don't." She pauses, alternately clenching her fists and splaying out her fingers. "Although in truth I haven't seen her since just before Christmas. We had a bit of a set-to."

"What about?"

Mum continues to look anywhere but at me. "About that witch of a sister of hers."

"Sarah?" I lean forward, staring at her. "What did she say about Sarah?"

Mum offers a little shrug. Her face is jammed tight and I'm suddenly petrified of what she's hiding.

"Mum. . ?" I can feel my heart pounding. This has something to do with Sarah's parents, rushing out of the café today. "Mum, please tell me."

Mum sighs. She untucks her legs so that she's sitting formally on the sofa, as if being interviewed. Her hands are folded tidily in her lap. "Hannah came over just before Christmas. She told me she had some news I might find difficult. Well, she wasn't wrong there."

She stops, as if unable to find the words, and I begin to feel sick. What happened to Sarah? **Oh God, what happened to Sarah?** My hands scrabble like spiders, although what they're clutching for, I don't know.

"What did she tell you?" I ask.

Mum doesn't say anything.

"Mum, it's very important that you tell me."

She clenches her jaw and her temples bulge. I can't remember the last time I felt so anxious. Eventually, she says, "Sarah's moved back to England. She moved back in August last year."

Blood rushes to my face, and I lean back in the chair. I thought she was going to tell me . . . I thought she was going to say—

I've wondered, again and again, who that funeral was for. Whose life was being mourned and celebrated by those beautiful wildflowers. I've done my best to talk myself down from paranoid theories, but those insidious questions never quite went away. **What if she died? What if it was Sarah in the hearse?**

Sarah is alive and well. She's in England.

It takes a while for all of these words to register. "Hang on," I say, sitting up. "Mum—did you say she moved back here? To **England**?"

Mum springs out of the sofa with an energy I seldom see. She stands in front of me, her tiny frame rigid with anger. "How can you look so pleased?" she hisses. "Look at your face, Eddie. What's wrong with you? She—"

"Where is she?" I interrupt. "Where has Sarah been living?"

Mum shakes her head and walks over to the window. "With her parents, from what I gather," she mutters. After a moment she turns round and walks back to the sofa, looking at Alex's photo. I suspect this is for my benefit. **Just look at your poor sister.**

"Living with her parents, like some sort of parasite. Penniless and . . . apparently . . . pregnant." She shoots a hand up to her mouth, as if she hadn't meant to say this. After a pause, she sits back down, closing her eyes and sinking back into the sofa. She shudders. "I mean, if at her age you still haven't got your act together, then what hope is there?"

I stare at her. "**Pregnant?** Sarah's pregnant?"

I feel a pain so sharp it's as if she's guided a blade between my ribs.

Mum doesn't answer.

"**Mum!**"

Just once, and with palpable disgust, she nods. "Pregnant," she confirms.

"No," I say, although the word doesn't quite make it to my mouth.

No. No, no, no.

Sarah can't be having another man's child. Mum slides out of focus and my head begins to explode with misery, a hundred different shades of it, spattering in all directions. But then the roller coaster dips, yet again, and another sensation bursts in: hope. The speed at which I'm feeling all these things is dizzying. But the hope stays—two seconds, three, four, five . . . It doesn't go away. **It could be mine**, I'm realizing. **It could be mine.**

"She came back because her grandfather died," Mum says tightly. "That funeral procession we saw was probably for him."

I register relief, somewhere, that it was her grandfather, but I'm far too shocked to feel guilty about such a thought. Sarah is pregnant, and it could be my child.

"What else do you know, Mum? Please tell me."

Mum picks up her still-full soup bowl and takes it to the kitchen. I follow her like a faithful dog. "Mum."

"It was Hannah who called her sister with the bad news," she says eventually. Her voice is barely audible. "Apparently the shock of hearing Hannah's voice on the phone almost killed her. Walked out into a road, nearly got hit by a truck, stupid girl. But"—she puts down her soup bowl and gazes around her spotless kitchen—"for better or worse, the truck swerved, so she stayed in one piece."

Mum stops. She's becoming agitated; her breathing is shallow and she can't stand still. Neither can I. Sarah is here in England, and she's pregnant. I follow her back to the lounge, where her breathing gets worse.

With a mechanical detachment I start talking her through one of Derek's breathing exercises. I guide her into long, slow out breaths, and I wonder why she's speaking up now, after having kept all this secret for so many months. It's not in her interest to be telling me Sarah's back, let alone pregnant. Mum hates the idea of me even thinking about Sarah Harrington.

It's got something to do with Sarah's parents, I think. It's something to do with them leaving the café at a run. I stare desperately at Mum as she gets her breathing back under control. **Tell me!** I want to yell. **Tell me everything!** Instead I go with a mild, "And do you know anything else? About how she is? How things have been?"

"I believe she has been in a very depressed state," Mum says, eventually. "Wouldn't tell any of them who the father was."

Hope starts to bud.

"The funeral was the first time she had seen Hannah in nearly twenty years. Hannah told me she and her sister . . . they . . . agreed that there had been enough loss. They agreed to patch things up."

Mum looks disgusted by the words coming out of her mouth, and I see now why she's fallen out with Hannah. Years and years, Mum's managed to keep Hannah on her side: it must have felt like a terrible defection.

"So Sarah's been living in Frampton Mansell all this time? Six months?"

Mum nods, glancing over at me. "I take it you haven't seen her then." I think it's probably fairly clear from my face that I have not.

"Are you absolutely certain she's pregnant, Mum?" My words get caught in a dry part of my throat.

Mum looks over at me, and her face clouds with disappointment. She can see what this means to me. "I'm certain."

"When is it due? The baby?"

"I don't know." Mum twists her hands. I can tell she's lying.

Whatever it is that's prompted her to tell me all this is waging a terrible war in her head. She starts the breathing exercise again.

"You really have no idea when it's due?" I prompt. I can't bear it. "Not even a vague clue? I'm going to find out anyway," I add. "So you might as well tell me."

Mum closes her eyes. "February 27. Six days ago," she says eventually. "Which means that the child must have been conceived in June last year." She flinches as the words come out of her mouth.

Absolute silence.

"And nobody knows who the father is?"

"Just some stranger, I'd imagine," Mum says primly, but she doesn't mean it. She knows perfectly well what these dates signify.

I'm shaking as I crouch down in front of her, and my legs aren't working, so I end up sliding sideways, onto my bum. I sit on the carpet in front of her like a child at story time. "Are you telling me this because you think it's mine? Mum? Is that what you think?"

She opens her eyes and they film with tears. "I can't let Sarah Harrington have my grandchild," she says, in a tiny voice. "Eddie, I can't cope with that . . . But I . . ." Her voice shakes. "But I can't stop thinking the child might have been born, by now, and it could be . . ."

I watch her, even though I can't see her anymore. Sarah. My baby. Everything sways like a cornfield.

I try to organize my thoughts. "Why do you think

her parents left the café so quickly? Do you think something bad has happened?" I have to lean heavily on my right arm to stay upright.

From somewhere in front of me, Mum's voice says, "I don't know. But I've been extremely worried about it ever since. That's why I decided to tell you." She resumes her long exhales for the third time.

I put a shaking hand on her knee while she takes a few breaths. I have to find Sarah. "Mum . . . ," I say. "Help me."

After an interminable pause, Mum takes a longer, deeper breath, and nods over toward the phone, sitting on the side table. "The Harringtons' number is probably still there. In the address book."

I pull myself up and cross the room, knowing how huge this gesture is, knowing what it will have cost her. She's still a good person, my mother. Still capable of love, no matter how bleak her life has become.

A great many years have passed since I last felt that way about her.

The number's still there. Under "Nigel Harlyn," an old accountant friend of Dad's, and "Harris Plumbing of Cirencester." Scribbled in by a busy mother from another lifetime: **Patsy Harrington—Hannah from playgroup's Mum—01285 . . .**

I start to write the number into my phone, but my phone—of course—already knows it. Sarah gave me this number last June, when this baby must have been no more than a few cells.

"Mum," I say carefully. "I have to go. Okay? I have to go and find out what's happened. If you need someone, you've got the emergency outreach number, and you've got Derek's number, and you've Felix's number. But you'll be okay, Mum. You'll be fine. I have to go. I have to—" My voice thins out. I kiss my mother on the head, and walk, on trembling legs, to the car.

And Mum says nothing. She knows it could be her grandchild, and that's bigger than anything else. She can't say it—would rather die than admit it—but she actually wants me to go and find out.

"You'd better not be calling me because you're bottling," Alan says, when he picks up the phone. "Seriously, Ed—"

"Sarah's had a baby," I tell him. "Or she's about to have one. And I'm certain it's mine. I've tried to call her parents, but there's nobody home. I need Hannah's mobile number. Do you have it?"

There's a long pause.

"What?" Alan says. He's eating something, as always. Alan works at an architect's practice. His colleagues have never quite been able to believe the extent of the provisions he keeps on his desk "in case of trouble." "Are you serious?"

"Yes."

"Wow," he says, after careful consideration.

"I need Hannah's number."

"Oh, mate, you know I can't give out a client's details." Alan recently drew up plans for a utility room at the back of Hannah's house in Bisley. We agreed, when he told me about the job, not to discuss it, but the agreement is now suspended.

"Gia and Hannah used to go for coffee after yoga," I say quickly. (About seven years ago.) "Gia would have her phone number. You're just saving time by getting it from the computer that is right in front of your face, rather than calling your wife. Alan, seriously, give me the number."

Alan starts whispering, as if that's going to make him less conspicuous in a silent office. "Fine. But can you also text Gia asking for it, so if I was ever questioned about it, I could say, 'No, he got the number through my wife.'"

I'm almost yelling. "Give me the fucking number, Alan!"

He does.

"I guess you won't be going on that date, then," he sighs.

Hannah's phone is switched off. She sounds tantalizingly like Sarah in her voice mail, only more brisk, more businesslike. Probably how Sarah sounds when she's speaking at a conference, or on the telly.

A child. My child. My head swims again. The sky is dirty white. My hands are still shaking.

I look at my watch: 3:45 P.M. It dawns on me that Hannah's children must have finished school. And that, with any luck, she or her husband will just have picked them up. Feelings are pitching through me faster than I can identify them. I know only that I have to find her.

I start up the Land Rover and head for Bisley. I try not to think about Mum, home alone, wrestling with what must feel like a nightmare. But then I think, **Three months, she's known. Three bloody months!**

She told me in the end, I remind myself, because I have to. Hating Sarah has prevented Mum from feeling the deepest pain—the most unbearable pain—for a very, very long time. It's been her best medication. That nod toward the phone, that reluctant blessing, is a gesture I must not underestimate.

The winter countryside flashes by, lank and dripping. I try to imagine Hannah coming face-to-face with her sister, after so many years of Mum whispering bile into her ear. And I picture Sarah, terrified and hopeful in equal measure. Desperate to say the right thing. To win Hannah back.

No wonder she hasn't told anyone who the father is. It'd be like throwing a hand grenade in among this recovering family.

3:51 P.M. "Please let Hannah not have a nanny," I mutter, as I reach the outskirts of Bisley. "Let Hannah or her husband answer the door."

I'm driving too fast, and to my surprise, I don't care. The last few months of stoicism, of Doing the Right Thing, have now been stripped back to the lunacy, the blind masochism they always were. I have known for less than fifteen minutes that Sarah's been carrying my child and already I have completely forgotten everything I'd been telling myself to keep myself away from her. All that matters is seeing her.

A baby. Sarah has been carrying my baby.

I recognize Hannah's husband as soon as he opens the door, from the night when I smashed my fist on the pub table. "Smelly!" he yells, as a black Labrador crashes past him and into me, a mangy comfort blanket in its mouth. The dog jumps up on me, its tail helicoptering with joy.

"Smelly!" he shouts. "Stop it!"

He grabs the dog's collar and does his best to hold it off.

"Smelly?" I say. It's the closest I've been to laughing in several hours.

"We made the mistake of letting the children name him." The man smiles apologetically. "Can I help?"

Smelly lunges at me again and I stroke him with one hand while trying to explain the impossible to a complete stranger.

"Sorry, yes. My name's Eddie Wallace. I've known Hannah for years. She—"

"Oh, right," the man says. "Yes, I know who you are. You're the older brother of Hannah's childhood friend—" He breaks off awkwardly, although whether it's because he's forgotten Alex's name or doesn't want to bring up my dead sister, I can't tell.

"Alex," I supply, because I haven't time for awkward pauses.

He nods. Deeper in the house, there is a loud thump and the sound of children screaming. He looks nervously over his shoulder but is reassured when one of them starts yelling something about preparing to die by the sword.

He turns back to me and I feel quite insane with desperation. I need information, now.

Smelly sniffs my crotch.

"So, this might sound strange, but . . . I believe that Hannah's sister might have just had a baby, or is just about to have one. I mean, I suppose she could even be having it right now . . ."

The man smiles. "Indeed! Hannah's at the hospital with her now. Poor Sarah's been in labor two days. Are you a friend of hers?" Then he pauses as he tries to square the fact that I'm Eddie Wallace with the idea that I might be a friend of Sarah's. Confusion becomes alarm as he realizes he might have told me something I'm not entitled to know.

For a moment I can't speak, so I just stand there, stroking Smelly. The dog smiles at me, and despite myself, I smile at the dog. Then I level with Hannah's husband. I don't have time to make up some excuse he'll never buy. "Not a friend, exactly . . . more, the father of her child."

Silence.

The man merely stares at me. "I'm sorry?"

"I had no idea, until about thirty minutes ago . . ."

The man frowns. It is inconceivable to him that I could be the father of Sarah's baby. I swallow. "It's a long story, but I wouldn't have come to your door if I wasn't certain it's mine."

Silence.

"Look—I'm just a decent bloke who's found out he's a father, or nearly a father, and I'm not going to force myself on Sarah or anything, but I . . ." I trail off, because, to my horror, my voice is beginning to crack. "I just want to be there for her. If I can."

"Right," the man says eventually.

Smelly sits by my feet, staring up at me. I can tell I'm a disappointment.

"Without meaning to pile undue pressure on you, I'm going out of my mind, wanting to just get there, and help if I can, or send her my love, or . . . I don't know. So I wondered if you could tell me if she's giving birth in Stroud or in Gloucester. Or some-where else."

The man folds his arms. "I'm going to have to run this past Hannah," he says at last. "I hope you understand."

Of course I understand. I want, also, to punch him.

I take a deep breath and nod. "I get it. Although if it helps, Hannah's phone's switched off. I tried it earlier."

The man nods. "Yes, that's most likely." But he persists with calling her anyway, moving off down the corridor so I won't be able to hear him when he says, "You won't **believe** this . . ."

A few moments later he's back. "No answer," he says. He jigs the phone up and down in his hand, uncertain as to what to do. He gets it, as a father—I can see he wants to help me. But this is no ordinary situation.

I begin to panic. He might not tell me.

"I could just turn up at Stroud, or Gloucester, I suppose . . . But would you be willing to tell me how the labor's going, at least?" I ask. I'll take anything, at this stage. Any crumb he's willing to throw from the table. Smelly sighs, leaning his big square head on my thigh.

He pauses. "All I know is that it's been going on two days. And that they've taken her out of the midwife unit and transferred her to the consultant-led bit."

"What does that mean?"

"When it happened to us with Elsa, it meant things weren't going brilliantly," he admits. "But it could be anything—she probably just got tired and wanted some decent pain relief. I wouldn't worry too much."

"Please tell me where Sarah is." My voice is too loud, but I think I probably just sound desperate rather than threatening or mad. "**Please.** I'm a normal guy. Not a psychopath. I just want to be there."

He sighs, defeated. "Okay . . . Okay. They're

at Gloucester Royal. I think the maternity complex is called the Women's Center. But be warned, they won't let you through the door unless Sarah tells them to. I'll text Hannah and let her know. I shouldn't do this, really, but . . . well, if I were in your shoes and all that."

I slump, my hand reaching instinctively for Smelly's shiny black head. It's a reassuring block, warm and—yes—probably smelly. "Thank you," I say quietly. "Thank you so much."

"Dad?" A child's voice from above. Behind the man, I see a head appearing, upside down, from upstairs. Auburn hair trails down toward us. "Who's that man?"

"Good luck," he says, ignoring his daughter. Sarah's niece, Elsa, whom she thought she'd never meet. He leans forward and shakes my hand. "I'm Hamish."

"Eddie," I say, even though I've probably already told him. "I can't tell you how grateful I am."

And then I'm off.

CHAPTER FORTY-SEVEN

The drive is one of the longest half hours of my life. By the time I hit the A417, I'm frantic. **Alex would have loved a niece or nephew**, I think, as I wait on a roundabout. (And: **How can this light still be red?**) She would especially have loved a niece or nephew related to Hannah.

And me? Of course I want a child. I've known for years, I think, but it's not something that ever felt possible—at least not until I met Sarah. Then it stopped feeling like a remote fantasy and started feeling like an obvious desire.

I love her, I think, as I accelerate ferociously out of the roundabout. **She made everything seem possible.**

Sarah Harrington has been carrying my child, all these months. Along with her grief, and her sadness, and the loss of her grandfather. She's moved to the other side of the world, back to a place to which she thought she'd never return, and has somehow patched up the scar that was riven down the center of her family. All on her own. Knowing I didn't want even a friendship with her.

I recall the unbearable sadness in her eyes when she talked of Hannah and her children, and I wonder again how it has been for these two women, trying to rebuild their relationship in such extraordinary circumstances. I hope it's made Sarah happy. I hope the fact that Hannah is with her for the birth means that they've become as close as they deserve to be. As close as sisters should be.

HOSPITAL 1 MILE, says a sign. One mile too far. I pass under a railway bridge and climb a hill, cursing the traffic. I drive, far too slowly, past a fish-and-chip shop. A man stands outside it in the fading light, a plastic bag of warm paper packages swinging from his wrist. He's on his phone, laughing, completely oblivious to the desperate man stuck in slow-moving traffic in a Land Rover.

A minute or so later there's a sign saying the hospital is half a mile away, but that's still not close enough. Another traffic light turns red. I seem unable to stop swearing.

The Land Rover is silent, save for the old-fashioned ticker-flicker of the indicator. I imagine Sarah, my beautiful Sarah, exhausted on a bed somewhere. I think of all the labors I've seen in films: terrible screams, panicking midwives, doctors shouting, emergency alarms going off. It's like someone's taken an ice-cream scoop and hollowed me out. I am weightless with fear. **What if something goes wrong?**

I turn left, reminding myself that problem-free

labors happen all day, every day—they have to: the human race wouldn't have survived, otherwise—and the brown hulk of Gloucester Royal slides finally into vision.

The hospital's busy. Illness, I suppose, is a 24-7 business. Several people cross the roadway in front of me. There are speed bumps everywhere. The first car park is full and I want to scream. I want to hurtle to the nearest entrance and abandon my car there.

And I know, finally, how Sarah felt the day she set off in pursuit of her boyfriend and her little sister. I know the terror that gripped her, the instinct that sent her spinning off the road to prevent a car crash Hannah would never have survived. I know she didn't swerve because she didn't care about Alex. It was love and fear that made her wrench that steering wheel. The same love and fear that, right now, I am feeling for her. I would do anything to keep her safe. I'd block a hospital car park. I'd break the speed limit. And I, too, in that same situation Sarah found herself in, in 1997, would have swerved left, if it meant saving the person I loved most.

CHAPTER FORTY-EIGHT

Hamish is right, of course: they don't let me in. The lady on the other side of the intercom sounds amazed that I'd even try.

"Is there anywhere I can wait?" I ask her. "I've told Sarah's birthing partner that I'm here . . . Um, and I am actually the father, if that helps . . . Or at least I think I am . . ." At that point the woman stops replying. I wonder if she's calling security.

I find a small waiting area at the entrance to the Women's Center and sit under an escalator, opposite a set of lifts I'd probably be arrested for attempting to use. And here, in the strip-lit reality of a hospital corridor—with proper families, proper couples everywhere—the stupidity of this enterprise is suddenly so blindingly apparent I almost laugh.

What was I hoping? That Hannah would pause from her duties to check her messages, maybe catch up on some e-mails? That she'd read Hamish's text and think, **Oh fantastic! The father's Eddie Wallace! And he's turned up here—how lovely!** and pop out to invite me in?

I sink my head into my hands, wondering if Hamish is doing the same back in Bisley.

If I stand any hope at all of getting Sarah back, it's going to take a damn sight more than a dash to Gloucester Royal. Six months she's lived less than a mile from me. Six months she's had to get in touch, to tell me I'm going to be a father, and I haven't heard a peep out of her.

But even though I know it's almost certainly pointless, I stay. I can't leave. I can't turn my back on her again.

The lift dings and I start, but, of course, it's not Sarah, holding a baby, it's a tired-looking man with a lanyard round his neck and a packet of fags already halfway out of his pocket.

We have a choice, I told her, the day we met. We are not just victims of our lives. We can choose to be happy. And yet I chose not to be happy, in spite of all I'd said. I turned my back on Sarah Harrington, and this once-in-a-lifetime thing that existed between us, and chose duty. A life only half lived.

An hour passes, two hours, three. People come and go, bringing with them blasts of icy air that quickly turn stale. A lightbulb breaks; it flickers intermittently, but a man comes to fix it before I've so much as thought of telling anyone. I offer silent prayers for the NHS. For Sarah. For my mother, whose feelings about this situation I can't even begin to imagine.

Maybe Felix will have popped round. Felix with his good humor and his determination to remain positive, no matter what life throws at him.

Sometime after dark has wrapped itself around the Women's Center, a family joins me in the little waiting area, a mother and father and a kid. The boy has a blond Afro and a naughty, impish little face that I immediately like. He assesses the waiting area, declares it boring, and asks his mum what she's going to do about it. She's fiddling with her phone, preoccupied. She says something to her husband about visiting hours.

Then the child says—and my heart stops—"Why hasn't Sarah's baby got a dad, Mum? Why is Sarah's sister helping her and not the baby's dad?"

I stare into my lap and my face burns.

The mother replies, "You're not to talk to Sarah about that, babe. If we get to go in and see her, you can ask about anything other than dads. Rudi, are you listening?"

"Yes, but—"

"If you promise me you won't, I'll take you to the ice cream factory tomorrow, the one I told you about near Stroud."

My heart is hammering. I chance a look at the boy, but he's not even remotely interested in me.

"Is it the man who broke her heart? The one who made her cry because he didn't call?"

And I feel like ripping off my skin.

● ● ●

The woman—Sarah's friend Jo—receives a call on her phone. She wanders off toward the lifts to take it, and Rudi plays with his father. Except it can't be his father, because after beating him at rock, paper, scissors five times in a row, he calls the man Tommy.

Tommy! Sarah's childhood friend! Although, I realize, that doesn't quite tally with what she told me in her life story. I know those messages off by heart: she never said Tommy and Jo were a couple. Maybe I misread? I wish I knew more about Sarah and her life. I wish I'd known what she ate for breakfast the day she went into labor, how her pregnancy has been, what it's like to have a relationship with her sister after all these years. I wish I knew she was safe.

When Jo returns, she starts packing up their stuff. Above Rudi's Afro, she catches Tommy's eye and shakes her head.

"Mum? Why are you going? Mum! I want to see Sarah!"

"We're going to stay with Sarah's mum and dad," she tells her son. "They just called to invite us for a sleepover. It's getting late, you need to go to bed, and Sarah can't have visitors today. She might not even be able to see us tomorrow."

"When can we see her, then?"

Jo's face is unreadable. "I don't know," she admits.

An ugly scene ensues: Rudi obviously loves Sarah and has no plans to leave. But eventually— furiously—he gets into his coat. And they're just about to leave when Tommy walks past me and does a double take. He carries on walking and then stops again, and I know he's looking at me. And after a beat I look up at him, because I'm desperate. If a crawlingly awkward conversation with Sarah's old- est friend is going to help, I'll take it.

"Sorry," he says, when our eyes meet. "Sorry, I thought you were someone else . . ."

Once again he turns. Once again he stops. "No, you . . . Are you Eddie?"

Jo, who's by the bottom of the escalator, wheels round. She stares at me. They both do. Rudi looks vaguely in my direction, but he's too busy being pissed off to take any real notice. I see Jo mouthing a few choice words—although I'm not sure if they're born of anger or shock—then she marches her son through an automatic door.

I stand up and offer Tommy my hand, which he shakes, although it takes him a while.

"How did you know?" he asks. "Did Sarah get in touch with you?" He's blushed a deep, livid red, although I'm not sure why. It's me who should be feeling ashamed.

"I only found out this afternoon. It's a long story. But Hannah knows I'm here, I think."

Before he's worked out what to say, I blurt, "How is she? Is she okay? Has the baby been born? Is Sarah all right? I'm sorry—I know I sound mad, and I know I gave Sarah a terrible time last summer, but I . . . can't bear it. I just want to know she's okay."

Tommy blushes even more deeply. His eyebrows

have taken on a life of their own, as if he's thinking up a speech, or solving a puzzle.

"I honestly don't know," he says eventually. "Jo's just got off the phone to Sarah's mum. I'm guessing she didn't want to update me in front of Rudi."

"Shit," I say. "Does that mean it's bad news?"

Tommy looks helpless and harassed. "I don't know," he repeats. "I hope not. I mean, her parents were here earlier and they've gone home, so it's probably just . . . Look, I have to go. I . . ." He trails off, backing toward the exit. "Sorry, mate," he says, and then he's gone.

It's the middle of the night. I'm pacing, like people do in films. I understand it now. Sitting down would be like staying still while someone pressed hot metal to your skin.

I'm sharing the waiting area with an aging man in his pajamas, but neither of us has spoken to each other. He looks as anxious as I do. A grandfather, maybe. Like me, he can do little else but yawn, jiggle his knees, and stare intermittently at the delivery suite entrance.

I've decided this must be what purgatory feels like. Perpetual postponement. Intense waiting in the key of fear minor. Nothing moving, other than the slow hands of a clock.

Alan's been trying to reassure me—keeps sending me articles about childbirth. Gia wants me to remind you that birth doesn't need to be like those horror shows you see on the telly, he wrote earlier. Women give birth all day long, all over the world. She says you should forget about all that overproduced drama and visualize Sarah taking long, slow breaths. Bringing a baby into the world in slow breaths.

Or something like that. I should take it seriously, but I'm too far gone.

In desperation, I start reading the messages Sarah sent me last summer. I read the whole lot, from the day she left my barn to the day before we met on Santa Monica Beach. I read them twice, three times, trying to find something I know they can't tell me.

Then the delivery suite door opens and my heart starts galloping. But it's just a staff member, pulling on a hat, yawning, plunging her hands deep into her coat pockets. She walks past us both with barely a sideways glance, patently exhausted.

I can't bear it.

I scroll back to the first message Sarah sent me, twenty minutes after we said good-bye.

Back home, it said. **I had such a wonderful time with you. Thank you, for everything. X**

I had a wonderful time, too, I write now. **In fact, I had the best week of my life. I can still hardly believe it happened.**

On my way to Leicester and thinking about you, she had written, a couple of hours later.

I was thinking about you, too, I write. **And while I admit my thoughts weren't as lovely and straightforward as yours, by that stage, I want you to know**

that underneath it all, I was hopelessly in love with you. That was what made it more painful than anything else—I was absolutely, totally, head over heels in love with you. I couldn't believe you existed. I still can't.

Then her messages started getting worried. **Hey— you OK? Did you get to Gatwick in time?**

I swallow. It's painful, watching her panic unfurl, knowing I could have stopped it.

I read a few more, but then I stop, because I feel too guilty.

You are the best and most beautiful person I have ever known, I write instead. **And I knew that the first day we spent together. You fell asleep and I thought, I want to marry this woman.**

I love you, Sarah, I write. I think I'm crying. **I wish I was there with you, cheering you on. I want only for you and the baby to be safe.**

> I'm so sorry I haven't been there for
> you. I wish I had been. I wish we could
> have done this together. I should have
> been braver. I should have trusted I'd be
> able to work something out with Mum.
> I should have stopped at nothing.

I'm definitely crying. A tear is pooling fatly across my phone screen. I try to clean it with a dirty cuff and the whole thing goes blurry. Then another one drips down and I realize I'm in danger of actually sobbing. I stand up and start walking again. I go outside, where the air is cold as an arctic sea, but it stops the tears immediately, so I stay there. The car park is quiet now. Coppery light, leafless trees swaying in a bitter breeze.

> I send you every ounce of strength and courage I have, although I know you won't need it. You are an extraordinary woman, Sarah Harrington. The best I know.

My fingers are shaking. Cold knifes in through the open front of my duffel coat, but I've stopped caring about me.

> Please, when you're ready, can we try again? Can we draw a line through everything—even the thing that I thought we couldn't get past? Can we go back to the start? There's nothing that would make me happier than being with you. You, me, this baby. A little family.

> I love you, Sarah Harrington.

An ambulance wails, and a gust of paralyzing wind punches me in the side of the face.

> I love you. I'm sorry.

CHAPTER FORTY-NINE

Sarah

I am rotating slowly, hovering above my life. There are hexagons and octagons, maybe ceiling tiles, or perhaps it's just the fine detail of the thing I was leaning my forearms on earlier, that chair . . .

There have been many tiny furniture details during this parallel time, things I have stared at so hard they've gone macro and taken on patterns, danced: a kaleidoscope in heaven.

Happy times. Positive images. Things that will stimulate oxytocin. That's what I'm meant to be thinking about. I play happy times on the screen in front of my brow bone. There is the fat little pony that belonged to the woman who lived in that house beyond Tommy's—

Pain. A roaring waterfall of it. But: **I trust my body,** I repeat, because that's what I was told to do. **I trust my body. It's bringing my baby to me.**

There is Hugo, Tommy's cat, the funny one that didn't drink enough water in the summer.

The midwife is doing something to my abdomen

again. Tightening straps. Since I moved into this room they've been monitoring my baby's heart with a device that looks like a laboratory experiment. **One sensor for your contractions, one for baby**, she reminds me, catching my expression. I nod, and try to take myself back to happy memories.

There is a child called Hannah; she is twelve years old. She wears a sling; her eye is swollen and green, her skin pockmarked with cuts and bruises. Her best friend is dead and she hates me.

No, this isn't happy. I search through layers of pain and exhaustion for something better. I breathe in for four, out for six. Or was it eight? **Trust your body**, they said at the classes. **Trust your body. Trust the process of labor.**

But I've gone into some sort of tunnel, and it's so deep I don't quite know where I am. I think there are drugs. That's right: there was an injection in my thigh, and there's the thing near my mouth. I clamp around it and breathe in sweet stories as I start to climb another mountain. It's floating—someone tries to take it away, so I hold on hard.

There is a room full of medical equipment, and that same girl, Hannah, only she's different now: she's my sister again, but she's a woman with a family and a career. She's my birthing partner. She's been having counseling because she doesn't like herself very much. She says she was awful to me.

But she wasn't awful. She was never awful. Hannah is in the bank of good memories getting me through this tunnel. I breathe in the wonder I felt in my heart the first time I saw her, when she turned up at Mum and Dad's house on the morning of Grand-dad's funeral. How she held herself stiffly in front of me and then crumpled forward, and the other-worldly joy when I hugged my sister for the first time in nearly two decades.

More shapes and patterns; a moving scrapbook. I am only half aware of the people in the room, the things they're doing to my body, the gentle com-mands.

I remember a café in Stroud, Hannah and I on our first date together as adults. The silences, the nervous laughter. The apologies, from both of us, and the sight of my father crying when I told him that Hannah had invited me round to her house to meet her family.

But . . . my baby. Where's my baby?

The sea falls in on itself, again and again, and a cuckoo sings its two notes into a dusky wood. Eddie is laughing. They're examining me again now. Peo-ple, lots of them, looking at a screen that's printing out jagged lines . . .

Where is my baby?

My baby. My baby that I made with Eddie.

Eddie. I loved him so much.

Eddie. That's the name Hannah's telling me. She's telling me about Eddie. She says he's outside. She looks shocked, amazed, but now I have to listen to a doctor, who takes the tube from me and starts talking slowly and clearly. "I'm afraid we can't wait any longer . . . ," she says. "We need to get this baby out: you're still not fully dilated . . . the fetal blood sample indicates . . . oxygen . . . heart rate . . . Sarah, do you understand what I'm saying?"

"Eddie?" I ask. "Outside?" But there are more words from the medical people and then the bedchair thing starts moving; it's leaving this room.

The tunnel is fading. There are ceiling tiles. Hannah's voice is close to my ear. "You agreed to have a cesarean," she's telling me. "The baby's struggling. But don't worry, Sarah, this happens a lot. You're going straight to surgery and the baby'll be out in minutes. Everything'll be fine . . ."

I ask her about Eddie, because it might just have been one of the stories from the kaleidoscopic tunnel. I am so tired.

Not enough oxygen?

But it's a real fact, not a tunnel fact: Eddie is waiting for me. He's outside. He's been messaging my phone; he says he loves me. "And he keeps saying he's sorry," Hannah tells me. She is astounded. "Eddie Wallace," she mutters, as someone takes her by the elbow and tells her she will need to put on a surgical gown. "Father of your child. I mean, what?"

Eddie says he loves me. My child is in trouble.

Then the doctors all just sort of cave in on me, all talking, and I have to listen.

CHAPTER FIFTY

Eddie

I sit bolt upright: the door to the delivery suite is opening. I realize I must have been sleeping. I feel terrible. And I'm freezing, shivering all over. Why didn't I take a a hat, or some gloves? Why didn't I plan this properly? Why have I messed up **everything**, from the moment Sarah left my barn back in June?

"Is there an Eddie Wallace here?" asks the woman standing in the doorway. She's wearing scrubs.

"Yes! That's me!"

She pauses, then nods over at the lifts, where we can talk without my waiting-area companion hearing. He'd fallen asleep, too, but now he's watching me with jealous eyes.

Arrows of fear circulate my body like the science videos they showed us at school, and I walk far too slowly. The woman in scrubs waits for me, her arms folded, and I realize she's looking at the floor.

I realize quickly that I don't like that.

I realize even more quickly that if she gives me bad news, my life will never be the same again.

And so, for the first few seconds, I can't hear what she's saying, because I'm absolutely deafened by fear.

"It's a boy," she repeats, when she realizes I haven't taken anything in. She starts to smile. "Sarah gave birth to a beautiful baby boy about an hour ago. We're doing a few tests at the moment, on Mum and baby, but Sarah asked me to tell you that it's a boy and he should be absolutely fine."

I stare at her in sheer astonishment. "A boy? A boy? Sarah's okay? She's had a boy?"

She smiles. "She's very tired, but she's okay. She did really well."

"And she wanted you to tell me? She knows I was here?"

She nods. "She knew you were here. She found out just as we took her in for a C-section. Her sister told her. And your son's lovely, Eddie. An absolutely gorgeous little thing."

I fold forward on myself, and a sob of wonder, of joy, of relief, of amazement, of a million things I could never name tumbles out of me. It sounds like laughter. It could well be laughter. I cover my face with my hands and cry.

The woman puts a hand on my back. "Congratulations," she says, somewhere above me. I can hear her smile. "Congratulations, Eddie."

Eventually I manage to straighten up. She is turning to leave. It defies belief that she's off to bring more lives into being. That this miracle is common-place for her.

A boy! **My** boy!

"Sarah's recovering in her room, and she'll need to stay a few days on the postnatal ward. I'm afraid you won't be able to come in tonight, but visiting hours on the ward start at two P.M.," she says. "Al-though, of course, it'll be up to Sarah."

I nod stupidly, joyously. "Thank you," I whisper, as she starts to walk away. "Thank you so much. Please tell her I love her. I'm so proud of her. I . . ."

I haven't cried like this since the day they told me my little sister was dead. But that was the worst mo-ment of my life, and this is the best.

After a long while I stagger outside, where the wind has dropped, and a thin gray is beginning to filter through the night sky. It's silent, save for the sound of my tears and sniffs. Not so much as a dis-tant car engine, just me and this towering, dizzying news. "I'm a father," I whisper, into the nothingness of predawn. "I have a little boy."

And I repeat this several times, because I don't have any other words. I lean against the cold wall of the Women's Center and try to recalibrate my vision of the universe, so it can include this miracle, but it's impossible: I can't imagine. I can't compute. I can't believe. I can't do anything.

A lone car enters the car park, makes slowly for a disabled space opposite me. Life goes on. The world is waking. The world contains my son. This is all his. This air, this dawn, this crying man whom he might one day call Dad.

Then my pocket buzzes and I see Sarah's name, and the word "Message," and I'm off again, crying uncontrollably, before I've even read the thing.

He's beautiful, she's written. **He's the most amazing thing I've ever seen.**

I watch, breathless, as she writes another message.

He looks like you.

Please come and meet our boy tomorrow.

And then the final one: **I love you too.**

CHAPTER FIFTY-ONE

Sarah

It's June 2. Another June 2 on the Broad Ride: my twentieth, I realize, as I try to pull my hair into an elastic band. There's a stiff breeze today, pushing clouds quickly across the sky, combing and whipping them into tight whorls. The breeze snatches at strands of my hair, dancing them away out of reach.

I think of the year when it rained so hard the nettles bent flat, and the year when my hat was lifted off by a rampaging wind. I think about last year, when it was so hot that the air around me compressed and even the birds were silent, dead-feathered in their trees. That was the year I met Eddie, and this began.

Eddie. My Eddie. Even though I'm exhausted, sleep-deprived beyond all reckoning, I smile. I smile hopelessly, and my stomach zips and zooms.

This is still happening to me, a whole year after I ran into him on the village green. He says it happens to him, too, and I know he's telling the truth because I can see it right there in his face. Sometimes I wonder if it's an aftereffect of the battle we had to find and keep each other. Mostly, though, I think it's because this is how it should feel.

As if sensing the swell of his mother's heart, Alex snuffles, burrowing tighter into my chest. He's still fast asleep, in spite of the number of people who have prodded and cooed at him in the last hour. I circle my arms around him, wrapped tight in my Stroud-issue sling, and kiss his warm little head, over and over. Having him on me—even when I'm so tired I would happily sleep in a dog bowl—is like turning on a light. I had no idea I could love anything, or anyone, so much.

The day after Alex was born, when Eddie walked into my room holding a toy squirrel, his hands shaking, his face white with terror, I knew we'd make it. I handed him his son and he stared at him in utter amazement, wept uncontrollably, and called Alex "Bruiser." Later, when a nurse prized Alex away from Eddie, he looked at me for a few moments and then told me he loved me. No matter what happened, he said, he was mine if I'd have him.

So he came back to Mum and Dad's with me when I was free to go home. We moved back to his barn a few weeks later. (He made a cot. A cot! He hung Mouse from the top.) And although his mother refused to talk about me, even though she took to calling him throughout the day, even though I had completely run out of money, and Eddie's roof had sprung a leak, and I got mastitis and felt dreadful, I was the happiest I'd ever been. We didn't get out of bed that first morning. We just lay there, with our son, feeding him, cuddling, drifting in and out of sleep, kissing, changing nappies, and smiling.

At first Eddie answered two, maybe three of his mother's calls each day, although it soon dwindled to one. It was hard for him— "Impossibly hard," he said, having woken one morning to three missed calls. "Night calls are the worst." His hands shook as he called her back, sitting up in bed as I fed Alex in a chair, and he went round there soon after. She was "okay," he said, on his return. "Just a bad night. But she's had a bad night at least once a month for two decades, and she's survived. I've got to trust more."

Even after years of tortured imaginings about the misery of the Wallace family, the extent of Eddie's responsibilities toward his mother have still come as a shock to me. But when he apologized for the number of phone calls, for the number of visits he still made to her, I told him he mustn't. Of all the women on earth, I pointed out, I was surely the best placed to understand.

I understand, too, that something even bigger than his mother's illness has happened to Eddie, and that's parenthood. Parenthood, and all the indescribable instincts and emotions over which it reigns. Alex arrived into Eddie's life, tiny, warm, looking like he was solving the mysteries of the world, and without saying so much as a word to his father—without so much as lifting a finger—he changed the landscape of Eddie's responsibilities forever.

When his mum phones now, he'll just cancel the call, message her later, but mostly his attention is on Alex. On me. "I just have to pray that Mum will be okay," he said one day. "That what I can still give her is enough. Because I can't give her more, Sarah. I won't. This little man, he needs me. He's the one I have to keep alive now."

Still. I know it hurts him that his mum hasn't turned up today. I knew she wouldn't turn up; he knew she wouldn't turn up—she's met Alex six times in three months, each time insisting that only Eddie be present—but the slump of his shoulders when we had to start without her broke my heart.

When Jenni and Javier announced their plans to fly over for the month of June, Eddie and I decided to hold a welcome party for Alex. With two atheists for parents he was unlikely ever to get a christening, so we planned a little ceremony for him. Just a couple of friends saying a couple of things, then on to the serious business of eating and drinking.

Jenni's found the last ten months very difficult. We've spoken at least twice a week, and there have been some heartbreaking lows, but I sense she's emerging from the worst of it. She's been on good form since they arrived yesterday morning. She told me earlier that she and Javier now feel ready to figure out what their life is going to look like without children (maybe some travel? she said)—she's even considering a postgrad degree in "something cool." Poor Reuben will be distraught if he loses her, too.

It was Eddie's idea to do it here, on Broad Ride, on June 2. Right where Alex and Hannah had their den. I thought that was perfect.

But, of course, as with every other part of our relationship, it has not been a polished affair. Smelly, my sister's dog, ate almost all the food during our ceremony—including a large chocolate cake—so Hamish is now with him at the emergency vet, and Hannah's children keep crying because they're scared he has finally eaten himself to death. Alan, Eddie's best friend, was very nervous about making his speech and drank so many beers that he'd fallen asleep by the time we were ready for him to stand up. His wife isn't talking to him. And then Rudi was discovered kissing the elder daughter of one of my mother-and-baby-yoga friends in a secret cow-parsley cave, even though he is eight years old and should be finding girls annoying for at least another four years, and even though the yoga friend was telling me just last week how happy she was that her daughter isn't inappropriately sexualized like most children these days.

Jo couldn't stop laughing, which did little to diffuse the situation.

Still, everyone is here, except Hamish and, of course, Eddie's mum. Jenni, Javier, my sister and her family, Alan and Gia, who have been so warm and welcoming to me—and Tommy and Jo, who are all wrapped up in a love story of their own. They are both the happiest I've ever seen them, although things with Shawn have been messy since Jo told him about Tommy. But she's got something she never had before: a real partnership. She'll deal with it.

And, of course, my parents are here, watching with great delight every last interaction between their two daughters. They still can't quite believe that I'm back, that Hannah and I have managed to become friends again, that we can be together as a family. And of course they're obsessed with Alex. Dad wrote a cello piece for him. I have a bad feeling he's going to play it later.

I take another piece of quiche, while I still can— Alex is going to wake any minute—and look for Eddie.

There. He's on his way over to us, hands in pockets, smiling. I don't think I'll ever tire of this smile.

"Hello," he says. He kisses me once; then he kisses me again. He peers down at our tiny little son. "Hello, Bruiser," he whispers. Sure enough, Alex is beginning to wake. He half opens an eye, screws up his face, then headbutts me in the chest, fast asleep again. His father kisses him on the top of his head, which smells like the most perfect smell in the world, and takes a crafty bite of my quiche.

Alex wakes again, only this time it looks like he's going to stay with us. He stares blearily at his father, whose face is like a ridiculous, beaming pumpkin looming into view, and—after a few moments' consideration—smiles. And Eddie falls to pieces, just like he always does.

He begins to extract his son from the sling, and I see us suddenly, the two people who watched each other over an escaped sheep last year. The gusts of hope and expectation, the unstoppable unraveling of a past of which we weren't even aware. A lot has changed since then; more is yet to come. But there is nothing to hold me back anymore. No dark corners, no pending avalanche. Just life.

And who would have thought that Eddie Wallace would have been the solution? That Eddie, of all people, would be the one to stop me running? Who made it possible for me to sit still, to breathe, to like myself? Who would have thought that it would be Eddie Wallace, from whom I'd hidden so many years, who would make me want so desperately to come home? Who would allow me to spread my roots and belong somewhere at last?

When I look up, I see Carole Wallace.

She's standing at the edge of our gathering, her arm tucked into that of a man whose other sleeve hangs empty by his side. It must be Felix. My body goes still, and my heart goes fast. I'm not sure I'm prepared for this. Selfishly, I'm not sure I even want it. I can't cope with a scene, not on Alex's day.

But here she is, and she's already picking her way across the gathering, making straight for me.

She's heading for Eddie, I tell myself. **She won't**

even look at me. Eddie's lifting Alex above his head, laughing at his son's expressions of wonder and confusion. I watch as Carole and my mother see each other at the same time. My mother stops her, puts a brief hand on her arm, says something, smiles. Carole just looks really shocked. She blinks at Mum, stands awkwardly still, and then manages to reply. There might be a smile, although if there is, it's brief. Mum says something else, points toward the picnic, and Felix smiles warmly at her, nods, and thanks her. He looks at Carole, but she's turned back toward me and Eddie, and she's walking again.

"Eddie," I say quietly. He's still talking to his son. "Eddie. Your mum's here."

He swings round and I feel his body switch to high alert. There's a febrile pause as he works out what to do. For a second he starts to move away, to intercept her before she gets to me, but then he stops. He stops, stands firm, and takes hold of my hand. With his other, he holds Alex close to his side, a thumb moving across the soft cotton of Alex's miniature dungarees.

I look up at him. His temple is pulsing. His neck is strained, and I know he wants very much to bolt, to waylay her. But he stays. He holds my hand more tightly than ever. **We are a couple**, he's telling her, and I love him for it. **I'm not just me anymore. I'm us.**

Carole is looking only at her son. As she approaches, the man, Felix, drops back. He smiles warmly at me, but it's not enough to make me believe that this will be okay. Over his shoulder, my parents are watching. Jo is watching. Alan is watching. In fact, everyone is watching, although most of them are pretending not to be watching.

"Hello, Eddie darling," she says, arriving in front of us. She seems only at this moment to realize that Felix isn't with her. She glances back nervously, but he doesn't move, and she seems to decide to stay put. "I thought I'd come and see Alex on his special day."

Eddie holds my hand yet tighter. It's beginning to hurt.

"Hey, Mum," he says. Cheerful and relaxed, as if everything's okay. And I think, You are so kind. You've done this for years. Made her feel safe, no matter what's happening inside you. You are an extraordinary man.

"Alex!" he whispers. "Alex, your grandma's here!"

Alex is getting hungry: he keeps diving toward Eddie's chest, even though he's not going to find much milk there. "Would you like a cuddle?" Eddie asks his mother. "I think he's going to want feeding soon, but you may get a few minutes of peace."

Carole doesn't look at me, but she smiles and opens her arms. Carefully, gently, Eddie hands her our baby. He waits until she's got him; then he kisses his son on the top of his head.

He steps back and takes my hand again. Carole

breaks into a smile I never imagined seeing on her face, the face that sat at the edge of my mind for so many years. "Hello, my darling," she whispers. Her eyes fill with tears, and I realize that Eddie's lovely ocean eyes are hers. "Hello, my lovely boy. Oh, Granny loves you, Alex. Oh, she does!"

Eddie reaches out to squash one of Alex's chubby little feet. Then he glances sideways at me and squeezes my hand.

"Mum," he says levelly. "Mum, I want you to meet Sarah. The mother of my son."

There's a long pause, during which Carole Wallace murmurs at Alex, as he begins to wriggle down her chest. Eddie drops my hand and puts his arm around me. Carole doesn't look up. "Aren't you a good boy," she murmurs at Alex. "Aren't you **such** a good little boy."

"Mum."

Then slowly, uncertainly, Carole Wallace looks at me. She looks at me, across my son's head, across two decades of pain that I can only now, as a mother, begin truly to comprehend. And for a second—a lightning crack of a second—she smiles. "Thank you for my grandson," she says. Her voice trembles. "Thank you, Sarah, for this little boy."

She kisses Alex and then moves away from us, back to the safety of Felix, and conversation resumes. The wind has slowed; the sun is warmer. People are taking off jackets and jumpers. The cow parsley sways violently as a child burrows through its stems, and a tiny shower of butterflies flickers over the wild grass that surrounds us all, screening us off from the past, from the stories that we told ourselves for so many years.

I slide my arm around Eddie's waist, and I feel him smile.